A Doctor's Journey

*From Czarist Russia
to Communist Poland*

Lois Gayle Chance
in collaboration with Anna Kowal

outskirtspress
DENVER, COLORADO

This book is a work of fiction based on the life of a real person. Some names have not been changed and others have been changed. The opinions expressed in this manuscript are solely the opinions of the author and do not represent the opinions or thoughts of the publisher. The author has represented and warranted full ownership and/or legal right to publish all the materials in this book.

A Doctor's Journey
From Czarist Russia to Communist Poland
All Rights Reserved.
Copyright © 2013 Lois Gayle Chance in collaboration with Anna Kowal
v2.0

Cover Image by Lois Gayle Chance.

This book may not be reproduced, transmitted, or stored in whole or in part by any means, including graphic, electronic, or mechanical without the express written consent of the publisher except in the case of brief quotations embodied in critical articles and reviews.

Outskirts Press, Inc.
http://www.outskirtspress.com

Paperback ISBN: 978-1-4327-9593-1
Hardback ISBN: 978-1-4787-1734-8

Library of Congress Control Number: 2012920917

Outskirts Press and the "OP" logo are trademarks belonging to Outskirts Press, Inc.

PRINTED IN THE UNITED STATES OF AMERICA

Acknowledgements

I am grateful to Mary Kay Shanley and Suzanne Wheeler for their encouragement and suggestions. I am especially grateful to my husband Geoff Chance for all his support.

Alexander Kowal circa 1913

Preface

Alexander Kowal, born in Czar Nicholas' Russia, lived through the Russian revolution, two world wars, and the communists' takeover of Poland, his adopted homeland. This is his story garnered from a circumspect account of his life that he wrote in Polish during his last years as well as from the memories of his son John and especially his daughter Anna. The events depicted in this story are true. A few names have been changed to protect people's privacy. Conversations and details are from the imagination of the writer.

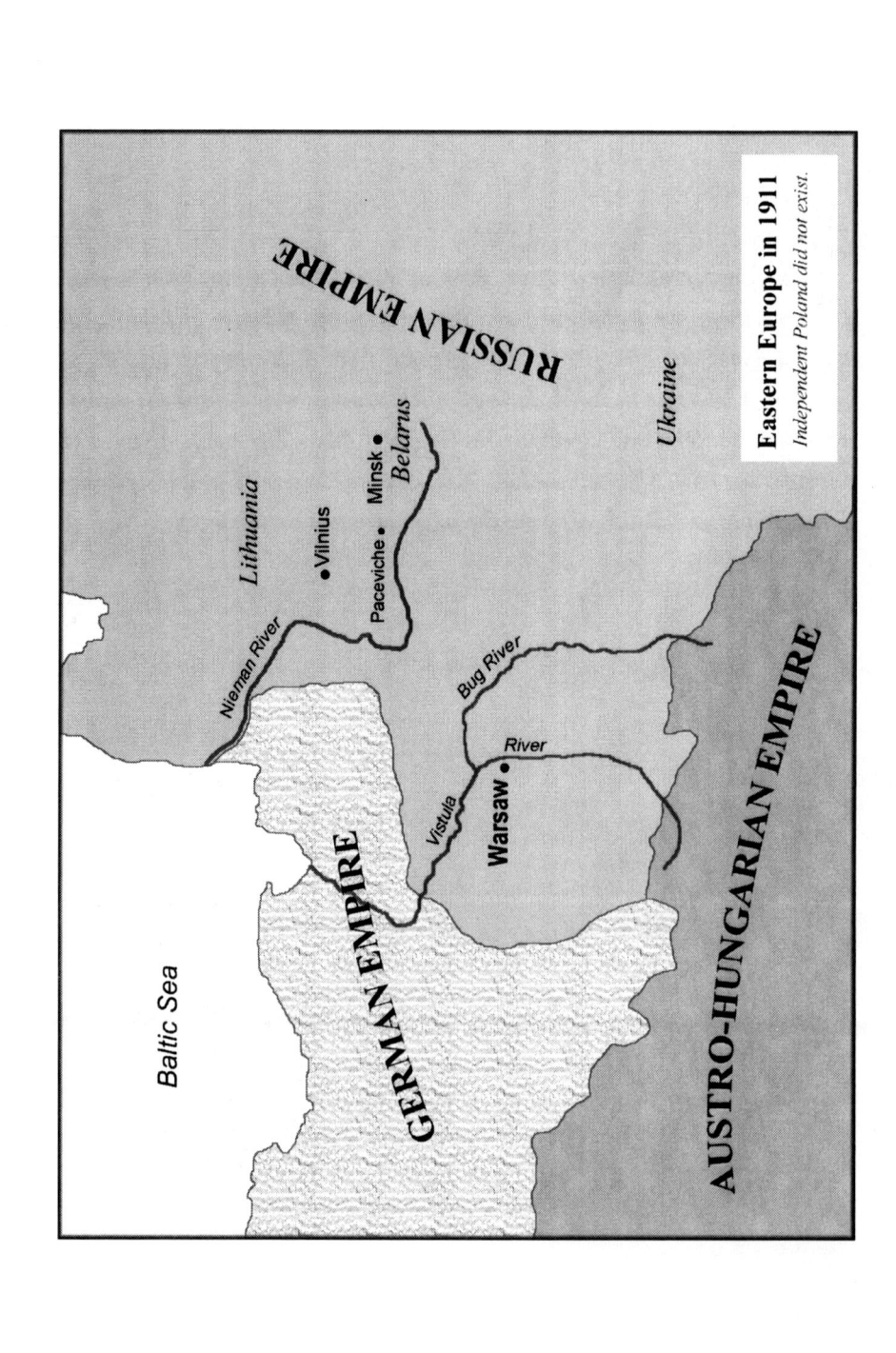

Eastern Europe in 1911
Independent Poland did not exist.

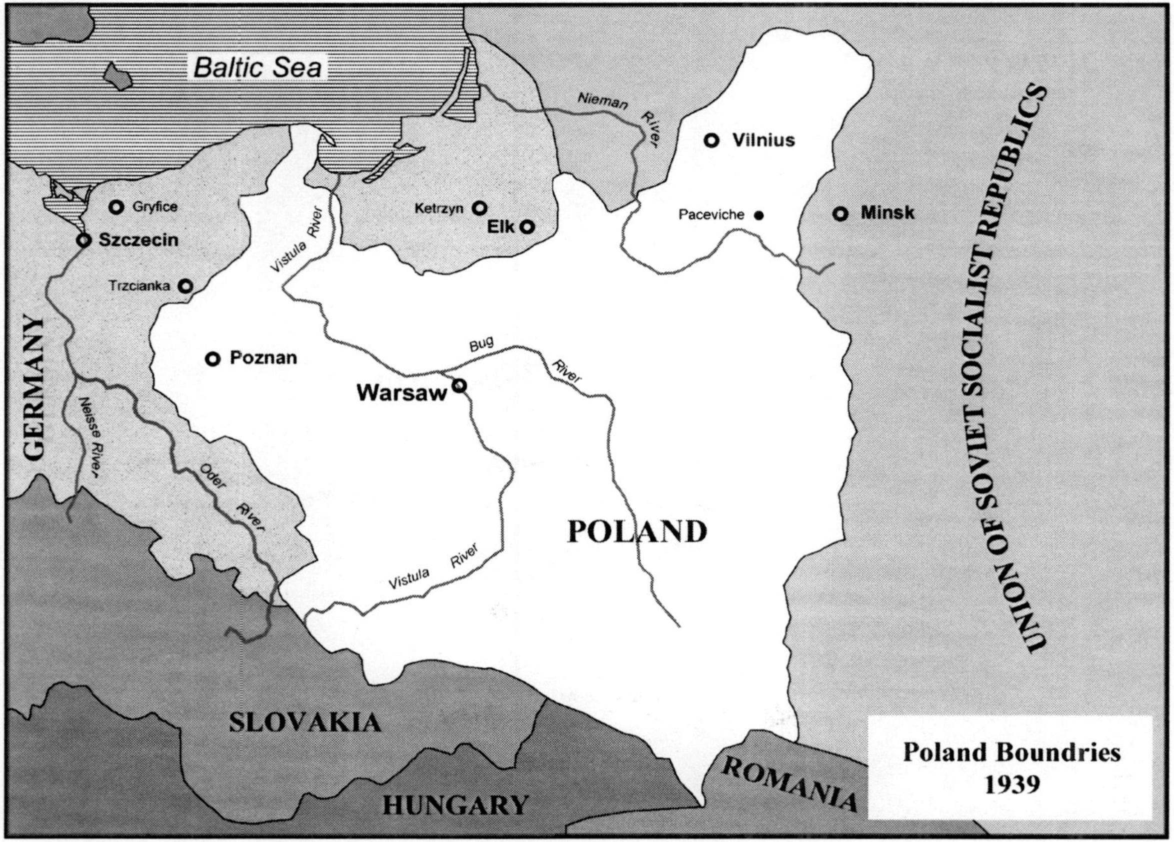
Baltic Sea
Gryfice
Szczecin
Trzcianka
Ketrzyn
Elk
Nieman River
Vilnius
Paceviche
Minsk
UNION OF SOVIET SOCIALIST REPUBLICS
Vistula River
Poznan
Bug River
Warsaw
GERMANY
Neisse River
Oder River
POLAND
Vistula River
SLOVAKIA
HUNGARY
ROMANIA
Poland Boundries
1939

Baltic Sea
Nieman River
Vilnius
Paceviche
Minsk
Gryfice
Szczecin
Ketrzyn
Elk
Vistula River
Trzcianka
Poznan
Warsaw
GERMANY
Neisse River
Oder River
POLAND
Bug River
Vistula River
UNION OF SOVIET SOCIALIST REPUBLICS
CZECHOSLOVAKIA
AUSTRIA
Poland Boundries
After World War II

Chapter 1

Paceviche, Czarist Russia, August, 1907

Early on a warm summer morning that would become a hot day, Alexander Kowal looked out the dusty window hoping to see that familiar figure striding towards their house, but as far as he could see, the road was empty except for an elderly neighbor shuffling across to the family garden. He sighed and sat back down at the table waiting for his father to finish his chicory coffee. Why was it taking so long? What if he was rejected?

Alexander Kowal's village, Paceviche, Belarus, in 1907 looked very much like it had for a hundred years. One-room rustic brown log homes topped with thatched roofs nestled on the east side of a rutted dirt road that was always either dusty or muddy. West of the road beside the Berezyna River birds flitted among the cattails in marshes. Between the river and the road vegetable gardens thrived from careful tending. Small neat flower gardens protected by stick fences in front of each of the two dozen homes gave a splash of color to the otherwise drab village.

For generations the plots of land that had been given to the peasants when feudalism died had been divided among sons until families had barely enough land to sustain themselves. However, unlike other peasant families, the Kowals passed all the family land to the oldest son, who was then expected to pay his younger brothers for their shares. By village standards, this made the Kowals a little more prosperous. But a stranger to the village would not have noticed. Their rough-hewn log home was no larger than the others in the village. The Kowals wore clothes made of homespun linen and hand-knitted wool and shoes woven from willow bark just as Paceviche denizens had worn for generations.

"You're the oldest, Alexander. You'll inherit the land," Afanasy Kowal repeated often to his son even though he knew Alexander had other ideas about the future.

Afanasy had inherited the twenty-five acres from his father Jacob, who had inherited it from his father Nicholas. He had received the deed to the land from the czar when the owner was drafted into the Russian army in the 1850s and never returned. However, Alexander dreamed not of being a farmer but of becoming a teacher and leaving Paceviche. Afanasy Kowal neither encouraged nor discouraged his oldest son's desire to be a teacher. Boys dreamed such things, but Afanazy believed that soon Alexander would realize being a farmer was his lot in life and forget his teacher dream.

Alexander was determined. He wanted to be like his teacher Szymon Kuzmicz, the smartest person he knew. His happiest moments were those in school. Alexander completed all the available seven years of school taught by Mr. Kuzmicz in nearby Bakshty. Still, he thirsted for more schooling so he could pass the entrance exam of the teacher's college in Nieswiez, which was a two-hour wagon ride to the nearest train depot plus a three-hour train trip.

"There's so much to learn," he told Mr. Kuzmicz. "So many books I want to read." For over a year Alexander worked for a lumber company after finishing his chores at home to earn money to hire Mr. Kuzmicz to tutor him and to pay for the train fare to Nieswiez.

Mikail, another village lad, had the same dream, and his father was willing to take the two fifteen-year-old boys to the train station so they could take the exam in Nieswiez. With high hopes they made the journey, took the oral exam, and went home to await the results. Alexander passed the test, but Mikail failed. Unfortunately, the school could only offer Alexander a half-tuition scholarship, and even if Afanasy had wanted Alexander to become a teacher, the Kowals had little money.

A DOCTOR'S JOURNEY

Disappointed, but not deterred, Alexander talked to Mr. Kuzmicz about getting into the medical school in Vilnius. The best students in each school were encouraged to apply. Opened in 1906 by Czar Nicholas, it offered better scholarships, and Trofim Sokolowicz, the best student in last year's graduating class, had been accepted. Maybe the school would take Alexander, too. If he couldn't be a teacher, perhaps he could be a doctor. Alexander remembered the doctor who had come to their house when he was six and ill with a throat infection. He remembered waking from a fevered sleep to see looking down at him a tall, slim man wearing black knee-high boots and a crisp dark-green uniform. The gold buttons marching across his uniform shined even in the dim light. The stranger's fingernails were clean and trimmed, and he spoke with quiet authority. To wear such a uniform and travel to villages to make people well—Alexander had not thought about this possibility before, but now it seemed exciting.

"I think you and Adam Gorodowicz should both apply," Mr. Kuzmicz told him. "You're the top students in the class." He handed Alexander the three-page form. "There's no entrance test, only an interview at the school if they like your application."

Both boys were invited for interviews, but Alexander was nervous. Perhaps they'd accept Adam because his father was the Bakshty town administrator, but deny Alexander, whose father was only a simple peasant.

"If they say no, I'm out the train fare and some time," he told his sister Melanie, "but I have to see if I can make it in."

The round-trip train fare to Vilnius depleted Alexander's meager savings. The interviews lasted more than an hour and were followed by a tour of the school. The building was the largest Alexander had ever been in, and he had never seen so many books. He wanted this. He wanted to go to school and learn about healing people. Neither boy could tell how well he had done in the interview. They went home to wait for the letter that would tell their fate.

As Afanasy gulped the last of the coffee and stood up, the rotund village magistrate appeared at the door of their single-room house. "Afanasy?" He knocked and opened the door. "Good morning," he greeted Alexander's father. "I have news from Vilnius officials." He turned to Alexander. "Did you cause trouble when you were there?"

Alexander paled. He couldn't think of anything he'd done that was wrong." The magistrate chuckled. "Don't look so worried. I bring good news. You've been accepted to the medical school. The letter came late yesterday." Because all mail for village residents was delivered to the magistrate, he knew everyone's business and enjoyed being the village news courier.

Alexander gasped, then shrieked and engulfed his mother in a hug. Blinking back tears, he turned to the magistrate, "May I see the letter?"

His eyes lit up as he read. "It says I got a full scholarship. I can be a doctor. They'll even give me clothes, and I'll live at the school."

Gregory, his younger brother, and his sister Melanie whooped and hollered. "My brother, Dr. Kowal," giggled eleven-year-old Gregory. Watching the commotion, Afanasy pursed his lips and furrowed his brow. He had never considered the possibility that Alexander's dream of leaving Paceviche might come true.

"No," he stormed. Afanasy's blue-gray eyes narrowed. "You're the oldest son. You belong here." Alexander stared at his father, the letter rattling in his quivering hands. Afanasy's jaw tightened, ready to deflect any arguments. A cloud of tension filled the room.

The magistrate turned to Jacob, Alexander's grandfather who had remained sitting quietly by the stove weaving willow-bark shoes, "I wish I had such good news about my son," sighed the magistrate. "Boris is not a good student and doesn't seem to care about his future." He put on his dusty brown hat. "You'll need to reply to the letter," he said to Alexander as he let himself out.

Silence again filled the room. Outside a rooster crowed. Alexander was too stunned to reply to his father. Stay here and farm instead of becoming an educated doctor? How could his father make such a demand?

As Afanasy turned towards the door, Jacob rose from the creaking chair. "He must go, Afanasy," he said to his oldest son. "Becoming a doctor for free is an opportunity that shouldn't be ignored. You'll still have Gregory. Give Alexander the money for a train ticket." Jacob's voice was quiet, but his steely blue eyes reflected determination.

Afanasy shook his head, strode to the door, ran his fingers through his thick graying hair, and took his worn straw hat from its hook. "Come on, boys. We have to finish raking the hay this morning while the weather is good."

"Papa," he said turning to his father, "will you be able to get that harness repaired this morning?"

Jacob, a robust man, prided himself on being able to fix almost any tool or piece of equipment that broke. "Yes, I'm almost done." Jacob rose and followed his son out the door.

All through the warming morning, Afanasy and his sons worked in sweaty, angry silence raking the neat rows of hay that they would begin piling into two high stacks tomorrow. Gregory kept his distance by starting on the opposite side of the field. At fifteen Alexander, six inches shorter than his father, worked hard to do the man's work he knew his father expected of him. He rhythmically pulled the wooden rake through the drying grass as small green frogs croaked and jumped to avoid being hit, but Alexander's mind was swimming. He knew arguing with his father would only make him more determined to say no. Afanasy was stubborn. "This is to be my life—planting, raking, and harvesting the same crops year after year. Live and die in the same house where I was born?" Alexander despaired softly to himself. He fought to keep the tears at bay.

At the end of the last row, Afanasy hefted his wooden rake over his shoulder and turned towards the house. Seeing Melanie waving from the edge of the field, he muttered, "Time to eat." Nodding, Alexander and Gregory followed him to the edge of the field and past the animal sheds. As they entered the house, Gregory patted his brother's shoulder.

Usually Alexander loved plunging hunks of dark, crusty, warm bread into the shared cast iron cooking pot filled with hearty cabbage and salt pork stew. But today it could have been dried grass that he chewed on. Only the clanking of wooden spoons broke the silence. Afanasy swallowed his last bite of bread, wiped his lips with his sleeve, and cleared his throat, "You really want to be a doctor?"

Five down-turned heads popped up and ten eyes snapped to the end of the table. Alexander felt his heart leap to his throat as he met his father's gaze. He nodded. Finally the words tumbled out. "Yes, more than anything. It would be even better than being a teacher. I could help people get well."

"All right. Go." The price of these words was evident in his set jaw. "I'll give you the train fare. But don't forget your family." Jacob smiled at his son, but Afanasy merely rose from the table and walked towards the door.

"Oh, I won't, Papa. I promise. And I'll be home for holidays."

Alexander's mother, Feodora, beamed and reached across the table and squeezed his hand. Gregory and Melanie grinned, but glancing at their father's troubled face, their joy remained wordless. For the second time today, tears filled Alexander's eyes, but this time they were tears of joy.

"When'll you leave?" Melanie asked.

"The term begins the first day of September. That gives me three weeks to help with the fieldwork before I go. Thank you, Papa. I'll make you proud. I will." Afanasy slipped on his hat and opened the door without acknowledging Alexander.

Jacob, still an inch or two taller than his son when he stood up straight, watched his grandson's excitement spread through the small house. He met his daughter-in-law's gaze and smiled. He had grown very fond of the tall, handsome woman. Feodora was a loving mother and submissive wife, and she treated him with kindness and respect, which he appreciated. She slipped around the corner of the table and sat next to him. "That was a good thing you did for Alexander," Feodora said softly as her children shared the happy moment with each other.

For a moment, Jacob said nothing. "Letting a son go is always hard, but Afanasy knows in his heart that this is the right thing to do."

On the other side of the room the siblings' laughter and chatter began to subside. "Do you think Adam was accepted, too?" Gregory asked his brother. In all the commotion Alexander had completely forgotten Adam. He'd walk the three kilometers to the Gorodowiczs' in Bakshty as soon as afternoon chores were done. Perhaps in four years they'd both be doctors. He hoped so.

Chapter 2

Paceviche, Czarist Russia, 1907

On his last night at home Alexander slept in fits and starts, lying awake for what seemed like hours listening to his family breathe and turn in their beds. In one more night he and Adam would sleep in a room with classmates they had yet to meet. At dawn he crawled out of bed and went out to do his chores one last time. After he had received his acceptance letter, the weeks until he was to leave had seemed like a long time. But the days had slipped away quickly, and this afternoon he was leaving to take the night train to Vilnius.

As noon approached, Feodora put the finishing touches on the basket of bread and sausages for Alexander. She had not been in good health for several years and even at this early hour after a good night's sleep, fatigue haunted her. She was grateful that each week Melanie took over more of the cooking and housekeeping. The simple task of packing food into a basket was an effort, but Feodora didn't complain.

Jacob, Afanasy, Alexander, and Gregory came into the house just as Melanie put the vegetable and sausage stew on the table for their mid-day meal. Alexander was anxious to finish and get on his way to Adam's house. "I'll miss your cooking," he said to Melanie and his mother. "I bet the cooks at school can't make stew like this."

"Then you'll just have to come home for something good to eat," his mother teased. "Don't forget the food I packed for your trip."

"I won't, and thanks for fixing it." Alexander turned to his father. "Are you ready? I don't want to be late getting to Adam's."

"I'm ready. Gregory, help your brother with his trunk."

The boys hefted the wooden trunk into the back of the wagon and Alexander bid his grandfather, sister, and brother good-bye.

A DOCTOR'S JOURNEY

"Go with God, my son," Feodora told Alexander as she brushed her thin hands over his cheeks. Tears glistened in her eyes.

"Thank you, Mama. Don't work too hard." After a final hug, Alexander hopped up next to his father and turned to wave to his family and look at his childhood home. A skylark swooped over the raked fields. Soft chirping came from the dark green forest at the edge of the field and on the other side of the road in the marsh by the river a stork searched for frogs. Alexander closed his eyes and breathed the sun-warmed afternoon air. This was the picture he carried with him for the rest of his life.

Afanasy drove Alexander to Adam's house. Mr. Gorodowicz would drive the boys the twenty-four kilometers to the train station in Juracishki. Alexander lifted his trunk into the back of the wagon and faced his father.

"Thank you, Papa, for ... ." No more words found their way out of Alexander's mouth. For the ride. For the new leather boots that still felt stiff on his feet. For agreeing to medical school. For being a loving father. He wanted to say so much, but words hid in his throat. Afanasy opened his arms and Alexander wrapped himself around his sturdy father. They hugged for a long moment. "I'll make you proud, I promise."

Afanasy patted his oldest son on the back. "I know you will. Study hard and write. Your mother will want to know how you are. And don't forget who you are and where you came from." He released his son and, after thanking Adam's father, climbed into the wagon and turned the horse towards home. Alexander watched his father's back until he disappeared in the grove of pine trees.

They headed to pick up Trofim Sokolowicz, the second-year medical student they had known at school in Bakshty. Even though Alexander and Adam had been to the medical school for their interviews, both boys were glad to have an experienced student with them. They were quiet for the first few kilometers, but excitement and anticipation soon caught their tongues, and before long they were chattering with Trofim and reviewing the letters of instructions they had received.

"They told you not to bring clothes because you'll get all the clothes you need. New clothes. They don't want anyone bringing lice into the school, and most boys have lice." Alexander felt a wave of embarrassment. He knew he had lice. So did Adam. It was common, but now Trofim's comment opened his eyes to the fact that not everyone thought lice were just a part of life. It was the first of many new worldviews Alexander would discover.

Adam and Alexander felt like seasoned travelers as they climbed aboard the train for the all-night trip to Vilnius. Yet, in their minds they knew they were riding into a new and foreign life. Unlike their Bakshty classmates, they were going to school to become doctors. They arrived in Vilnius at seven o'clock the next morning, and Trofim got a carriage to take them from the station to the school.

A staff member greeted the new students at the front reception room. When all twenty-four boys had assembled, he directed them to go down the street to the public bath house. A second-year student led the way.

In the dressing room another staff member awaited them. "Good afternoon, gentlemen," he said gruffly. "Take off all your clothes and place them in those willow baskets. Write your name on the tag. They'll be washed and stored until you go home for Christmas holiday; but after you bathe, you'll be given pants, a shirt, a jacket, underclothes, boots, and a hat. You'll wear them until you're fitted for uniforms. The bath is through that door. You have fifteen minutes. Use the soap that is provided. Use as much as you need, and be sure you wash thoroughly, especially your hair. After you bathe, go to those two gentlemen." He pointed to two balding barbers standing by stools at one end of the room. "They'll cut your hair short. Very short." Both barbers smiled, and Alexander noticed they had razors as well as scissors. He guessed that they were all going to have their heads shaved to get rid of lice.

"Then we'll return to the school." The boys scurried to follow orders.

They were back at school by the time dinner was announced, dressed in their new underwear and socks, gray linen shirts, black wool pants, and black leather boots. And their heads were shaved. They put their new caps and boots in storage cubicles in the entry hallway. They put on their new felt slippers they would wear indoors and went to find their beds in the sleeping room.

"Look at these pillows and blankets, Alexander." Adam ran his hand over the white linen sheet and blanket cover and heavy gray wool blanket. "Mine at home weren't nearly this nice."

"Mine either." The wool blanket was scratchy to the touch. A beige linen night shirt was on each bed. Alexander had always shared a bed with Gregory, but tonight he would sleep alone. He wondered what that would be like. The boys scanned the large room filled with beds, each identically covered. The students chatted as they examined their new quarters. Like Alexander and Adam, most came from humble homes and were amazed by the luxury of single beds and new heavy blankets. At one end of the room, which was larger than many of the boys' homes, stood a coal stove that would keep the room warm during Vilnius' cold winter nights. At the other end of the room two windows looked out over the town.

They spent the afternoon listening to a professor explain rules and schedules. They had just enough time after supper to change into their night shirts and brush their teeth and say evening prayers before the kerosene lamps were turned off. Alexander tossed and turned when he tried to sleep. He missed Gregory's warmth, but finally exhaustion from not having slept much on the train or on his last night at home caught up with him. The next thing he was aware of was a voice saying, "Everyone up. Be in the common room in thirty minutes." Breakfast that morning was oatmeal with milk, thick slices of bread with butter and, to the boys' surprise, tea, which for them had always been only a holiday treat. They marveled at the tall coal-heated samovar filled with steaming hot water for tea on a table near the kitchen.

At eight o'clock the boys met their instructors, but the first few days were not devoted to studying medicine. Personal hygiene, regulations, study skills, and manners were taught before textbooks were distributed. The new students were instructed to wash each day, brush their teeth with their new toothbrushes in the morning and the evening, and they were given a schedule for going to the public bath house. They were fitted for uniforms and overcoats and shown how to treat their new boots with boot grease. Second-year students sat with the first-year students at each long table during meals and explained proper etiquette. Every hour was filled with something new to learn.

"Chew with your mouth closed," the blond second-year student at Alexander's table instructed his younger peers. "And hold your fork and knife like this." He demonstrated again how to cut with a knife and pick up food with a fork. The boys were accustomed to eating with spoons, and most of their families, like the Kowals, ate out of a communal cooking pot placed in the middle of the table. Knives and spoons felt cumbersome as they tried to use the utensils correctly. The first-year students listened and learned. They quickly understood that becoming doctors in the czar's medical corps meant becoming gentlemen, too.

Chemistry, biology, and anatomy classes soon filled the medical students' days. Alexander thrived. His love of learning was fulfilled, and nearly every morning he woke before his classmates, slipped out of bed, dressed, and eagerly hurried to the common room to study. In the kitchen the cooks bustled around fixing breakfast, but otherwise it was quiet as Alexander absorbed formulas and facts. And he didn't forget his promise to write home.

> Dear Grandpa, Mama, Papa, Melanie, and Gregory,
> I am well and studying hard and doing well in all my classes. The instructors expect us to give our best, but I don't mind. Our meals are good. I miss you all and hope you are well.
> Love, Alexander, your grandson, son, and brother

A DOCTOR'S JOURNEY

The days flew by. Vilnius was blanketed with snow in mid December when the students prepared to go home for Christmas holiday, but to Alexander it felt like he had arrived just last week. Now he felt the same excitement about seeing his family for the Christmas holiday that he had felt when he was getting ready to come to Vilnius.

No one slept much the last night before vacation. Quiet hours were not enforced. The boys played cards most of the night, then slept on the train to Juracishki.

"There he is." Gregory pointed to his brother descending the train steps. "Look at his overcoat. Alexander! Over here." Alexander rushed towards his father and brother and embraced them. Adam and Trofim followed and waited to shake hands.

"I can't wait to get home," Alexander said to his father. They bundled up in sheepskin coats for the trip over snow-covered roads to Trofim and Adam's houses and then to Paceviche.

The last kilometer seemed like ten. Alexander leaped from the sleigh and ran into the house. Respectfully, he went to his grandfather first.

"Welcome home, Alexander. It looks like school agrees with you."

"It certainly does. You look well, too."

Then Alexander turned and gathered his mother into his arms. His first reaction was how fragile she felt. Her cheeks were sunken and dark circles made her eyes seem larger, but her face still glowed with happiness. His hug was gentle for fear of hurting her.

Alexander stepped back and took off his wool overcoat so his mother could see his uniform. She took a gold button in her hand and kissed it. "Don't you look handsome." She beamed at him. "What a fine uniform." She rubbed her hand over the button again. Happy tears filled her eyes.

Alexander laughed. "Do you like it?"

"Oh, my, yes," she laughed.

Melanie waited until Alexander turned towards her before

throwing her arms around him. How she had missed him.

Feodora and Melanie brought out cheese, bread, milk, and hard boiled eggs, as was the custom for a visitor. Although Alexander was the son, he was now also a visitor for the holidays. A smiling Afanasy sat next to his oldest son. The family gathered around the table hanging on every word as Alexander talked about school.

He folded his uniform and placed it in his trunk and put on the regular clothes that he had worn when he went to Vilnius. They were snug and didn't completely cover his wrists or ankles. He hadn't realized he had grown in four months. For three weeks he slid back into the role of son and peasant. As glad as he was to see his family and, as much as they laughed and talked and enjoyed visits with friends and relatives, he knew he had changed. Home would never feel quite the same to him. He was anxious to go back to school.

At school Alexander quickly settled back into his routine. He studied in the common room early in the morning, and asked for permission to go to the public library in the afternoons.

"You're doing well in your classes, so yes, you may go to the library, but for no more than two hours," Professor Lubowski told him. Alexander was pleased. Time in the library was often the happiest part of the day. He read whatever caught his fancy and soon became friends with the librarians.

The snow disappeared and the trees leafed out. A week before Easter holiday, Alexander was summoned to Professor Lubowski's office.

"Please, sit down." The professor pointed to the wooden chair in front of his desk." Alexander sat and waited for the solemn-faced professor to continue.

"I've just received this telegram, and it has sad news for you." The professor paused. "Your mother died yesterday, Alexander. I don't know of an easy way to tell you. I'm sorry."

He felt the blood drain from his face. Mama? He knew she was ill, but he didn't expect this. Alexander rocked back and forth in his chair and then put his hands over his face and sobbed. The usually undemonstrative professor stood beside him and put his arms around him. After a few minutes Alexander sat up. "Can I go home tomorrow?"

"Of course, I'll get your ticket as soon as the depot office opens. It's only a few days until our holiday starts and you're in excellent standing in your classes. It won't hurt for you to miss a few days."

The trip was a blur. Alexander stared out the window remembering his mother comforting him when he was sick, remembering her baking rye bread every week, remembering her proud smile when she first saw him in his school uniform. He couldn't imagine life without her.

Many years later he told his children, "When I got home, I went right to the cemetery and cried. She was so proud of me. I'm glad she got to see me in my uniform. It meant a lot to her and to me."

It was a sad holiday. Alexander returned to Vilnius with a heavy heart.

Once back in his routine, he found solace in studying and the rest of the term flew by. Alexander earned the highest scores in most classes. One of his professors offered to lend him books for the summer. Alexander gratefully accepted. Back in Paceviche he once again became a peasant, milking the cow, cultivating potatoes, and helping with the harvest. Home, however, was not the same place without his mother. Melanie did the household chores. She couldn't fill the emptiness.

In the evening light, Alexander devoured the books his professor had given him, reading many of them more than once before sharing them with Adam. Reading and learning were his refuge, and Adam was his closest friend. They fished in the river and attended the local dances that the young people of Bakshty held whenever someone's father was convinced to allow his barn to be cleaned out for a party. But they both felt as though they had a foot in two different worlds. Bakshty and Paceviche had not changed, but they had. As much as they loved their homes and families, they couldn't wait to be on the train back to Vilnius to become second-year students and to help new students become a part of the fabric of the school.

For the next three years Alexander's life had two seasons—school from September to June, working on the farm during July and August. He climbed aboard the train to Vilnius for his last year of medical school focused on his future profession. He didn't expect to meet the girl who would change his life.

Chapter 3

Vilnius, Czarist Russia, 1911

Snow began falling in early November. By the first day of classes in 1911 after the Christmas holiday, two feet of snow covered Vilnius, the temperature seldom rose above freezing, and the sun seldom broke through the waxed paper sky. Alexander and his classmates scurried from the public bath house, knowing their wet hair would be frozen by the time they returned to the school.

Professor Boris Ivanovich ended his lecture a few minutes early the first Monday of the new term to tell the boys some good news. In two weeks they would be hosting a winter dance for the girls from Madame Kaminska's School for Young Ladies. Since many of the boys only knew folk dances, beginning tonight, there would be formal dance lessons each evening before supper, taught by the wives of faculty members. The news was met with surprise, laughter, and some trepidation. But the idea of meeting girls pleased the boys. This was a welcome break from the arduous study of pathology, physiology, and anatomy. Like Alexander, most of the boys came from small villages, had little knowledge of formal social events, and were unsure of what such a dance might be like. Doctors, however, were expected to take part in society, and this dance, they realized, was an important part of their preparation. The czar had high expectations of the young men he was training to go out and care for people's health.

Meeting pretty girls was motivation enough that snowy afternoon to get the medical students to move the common room tables for dance instruction even before the faculty wives arrived. Professor Sokolovich provided music with his accordion and after an hour, most of the boys were able to hesitantly waltz to the music. Each night they improved, and by the end of the second week, they were moving confidently under the tutelage of their teachers' spouses. Every day they worked on social graces—introducing themselves, carrying on a conversation, serving a young lady a cup of tea, and being socially astute. On the final day of preparation, the young doctors-in-training danced, conversed, and deftly served tea. Professor Boris Ivanovich declared that they were perfect young gentlemen ready to meet the young ladies from Madame Kaminska's school.

On a Saturday evening in frigid January, Alexander in his freshly brushed uniform entered the common room with his classmates, unaware that this night his life would change forever. A table near the coal stove at the far end of the room was covered with a white lace cloth brought to the school for the occasion by Professor Ivanovich's wife. A tall polished brass coal-heated samovar held steaming hot water and a small gleaming brass teapot of strongly brewed tea stood at the center surrounded by china cups and platters of ginger cookies. Dark wood chairs encircled the open space of the room like guards. At one side of the room, three men in dark blue wool tunics and brown knee-high leather boots sat in a semicircle, one playing an accordion, one a violin, and one a balalayka.

Kerosene lamps flickered. As the boys fidgeted with their freshly brushed uniforms, the unfamiliar high tones of girls' laughter and chatter floated into the room and mingled with the music. Under the watchful eyes of the faculty and their wives, the boys walked to the door, each greeting a girl by kissing her hand and saying the practiced, "Hello, my name is ---. May I have the privilege of the first dance?" The initial awkwardness soon dissipated as couples swirled around the room waltzing and talking. Madame Kaminska's was a finishing school for young ladies from families of well-to-do landowners, and these families expected daughters to become the wives of other landed gentry. Proper manners, the care and running of a household, needlework, and social graces were important parts of Madame Kaminska's lessons. The dance was an opportunity for the girls to practice the social skills they had been learning.

Alexander had danced with several partners when he saw a girl with porcelain skin and a waist so tiny he thought he could encircle it with his hands. Ivory combs held her long thick chestnut hair in a chignon. She stood by the refreshment table as one of his classmates lifted the gleaming teapot, poured a small amount of strong tea into a china cup and filled it with hot water from the samovar. He handed the cup to her with a smile. She took it in her white-gloved hands with ease. Using the conversational skills Madame Kaminska taught her students, the girl chatted effortlessly. She's the prettiest girl here, Alexander thought as he watched her from across the room.

Almost without realizing what he was doing, he walked over to the girl and her partner never taking his gaze from her. "Hello," he said, his voice cracking slightly, suddenly overcome with shyness. She smiled.

"I'm Alexander Kowal." He bowed slightly, remembering the etiquette lessons from the faculty wives.

"I'm Olimpia Legutko," she answered extending her gloved hand for him to kiss.

His hand trembled slightly as he inhaled the floral fragrance of her perfume. "Olimpia," he said silently, "what an unusual and beautiful name."

"Would you care to dance after you finish your tea?" Alexander asked before he had actually listened to the music. He was glad to hear a familiar melody that had been played during last week's lessons. Olimpia handed her empty cup to her previous partner, and Alexander led her to join the wave of dancers. Her emerald velvet dress felt soft and luxurious under his perspiring hand as he guided her around the room. He was surprised that she followed his steps with ease as though they had danced together often. With practiced grace the petite girl engaged him in conversation and to Alexander, the music ended much too soon.

Alexander wanted to dance with Olimpia again, but the medical students had been admonished to dance only once with each young lady to be sure no one was left out. Alexander led Olimpia back to a chair, bowed slightly as she smiled at him and held her hand out for him to kiss. He continued to ask other young ladies to dance, but out of the corner of his eye, he kept track of Olimpia.

The evening was the highlight of the long cold month. Much to the students' delight, the two schools agreed to hold more dances during the winter with the next one in two weeks to be at Madame Kaminska's. As he lay each night in his narrow bed in the cold sleeping room under the heavy blankets, Alexander found himself thinking of Olimpia and her dark blue eyes, remembering her intoxicating perfume, which was unlike the fragrance of any girl he had ever known.

Madame Kaminska's school was housed in a large red brick building. On the appointed night the dining room with its heavy emerald-green silk drapes, polished dark pine floors, and candle chandeliers was cleared of tables. The same musical trio that had played at the last dance was ensconced at one end of the room. Alexander entered the foyer searching for Olimpia, but not seeing her. He escorted a tall blonde, who introduced herself as Celina, to the dining room and waltzed with her for the first dance. He led her to a chair, bowed, kissed her hand, and turned to scan the room. He saw Olimpia entering the room with his friend Nikolas. Her yellow brocade dress with a dark brown sash and full skirt emphasized her tiny waist. Alexander felt a pang of jealousy as Nikolas guided Olimpia smoothly around the floor, obviously charming her with his conversation. Alexander turned to a round-faced girl he remembered dancing with last time and invited her to dance. He forced himself to be attentive and talkative. When the music ended, he led the girl to a chair near Olimpia. As quickly as he could while still being polite, he thanked her and turned toward Olimpia.

When Olimpia saw him, she smiled. "Alexander, how nice to see you again."

He felt himself blushing. She remembered his name. Perhaps she had been thinking of him, too. And as he brushed his lips on her gloved hand, he inhaled the familiar fragrance of flowers. The music started, and she took his arm before he had asked for a dance. He led her to the middle of the floor and they began to waltz. Alexander had rehearsed this moment in his head every night, but inhaling her floral scent and feeling the smooth yellow brocade under his palm emptied his mind. Fortunately, Olimpia, asked, "How are your studies going?"

He looked down at her and smiled. "The professors are working us hard," he answered. "There's so much to learn this last year. Sometimes I think my head will explode from all the facts I've memorized. But we're all excited for May 1. That's when we'll learn where our first jobs are."

The rest of the dance flew by and the conversation flowed easily. Alexander realized that Olimpia was not only beautiful, but also very bright and well-read. They made their way to the refreshment table, and over tea, discovered they both liked to read similar books.

The two schools scheduled one last dance at Madame Kaminska's a few weeks after Easter. This time Alexander waited in the foyer until Olimpia appeared on the stairs. She scanned the waiting faces until she found his. She smiled at him. He moved to the banister and extended his hand to take her gloved one and inhale the now familiar rose scent as he kissed her hand. "You look lovely, Olimpia."

Their classmates understood that Alexander and Olimpia preferred each other's company and allowed them space. They danced with others as was proper, but most of the evening they spent together. Madame Kaminska announced the last dance, and Alexander and Olimpia put down their tea cups.

"May I write to you when I get to my new job?" Alexander asked as they danced.

"I'd like that." This serious young man was not like any of the landowners' sons she knew at home. His intelligence and intensity drew her to him. He was the first young man who seemed to love learning new things in the same way she did. Olimpia smiled. "Will you be in the park on Sunday? Several of us are going there in the afternoon to paint. I could give you my address."

Alexander grinned. "I think I can give up studying for a little while."

And that was the beginning of their romance that would be filled with great joy, separation, and sadness.

Although Alexander and Olimpia saw each other a few times that spring, Alexander was consumed with his studies. Passing final exams and getting a physician's certificate was utmost in his mind. It had been a long four years. He had come to Vilnius as a naïve fifteen-year-old wearing homemade clothes, and now four years later he was poised to accept a position as a doctor in a clinic caring for ill peasants, earning more in a month that his father had ever earned in a year.

He was about to become a doctor, but he still saw spring through a farmer's eyes. Walking by the greening grass and blooming flowers outside the medical school, he thought of his father and brother sowing oats and barley and of his sister nurturing the new garden plants. He remembered the feel of the dark soil in his hands and the delicate green of the new crops as they rose from the ground. This would be the first summer he had not helped harvest the crops. Back at a table in the study room, those images were buried as he memorized the symptoms and signs of illness that would soon be his daily work.

Chapter 4

Paceviche, Czarist Russia, 1911

"She smelled so wonderful," he told his sister Melanie as they sat outside the family home that June between graduation and the beginning of his first medical assignment. Even though Melanie was now married and would soon give birth to her first child, she was still Alexander's confidant. "Sweet Rose is her favorite fragrance. I don't remember what we talked about," he said as he recalled the evening of the first dance, "but by the end of the evening, my heart was hers. Now I have to convince this beautiful girl that her heart belongs to me."

Melanie reached for her brother's hand. "Why wouldn't she be attracted to such a handsome doctor? She may already be smitten with you. But Alexander, are you sure you aren't setting yourself up for disappointment? Why do you think her father would ever give his blessing to anything serious between the two of you? You're definitely below her social class."

Alexander laughed and squeezed his sister's hand affectionately. "I suppose that's a possibility, but look how far I've come in four years! I can't let the chance that he'll disapprove keep me from trying. I don't give up. You know that better than anyone else, Melanie."

That unwillingness to give up would prove to be one of Alexander's most important personal attributes, although he certainly wasn't aware of it as he and Melanie sat talking and enjoying being together that June evening. Persistence was a legacy he would pass on to his children, especially his youngest daughter who would cling to it in her darkest hours.

In May Alexander had graduated at the top of his class. Medical reference books, a set of medical instruments, and the best position in the

Vilnius district were his reward. He was to be a physician's assistant to the doctor at the free community clinic for peasants in Kryviche. This plum assignment was especially pleasing since Olimpia Legutko's Polish family lived on their large estate nearby. Alexander had grown up speaking Russian and had been taught to write in the Cyrillic alphabet. Because Kryviche was a part of what had once been the commonwealth of Poland until it had been subjugated by the czar in the eighteenth century, the noble class of the Vilnius region, including the Legutkos, spoke Polish at home. Although learning Russian was required, they preferred speaking and writing in Polish, which is based on the Latin alphabet. They were officially a part of Russia, but they cleaved to the culture of their ancestors. The peasants, who were to be Alexander's patients, spoke Russian. However, Alexander wanted to learn Polish. He wanted to bring himself up to the social level of Olimpia's family, and speaking Polish was, he decided, one way to do that. Alexander could not believe his good fortune to be this close to the beautiful petite girl he met at the winter dance. Instead of long train rides to see her, he needed only a horse or horse and buggy. He set about preparing for his first medical assignment with Olimpia's smile and dark eyes in his mind.

While visiting his family in Paceviche, Alexander learned that Dr. Filmon Muszczun, the physician at the clinic in nearby Bakshty, had previously been assigned to the Kryviche clinic, and so he sought him out for advice.

"Kryviche's a wonderful place. I have many good friends there. You'll like them," Dr. Muszczun told Alexander. In fact, I'll go with you and introduce you. It'll be great fun to see everyone, and I'm due for a holiday." It was an unexpected offer that Alexander readily accepted. "We must take them something to drink. A good quality drink. They like parties, and a party will be an excellent introduction. I'll let the magistrate know we're coming, and he'll make the arrangements."

With his new medical books and instruments, his trunk of clothes, a few household items, and a fifty-liter keg of the best beer brewed by the most popular brewer in Bakshty, Alexander and his new friend Dr. Muszczun stepped off the train at the Kryviche depot at noon on the last day of June. The gregarious magistrate, with freshly shined brass buttons on his black uniform, was waiting to take Alexander's trunks to the hospital and then to take the two doctors to his well-kept bungalow where the elite of the town had gathered to meet the young Dr. Kowal.

Entering the magistrate's house through the kitchen, Alexander and Dr. Muszczun were greeted by a table laden with sausages, fresh radishes, cheeses, and breads of all shapes and sizes that the guests had brought to go with the beer. Landowners, government administrators, and other professional people filled the magistrate's home with laughter, singing, jovial conversation, and welcome. The school teacher, much to Alexander's surprise and delight, had been his teacher in Bakshty. Two prominent people were not among the party goers, the priest and Dr. Bogdan Niewiadomski, Alexander's supervisor. As beer flowed and the noise level rose, it was decided that the party, which finally ended at midnight, would continue the next night as a housewarming at Dr. Kowal's apartment at the clinic.

"But I don't have anything to feed them, Filmon. What'll I do?" Alexander worried.

"Don't worry," his new friend assured him, "they'll bring the food and beer. It's good they like you."

Alexander slept well that night in his sparsely furnished two-room apartment in the center of the Kryviche Clinic compound. He woke at dawn to the unfamiliar sounds of his new home. He could hear doors opening and shutting and the murmur of voices in distant rooms. He rose groggily and shuffled from his bedroom into his sitting room and looked out the single window in his living quarters. While trying to clear sleep from his brain, he looked at the hospital garden where carrots, potatoes, cabbages, and other crops thrived. It reminded him of the family gardens beside the river in Paceviche, and he thought of Melanie who was probably hoeing weeds this morning. This garden was larger, of course, but showed the same attentive care Melanie gave her garden.

After growing up in a one-room house and spending the last four years in a dormitory, his two-room apartment felt quite large. From his sitting room, one door led to the pharmacy storage room, one door to his small bedroom, and one door opened into the clinic's reception room, the only entrance to the apartment. When someone needed medicine, Alexander noted, he would have to get it from the storage room. Dr. Muszczun had told him that the midwife, Julia Wieckowska, and the cook also had small apartments in the clinic and that women from the village were hired as nurses' aides to clean and help care for patients.

Alexander brushed his new uniform and cleaned up as best he could before leaving his apartment. Julia Wieckowska was waiting for him in the reception room. She appeared to have been awake for quite some time.

"Good morning. It was a good welcome party? Yes?" Julia smiled at the new doctor's bleary eyes.

"Very good. Yes." Alexander smiled. His head ached from the beer and lack of sleep, but he did his best to look alert and professional.

"Why don't we start the day with a tour of your new home," Julia suggested. She looked at Alexander. "But first let's get some tea in the dining room and maybe something to eat."

The tea, crusty bread, and soft-boiled eggs helped clear Alexander's head.

Julia's pride in the clinic was evident as she showed him around. Separate five-bed wards and isolation rooms for male and female patients filled the east and west wings of the small hospital. The reception room and an examination room near the front door, storage rooms for linens and supplies, a kitchen at the back of the building, and the other two apartments completed the hospital. They walked through the kitchen to the garden Alexander had seen from his window. It was larger than he had realized.

"The garden and those apple and plum trees are tended by the cook and maintenance man and provide fresh food for all of us staff and patients in the summer." Julia pointed to the dozen or so trees growing in neat rows at one side of the garden. "And they store vegetables and fruits in the root cellar for winter. The cook knows her way around the kitchen. We eat well. You already sampled her bread."

Alexander nodded in agreement as Julia led him on. Behind the garden she showed him the barn and shed for the milk cows, pigs, and chickens, and the other small shed for the hospital's horse and buggy. At last they stood outside a small one-room house behind the barn where the maintenance man lived.

"That's pretty much everything. Dr. Niewiadomski lives about five kilometers away in his own home," Julia explained. "We see him during the day and can send someone to get him if we need him for an emergency during the night. But that doesn't happen very often. I hope you'll like it here, Dr. Kowal. It's the best place I've ever worked."

"I'm impressed," Alexander told her. "I can see why you're proud of it."

Julia smiled. She liked this young man. "Time for us to start our day. Dr. Niewiadomski will be here soon. He expects us to be ready to work when he arrives."

Alexander's first day was underway. Dr. Niewiadomski arrived at the clinic before eight o'clock ready to continue Alexander's orientation. The day was a blur of introductions to staff, explanations of procedures and expectations. By three o'clock, Alexander was relieved when Dr. Niewiadomski took his leave. He sat in the only chair in his new home and fell asleep. But his day was not over.

True to their word, the party goers from the previous night arrived with beer, food, and a few household items for Alexander's new home. Dr. Niewiadomski and his wife came to the party, but stayed only an hour. He was cordial, but Alexander could not help but notice that his new supervisor remained aloof from the other members of the elite.

Alexander pulled Dr. Muszczun aside and asked him about this. "He's Polish and holds himself above the others," Dr. Muszczun explained. "And I suppose that some of the old wounds are still unhealed." Alexander knew he was referring to the 1863 Polish uprising against the czar when the Polish people strove to declare their independence. The uprising had been crushed; Polish culture and language had been stifled. Even now Roman Catholicism, the faith of most Poles, was tolerated, but marginalized. Alexander was glad to have this insight about his new supervisor. And it occurred to him that Dr. Niewiadomski might be pleased that he wanted to learn Polish.

The parties were the beginning of a good relationship between the young Dr. Kowal and the educated elite of the town. The fact that he was a handsome, eligible bachelor didn't hurt. Families with unmarried daughters saw his potential as a husband. The Russian Orthodox priest in particular had two daughters in need of husbands, and his interest in Alexander as a son-in-law was too great for him to completely hide. It was a heady experience for Alexander, but his thoughts of Olimpia tempered any interest he may have had in a village girl. He was polite and gracious, but was sure to show no special interest in any of the young ladies, no matter how charming they were. But he did enjoy the lively social life.

Alexander set about learning his duties and the routines of the clinic. During the first weeks Dr. Niewiadomski came every day to supervise and demonstrate how things should be done. By the time the leaves on the trees changed color, Dr. Niewiadomski was spending only a few hours at the clinic every week, and by the first snowfall, he appeared sporadically. Dr. Niewiadomski trusted the young Dr. Kowal to be in charge of the hospital, which left him free to see paying patients, members of the landed gentry and professionals who could afford to pay for a doctor's services. Alexander loved his work at the clinic, and he enjoyed taking the horse and buggy to make house calls. Walking or riding through the village in his dark green uniform, he was greeted with a kind of respect that was new to him. Having money to spend was also an exhilarating experience. Taking the train to Vilnius, he purchased clothes, ate in cafes, and checked out books from the library to take back to Kryviche. He also sent money to his family, and every month he saved ten percent of his salary.

Soon after his arrival, Alexander approached Dr. Niewiadomski about his desire to learn Polish. "I'd be delighted to lend you books in Polish, Alexander. It's a beautiful language. Come to my house after you finish here at the clinic today, and I'll give you some books to read and study."

Alexander was amazed at the vastness of Dr. Niewiadomski's personal library. One wall of his office was floor-to-ceiling bookshelves filled with books. At that moment, Alexander knew he, too, wanted one day to have such a library.

The doctor pulled several books from the shelves and handed them to Alexander. "Here's one by Henryk Sienkiewicz, my favorite Polish author. What a storyteller. Once you master the language, you won't be able to put his books down."

Alexander began learning Polish as quickly as he could. He devoted time each night to learning to read Polish. No matter how tired he was, he read at least one page of a book. The village people liked to have fun, and the handsome, unmarried young doctor seldom was without an invitation to someone's house for a meal or a party, but every night he read something in Polish. At first reading a Polish book was a slow, painful process, but his affinity for languages and the thought of talking to Olimpia in Polish kept him at his studies.

When he told his new colleague Julia that he was learning Polish, she was delighted to practice speaking the language with him. "*Dzien dobry*," she greeted him each morning. Good day. She wove Polish words into their conversations, and their noontime dinners often became a language class. Before long he knew the Polish words for every food and dish the cook served.

"Dr. Niewiadomski, you're certainly right about Henryk Sienkiewicz. I can become so engrossed in his story, I don't realize how much time I've been reading," Alexander told his supervisor.

Dr. Niewiadomski smiled. "You have good taste in literature, Alexander. I have more books of his when you finish that one." Perhaps it was his desire to speak Polish that cemented his relationship with his supervisor and the midwife, for they got along very well. One night he felt confident enough to write a letter in Polish asking Olimpia if he might call on her. He copied it five times before he was satisfied with the wording and spelling.

She responded:

Respected Dr. Kowal,
My father says that you may visit for a Sunday afternoon. My mother and I will be visiting my aunt and cousins for two weeks beginning September 18. Perhaps you can come before then. I didn't know you could write in Polish.
Respectfully,
Olimpia Legutko

It was early September when Alexander borrowed the hospital's horse and buggy for his first visit to Wincentow, the Legutko's estate, an hour's drive from Kryviche. His Polish was improving, but still rudimentary, so he practiced with only the horse to listen as he drove through the countryside and then past the orchards and fields of the Legutko estate. Five years ago he was a farmer in his family's fields helping his father coax crops to prosper. Now he was a professional, a doctor wearing a new black suit he had purchased from a Vilnius tailor, and he was calling on a female member of the gentry. In 1911 in the czar's world, such a life transition was rare, and Alexander knew he still had much to learn about his new role in society. With no one to teach him, he had to be observant and cautious.

Chapter 5

Wincentow near Kryviche, Czarist Russia, 1911

The Legutko's one-story house appeared through the trees. It was a grand house to Alexander's eyes, a far cry from the Kowal's one-room house in Paceviche. Its wood exterior was painted dark gray, almost black, as was the custom, and a wide porch greeted visitors. A housemaid in a gray dress and starched white apron answered his knock, led him into the sitting room, and indicated he should sit in the chair near the window. Alexander looked at the elegant furnishings, heavy draperies, and paintings that lined the walls. He could see into the dining room and marveled at the glass chandelier hanging above the long rectangular table. He had never been in a house as magnificent as this. His stomach tightened. Whatever made him think a girl who was raised in a home like this would even consider him?

Then Olimpia and her mother appeared in the doorway. He stood, trying to gain his composure. Olimpia smiled brightly as she introduced him to her mother as the "brilliant Dr. Kowal who graduated at the top of his class." He greeted them in Polish. Mrs. Legutko, whatever she may have been thinking, was as gracious as her daughter and made Alexander feel welcome. His knees ceased shaking. Olimpia was more beautiful than he remembered. She wore a dark blue wool dress with a white collar and tiny white buttons from waist to neckline. Her hair was braided and coiled on top of her head. She seemed as happy to see him as he was to see her. As was the custom, the visit was chaperoned at all times, and Alexander was invited to share tea with the family. Olimpia's father and brothers were politely formal and reserved. Alexander left, never having spent a moment alone with Olimpia. But seeing her again reignited his feelings for her. As she talked, he was sure that she was favorably inclined towards him, even if her father seemed a bit distrusting of this stranger who his daughter had met at school. Alexander hummed to himself all the way back to Kryviche. The rising turmoil that was sending tremors throughout Russia and Europe was far from his thoughts. But these tensions were sending their tentacles towards Kryviche.

"Unfortunately," Alexander wrote to his sister Melanie soon after that first visit to the Legutko's, "when I met them, they didn't seem to feel any warmth for me. They were very polite, but I am little more than an educated peasant in their eyes. She is her Polish family's princess—her father's darling—the only girl with four brothers. They expect her to be courted by young, wealthy, Roman Catholic Polish noblemen, not a young Russian Orthodox doctor who is paid by the czar. I could hardly be a less suitable suitor."

Persistence, however, was one of Alexander's strongest traits, and fueled by ardor, he was determined to win over Olimpia's father and mother. He continued courting her. He wrote letters to her and made more hour-long buggy rides to the Legutko's. His cause was helped by Olimpia's growing fondness for him and her sweet way of swaying her father, who doted on her and could see that Olimpia was smitten with the young doctor. Mr. Legutko couldn't bear to break his daughter's heart. So, he didn't demand the cook serve this young Belarusian, who spoke Russian-accented Polish, the traditional black soup, a thick vegetable broth made with pig's blood that was the customary culinary notice to a young man that he should not call on a young lady again.

Alexander's Polish improved, and he became a familiar visitor at the Legutko's during the next two years. After the first year, Olimpia's mother would excuse herself from their company and allow the young couple time to be alone, but she was never far away. Then came walks through the orchards. Eventually, they took short buggy rides around the estate and had picnics by the river that ran near the edge of the estate. Olimpia's fondness for Alexander grew into love, and they discussed their future. Religion was an issue for the family, and Alexander told Olimpia he would convert to Catholicism. His family had never been particularly religious; he felt no strong ties to the Russian Orthodox Church. A larger hurdle in his mind was how to approach Olimpia's father for his beloved daughter's hand in marriage. Although always gracious towards Alexander, Mr. Legutko was an imposing man, and Alexander felt disapproval bubbling under the surface of his polite exterior.

But almost three years after his move to Kryviche, the same determination that had enabled Alexander to confront his father about wanting to leave the village and become a doctor, enhanced by his love of Olimpia, gave him the courage to seek Mr. Legutko's permission to marry Olimpia. The apple trees were blooming and chirping birds flitted from one flowering bush to another when Alexander drove down the lane to the Legutkos' estate in the spring of 1914. He had rehearsed what he would say dozens of times.

Turning into the lane that led to the Legutko's house, he saw Mr. Legutko in a field supervising the peasants sowing barley seeds. Alexander pulled on the reins and the horse stopped, happy to nibble on the new green grass by the side of the road. Alexander ran his fingers through his hair, climbed out of the buggy and over the fence, and walked towards Mr. Legutko. He stood back waiting until Mr. Legutko finished his firm orders to the workers. Then he stepped forward extending his hand.

"Good morning, sir."

"Well, Dr. Kowal, you're out and about early today."

After a few minutes of polite conversation, Alexander plunged into his mission of the day. "I'd like to speak to you about something important, if it is convenient," Alexander said.

Mr. Legutko nodded. "Of course, why don't we sit under those trees?" He motioned to a grassy spot near a stream. It wasn't quite the setting Alexander had envisioned, but he agreed.

After settling in the shade on some rocks on the bank by the stream, Alexander looked directly at Mr. Legutko, took a deep breath, and forged ahead with his request. "Your daughter and I have been seeing each other for almost three years, and I believe we are well-suited to each other. I love Olimpia."

Alexander paused and sat up a little straighter. "My position at the clinic supplies me with adequate income to support a wife, although certainly not in the lifestyle in which Olimpia has been brought up. But she'll have a comfortable life as a physician's wife." Alexander swallowed, inhaled, and let his breath out slowly. "Sir, I'm asking for her hand in marriage. Will you give your permission for Olimpia to marry me?" The spoken words didn't sound quite as caring and confident as they had when he rehearsed them. Alexander felt his heart beating.

He paused, waiting for Olimpia's father to say something. Mr. Legutko looked away but said nothing. Muffled voices of the field hands and water splashing over the rocks in the stream bed filled the silence. Rivulets of perspiration trickled down Alexander's forehead.

Finally Mr. Legutko's gaze met Alexander's. "I know my daughter cares for you. She lights up when she sees you coming up the lane. I suppose I knew that this day was inevitable." He looked in the distance and then turned his eyes back to Alexander.

He hesitated. Was he going to say no? "You're an honorable young man, even if you aren't Polish. But there's the matter of religion."

"I've told Olimpia that I'll take instruction in the Roman Catholic faith," Alexander blurted to counter that argument. "It won't be a problem."

Mr. Legutko pulled up a long blade of grass and rubbed it between his fingers. "Well, that's good. Our faith is important to us. I suppose you two have talked about it. Her mother is fond of you and has spoken to me in your favor, although I suspect she did so at Olimpia's behest."

Mr. Legutko paused and remained silent. Alexander was trying to decide what else he could say to make his case when Mr. Legutko sighed deeply as though it came from his soul. He put his hand on Alexander's shoulder. "Yes, you have my permission to marry my sweet Olimpia. But first, you must complete the instruction and take communion in our church. And there must be a proper engagement. Weddings can't be rushed."

"Thank you, sir. Thank you. I'll take good care of your daughter, sir." Alexander's heart was pounding.

His future father-in-law nodded. "I'm sure you will. Of course," Mr. Legutko smiled for the first time, "Olimpia must accept your proposal."

"I believe she will," Alexander laughed. Relief swept his body. "I'll always take excellent care of your daughter. I promise." He shook Mr. Legutko's hand.

"Come up to the house. We must seal this with a bit of vodka, don't you think?" Mr. Legutko laughed.

"Absolutely." Alexander beamed.

Olimpia and her mother were sitting on the veranda when the two men drove up in Alexander's buggy.

Mr. Legutko looked at his wife and took Olimpia's hand. "My little one, Dr. Kowal has asked for your hand in marriage." He paused and looked at the beaming doctor standing slightly behind him. "I've given my permission." He looked again at his wife whose eyes were brimming with tears.

Olimpia's smile lit up her face. "Thank you, Father. Thank you." She hugged him and grinned at Alexander, who stood off to one side not quite knowing what to do next. He actually hadn't thought about what would happen after Mr. Legutko said yes.

Olimpia turned and embraced her mother. "Be happy, my daughter," she whispered in her ear. "Be happy."

Olimpia turned to Alexander. He reached for her hand, held it for a moment, and kissed it. She smiled, held his hand in both of hers, and looked at him adoringly. Although they may have wanted to be alone, this was a formal occasion, and a kiss on the hand in front of her parents was as intimate as they could be. Alexander bowed to Olimpia's mother and kissed her hand. Then Mr. Legutko led them all into the house. After the vodka toasts and some cheese and bread, a very happy Alexander drove back to the clinic.

Chapter 6

Kryviche, Czarist Russia, 1914

That night Alexander fell asleep smiling. Just as he had told his sister Melanie before he left for Kryviche, it wasn't in his nature to give up when he wanted something, and he had known almost as soon as he met Olimpia that someday he wanted to marry her. He had courted her with measured persistence, knowing he had to win her father's approval. He laughed silently realizing that he had really courted her father as much as he had courted Olimpia, understanding that he would decide whether or not Alexander would be his son-in-law. Now Alexander had permission to marry Olimpia. His heart was full.

This was the second major life-changing decision he had made since leaving medical school. The first one had been two years ago. It had changed not his life path, but that of his brother Gregory. Tensions between countries were high and rising in Europe. Things were changing in Czar Nicholas' Russia, but the Kowals in Paceviche were not aware that world events were aligning to impact their lives. During Alexander's four years at medical school, he and his fellow students had heard more and more rumblings of dissatisfaction spreading across the vast Russian empire. However, they were insulated within the walls of the Vilnius Medical University, focused on memorizing muscles and disease symptoms. But while these teen-aged boys studied to become doctors, envisioning themselves in handsome dark green wool uniforms tending to ailing people, poverty-stricken workers' anger and resentment grew towards the wealthy.

While Alexander was still living at home in Paceviche in 1905, these feelings of anger in cities had exploded in the Bloody Sunday uprising. In response the czar had issued his "October Manifesto" which instigated some reforms, including the formation of medical schools such as the one in Vilnius. That Alexander had the opportunity to attend medical school without paying any tuition was in reality the result of Bloody Sunday. Czar Nicholas had also created the Imperial Duma, a parliamentary body that was supposed to give citizens some say in government, but the disparity between the very wealthy and the very poor did not diminish. The Bolsheviks continued fomenting unrest among peasants and workers against the czar, nobility, and large landowners. Workers' strikes erupted in cities, including St. Petersburg. But Vilnius and Paceviche were far removed from St. Petersburg, which was hundreds of kilometers away, and life remained much the same as it had for generations. Sometimes young men from large cities mysteriously appeared in small towns and villages and tried to lead the peasants to revolt. Letters from Melanie in Paceviche rarely mentioned any unrest, although once in a while a Bolshevik arrived in Bakshty to spread a message of a need for change, planting the seed of discontent in the peasant's minds. However, the Kowals, like their neighbors, had owned their small farms for generations and weren't willing to risk doing anything that might harm their survival. They didn't know that political unrest was about to change Mother Russia.

As he treated patients almost eight years after Bloody Sunday, Alexander heard more about strikes and uprisings during evening talks with the magistrate. These events were unsettling. Hearing about this spreading violence, Alexander realized his brother Gregory was at risk. If he were drafted into the army, and most certainly he would be drafted, his lack of education and skills would put him on the front lines of any conflict. The only way to avoid the draft was to leave the country.

The more Alexander heard about the turmoil, the more apprehensive he became for Gregory. He decided that he must act. He confided his concerns to Julia as they ate dinner each day.

"Gregory has to go to America," Alexander told Julia as they finished their rich pork stew, one of the cook's best dishes. "If I don't send him away, I'm afraid he has no future."

"Then do what you think is right. He's fortunate to have a brother who can afford to help him. America. A family from my village went there a few years ago. I hear they're happy and doing well." Julia confirmed his feelings. Gregory had to leave. They'd just have to convince his father.

Afanasy had come to accept Alexander's choice to be a doctor. It had raised his status in the village. Lifelong friends never failed to praise him for having such a smart successful son. Sending Gregory to America knowing he might never see him again would be heartwrenching. Afanasy was a strict father, but his love of his children could never be questioned.

Alexander knew a meager future lay ahead for Gregory after army service (if he survived) when he returned to Paceviche, so in late summer of 1912, he checked on the cost of a steamship ticket to America for Gregory and wrote to his family.

The letter was brief:

I have asked for a week's leave. Gregory, meet me at the train station on September 18.

Gregory was there with the family cart and horse when Alexander stepped off the train. "You're soon going to be taller than I am, Gregory!" Alexander laughed as they carried his bags to the cart.

"I'm fifteen. I'm not just your little brother anymore," he said as they climbed into the cart and headed down the hard-dirt road towards home.

"I know. That's why I've come home. Don't rush the horse. We have much to discuss." Gregory looked puzzled. Alexander turned his head towards his slim muscular brother.. "I don't know how much you know about what's happening in the big cities and the government, Gregory, but things are changing. I'm not sure what's coming, but I don't think it'll be good." He paused and looked at the familiar landscape and houses that had changed little since his first train trip to apply to the teacher's college.

"Lots of people are unhappy, and there's talk about getting rid of the czar. I can't imagine that happening, but from the people I talk to in Kryviche, most think trouble is on the horizon. I hear about conflict between European countries, too. The kaiser in Germany says all sorts of inflammatory things that I read in the newspaper. Who knows if Russia will get pulled into a war if one's started? The czar has so many alliances with other countries. I really don't understand all of it, but what I read worries me."

"We hear about strikes in the cities, but everything here is fine," Gregory said. "And I don't know anything about those countries in Europe."

"Well, yes, it's quiet here, but when you're drafted, you'll be sent who knows where and you'll be in the thick of any fighting the army sends you to."

"I haven't thought much about the draft. I'm still too young. I suppose I will have to go when I'm eighteen, but what can I do? Run away?"

"Actually, yes. I want to send you to America."

Gregory's eyes widened. "America?"

"I've checked it out. I'll pay for your ticket. I've already written to the brother of one of my classmates. His name is Peter Czernik and he's been in America in New York City for about five years. He has a good job and wrote back to me agreeing to be your sponsor." Gregory couldn't speak. He gripped the reins tighter. Leave Paceviche? He'd never thought of leaving the farm.

"I don't know. Papa needs me. He can't take care of the place without me. It's too much for him."

"That's true, but if you're drafted, you won't be home to help him either. Maybe Melanie and Pahom will move in to help him."

Drafted? Gregory shuddered. His brother's words made the draft seem imminent. Three years wasn't that long. He knew that young men who were drafted often didn't ever come home. Alexander gave his brother time to digest the idea of leaving.

Gregory relaxed his grip on the reins and breathed deeply. He'd heard stories of people who had gone to America and became prosperous. They had good jobs and nice houses. It was a future he'd never dreamed of. But now his brother was making it possible. "I suppose it could be all right for Papa. He might like having Melanie back in the house, and he's crazy about the baby." Alexander nodded, but said nothing. He wanted Gregory to make his own choice.

They rode in silence for nearly half-an-hour. Gregory broke the reverie. "Alexander, I think you're right. I'll go." Alexander wrapped his arm around his brother and pulled him close.

"It won't be easy. I missed all of you a lot when I went to Vilnius, but I learned to adjust. You'll have to work hard, but you're smart. You know how to watch and learn."

"It's funny that you came home with this idea now. Just last week when I was chasing that sow that keeps digging under the fence and escaping, I talked to Wasyl Makowczyk who lives three farms over from us. Remember him? I think his youngest brother went to school with you in Bakshty. He told me he envied you getting out of Paceviche and wished he could, too. He's talked about going to America." Gregory pulled on the reins to move the horse to the side of the road as they passed another buggy.

"It sounds like he's been thinking about it for a long time. He works as a logger every summer when he can and has saved the money that American immigration information says he must have to enter the country. He said that he'll be thirty-four next month. He wants a better life and maybe a little adventure. He's talked about those agents that pay your way and let you pay them back when you get work in America. He said that he's ready to sign up with one."

"Really? I wonder if he's ready to go now. You could go together.

That would certainly make Papa feel better."

"We go right by his house. Maybe we can ask."

Wasyl agreed more quickly than they thought he would. It was as if this was the sign he was waiting for. Alexander couldn't believe such good fortune. He felt even more confident that this was the right thing to do.

By the time they reached their childhood home, they had a plan. Alexander would write to Peter Czernik to ask if he would also sponsor Wasyl. Gregory would stay home until all the crops were harvested and stored. He and Wasyl would take the train to Hamburg, Germany and board a ship there. Alexander would arrange and pay for his brother's passage through a ship's agent in Vilnius. They'd ask Melanie and Pahom to move in with Afanasy. It was all set. Now they just had to tell their father. Papa expected Gregory to marry, bring his bride to live in the family home, and beget the next generation of Kowals to nurture the land.

Afanazy's shoulders slumped as Alexander finished his case for Gregory leaving.

One son gone from the land and now the other, and he was beginning to feel the slowing of his own body. This land was all he had. It was his legacy for his grandchildren. But he knew the truth in Alexander's words. Even in this isolated village, he had heard the winds of discontent. Alexander certainly knew more about this than he did. His heart breaking, he reluctantly muttered, "All right, go."

Melanie and Pahom agreed to move into the Kowals' home to help Afanazy. Alexander gave Melanie money for expenses. She assured both brothers that Afanazy, she, and her family, soon to include two small children, would be fine.

"This'll be better for us, Papa," she told her father. "Pahom can help you and still help his father and brothers when they need him. You'll see, we'll make it work." Actually, Melanie was happy to be moving back to her home. She and her family were living with her husband's parents, grandfather, and two siblings in a one-room house. Now she would share a home with only her father and grandfather instead of seven people.

"From what I hear, you'll have a good life in America, Gregory. I think Mama would want you to go. She always wished the best for us. You know that. Alexander is giving you an incredible gift. It's a blessing," Melanie said as she hugged her youngest brother.

And so it was settled. Alexander took the train back to his post, knowing he would not see his brother for many years. Melanie set about preparing Gregory for his journey. When they butchered the pig after the first frost, she made sure two small hams for Gregory cured in the attic next to the family hams. She set about spinning wool she bought from a neighbor into yarn and then knitting socks and a sweater for Gregory. She made cheese and wrapped it in cloth. Alexander sent a coat he bought from a tailor in Vilnius. Melanie made Gregory new underwear, and with some of the money Alexander gave her, she had a pair of leather boots made. She had them made a little too big. She knew Gregory was still growing.

"This leather is so smooth," Gregory said as he tried on his first-ever leather boots. "I'll just have to put a little paper in the toes until I grow into them. Leather boots and all these new clothes! I feel like royalty!"

"Take good care of them," Melanie admonished. "I won't be with you to remind you to oil your boots or brush your coat." She was too busy to think much about Gregory's leaving, but when his departure grew near, she found herself watching him as he went about his chores. He looked so young.

The days had grown short and snow covered the ground when, with excitement, sadness, and apprehension, fifteen-year-old Gregory packed a trunk with his few belongings and the food his sister had prepared, and left the Kowal farm hoping to return after he passed draft age. With good fortune and hard work he would earn enough money to make life easier for his family.

Melanie smiled through her tears. "God go with you. Write to us. And be careful. I'm glad Wasyl is going with you. He's older, so ask him for advice."

Wearing his new gray wool coat and brown leather boots, Gregory hugged her and his niece and shook his brother-in-law's hand. "Thanks for all you've done, Melanie. I'll write. I promise."

Afanasy hitched the horse to the sled and drove his son and Wasyl over the snow-covered roads to the train depot. As Gregory bid his father good-bye, he realized it was unlikely he would see his father again. Until that moment he had been too caught up in his own excitement about the adventure to realize just how much his father had aged.

"Thank you, Papa." Gregory choked out the words. "Thank you." He could get nothing else out. He hugged his father.

Afanasy held his son tightly, nodding. "Good-bye." He wanted to say more, but the words caught in his throat.

The tears Afanasy managed to hold back as he bid his youngest son farewell flowed freely as he drove back to his one-room home. It was the last day of 1912 when Gregory and Wasyl sailed for America from Hamburg, Germany. Each had the twenty-five dollars needed by the emigration officials before they could board the ship. Gregory would celebrate his sixteenth birthday and every birthday thereafter in a new world. Afanazy did not know then that his consent saved Gregory from the unimaginable horror that was coming, nor did he know that seventy years later a yet unborn granddaughter fleeing oppression would have a safe haven in America because her grandfather had consented to letting his son leave and go to an unknown land.

Chapter 7

Kryviche, Czarist Russia, 1914

"You're in an exceptionally good mood this morning," the young nursing aide said when Dr. Kowal came into the men's ward whistling.

"Well, I have a good reason," Alexander beamed. "The father of the girl I've been courting just agreed to allow his daughter to become my wife. I'm engaged!"

"Congratulations. Who's the lucky girl?"

"Olimpia Legutko."

By the time the noon meal was served, news of Alexander's engagement had spread through the clinic, and by nightfall the whole village knew. During the next few days Alexander drank many vodka toasts with his friends celebrating his good news.

"Marriage will make you a happy man," his friend Boris told him as they drank beer and ate hard cheese and rye bread that Boris' wife, round with her fifth child, placed on the table. "Look at me," Boris laughed. "I've a house full of children, and so will you, I've no doubt." Alexander smiled broadly. Having children with Olimpia was a wonderful thought.

However, Alexander's engagement pleased not everyone in the village. The families who'd hoped Alexander would look favorably on their unmarried daughters were, of course, disappointed. And several young women were quite sad. There weren't many handsome professional single young men in the village. Every one of these girls had smiled hopefully each time they saw Dr. Kowal, looking for a glimmer that indicated interest.

A few people were very upset. The Legutkos were Polish. They were the upper crust of society and Alexander was not. Crossing class lines unsettled them; it shook the social order where everyone knew their place. Alexander's socializing with the Poles, someone decided, must be from the influence of Dr. Bogdan Niewiadomski and Julia Wieckowska, the two Polish people at the clinic with whom Alexander worked most closely. In this western corner of the Russian Empire, Poles, Belarusians, and Jews lived peacefully, trading and working harmoniously. Each group knew its place in the social hierarchy. Poles were the landed gentry at the apex of the local social classes. Jews owned the retail businesses, lumber mills, flour mills, and taverns. Belarusians were the peasants at the bottom of the structure. Within this social web, the intelligentsia—priests, rabbis, doctors, teachers—were a special group who socialized together. But marriage between classes? Unacceptable.

News that Alexander studied Polish and took frequent trips to the Legutko's estate caused a few people to wonder. What were the doctor and the midwife telling Alexander? Did they like this young man so much that they were encouraging him to court and now marry a Polish girl, one above him socially?

For a very few people the memory of Polish rebellion caused distrust of the Poles in the area. The Poles spoke Polish at home and worshiped at the Roman Catholic Church instead of the Russian Orthodox Church. The czar was not only the head of state, the pinnacle of the social order, but also the head of the Russian Orthodox Church. Someone like Alexander deciding to attend the Catholic Church and learn Polish knowing the czar had paid for his education and paid his salary seemed like an insult to the revered ruler.

The Poles had staged rebellions in 1830, 1848, and 1863 seeking independence, but every attempt had been quashed. After each unsuccessful rebellion, they had been repressed. This caused them to cling together, and made a few people wonder if they might rebel again. The czar's agents were always on the lookout for signs of another uprising.

A DOCTOR'S JOURNEY

Why was Alexander going to marry a Polish girl and join the Catholic Church when there were many nice young single women of his class in the village? He knew the Poles were a part of the upper strata of society, and even though he was educated, he came from the peasant class. What didn't he understand about this? Ignoring the class hierarchy was for Olimpia committing *mezalians*, a social sin, and he was encouraging this. However, Alexander and Olimpia, young people deeply in love, were willing to cross those boundaries. Her father had begrudgingly overcome the stigma of Alexander's background, won over by the young doctor's intelligence, courtesy, and devotion to his cherished daughter.

Alexander's only concern was Olimpia's family's acceptance of him. He was in love. He was certainly aware of the extraordinary situation. He knew that one word from Olimpia's father could end the relationship. To him the minority dissent about his personal life was little more than village gossip until a letter appeared in the Vilnius newspaper.

A few weeks after his engagement, Julia Wieckowska brought the weekly paper to Alexander as he drank his morning tea before seeing patients. "You'd better read this," she said handing him the newspaper opened to the third page. She walked to the other side of the table, took a cup from the shelf, and fixed herself tea. Alexander read with growing dismay. A letter to the editor filled one whole column. The letter was a long vitriolic tome. The essence of the writer's sentiments appeared in the last paragraph.

"How can we let this go on at the Kryviche clinic? Dr. Bogdan Niewiadomski and Julia Wieckowska are spreading Polish language and culture at the hospital. What they are doing is wrong and must be stopped! The clinic is sponsored by the czar, and people employed there should speak Russian and show their loyalty to Czar Nicholas and not be a negative influence on other people who work there," Alexander read aloud.

The letter was signed Father Gregori Buszman and Josef Zubiec, the priest at the local Russian Orthodox Church and the school principal. Alexander knew from their attitude towards him at social functions that these men thought he was being wrongly influenced at the clinic. But this? Alexander shook his head as he stared at the paper. What would Olimpia's father think when he read the letter? Would he withdraw his approval of the marriage to avoid social unpleasantness? One word from Mr. Legutko and the engagement would be over.

Alexander shook his head and looked over at Julia. "I haven't hidden my interest in learning Polish. Do Buszman and Zubiec think you're encouraging me to cross the ancient social lines because you're Polish? Do they think my marrying Olimpia is somehow disloyal to the czar? How ridiculous!" But in his heart he knew that beneath his stethoscope and fine new clothes, he was still a peasant in the eyes of society.

Julia sat across the table from him and sipped her tea. "It looks like they do, doesn't it." She shook her head. "This is probably the end of my job."

But it was actually the beginning of the end of Alexander's job in Kryviche. The toxic letter quickly made its way to the regional medical offices in Vilnius. The next week a letter for Alexander arrived from his supervisor.

> Respected Dr. Kowal:
> I have been informed of the unfortunate influence you are subjected to at the clinic in Kryviche. I regret that this has happened, and it is my duty to see that you are protected from such pressure. I believe that the best way for me to protect you is to transfer you to another clinic. To that end, you are being transferred to Ostryn. Your duties there begin on July 1, 1914. It is a well-run clinic, and I am sure you will find that your excellent medical skills will be appreciated. A one-way train ticket is enclosed.

A DOCTOR'S JOURNEY

It was signed by the senior regional medical officer who Alexander knew from his medical school days. Politically, he supposed, the authorities understood he must be moved, but dismay filled his heart. His career and personal life were at the mercy of a government official in a distant office responding to a letter in a newspaper. Alexander shook his head, folded the letter, and slid it into his pocket. He did not know that politics would play an even larger role in his life in years to come.

Hardly more than a week to prepare to move. Ostryn was a day's train ride west of Kryviche, a long day's ride away from Olimpia. But Alexander must go. He served where he was told to serve. Dr. Niewiadomski gave him permission to drive to the Legutko's estate Saturday afternoon to tell Olimpia the news.

"We'll have to write lots of letters," Olimpia told Alexander. "We can't change this, so we'll just have to make the best of the situation." Tears almost welled, but she held them back. "We'll get through this," she said, looking at him with those deep blue eyes that made him melt. "Mother and I will continue to prepare for the wedding. You must promise to take good care of yourself and write every day." Alexander realized for the first time just how strong his fragile-looking fiancée was. She was saddened by this turn of events, but it didn't crush her. Immediately she started figuring out what needed to be done. They walked hand in hand in the garden savoring their last few moments together. How he loved her! And today he had a newfound respect for her strength. He didn't know that day how much Olimpia would need that backbone of steel in the coming months and years as the turmoil on the horizon engulfed them.

A whirlwind of farewells to friends and tying up loose ends at the clinic filled Alexander's last days in Kryviche. He had become fond of the village and the people. Dr. Niewiadomski was upset at this turn of events. Alexander was a good doctor and well liked by the patients and staff. But he also had to follow orders.

While packing, Alexander decided that as soon as possible he would ask his supervisors in Ostryn for permission to marry Olimpia. As a member of the czar's medical corps, he could only marry with consent of the medical administrators. If he was going to be transferred wherever they wanted, he wanted Olimpia with him. In early morning under a cloudless sky Alexander boarded the train on the last day of June, 1914, bound for Ostryn with the trunk he had brought from home and two more trunks filled with books and clothes acquired during his time in Kryviche. Alexander might not have packed so much had he known how brief his stay in Ostryn would be.

At the end of his first day in the Ostryn clinic, Alexander's supervisor handed him a copy of the local paper. "Big news, Dr. Kowal. You might find this interesting reading."

Alexander took the paper to the wide porch at the side of the clinic and read the headline: *Austrian Archduke Assassinated*. He sat on the top step and continued reading. Serbian nationalists were being blamed for killing the heir to the Austro-Hungarian throne. Alexander closed the paper, ruminating on the article. This tragedy in Sarajevo did not bode well for these nations who had such a tenuous relationship.

Will Austria declare war on Serbia? Alexander wondered. He knew Russia had signed an agreement to support Serbia if it were attacked. He thought he remembered that Germany had a similar agreement with Austria. If they did, would Russia be pulled into a war with Austria and Germany? "Politics. I hope they don't drag us into a war," he muttered. He shook his head and sighed. So much discontent in the world. He continued to read the local news, but it meant nothing to him. It had been a long day and he was exhausted.

The events he read about would soon change his life path in ways he couldn't have imagined. On July 15, just two weeks into his assignment, his supervisor called him into the clinic office. He held a letter in his hand. "I've just received some unexpected news. You've been drafted, Dr. Kowal, as a medical officer. You're ordered to report to

Dwinsk. The army is mobilizing there. The German kaiser has promised to support Austria against Serbia, and you know we're pledged to support Serbia. I think we're headed for war. The army expects you to leave here the day after tomorrow." Alexander stood silent a moment absorbing this.

"So quickly?" Alexander asked. His supervisor nodded.

"Well, I have no choice, do I?" He thought of Gregory now safe from the draft in America and was glad for it. As a doctor, Alexander hoped he was at less risk of being in danger than his brother would have been if he had stayed on the farm. He would be armed with a stethoscope not a gun, but Gregory would have been sent straight to the front lines. Dwinsk, near the Baltic Sea, was far from where the front lines were likely to be, and was just a place for mobilizing. Of course, who knew where he would be sent from there. Kryviche, Alexander realized was on the way to Dwinsk. He could stop and see Olimpia. In the army, traveling to see her would require permission, which he doubted would ever be granted. War had disrupted their plans. Now he would need the czar's permission to marry his Polish fiancée.

There was no time to write and tell her of this change of plans. He packed a portmanteau, the only luggage he was allowed, and boarded the early morning train. As soon as he reached Kryviche, he found a friend to take him to the Legutko's.

"Alexander! What are you doing here?" Mrs. Legutko couldn't believe her eyes as she recognized him climbing out of the buggy. "Is something wrong?" she asked noticing Alexander's serious expression. "Olimpia! You have a visitor," she called through the open door.

Olimpia appeared in the doorway. "Alexander!" She rushed down the steps to greet him. Alexander kissed her hand and then walked up on the porch to kiss his future mother-in-law's hand. "Alexander, is everything all right?"

"I'm on my way to Dwinsk. I have to catch the late afternoon train," Alexander said.

"Dwinsk?" Why Dwinsk?"

"I've been drafted, Olimpia. That's where the army is mobilizing." He stood beside his future mother-in-law. Olimpia's hands pressed against her cheeks and her eyes widened.

"Are you going to war?" Shallow wrinkles of alarm sprang across her pale forehead. "Oh, Alexander, I can't believe this is happening. The army?"

"Please don't worry. I won't be on the front lines. I'm a doctor. I'll be taking care of the wounded. It won't be pleasant, but I'm strong. I can handle it." He descended the wood steps and took her hand, the most affection he could properly show even though her rose cologne filled his senses. He wanted to wrap his arms around her and hold her close. "I'll be fine. I promise. You know I can take care of myself."

Mrs. Legutko interrupted. "You must be hungry. Come inside. We'll have tea and something to eat." Even in a time like this she didn't forget her manners. When someone arrived at her house, she always served food. It was tradition, and to forget would be rude.

As Mrs. Legutko heated the water in the samovar and the cook brought out rye bread, fresh butter, and thin slices of ham, Alexander told them what he knew of the mushrooming tensions. "But Russia is very strong," he assured Olimpia and her mother. "The war shouldn't be long. I'll be back in a few months and we can resume our lives."

"I certainly hope so," Mrs. Legutko said. "Do you know where you'll go after Dwinsk?"

"No, I just found two days ago that I was drafted, but I should know soon where they'll send me. I do have a favor to ask." Alexander turned to Mrs. Legutko. "I had to leave all my belongings in Ostryn. I have only that portmanteau on the porch. Would you allow Olimpia and one of your sons to take the train to Ostryn, gather my things, and bring them back here?"

"I'll have to speak to her father when he gets home from the far fields later, but I'm sure he won't mind. We can work out something."

A DOCTOR'S JOURNEY

"I'm in your debt," Alexander replied. "Olimpia, the doctor at the clinic has my medical diploma, and he wouldn't give it to me when I left. See if he'll give it to you. When this is all over, I'll need those credentials wherever I'm sent. My trunks are locked in a room at the back of the clinic, and they should be safe until you can get them."

The hour visit was brief, but he was glad to be able to leave with the memory of Olimpia's smiling countenance watching and waving to him from the porch. He didn't see her tears.

Alexander stared at the changing countryside as the train took him to his new life. He felt that his fate was completely out of his control. Military officer. It was certainly not what he planned for himself. He stepped off the train in Dwinsk to a sea of confusion, but finally found an soldier who directed him to the check-in tent.

On July 28, 1914, Austria declared war on Serbia. On August 1, 1914, Germany declared war on Russia. What Alexander had feared when he read about the archduke's assassination had happened. He did not realize, however, that the assassination did not ignite just a fight between these countries, but a firestorm that would leave all of Europe in ashes.

The commandant of the Dwinsk camp announced the declaration of war at the morning convocation. Alexander had little interest in politics being somewhat naïve about world affairs. His world was medicine.

"Russia is strong," Alexander said to the two young men who shared his tent," repeating what he had told Olimpia. "It'll no doubt end quickly."

Alexander wrote to Olimpia as often as he could and she to him, but the war made mail service slow. He was disappointed when he heard from her that the doctor in Ostryn would not give her his medical diploma. It was his most valuable possession and meant everything to him. But rules were rules. He was still technically an employee at the clinic.

In Dwinsk Alexander was made supervisor of the hospital that would care for the soldiers who worked in an army bakery. He was in charge of two, sometimes three physician assistants and several medics. As the army moved closer to the fighting, the bakery moved, so the hospital and Alexander moved, too. In September, only three months after he was drafted, Alexander's hospital was moved by train to a camp near Warsaw, which fortunately was still a long way from the front lines. The area was reasonably quiet, and Alexander had time to explore and even do some shopping in the city.

In December Alexander's supervisor came down with pneumonia. The commandant decided to send him home to his family near Kryviche and, since the man was too ill to travel alone, appointed Alexander to accompany him. He spent four days at the Lugutkos' before returning to his unit. Olimpia was thrilled with the dressmaker's form that Alexander had bought for her in Warsaw. A naturally talented seamstress, she enjoyed sewing. It was a joy-filled visit shadowed by the knowledge that the fighting might be moving nearer to Kryviche. He returned to the relative calm of Warsaw with an uneasy feeling. The city remained a haven from the fighting during the spring and early summer of 1915. However, the front lines inched closer. The Germans captured Warsaw on August 5. Alexander's medical unit moved away as the Germans approached, and after the city fell, he was shipped to Maloryta, a small town in the Polesie region.

Chapter 8

On The Russian Front, 1915

Alexander soon realized that the war wasn't going to be won as quickly as he had thought. He spent most of his days treating burns and minor injuries, but was sometimes needed to care for wounded soldiers who were brought back from the front lines. Letters from Olimpia took weeks to catch up to him. She wrote cheerful letters meant to make him feel good, leaving out anything that might be censored. Soldiers shared news they heard from home trying to discern what the real situation was throughout the country. It was hard to sort rumors from real news, but Alexander knew the fighting was getting close to the Legutko's and to Paceviche. He kept busy to keep from worrying, and he filled his off-duty hours playing cards with his fellow officers, writing to Olimpia, and even joining a choir the soldiers formed to sing Russian folk songs.

Sometimes the separation from Olimpia was heartbreaking. When Olimpia wrote that her father had died, Alexander wanted to go to her, but that was impossible. Mr. Legutko had not felt well for several days, Olimpia wrote, and had collapsed after supper one night and died in his wife's arms. His sons were taking care of things, but the family missed their patriarch's strong influence.

Alexander had written to Melanie, but had received no letters from her for several months. He heard that the fighting had been heavy in that area and worried about his family, but could do nothing to reach them. Life took on an army routine—seeing patients, doing paperwork, trying to requisition supplies, supervising the medics assigned to help him, and playing cards. Months of war turned into years of war.

Olimpia wasn't free to say much about her family's situation in letters, and he tried to read subtle meaning into the hopeful picture she painted, which only made him more concerned for her and her family. He was quite sure her words hid the whole truth. It was not the short war I'd anticipated, Alexander mused, as he held her last short letter. Just surviving will be victory, he thought as he listened to the weary, homesick voices of the soldiers in the next tent.

The Germans were more prepared for war than the Russians, but thousands died on both sides of the lines. Rumors fueled more rumors. The Germans were fleeing. The Russian troops were decimated. The Germans occupied Vilnius. No one knew for sure what was really happening. Alexander listened for news as soldiers passed through his field hospital, hoping they would shed light on what was happening around Kryviche and Paceviche, but information was spotty at best. Food shortages in Russia grew. The army commandeered most of the animals, grain, and produce for its soldiers, leaving the populace with little to eat. This fanned unrest against the army and the government. Listening to the soldiers talk, Alexander wondered if the Legutko's crops had been seized. Olimpia's letters never mentioned it.

One spring day in 1916 as the last patient of the day left, a nun appeared at the door of the small building the army had taken over as a clinic in Maloryta.

"Good afternoon Sister, may I help you?" Alexander asked. Nuns served as nurses in the army, and their stiff black habits were a common sight. People in nearby villages and homeless refuges sought them out for help. He was used to late afternoon knocks by sisters requesting that he see an ill child or feverish mother, and this was probably another mercy mission. Alexander's day was not over since he would agree, as he always did, to go and see if he could help.

"Alexander, it's me!" The voice was familiar.

Alexander gasped. He looked more closely at the young woman in the crisp black habit. "Olimpia? How did you get here?" he asked incredulously as he reached for her hands. They were reddened and chapped, not soft as they were when he had last held them in the Legutko's garden.

"On the train. People are very respectful and kind to nuns, and there were several nuns on the train going to nurse wounded soldiers." She smiled as she squeezed his strong hands. It felt like a dream. Often at night Alexander fell asleep on his narrow cot imagining Olimpia appearing in his room. This time she was real, but she was in a nun's habit. It made no sense. Surely she hadn't joined a convent?

"But why? Why did you risk coming? It's not safe to be traveling these days."

Olimpia's face darkened. "It's probably safer here than at home. My brothers felt it was the only way to tell you quickly."

Olimpia trembled. "The fighting is very close to us, Alexander. The army has taken all our grain except for the little bit we managed to hide. We don't have enough food to last through the winter. Bronis has gone to Orenburg. It's so far east the fighting will never reach there. He says Orenburg is at the edge of a desert and it's safe." She rubbed her fingers over Alexander's smooth hand.

Her words poured out. "He has a place waiting for us, and a neighbor has agreed to lease our land, but no one else knows about that or our plans. We want to go to Orenburg, too, but it's almost impossible to get on the train. The army's needs supersede ours. My mother agreed to let me come and ask for your help. It might be risky, but not as risky as doing nothing and waiting for the fighting to engulf us. And it will soon. The Germans are headed our way. Can you help us?"

Alexander's mind whirled. His worst fears were realized. The waves of war were lapping at the edges of the Legutko's land. If the two armies collided there, the chances of everyone surviving were small. It would be difficult, but somehow he would pull strings to help.

"It may take a few days, but I think I can get passage. Don't expect more than a seat for each of you and space for a few belongings. The latest word is that the front is moving to Romania. I'll have to go there, too, and I want to be sure you're safe before I leave." His heart felt as though it would burst. Even in a nun's habit with her chestnut hair hidden, Olimpia was beautiful. How he had missed her.

"How long can you stay?"

"My train leaves at eight o'clock."

"Let's go see my commander now. I've done a few favors for him, and I think he'll help."

Alexander introduced Olimpia to the general. When they explained their situation, the commander was sympathetic. "Take this order to the stationmaster. He'll see that you get the tickets. If you have any vodka, he'll find available tickets faster." The tired-eyed general smiled. "Isn't it always that way? Will you want an emergency leave to help your fiancée and her family?"

"Yes, sir, that'd be wonderful. Thank you," Alexander replied. "And we have another favor." He smiled at Olimpia. "Would you fill out the paperwork to go with a letter to the czar requesting permission for us to marry? I submitted the forms to the regional medical office before I was drafted, but now their permission is meaningless. I need the czar's consent. The war consumes so much of his energy, I'm sure it will take a long time, but we'd like to start the process."

"Of course. I have no forms. You write the letter, and I'll write my approval of your request. It's good to do happy work for a change." He smiled at the young couple. "I remember being engaged. It's a beautiful time in life." Alexander and Olimpia left the office encouraged and hopeful. It had been a long time since they had felt happy.

In the midst of the cacophony of the hundreds of soldiers hollering at one another, milling grain, and baking bread, Alexander and Olimpia carved out a brief sweet space to be together until she had to board the train to return home. He escorted her to the station as if she were a nun he barely knew.

Alexander set about securing arrangements for Olimpia, her mother, and her brothers to go to Orenburg. The general's order and a bottle of vodka produced tickets for Olimpia and two of her brothers on the same train. Her mother and one brother's tickets were for the following week.

In spite of everything Alexander had to do, the rest of the week crept by. He was awake well before dawn on Monday and at the depot long before the morning train was due. He was exhausted but couldn't sleep. At noon he ate the bread and cheese the cook had given him, grateful for something to put in his stomach. When he saw the man across the aisle staring at his food, he broke off a piece of the coarse rye bread and a hunk of cheese and offered them to him. The man thanked him, broke the food in half, and shared it with his seatmate. Neither man looked as though he had eaten much lately.

For Olimpia, the week flew by. She packed and unpacked her trunk trying to decide what she needed.

"Mother, should I pack my heavy winter coat? It takes up so much room."

"Yes, Bronis said it gets very cold in the winter. And take your fur muff, too."

Olimpia looked at her partially finished wedding dress on the dress form in her room. "Should I take my wedding dress, or do you think we'll be back here for the wedding?"

"Better take it so you can finish it. But wrap it carefully. That fabric is delicate. The veil, too. It's safer to take it than leave it."

Olimpia filled her trunk with practical clothes and necessities. At the last minute, her mother gave her and each brother a metal plate and spoon and a cooking pot to squeeze in. "We'll need these." The brothers also took a few tools and some seeds for planting that Bronis had requested. They were ready before Alexander arrived.

An hour late, the train pulled into the Kryviche station, Alexander hired a horse and buggy and went directly to the Legutkos. The usual boisterous brothers went about preparing to leave with a sense of mourning. When, if ever, would they come back here?

The next morning Alexander took Olimpia and her brothers Julak and Lambert to the train. In the warm June morning, watching them board with their trunks and baskets of food, Alexander was swept with relief and sadness. Orenburg was at least a five-day trip east if there were no unexpected delays. It was far from the front; they would be safe there, but he wondered when he would see Olimpia again.

Alexander returned to Maloryta just in time to pack and leave for Romania. It was a busy summer. Fighting was intense. Seldom was the makeshift clinic less than filled to capacity. By the end of summer, the Russian army had defeated the Germans, their only major victory of the war. After the area was secured, the pace at the clinic slowed, and Alexander had time to play cards with the other officers. As autumn turned to winter, the men fought boredom.

It was December when fortune smiled on Alexander. "The commandant wants to see you within the hour, Dr. Kowal," the shivering young man said as he came unannounced into the makeshift examining room. Alexander was wrapping a middle-aged man's burned arm.

Glancing at the three patients waiting, Alexander nodded. "I'll be there." He looked at the medic. "I'll take care of those three, but if anyone else comes, tell them to wait."

"Yes, Dr. Kowal," the young man replied.

Alexander applied salve to the burn on the patient, dealt with the remaining three patients' needs, and walked across the frozen field to the commandant's office.

"You want to see me, sir?"

The commandant looked over the top of his glasses and indicated Alexander should sit down. "Could you use some good news, Dr. Kowal?"

"Good news has been in short supply, sir. Yes, I could certainly use something cheerful."

The commandant handed Alexander a piece of paper. It was the letter he had written to the czar asking for permission to marry Olimpia.

One word and a signature were written at the bottom of the page:

Agree. Nicholas II

"Congratulations, Dr. Kowal," the commandant said. He pulled a bottle of vodka and two glasses out of a drawer and poured some of the clear liquor into each glass. "To better times and happiness, Doctor." They lifted their glasses and drank.

"Thank you. I thought the war might keep us from ever getting this." Alexander's eyes glistened, and he couldn't stop smiling.

"Where's your intended?"

"She and her family are in Orenburg. They settled there about six months ago to get away from the fighting in Kryviche."

"That's where you were stationed, wasn't it? Did you meet her there?"

"No, we met while I was still in school in Vilnius, and fortunately, her family lives in the Kryviche region. We've been engaged since the spring of 1914." Alexander paused and looked at the commandant. His future was in this man's hands. "Might it be possible for me to have leave to go to Orenburg?"

The commandant poured himself another shot of vodka. "It's quiet here, and I think some time off is in order, Dr. Kowal. How about a month's leave? It's time you marry this young woman."

On the morning of Alexander's departure his superior officer gave him a hundred rubles as a wedding gift and his fellow officers celebrated his impending nuptials with vodka toasts. Then with the army band playing, they escorted him to the train.

He was in Orenburg before Christmas, and on January 8, 1917, Alexander and Olimpia were married. Olimpia wore the delicate white dress and lace veil that she had started sewing before leaving Kryviche. It had been finished for months, wrapped in muslin in her trunk. From silk scraps she and her mother made flowers for a bouquet and boutonniere. The temperature was below freezing and the war was raging on, but inside the small Catholic Church it was peaceful. Olimpia's mother and brothers, and their new Orenburg Polish friends shared the young couple's joy. Alexander smiled at his bride. She was even more beautiful in her wedding dress and veil than she was the night they first danced at the medical school. So much had changed, but their love had remained constant. The family returned to the small house near the Ural River. Here in their home in Orenburg they celebrated late into the evening. Alexander and Olimpia envisioned a long and happy life together, but the turning of fortune's wheel was unstoppable.

Chapter 9

Romania, 1917

Ten short days later Alexander returned to his post in Romania. He regretted leaving his bride, but he felt fortunate to have been given an entire month's leave. While the war against Germany continued, each day the political situation in Russia grew more chaotic. On a cloudy February morning just as Alexander had taken out paper to write a letter to Olimpia, the bugle sounded calling everyone to the field by the general's quarters. Soldiers poured out of their tents and organized themselves in formation. They were a disheveled group wearing uniforms in various states of disrepair and almost soleless shoes with newspapers replacing socks, and they were hungry. The hot tea and palm-sized piece of coarse, chewy bread they had been served for breakfast didn't come close to filling their bellies. The commanding officer stepped up on a makeshift platform to address them.

"We've just received word that Czar Nicholas II has abdicated. He and his family have been taken prisoner." The soldiers looked at each other with bewilderment. The czar was gone? Why had he been arrested? With his eyes the general sought the reaction of the troops and saw their puzzled looks. "We now fight against the Germans for the new provisional government." The general paused and looked down at the paper he was holding, unsure of what to say next. The soldiers shivering in the chilly February morning looked at one another. What did this mean for them? They had never known Russia without a czar. If they weren't fighting for the czar, who or what were they fighting for?

The general gathered his thoughts. "We'll continue to defend Russia against the kaiser's invading forces. Only one thing will be different. The new government wants all people to be represented, so we'll have elections. We'll choose one officer and two soldiers to form a committee. This committee will be a part of the new government." He paused again looking out at the assembled troops. He didn't understand exactly what this meant for him or them. He was merely repeating the words on the order he had been given that morning. Decisions had always been left to the czar and the ruling class. He could think of nothing else to tell the men he commanded. "Fall out," he ordered before quickly turning, stepping off the rickety platform, and disappearing into his tent.

Soldiers shuffled back to their campfires. Life was suddenly foreign. Elections? Representatives? For what? The usual mumbling and grumbling about hunger and loneliness changed to questions about who was ruling Russia and what the commander's announcement meant. One grizzled soldier finally summed it up when he told his bunk mates, "Well, whatever has happened, we'll still be hungry tomorrow morning."

A provisional government was supposedly in charge, but in reality, no one was in charge. The Bolsheviks, the Miensheviks, and other groups were struggling for power in the vacuum left by the czar's absence. The war with Germany, now in its third year, had drained Russia's financial and human resources. Anger, fanned by the growling of empty stomachs, was the overwhelming mood of the people. Uncertainty was the only certainty. Besides fighting a hopeless war, Russia was now thrown into a revolution.

The soldiers voted for the first time a few days after the general's pronouncement, not really sure of why they were electing representatives. The officers chose Alexander. He had more schooling than any of them, and his abilities as a doctor had garnered much respect. As a part of his new duties, he was sent to Odessa for a joint meeting of the Romanian army contingent; the Black Sea Fleet and emissaries from France, Belgium, and England who came to encourage the Russian army to keep fighting the Germans. However, the Bolshevik delegation from St. Petersburg asserted leadership. They did not want to continue fighting Germany. They defiantly urged the Russian military to stop. The meeting accomplished nothing.

It was one more crack in the disintegrating Russian army. Hearing of the Bolsheviks' actions, more soldiers were emboldened to desert. The front quickly crumbled. During lulls in fighting, German and Russian soldiers sometimes climbed out of their trenches and befriended each other. One by one many soldiers simply left and melted into the countryside. No one went after them.

Alexander knew his country was rapidly unraveling and was overjoyed when his application for a transfer to Orenburg was approved. He didn't want to be separated from Olimpia if rail lines were cut or fighting factions made travel impossible. Now that they were married, he wanted more than ever to be with her. His superiors granted his transfer. They, too, wanted to be home with their wives and children. Once in Orenburg, Alexander took advantage of the political confusion and requested release from the army. Russia was on the brink of defeat, and the army generals realized the war would soon end.

In what came to be known as the October Revolution of 1917, the Bolsheviks gained power. Vladimir Lenin, a cruel yet charismatic man, triumphantly returned to St. Petersburg to lead this new wave of revolution. An unexpected attack was the final blow to the Provisional Government. The attack came from a ship in St. Petersburg's harbor that was supposed to protect them. News of this dramatic turn of events made Alexander uneasy, but not as uneasy as it made the generals who knew that most of those they commanded had lost their will to fight months ago. They saw themselves in a hopeless situation. They had loyally served the czar. Were they supposed to switch their loyalty to the Bolsheviks? In the confusion Alexander's request for termination was granted. Soon after, on December 23, 1917, the Bolsheviks signed an armistice with Germany, ending the war. Now the Bolsheviks and their Red Army turned their energy to harnessing the Russian people and destroying anyone who opposed them, especially the counter-revolutionary White Army and those deemed a threat, particularly the intelligentsia.

Thanks to his medical degree, Alexander had survived a brutal war unharmed, but he knew the revolution swirling around them still held great peril for him and his family. Because he was educated, he was considered a threat to the Bolsheviks.

Even in this tumultuous time Alexander hoped for a better future. The treaty with Germany was signed on March 3, 1918. A few weeks later Olimpia gave birth to Aleksy, their first son. This new life, so innocent and beautiful, brought a new level of love into the crowded home.

"The Bolsheviks and Red Army's fighting can't last forever," Olimpia whispered to her infant son. "When it's over, we'll go home. I promise."

World War I was over for Russia but not for Germany. The following months the tide turned against Germany, even though the kaiser put all his efforts on the Western Front fighting France. By July the German army was collapsing as France and her allies wore down the war-weary Germans. November 11, 1918, brought the end of the war when Germany surrendered to France. Meanwhile, revolution engulfed the former czarist nation.

The three oppressors, the kaiser's German Empire, the Austro-Hungarian Empire, and the czar's Russian Empire that had divided Poland at the end of the eighteenth century were gone. Germany and Austria-Hungary had been defeated, and czarist Russia had disappeared into the new Bolshevik-run communist Russia. When the Treaty of Versailles was signed in June, 1919, new national boundaries were drawn. Poland once again appeared on the map as an independent country, no longer a part of Russia, but its borders were fluid as countries' perimeters were drawn and redrawn. The area around Kryviche remained in the grips of the Russian Bolsheviks. The Kowals and Legutkos dreamed of going back to their home, but the political situation made it an impossible dream. Their homes were still in communist Russia engulfed in the same turmoil that shaped their lives in Orenburg.

Now that Alexander was no longer paid by the army, he had to find work. Orenburg, a major railway center, had been thousands of miles from the war with Germany and had been a peaceful haven during World War I. But the Russian revolution swept eastward to Orenburg, and the power struggle echoed in the streets. What was most frightening as the revolution ground on was not knowing who could be trusted. Who was the enemy? To save his own skin or make trouble for someone he didn't like, had a neighbor reported seeing something suspicious? Had someone told those in charge about true or untrue rumors of counter-revolutionary activities? The most innocent remark could bring the revolutionary guards to the door. People who were arrested often disappeared never to be heard from again. Families didn't know if their loved ones had been sent to Siberia or killed, and they were left forever with unanswered questions. It was not safe to write letters as they were opened and censored and their contents used against the writer. Alexander feared Gregory would try to come back from America, but dared not write to him. They hadn't exchanged letters since the beginning of the war. Nor had Alexander heard from his father or sister in years. He heard rumors of fighting in Paceviche, but didn't know if they were true. Worries about them gnawed at him.

Food was in short supply and few jobs were available. For a month Alexander worked as a civilian for the army in Orenburg, but the army division was suddenly transferred. Once again, being a doctor proved useful when the railroad hired him to care for its workers. He supplemented his income by seeing local residents and nearby tribesmen who came to him seeking medical care. He was the family's main wage earner, although Olimpia put the sewing skills she had learned at

Madame Kaminska's to good use. Using her natural talent as a seamstress, she sewed for people in return for food. Meat was especially hard to come by, and sometimes they ate meat only when a member of one of the nomadic Kirgiz tribes, who lived in the desert outside Orenburg, rode to their door on a camel or horse seeking Alexander's medical help. He'd go with them to their yurts in the dessert, treat an ill tribe member, and be paid for his services with mutton or game birds. Occasionally they paid him with a bag of wild oats or barley they had gathered.

The Legutkos had established a garden when they first arrived in Orenburg with seeds they had brought with them and some given to them by neighbors. They grew vegetables each summer and, if they were careful, had enough potatoes, carrots, and turnips in the root cellar to last the winter. Preserved seeds and seed potatoes were saved for the next season. The family was introduced to a new crop, tomatoes, which had not been grown in Kryviche or Paceviche. It took some time for them to appreciate the flavor of this vegetable, but they grew them and sold them. Life was not easy, but they survived.

Alexander was occasionally required to take the arduous train trip to Moscow, the capital city, to get medical supplies for the railroad's clinic. The days-long ride was a journey into a different culture. He marveled at Moscow's large stone government buildings, wide busy streets, and tree-filled parks.

The diplomatic embassies, their flags flying in the crisp air, particularly drew his attention. In a casual conversation with a medical supply clerk, the idea of contacting Gregory through one of them took root.

"I've never seen anything like those embassies I passed on my way here. It looks like they're their own countries within this country," Alexander said as he watched the clerk carry boxes of medicines to the warehouse counter.

"Well, I guess they are in a way," the clerk replied. His job was often solitary, and he relished chatting with anyone who came to the small warehouse. "The ambassador and people who work there seem to have their own laws. They travel in their own railway cars when they come and go. Even their food and supplies are shipped from their own countries on those cars and taken directly to the embassy." He checked off two more items on Alexander's list. "And their packages and correspondence travel with them in those railcars when they go back to their own countries." He put down the list.

"My cousin works at one of the embassies sometimes, and he told me they have these boxes called diplomatic pouches that our government can't open. It's some sort of agreement between countries so our government can have the same privileges in their countries. I think they live pretty well behind those walls. My sister sometimes works in the Turkish embassy when they have big parties. She says the food isn't anything like what we can buy."

Alexander thought about this for the rest of the day. Was this the answer to one of his nagging worries about Gregory? It was risky, but was it worth the risk? The next morning he walked to the Lithuanian Embassy, the one nearest his lodging, and approached the young uniformed man at the door.

"I'd like to speak to someone on the ambassador's staff," Alexander said.

"Your purpose?"

Alexander hesitated. Was it safe to say? "A letter. I want to send a letter." He took a breath. "Through diplomatic mail."

The young man nodded. "I see. Take a seat. I'll find someone."

Alexander's heart raced. Was the young man going to find a policeman to arrest him? A bushy-haired man appeared in the reception hall with the receptionist. Alexander extended his hand, controlling the nervous feeling in his stomach.

"I'm Dr. Alexander Kowal."

The bushy-haired man's handshake was firm and friendly. He

introduced himself as an assistant to the ambassador and invited Alexander to follow him into an office.

Seated behind his desk, the man asked, "Tell me who you want to send a letter to?"

"My brother. He lives in America. I haven't heard from him in nearly six years. You understand how the mail system in our country is disrupted. I would greatly appreciate using your diplomatic mail system to reach him. Is that possible?" The look on the assistant's face made clear he understood that Alexander was referring to the censorship of Russian mail.

"Do you live here in Moscow?"

"No, my family and I live in Orenbug. It's at the edge of an Asian desert, a long way from Moscow." Alexander pulled out his identification papers and handed them to the man, trying to discern his reaction. "I'm here in Moscow getting medical supplies for my clinic. My train leaves in a few hours. I was hoping you might help me send a letter to my brother." The assistant perused Alexander's papers and handed them back.

The official looked at the neatly groomed man seated before him. He was unlike so many of the unkempt men he saw on the streets in Moscow. "Dr. Kowal, I think we can help you. I'll get you some paper and an official envelope. You may use the desk in the next room." Alexander's breathing returned to normal.

He wrote a brief letter to Gregory:

> Olimpia and I are married. We are well and living in Orenburg with her family for now. You have a nephew. I have not heard from our family in Paceviche. It is not safe yet to return home. Stay in America. I wish you well. Your brother Alexander.

He addressed the letter, sealed it, and gave it to the bushy-haired man, not knowing if it would actually reach Gregory, but he had done all he could do. He thought of Melanie and his family in Paceviche and wished he could write to them, but any letter could be misinterpreted and cause trouble. Wouldn't it be nice, he thought as he walked past the large Moscow buildings, to practice medicine in Paceviche? He smiled. When he was young the thought of living on the family farm for his whole life depressed him. Now a quiet life as a doctor with Olimpia and Aleksy in a small village sounded wonderful. He went to the medical supply warehouse, checked his order, loaded it in the hired wagon, and went to the depot to return to Orenburg.

The revolution in Orenburg, hundreds of kilometers southeast of Moscow, had its own flavor. Newspapers and rumors from the center of power came with the steam-run trains that came from Moscow and St. Petersburg. Alexander brought a copy of the weekly newspaper home, and the rest of the family poured over it, reading every word and then talking about the news. Then Bronis took the newspaper to a neighbor, and it was passed from neighbor to neighbor. The czar's tragic end in July, 1918, was the topic of conversation for many days. The announcement of his death and that of his wife and children at the hands of the Bolsheviks stunned people. It was the demise of the centuries-long Romanov reign. Rumors and stories of the power struggle in Moscow, such as the failed assassination attempts on Vladimir Lenin, added to the uneasiness that pervaded the countryside.

More immediate revolutionary struggles in Orenburg revolved around the nomadic desert Krigiz tribes who wanted to rule their own region. They had no desire to be under the thumb of the Bolsheviks. Occasionally, skirmishes between the tribes and Bolshevik troops brought fighting to Orenburg. On one trip home from treating a Krigiz tribal leader, Alexander noticed a larger than usual number of troops near the road at the city's edge where the Kowals lived.

"I think there may be trouble soon," he told his family as he described what he had seen. "We should stay close to home."

"Let's just stay in the house for a day or two," Bronis responded. "They wouldn't be here if they didn't expect trouble." Sure enough, early the next morning distant rifle shots shattered the quiet. The family gathered around the kitchen table. They and their neighbors who lived by the Ural River at the outskirts of the city were more likely to be caught in the crossfire. The vegetation in the marsh area by the river gave cover to the nomads and made it easier for them to surprise the Red Army protecting the city.

When the noise of the fighting grew closer, Bronis, as the oldest brother, took charge. He turned to his younger brother. "Go across the road and ask Mr. Tarasiewicz if we can stay in their basement with them. We don't have good protection in this house."

As soon as it was confirmed that they were welcome, Olimpia and her mother collected food, water, candles, and blankets, and they all scurried across the road. As small as he was, even little Aleksy seemed to sense that something was amiss.

"Krigizs warriors are crafty. They'll appear seemingly from nowhere, attack the troops, cause havoc, and then fade back into the desert," Mr. Tarasiewicz said to the group crowded in the small dirt-floored basement.

The fighting drew closer. Shouts and cries of pain interspersed the rifle fire of the skirmish. A bullet shattered a window of the Tarasiewicz's house. A Krigiz horseman halted his horse by the front porch, shouted in his tribal language, apparently giving orders, and galloped off. Bolshevik fighters raced by on horseback shooting at him. In the basement the innocent bystanders listened. Then the fight moved away for the moment.

Mrs. Legutko said nothing, but her eyes and clenched hands betrayed her fear and memories of the attacking German soldiers. She winced at each cry of pain or echoing round of gunfire. Her lips moved in prayer. "We're going to be all right," Alexander told her. His voice was firm and quiet, and she relaxed a little. He hoped he was right. If a shot ignited a kerosene lamp in the house, they'd perish.

Alexander watched his mother-in-law as Bronis tucked a camel hair blanket around her shoulders. Her resilience was remarkable. She was a widow living in a crowded two-room house thousands of miles from her home. It was not the life she was prepared for, yet she persevered. He realized Olimpia got her quiet strength from her mother.

All day shouting and gunshots filled the air. The smell of burned gunpowder seeped into the basement. Bullets struck trees and houses as the afternoon sun descended towards the horizon. They huddled together shivering with fear.

Mr. Tarasiewicz turned to Bronis and Alexander. "Living on the edge of town is becoming more dangerous. We're right in the middle of the crossfire. Have you thought about moving closer to the center of the city?"

Bronis shook his head. "We really haven't talked about it, but tonight makes me think it would be a good idea. Alexander, what's your opinion?"

That Bronis would ask for Alexander's opinion was a sign he was becoming more accepted in the Polish family. "I think it's a good idea. I don't like having your mother, Olimpia, and Aleksy in this situation." Mrs. Legutko nodded in agreement but said nothing.

At nightfall the guns around them fell silent, and the families dozed fitfully on the cold basement floor. At dawn shots again resounded, lasting all day, finally ceasing at dusk. The families remained huddled together in the dark, damp basement afraid to go outside to perhaps be mistaken for a soldier or nomad. Aleksy curled in his father's lap as they slept wrapped together in a thick camel-hair blanket next to Olimpia for a second fear-filled night.

Alexander woke before dawn and lay listening to the rhythmic breathing and soft snoring surrounding him and waited for the gunfire to return. The chirping of a bird caught Alexander's attention. No gunfire! The tribesmen had left. The families climbed the wooden stairs into the morning light. For the moment, life returned to normal, but another outbreak of fighting was inevitable. Alexander changed clothes and went to his office. He knew that soldiers who the day before had been in the fight were waiting to have their wounds treated. In a few weeks the family found two small rooms, really a larger room with a temporary partition dividing it, to rent in a house just a few blocks from the marketplace.

Since work was scarce for Olimpia's brothers, they did most of the gardening. But their most important task was finding material to burn in the stove to heat their rooms in the winter. Orenburg had hot humid summers and bitterly cold winters with weeks of below freezing temperatures and winds that seeped under the door no matter how many rags they stuffed beneath it.

The only trees were near the river and to cut them was illegal. Being caught chopping down a tree could mean prison or a bullet to the head. But the Red Army didn't patrol at night, so the brothers cut trees by moonlight, and all the adults, except Mrs. Legutko, hauled them home on their backs to build a stack of firewood for the winter.

Long-term Orenburg residents showed them how to dig saksaul roots in the desert. These roots burned almost like coal and their warmth was welcome on freezing winter days. Digging the roots and carrying them from the desert was hard, back-breaking work, but the three brothers did it because it had to be done.

Four years had passed since the Legutkos had fled to Orenburg. They had Polish friends, a church they attended, and Alexander's job with the railroad. They were much better off than most of the people in post-Czarist Russia.

One evening Olimpia, having put Aleksy to bed, was sitting next to her mother at the kitchen table reading *Izviestia,* the newspaper Alexander had brought home. *Red Army Triumphant* was the headline over a story about the White Army succumbing at Odessa to the Red Army. It appeared that the Bolsheviks were going to be the victors in the civil war. At the other end of the table Alexander, Lambert, Julak, and Bronis played a card game that Bronis appeared to be winning. A sharp knock at the door stopped them all. Lambert stood, walked to the door, opened it, and was pushed aside be three members of *Cheka*, the secret police. The family froze. Guns drawn, the glaring strangers studied the four men. "Bronis Legutko," barked the tallest of the three intruders. Bronis rose from his seat.

"I'm Bronis Legutko."

"You're under arrest for treasonous activity," the man said. "Come with us."

"Can you tell me what the charges are?"

"As if you don't know," the man sneered. "Come with us." He waved his gun towards the door.

Lambert, his hand still on the door, started to say something, but Alexander shook his head and mouthed, "No."

Bronis looked at his mother, "Don't worry, Mama, I'll be all right." He turned to the men. "May I take my coat?" He nodded towards the coats hung on pegs next to the door.

"All right, but that's all. No tricks." Lambert reached for his brother's coat and cap and handed them to him. Two of the men clenched Bronis' arms and hustled him out the door. Lambert peered into the darkness watching his brother being led away, and then closed the door.

"No. No. Not another son," Mrs. Leguto moaned. "I don't know where Stas is and now Bronis is gone." Olimpia held her mother in her arms and looked helplessly at Alexander. None of them had understood why Stas had joined the Red Army, and they hadn't heard from him since he'd left almost two months ago.

"I don't understand. What's Bronis done?" Julak asked.

"Nothing. Someone simply had to say he's done something," Alexander replied. "It's just like the Bosco boy down the road. A coworker was angry at him and told the NKVD that he was reading forbidden pamphlets. He's still in jail. You can't trust anyone these days. You never know who is an informant or a member of the secret police."

No one felt like sleeping, so they sat in the kitchen talking until the night was half over. "This isn't any way to live," Olimpia grumbled. She had recently given birth to their second son, Arkady, and living in this state of fear was wearing on her. "I wish we could go home." Everyone nodded.

They read the weekly papers for news of the civil war, wondering if the Bolsheviks would actually triumph. Then in November, 1920, the Russian civil war ended as the Red Army defeated the last of the counterrevolutionary forces. Russia was now ruled by the communist party. Private ownership of land was outlawed. All farms were now collective farms owned by the state. The Legutko family had fled to Orenburg in 1916 so they could be safe from the war, hastily renting their estate to Mr. Nalkowski, a neighbor, who they hoped was still tilling the land, but now it would belong to the government. The social hierarchy that had defined society for centuries was gone. Everyone was equal, at least in theory. All power was in the hands of the communist party who was making the rules. And they were ruthless, destroying anyone who appeared to threaten their control.

The family's fate lay in the hands of nebulous forces. Bronis' arrest made it clear that Orenburg wasn't safe anymore. But returning home wasn't the answer. They were landowners, and the new communist rulers of the country had declared all landowners enemies of the people. If they returned and acknowledged ownership, they would be arrested and sent to Siberia. Kryviche was not safe either.

We're pawns of the state, Alexander thought as he finished his morning paperwork in the railway medical clinic. He hated the culture of bribery and black markets in which they lived; yet to survive, he participated. He was given large quantities of coupons for *spirytus*. It was pure alcohol that he used as a disinfectant. It was also used as the base for making vodka. He didn't need as much spirytus as he could get with the coupons he was given, so he took home what he didn't need. It was a popular bribe and, although he didn't know it as he was increasing his supply, it would be crucial to their escape.

The skies threatened more snow. Before eating the bread and cheese Olimpia had fixed for his dinner, Alexander picked up the newspaper the stationmaster had left for him to read. On the front page of the February 20, 1921, paper was a map and the headline: *New Polish Border Decided*. He looked at the map and could hardly believe his eyes. Kryviche and Paceviche were now in Poland. He read the accompanying story just to be sure. The map was correct. The Legutko land was now in Poland. Alexander put the paper down. "Is getting there even possible?" he muttered to himself. He knew that as soon as his wife, brothers-in-law, and mother-in-law saw this story, they would want to go. How could he make this happen? Their land would still be there, and in Poland it was still theirs, not the government's. "Bronis," Alexander muttered, "we have to figure a way to get him out of prison."

That night the family sat at the table reading the paper over and over. "To do this we have to get Bronis released and make arrangements to leave quickly.. I don't think we'll get more than one chance. But before we do that, I have to make sure we can get permission to leave."

The next afternoon Alexander approached a physician he trusted. It was still a risk. Even the most trusted friend could turn out to work for the Bolsheviks, but Alexander saw no other way.

"Of course, I'll sign whatever you need," the bearded doctor said as he and Alexander shared an after work glass of spirytus. "And don't worry, it's just between us. You're wise to leave, and if I can figure out a way to get out of this god-forsaken country, I'll be gone, too."

It took a few weeks and a bribe of firewood and spirytus for the guards, but on a moonless night, Alexander and Lambert, hearts pounding, stood in the shadows near the prison as the front gate opened and a bewildered, malnourished Bronis appeared.

When the three men arrived, Olimpia and Mrs. Legutko laid out ham, sausage, and bread for the homecoming. Bronis was thin and bruised from beatings, but he was alive and home. It was a tenuous situation. Bronis could not be seen by the neighbors. Anyone could turn him in and ruin their plans.

It was time. Alexander filled out the forms, and the corroborating doctor signed them. The cost was a few rubles. The forms certified that the Legutko family was infected with malaria and the doctor prescribed moving them to Minsk. That was still in Russia, but very close to the Polish border. With the diagnosis and prescription in hand, Alexander went to the government officials to get the papers that allowed travel to other regions. A few more rubles and the permits were approved, stamped, and in Alexander's hand.

With more rubles and another half-liter of spirytus, Alexander reserved an entire railcar for the trip to Minsk. The next day he purchased the tickets and the family prepared to leave. Trunks were packed and food baskets were stuffed to overflowing. Aleksy was three and Arkady was eight months old as the family of eight boarded the westbound train for Minsk. They fashioned sleeping palettes of straw and blankets at one end of the car next to their luggage and settled in for the long trip.

Every stop as the train wended its way closer to Poland was fraught with danger. Bronis' papers were forged, and each time an official boarded to check their credentials, their hearts raced. Of course, having been in prison for a year, he looked more like he had malaria than anyone else, and he was "asleep" on one of the pallets at each stop. Just one suspicious official could destroy the family's flight. The two cases of spirytus proved useful each time their papers were checked. At every stop they repeated their story. The family had malaria and was going to live in Minsk where the climate was better for them.

"A gift for you," Alexander said to each Bolshevik official as he handed him a half-liter of spirytus. The official would nod, stamp his approval on their documents, and leave. Each time the family breathed a collective sigh of relief and girded themselves for the next stop. It was almost two weeks of tension before they reached their destination.

In Minsk they went directly to the government offices and applied for permits to go to Poland. They had become deft at playing the bribery game; and in six days they had official permits to leave Russia. All of them, that is, except Bronis. His papers, he was told, were not in order, and he would have to stay behind for another month while permission was sought.

Alexander gave Bronis bottles of spirytus. "With these and the rubles you have left, you should be able to bribe the clerks to stamp your papers in a few days."

Mrs. Legutko didn't want to leave any of her sons behind, but Bronis was firm. "I'll be home soon. I'm not going to be stopped this close to home."

Once again they boarded a westbound train. Poland was a short ride from Minsk. At the border crossing, guards ordered everyone to get out. They could see Poland, but they had to get through this checkpoint before they were free. A portly guard wearing rimless glasses gruffly took the family's papers Alexander proffered. He read each permit slowly, scowling as he read. "A gift for you," Alexander said to the guard as he handed him a bottle of their dwindling supply of spirytus. The guard stuffed the bottle in his pocket.

"Your papers appear to be in order." Without looking at him, he handed the forms back to Alexander. "Board the train."

The family sat in silence as the train pulled out of the border crossing. Then Olimpia whispered, "Look! The flag. We're in Poland!" Alexander patted her hand and smiled. They had survived the war and the revolution. They were almost home. They reached Baranoviche, the first town inside the Polish border. The train halted and the repatriates were taken to a quarantine barracks for a two-week stay before they could proceed. Malaria was stamped on the Kowals' papers, and they had to show the Polish officials they were healthy.

"Your family looks healthy, Dr. Kowal," the quarantine official said, "and I understand why your papers say otherwise, but I have to follow the rules. We'll make you as comfortable as we can and won't keep you any longer than necessary."

It was an exhausted family that on July 21, 1921, loaded a rented wagon at the train depot in Kryviche to take them to their estate. Arkady slept peacefully in his mother's arms, but the rest of the family scrutinized the familiar landscape noting the leftover scars of war. Mrs. Legutko's mouth moved in quiet prayers of thanksgiving. Then as they rounded the last curve, they saw it.

"It's still standing. Our house is still here!" Lambert shouted. The family erupted in cheers. Mrs. Legutko sobbed and repeated her prayer. Lambert and Julak leaped from the wagon and ran full force the last hundred yards to the house. Some windows were broken, it was in drastic disrepair, but the family home still stood. The war had come to the edges of their land, but their house had mostly been spared.

Olimpia, pale and exhausted from the long journey, hugged her sons. "This is home," she whispered in their ears.

"By next spring we'll have crops in the ground," Lambert declared. "We'll make this place look just as good as it did when our father was alive. And now it's in free Poland!"

Chapter 10

Poland, Legutko Estate, 1921

Alexander's relief at being free was tempered by not having his medical diploma and by Bronis being held up in Minsk. But three weeks after they arrived home, Bronis, thin and weary but in good spirits, joined them. "I gave the last pint of spirytus to the Russian border official," he told his family, "and the Polish quarantine officer feed me and sent me on my way when he realized I was another Legutko."

Alexander's missing diploma was still a problem. "There are some open positions at clinics in the district, but I can't hire you if you don't have proof you're a doctor," the medical officer told Alexander.

Alexander had a wife and family to support, and he was anxious to have a home for Olimpia and the boys.

"I have to try to get my diploma from the clinic in Ostryn. The prewar files may still be there," he told Olimpia as they lay in bed a few days after their return. "If it's not there, I don't know what I'll do. The medical school in Vilnius is gone. I can't get a duplicate to prove I graduated. Without that diploma, I'm not going to be able to find work."

"Write to your friend Ziegler in Ostryn and ask if you can visit. Then go. The boys and I'll be fine. You being a doctor has already saved us more than once. And if you aren't back in a week, I'll just have to put on a nun's habit and come find you," she joked.

"My favorite nun." Alexander laughed and hugged her.

The day after Ziegler's reply arrived, urging Alexander to come as soon as he could, Lambert drove Alexander to the train depot to retrace the trip he had taken that hot July day in 1914 after his abrupt transfer. Alexander found Ostryn in the process of rebuilding after the war. He saw several new buildings. Konrad Ziegler met Alexander and took him to his two-room house where his wife had sausages and beer waiting. It wasn't long before the conversation turned to the purpose of Alexander's trip.

"Dr. Rusinka, the new clinic supervisor, has most of the papers from the old clinic, I believe," Konrad said, "But whether or not he has your diploma, I'm not sure. If he does, it's probably not at the clinic. He keeps lots of files at home. And if he has it, I'm not sure he'll give it to you. He's a stickler for rules and control. Liquor is the best way to loosen him up. He's fond of it. If he has your diploma, he's much more likely to give it to you if he's a bit drunk."

"I'll get him drunk if I need to," Alexander replied.

The next afternoon, with a bottle of vodka and some food in his satchel, Alexander walked to the medical clinic. A young woman sat at a small desk just inside the door of the medical clinic. She looked up from her work and greeted him. "Dzien dobry."

"Dzien dobry. My name is Dr. Alexander Kowal. May I speak to Dr. Rusinka please?"

She went into the next room and soon came back with a thin, balding man whose face was defined by a heavy five o'clock shadow. "Dr. Rusinka, this is Dr. Kowal."

As the men shook hands, Dr. Rusinka looked Alexander over with thinly disguised distrust.

"I was stationed here before the war and have come back to visit hoping to find my medical school diploma, which was left here when I was drafted," Alexander said.

"Well, I don't know if I have it," Dr. Rusinka replied.

"I understand. Perhaps we could have a drink and you can tell me about the clinic now. I'd like to hear." Alexander pulled a bottle of vodka out of his satchel. Dr. Rusinka glanced at it and his glower changed to a smile. "I suppose we could do that."

He turned to his nurse. "If any more patients come, tell them I'll see them tomorrow." He turned to Alexander and touched his elbow. "Come, Dr. Kowal, let's go to my house to talk of old times."

They sat in the doctor's small kitchen and the doctor brought two glasses to the table. Alexander filled them. He brought out the gefelte fish, ham, and bread that Mrs. Zeigler had given him and cut some for each of them. As they talked, Alexander slowly sipped from his glass and readily refilled Dr. Rusinka's glass each time it became half-empty, gently engaging him in conversation and encouraging him to talk. An hour passed and Dr. Rusinka became more animated and less coherent. Alexander waited another half hour before he made his move.

"I'd like to look at your files. I think my medical diploma might even be in them. Could I see them?" He poured the bleary-eyed doctor another drink.

"Sure, why not," Dr. Rusinka replied taking another drink and stuffing a slice of ham in his mouth. He weaved into his bedroom and came back with a thick gray file. "Here's what I have." He handed it to Alexander, sat down, leaned back, and took another drink.

Alexander opened the bulging gray file and started turning over papers. After flipping through only a few papers, he saw it. An envelope with his name on it. Without saying a word, he took out the envelope and pulled out the folded diploma. He looked at Dr. Rusinka, who was humming to himself and totally uninterested in Alexander's actions. Without saying a word, Alexander slipped the diploma back into the envelope and casually slid it into his own satchel. He flipped through a few more papers in the file and then closed it and put it back into the middle of the desk.

"Well, Dr. Rusinka, I must be going. I don't want to miss my train. Thank you for the conversation and pleasant afternoon. Please keep the rest of this and enjoy." He screwed the cap on the now half-empty vodka bottle and handed it to the inebriated man.

Alexander hurried back to the Zeigler's. "Success," he beamed as he showed them his long-lost diploma.

He held his satchel on his lap all the way back to Kryviche wishing the train could go faster. Once home, his family gathered around and he showed them this precious possession, his medical diploma. He never dreamed that nearly a century later it would be cherished by a daughter who hung it proudly in her office and looked at it for inspiration on difficult days.

Chapter 11

Paceviche, Poland, August, 1921

Alexander was anxious to return to Paceviche to see his family and fulfill his dream of practicing medicine where he had grown up. He had worked for the czar, the Russian Provisional Government, and the railroad. Now he would work for himself. He bid good-bye to Olimpia and the boys and took the train south to Juracishki, the nearest railway stop to Paceviche. There he found a ride with a man going the last twenty-four kilometers to Bakshty, the town of 2,000 where he had first attended school. He walked the last two kilometers to the Kowal farm in Paceviche.

As Alexander drew closer to his childhood home, remnants of the war littered the landscape, but the resilient farmers had begun rebuilding houses and barns, planting potatoes, rye, and barley. He wondered if he would have left for Vilnius that day when he was fifteen had he known what lay ahead. He thought of himself boarding the train in Juracishki wearing his new leather boots, so eager and excited. He smiled. If he hadn't left, he never would have met Olimpia. Leaving had been a good choice.

The first thing he saw as he reached home was that the house and barn were gone. But across the road near the river a garden bloomed. The pole fence he and Gregory had repaired so often was mostly gone. A hawk hunting for mice circled above a silent field of rye stubble. With no buildings the place looked deserted, but it wasn't. A field of potatoes thrived and a thin puff of smoke rose from the ground at the far edge of the field. He crossed the meadow and walked towards the smoke that was coming from a dugout in the side of the small grassy hill where he had once chased rabbits. He knocked at the makeshift door and then noticed a woman coming toward him from the other side of the hill. She drew closer and began to run and scream. "Alexander?" "Is it you?"

He peered at the woman in the threadbare blue dress who knew his name. "Melanie? Melanie!" He rushed to her zigzagging around a pile of composting weeds.

"Yes, it's you!" she cried throwing her arms around him. "Oh, Alexander! You're a vision. When you didn't come back after the war, I thought you were probably dead like everyone else." She sobbed and laughed at the same time. "I can't believe it. You're home."

"Melanie, Melanie, I was so afraid you...." He couldn't stop the tears as he held her thin frame. They stood gently rocking back and forth for a few moments before he released her and touched her ruddy check. She smiled and hugged him again.

Two young girls carrying baskets of mushrooms appeared at the edge of the forest. They hesitated. From behind the chicken coop a tall thin girl walked cautiously towards her mother and this mustached man. A boy of about six ran from the other side of the hill, stopped and looked wide-eyed at his mother embracing a stranger.

Melanie motioned the children to come closer, "This is your uncle, my brother the doctor I'm always talking about. Come give him a proper greeting." She laughed as she and Alexander stood arm in arm.

"Hello," Alexander smiled at the stair-step brood. "You must be Maria," he said to the oldest, a skinny ten-year-old. "You were just a baby the last time I saw you."

The girl nodded, looked at the ground and smiled. Alexander patted her shoulder. Glancing up at the stranger, she twisted the side of her thin cotton skirt with her fingers.

"Anna," Melanie said pointing to the next oldest girl. "Nastia," she nodded towards the youngest girl. "And this is Alosha, the man of the house." Melanie smiled at the young boy.

"Fine looking children, Melanie." Alexander smiled at them. "I can hardly wait for you to meet my children."

"Children?" Melanie asked.

"Yes, two boys," Alexander replied. "But before I tell you about me, tell me about you. Where's your husband?" Alexander asked his sister.

"Dead. Grandpa, Pahom, Papa, a lot of the people you grew up with." Melanie's countenance grew sad. "The Germans and the Russians destroyed everything they didn't steal. We had no food except what we foraged in the forest during the summer. So many people starved or became so weak from lack of food, they died of sickness. The kids and I are all that's left, Alexander."

Alexander shook his head. Tears slipped out of his eyes. "Looks like the fighting was bad here." He surveyed the remnants of the carnage that remained.

Melanie nodded. "During the summer of '16 it was constant. The Russians on this side of the river and the Germans on that side shooting at each other." She motioned with her arms. "We were just in their way. Haystacks caught on fire from cannon shots, then houses and crops in the fields. Livestock and chickens disappeared. We gathered what we could carry on our backs, harnessed the cow, and fled into the forest to hide."

Melanie raised her head and focused on the trees at the edge of the fields. "For months we lived in caves we fashioned in the sides of gullies. We searched for mushrooms and other wild plants, dug roots we could eat, and trapped rabbits to roast over the fire. We couldn't get to the river to fish. We existed day to day. After the cow died and we ate her, food was pretty scarce." She paused for a moment. "Grandpa died first. A summer afternoon during a rainstorm. Papa and Pahom dug a grave deeper in the forest. We buried him at dusk."

She stopped lost in memory for a moment. "Just as the snow started falling, the soldiers moved on to fight someplace else, and we came back home. Pahom, Papa, and I made the dugout, and Pahom fashioned the stove from river rocks and clay. But we hadn't been able to plant because of the fighting. We didn't have any potatoes or vegetables or rye flour stored for the winter. All the fighting even drove off most of the fish. We caught a few, but they weren't enough to stave off our hunger."

Melanie took a breath and looked across the field of potatoes. "Papa died in October. He gave some of his food to the kids and slowly starved. His stomach swelled from not having food. One morning he just didn't wake up."

She bit her lip. Her voice was flat. "Pahom lasted a few more months. He worked so hard to find food for all of us even though he was also starving. He fell in the river one day when he was ice fishing with the neighbors." She stopped and took a deep breath. "Chilled to the bone by the time they pulled him out. He was already weak. Within a few days I knew he wasn't going to make it. I think he had pneumonia. Couldn't get his breath. He died ten days after the accident."

She looked at where the family home had stood. "There was nothing here, but I couldn't give up." She looked at her children. "I had to keep going for them." She related her travails in a matter-of-fact tone. "Spring finally came. Neighbors gave us seed potatoes, and with the few seeds I had saved, I planted a garden. So here we are. We survived."

"Oh, Melanie, I'm so sorry. I had no idea how dreadful it was." He thought of how distressed he had felt at being separated from Olimpia. Now that seemed trivial. Even the difficult times in Orenburg paled in comparison to what Melanie and these children had endured.

Alexander looked at the surrounding landscape. The house, barn, and fences all gone. Weeds and wildflowers grew through the ashes of the Kowal's home. Alexander's eyes filled with tears. Generations of sweat and toil incinerated.

"It's been hard. Lots of days I didn't know if we'd make it. But look at those potatoes. For the second year we'll have enough to last through the winter. And over there we have onions, carrots, fava beans, beets, and cabbage." She pointed to the thriving garden across the road. "I couldn't do all this without the kids. Maria is quite the gardener. Even Alosha works in the garden every day. I've found neighbors willing to help with the rye in return for some of the crop. I trade rye for chickens, so we have eggs. And I trade eggs for milk."

She was quiet for a moment and then looked back at Alexander. "So what about you? Where've you been?'

"It's been difficult, but nothing like this." He swept his hand encompassing the farm. "I was drafted in 1914, just after Olimpia and I became engaged, but I think you know that. I was in charge of an army medical clinic and moved around a lot."

Alexander told his sister about marrying Olimpia, briefly talked about life in Orenburg, and described their perilous journey back to Poland. "I came here as soon as I had Olimpia and the boys settled at her mother's. I didn't know what to expect. When I saw the house was gone, my heart sank."

"It's behind us," Melanie said. "I've learned that looking back doesn't do much good. It doesn't bring back anything lost. I've learned to think about today and what we can do to make tomorrow better."

"Seems like you've done a good job of that," Alexander smiled at his sister. "I think you must be one of the bravest, strongest people I know."

Melanie almost blushed. She wasn't used to compliments. "Speaking of today, you must be hungry after your trip. The cabbage and salt pork should be ready. Girls, those are nice mushrooms. Clean them up, and I'll fry them with potatoes and onions. Maria, dig some up. Alosha, check and see if the hens have laid any eggs today so we can have scrambled eggs. This is a day for a celebration." The children dashed off to do their chores while Melanie and Alexander walked to the dugout.

Melanie peppered Alexander with questions as she chopped and stirred. "Have you heard from Gregory?"

"No. I managed to get a letter sent to him about four years ago telling him not to come home, but, of course, he couldn't answer, so I don't know if he got it. I haven't written yet. I was waiting until I got here. I'll write now that I can tell him about you and the rest of the family. I hope he's all right."

Alexander looked around the dugout and was impressed with how much Melanie had done with so little. Two benches and a table took up most of the room, but there was a bed for the children and one for Melanie.

The long-separated siblings laughed and chattered trying to fill in the missing years. Joy filled the corners of the warm dugout as the children listened intently to their mother and uncle. They had no memory of their mother ever laughing and being this happy. And while they ate the cabbage stew, scrambled eggs, and fried mushrooms, Alexander confirmed to himself that he wanted to live in Paceviche. This was where he belonged. At fifteen he couldn't wait to leave. Now he couldn't wait to get back. This was home. He was anxious for his seven-year odyssey to end.

"It's time for me to come home, Melanie. I'm going to build a new house, bring Olimpia and the boys to live here, and practice medicine. Speaking Polish will be an advantage now. I'll be able to get a government job but still speak Russian to patients." He smiled remembering the abrupt transfer from his first job because he had learned Polish.

"We'll actually build two houses, one for us and one for you." He hadn't planned to say he'd build two houses, but once he'd said it, he knew it was what he wanted. Alexander scraped up the last of the wild mushroom stew with a piece of rye bread.

Melanie looked at him with disbelief. "You'll really do that? Come home? Nothing would make me happier!" She looked at her children who were all grinning. "This is a wish come true."

Alexander's first task was finding a place for Olimpia and the boys to live while a house was built. It would be late autumn by the time they arrived, and a new house couldn't be ready before the next fall since the logs once cut had to be dried before being used. A neighbor agreed to rent them a one-room house that he wasn't using. Alexander set about building wood chairs, beds, and a table for his family. He discovered immense satisfaction in this endeavor. This would be the first home that belonged to them.

"You're like a papa bird building a nest," Melanie teased him as she watched him nail together a chair.

Alexander, Olimpia, and their sons moved into their first-ever home with only the four of them. The rental house was small and cozy. They were poor, Alexander told his youngest daughter years later, but it was a very happy time.

After the years in Orenburg squeezed into two rooms with her mother and brothers, having only her husband and two small sons in one room felt spacious to Olimpia. On cold winter days she filled the cabin with the aroma of fresh bread and hearty stews. She read to the boys and sewed. Maria, Anna, Nastia, and Alosha loved coming to visit. They doted on their young cousins, ever ready to play with them when chores and studying were done. Alexander, called to ill neighbors who could not pay, agreed to accept their help in the fields next spring in return for his giving them medical care.

As they had for generations, neighbors joined together to help Alexander harvest the timber for his new house. It was Paceviche tradition that the person needing help roasted a calf or pig and bought vodka for supper. Alexander applied for a government timber permit at the Bakshty office. On a crisp autumn morning in 1921 just after daybreak, the Kowals' neighbors showed up to help cut trees. A government forester, responsible for deciding which trees could be cut, led them. While they were gone, Olimpia and Melanie roasted a pig and boiled cast iron pots of potatoes and fava beans. In one day the men cut, trimmed, and dragged back logs for two houses, one for the Kowals and one for Melanie. Late that afternoon, the logs stacked for drying, they celebrated the day's work, drinking vodka and feasting on roasted pork.

By summer, the logs had dried and building began by hired workers grateful to have a job. The Bakshty craftsman with the reputation for making the best weather-proof roofs crafted the thatched roof. Late in the fall of 1922 the Kowals settled into their new three-room log home. Then the hired men built a barn and a small two-room house for Melanie and her children.

Alexander and Melanie were relieved when a letter from Gregory arrived telling them he was doing well. But his query about their Uncle Osif was disconcerting.

"I don't understand, Alexander." He should be here by now if he boarded the ship for Ryga months ago," Melanie said.

"I agree. I'm worried." Alexander reread the letter. "Maybe those rumors about the Bolsheviks robbing and killing people returning are true. We saw how ruthless they were in Orenburg. Gregory said Uncle Osif had saved enough money to buy some land so he'd be a good target. I suppose we'll never know unless he shows up. I'll have to let Gregory know he's not here. He folded the letter and walked back home.

Alexander's medical practice grew. Families who could afford to pay in cash did. Others paid with a chicken or a few eggs. Olimpia's skill as a seamstress also brought in income. They worked hard and enjoyed the work. After their years of fear and oppression in Orenburg, they appreciated freedom. They had enough to eat, one of the nicest houses in the village, and neighbors who were always willing to help if needed. After the boys went to sleep, Olimpia and Alexander read and talked quietly, enjoying being together alone. The bond they had first felt as young students in Vilnius deepened and grew. Their love for each other and their sons filled the simple log cabin with wealth money could never buy. Olimpia expressed her contentment in letters to her mother.

A DOCTOR'S JOURNEY

Dearest Mama,

Life is so peaceful here, and we have such a full and happy home. I understand why Alexander wanted to come back here. He is a very good doctor and is held in high regard by everyone. I am so proud of him. He works harder than I think he should, but that's his nature. He comes home tired, but never too tired to play with the boys and read them a bedtime story. Aleksy seems most like his father in temperament. They can both be stubborn when they are determined to do something. Alexander has been especially happy since he received a letter from his brother in America. Gregory is married and has a good job as a welder. You may remember that while we lived in Orenburg, Alexander sent Gregory a letter through diplomatic mail, hoping it would reach him. But he never knew if the letter actually got through. Well, Gregory did get that letter and took his brother's advice to stay in America. Of course, he couldn't write back. Alexander wrote again just after he got to Paceviche and Gregory answered.

We are all well, and I hope you are, too.

Love, Olimpia

In 1922 the Kowals traveled to the Legutkos' for the Roman Catholic Christmas. On Christmas Eve they enjoyed a traditional Polish supper and attended midnight mass. After a week-long visit Olimpia, Alexander, and the boys journeyed back to Paceviche and prepared to celebrate the Russian Orthodox Christmas with Melanie and her children. It was the life the couple had dreamed of when they were courting, and they looked forward to growing old together.

In the spring of 1923 Alexander secured a government post running a medical clinic in Bakshty. His increased salary gave the family more financial security. In addition, he became the doctor for the Jewish community. Each member of the temple paid a set fee to the rabbi, who then contracted and paid Alexander to take care of the whole community. The Jewish merchants' confidence was a tribute to Alexander's reputation as a good physician. He also saw patients at home and made house calls. Alexander was busy.

"At last I can provide for you as I promised your father I would," Alexander told Olimpia as they talked in the light of their new kerosene lamps. "I can hire men to plant more rye, barley, and a little wheat. Maybe I can build a bigger barn. Life is good, isn't it?"

She smiled and agreed. Life as the wife of a doctor in Paceviche was certainly more rigorous and less luxurious than her life would have been had she married one of the Polish landowners her parents preferred as a son-in-law. She would be managing a household with servants and spending her time preparing for parties and sewing with silk instead of cotton.

I'm happy, she mused, and I don't think I'd be any happier if my life were different. The difficult years in Orenburg had made her appreciate her husband. She knew people still thought she had married beneath her, but that no longer mattered. The social class into which you were born did not define your character or intelligence. She admired Alexander's intelligence, and she saw how people respected him. More importantly, she knew he adored her and worked hard to provide well for her and their sons.

Later that spring Olimpia developed a cough that became chronic. She lost weight and constantly felt fatigued. Alexander treated her with the medicines he had, but none were effective. Thoughts that his wife had tuberculosis crept into his mind. Olimpia's cough grew worse and her beautiful skin took on a gray tinge. Alexander couldn't bring himself to tell her what he suspected was a certain death sentence. As the chilly wind blew the last leaves from the trees, Alexander grew more despairing.

Olimpia sat near the kitchen stove wrapped in a thick camel hair blanket they had brought back from Orenburg. Alexander pulled a chair close to her and took her small pale hand in his. "Olimpia, I'm taking you to see Dr. Legier in Oshmiana. I want his medical opinion. Maybe he has something that will make you feel better. He's an excellent physician."

Olimpia put her other hand over his and nodded, her head barely moving. "Of course, if that's what you think is best." She closed her eyes.

Alexander feared this was the beginning of the end, but he couldn't bring himself to accept that fact. He looked at his beautiful Olimpia, love welling up in his throat. They sat with hands entwined for a quarter of an hour before he carried his sleeping wife to bed and pulled the blanket securely around her shoulders.

The next morning he heated bottles of water and wrapped her as warmly as he could for the trip to Oshmiana.

After Dr. Legier examined Olimpia, he took Alexander into his office and closed the door. "It's tuberculosis, Alexander, but you know that already. I'm sorry. I have nothing to offer that you haven't already tried. The disease is moving quickly."

Alexander's shoulders slumped and he stared at the floor. "I know. I don't want to believe it. I've loved her since I first danced with her in Vilnius. She gave up so much to marry me. And now I can do nothing to save her."

Knowing the boys risked catching tuberculosis from their mother, Alexander sent them to stay with their grandmother. Not willing to give up hope that something could be done for his wife, Alexander decided to take her to the hospital in Vilnius. Olimpia was placed in an isolation ward because of the infectious nature of tuberculosis. Alexander felt helpless as he watched his wife wither and grow weaker each day. He was able to stay with Bronis, Olimpia's oldest brother who had moved to Vilnius after his marriage, but he seldom left the hospital.

"Alexander, you know there's nothing any of us can do to stop tuberculosis. I suggest you take Olimpia home," her doctor told him. "You can treat her as well as I can."

Alexander and Olimpia left the city where they had met and returned by train to Juracishki. A neighbor met them with a sled for the chilly trip over snow-covered roads back to Paceviche. They arrived home in early December. Olimpia knew she did not have long to live. She wrote to Bronis.

> 6 December 1923
> My dear brother,
> I'm constantly sick, and I know for sure I will not leave this bed. I am like a skeleton and can't get out of bed without help. Oh, how much I don't want to die. Poor Alexander is losing his head. He runs around crying like a child. He's asked me to write to you and ask you not to leave him alone when I am gone. So, I'm asking from myself to you, my brother, take care of him and my children. My poor children, they are so little. When you write to our brothers, please ask them also to take care of Alexander and the boys. I am too weak to write to them separately. I kiss you perhaps for the last time. Don't forget me.
> Olimpia

Olimpia died three weeks later, leaving Alexander with a five-year-old and a three-year-old to raise alone. The ache in his heart after the death of his beloved wife made Alexander's days long and nights even longer. His life was empty without Olimpia, and the boys were bewildered by the loss of their bright-eyed cheerful mother. Alexander sank into depression, and gloom wrapped the once joy-filled house.

Olimpia had been their sons' primary caregiver, and Alexander was baffled by their needs. Trying to work and be father and mother was overwhelming. Alexander took Aleksy and Arkady to their grandmother's thinking she could care for them, but Mrs. Legutko was now elderly and didn't have the energy to keep up with two active boys. Alexander tried leaving just Aleksy with her and then just Arkady. But even one little boy was too much.

"Alexander, I know how much you loved Olimpia, but you must find another wife. You can't raise these boys by yourself. Olimpia would want them to have a good mother," Mrs. Legutko told him when he went to get Arkady in response to her letter that she wasn't strong enough to care for him.

"I can't imagine being married to anyone else," Alexander told his mother-in-law. "I miss her so much. Life is not the same without her."

"Look Alexander, you can't live in the past. You must move on. Olimpia died almost two years ago, but you mourn like she left us last week. It's not good for you or the boys," Mrs. Legutko admonished. "I know what it's like to lose a spouse. It's difficult. But you have to think of your sons. Find someone, Alexander."

Alexander took the children home and hired a neighbor to care for them. But the cloud that hovered over him didn't leave. He went through the motions of living but really just existed.

The rye and barley were safely stored in the grain shed when Melanie broached the subject of marriage. "Remember when you told me about meeting Olimpia and wanting to marry her in spite of her family's reservations about you? You said that you never give up. That you are strong and can deal with whatever comes your way. Now you seem so lost. I know you never dreamed you'd lose Olimpia. But you have to think of Aleksy and Arkady. They need a mother. You need a wife," Melanie told him as they watched the sunset from a bench by Alexander's front door. "It's been two years. Please think about it."

"I suppose, but I don't know anyone. I think a woman who was an orphan might be a good mother for them. She'd understand what they've been through."

If he thinks a woman who was an orphan might work, I guess I just have to find one, Melanie thought as she walked across the yard to her house.

The next week Melanie went to Bakshty to visit Julia Sokolowska, her friend since childhood. "I'm trying to help my brother. He's been a widower for almost two years and he needs a wife. He thinks his boys need an orphan as a mother so she could understand them. Do you know anyone? A Polish woman would probably be most appealing to him. Olimpia was Polish and the boys are used to Polish customs."

"Hmm, actually I do. My sister, Zenia Majewska, raised her husband's orphaned niece Katherine. I don't think Katherine has any marriage prospects. She's a few years younger than your brother, but maybe..... Do you want me to find out? The Majewskis live in Traby. I'm going to see them next Saturday."

"Oh, yes, please. Alexander has to get on with his life."

And so it was arranged. With reservations, Alexander agreed to go to Traby to the Majewskis' and meet Katherine. He needed a housekeeper, and he approached the possibility of marriage as a way to get a housekeeper who could take good care of the boys.

"Come in, Dr. Kowal," Mr. Majewski greeted Alexander heartily. Katherine and her aunt stood behind him.

"Dr. Kowal, my wife, Zenia, and my niece, Katherine."

Mrs. Majewska shook Alexander's hand and greeted him warmly. "Welcome, Dr. Kowal." She turned to her niece who was observing the well-tailored brown wool suit Alexander was wearing.

"Nice to meet you." Katherine shook his hand and forced herself to raise her head and look directly into Alexander's eyes. Katherine's shy smile emphasized her round face, ruddy cheeks, and pale blue wide-set eyes. Her curly, frizzy light brown hair, pulled back in a twist, made her face look even wider. She wore a brown cotton dress on her plump frame. Katherine blushed as she greeted the doctor. Neither of them seemed to know what to say. After a few minutes of stilted conversation, they all gathered around the kitchen table. Mrs. Majewska and Katherine brought steaming stew and fresh warm wheat rather than rye bread to the table. The wheat bread was the only indication that this was a special dinner.

Their conversation was halting and awkward. Katherine, a simple girl with little education, had nothing in common with Alexander. Her aunt and uncle did their best to keep the conversation going. Alexander left as soon as it was polite to excuse himself.

Katherine, in spite of the clumsiness of the dinner, was excited. That an educated doctor looking for a wife had called on her was remarkable. He was handsome and so finely dressed. She wished he would call again but was afraid to be hopeful. Her aunt told her that Alexander owned one of the nicest houses in Paceviche. Katherine was now past twenty. Most girls her age were married and had children. She knew her aunt and uncle expected her to marry and move out of their small house, but she had not received any proposals. She had nothing for a dowry, and young men wanted to marry someone whose family could improve their state in life. Her prospects of marriage were slim. That she might marry a doctor and have a nice home was more than Katherine had ever considered possible. Would not having a dowry make a difference to him? She hoped not.

She's rather plain, Alexander thought. He picked up the wedding picture with Olimpia so delicate and beautiful in her wedding dress. "I don't think I can ever love this Katherine," he whispered to the picture. She wasn't homely, but she certainly wasn't beautiful. And she had so little education. "I don't know," Alexander muttered to himself. "I just don't know."

Chapter 12

Paceviche, Poland, 1925

For the next few months Alexander mulled the idea of marrying again. At the end of a long day after the boys went to bed, he decided. He needed help, and at the moment Katherine seemed like the best solution. The next day he went to see her uncle and asked for her hand. It was more of a business proposition than a marriage proposal, but the uncle accepted. Katherine was delighted. More than anything else in the world, she wanted a home, and the thirty-four-year-old widower's offer of marriage would give her one that was better than she had ever imagined.

The wedding on January 27, 1926, was a small, quiet, serious affair in the Catholic Church in Traby. Katherine wore a simple white cotton dress and a lace-trimmed veil she and her aunt had sewn. After supper at the Majewskis', Alexander drove Katherine and her belongings home. Words did not come easily to either of them, and the trip through the frozen countryside was mostly silent except for the jangling of the horse's bridle and reins.

It was, Alexander told his youngest daughter many years later, a marriage of convenience. "I needed a housekeeper and someone to take care of my sons, and she wanted a home."

Katherine was an adequate housekeeper and stepmother. The boys accepted her, but their affection for her was muted. Katherine kept them clean and fed but perhaps because she had been an orphan, her mothering was more care giving than loving. Her cooking was plain, and her sewing ability, like her reading and writing, was rudimentary. She was very unlike Olimpia whose cooking, baking, and sewing showed creative flair. But Katherine brought a sense of order and completeness to Alexander's and the boys' lives, and the Kowal household settled into a comfortable routine. Alexander's growing medical practice consumed his days. With Katherine to care for the boys, house, and garden, he was free to devote his energies to the profession he loved. Even though it was not a marriage of love or passion, Alexander and Katherine developed a compatible relationship of respect and appreciation for what each gave to the other.

Alexander showed his appreciation of Katherine a few months after their marriage in a gesture that made Katherine feel like the most fortunate woman in Paceviche. While treating one of his Jewish patients, Levi Berkowitz, the owner of the local grist mill, Alexander learned of a new sewing machine by the Singer Company. It was supposed to revolutionize home sewing and improve any woman's sewing skills. Levi was buying one for his wife and sending her to Volozyn, thirty-two kilometers from Paceviche, for a three-month class in using the machine and refining homemaking skills.

"You should send your new wife, too," Levi said after describing the machine and class. Alexander thought about it for several days; then he picked up a Singer pamphlet at the general store which was owned by another of his patients. He read the two pages several times and examined the picture of the new machine.

"Katherine, I learned about a new sewing machine last week. I think it will make sewing easier for you," Alexander told his wife at supper. Her eyes widened in surprise. She had heard about this new machine from women in the village, but never expected she would own one.

Alexander pulled the folded pamphlet out of his pocket and handed it to her. Katherine slowly read the claims about the machine. It looked complicated.

"It looks nice, but I wouldn't know how to use it." She was flattered by her husband's offer, but fear rose in her throat. She could never learn to use such a wonderful machine, and if he spent all that money and she failed, she would disappoint him. What would he do then?

"The Singer Company's offering a course in Volozyn to teach women how to use it. I've signed you up. It's a three month class, and they teach other homemaking skills, too. You'll stay with a family that takes in boarders. The class doesn't start until after the gardening season ends, so you'll be able to get your summer work done." The matter was settled.

Three months to learn to use one machine? Katherine tried to wrap her mind around this unexpected prospect. For the rest of the summer Katherine quietly fretted. A sewing machine was a luxury she had never imagined, and she worried about learning to use it. She was determined to work hard in the classes and make her husband glad he had decided to buy the machine and arrange for the lessons. Intermingled with her worries about doing poorly in the class came the realization that three months of going to class would be a vacation with no cooking or cleaning. That was exciting. What a wonderful turn her life had taken.

The mornings were growing chilly when she stripped the garden of the last vegetables and filled the root cellar with the rest of the potatoes, carrots, cabbage, and onions. A neighbor was employed to cook and care for the Aleksy and Arkady. Alexander and the boys drove Katherine in the wagon to Volozyn and located the family with whom she would stay. After they had all walked to the general store where the classes would be held so Katherine knew where to go, they said good bye. Before leaving town Alexander stopped at the Jewish bakery and bought the boys *Obarzanki*, little hard donuts on a string. It was one of their favorite special treats and the highlight of their day.

The first snow of winter dusted the countryside when Alexander and the boys drove Katherine home three months later. She was proudly wearing a dress she had sewn on the new machine, and she had a bundle of cloth for clothes for the boys. The sewing machine was her most precious possession. During winter afternoons the Singer's rhythmic sound filled the house.

After Olimpia's death, Alexander had no interest in the family farm, but now that he had a wife, he again started thinking of the future. He hired men to build a new barn and he began reading agricultural journals, studying new ways of improving soil and increasing crop yield. He bought another horse and hired a neighbor to do some of the chores. When he saw tomato seeds listed in an agricultural journal, he ordered some and grew the first tomato plants in the Bakshty region. Alexander started the seedlings in the house, carefully transplanting them to a corner in the garden when the weather warmed. He was pleased with the success of this new crop. Not everyone was as enthusiastic about tomatoes as he was.

"These look like apples on a vine. Are they?" Melanie queried as she reached for a ripening tomato. He said nothing, watching for her reaction. She picked one, took a bite, and spit it out.

"It's terrible," Melanie sputtered as she threw the juicy, seedy fruit to the ground.

"You don't like my tomato? We ate them in Orenburg, and I think they're delicious."

"I'll stick to apples, thank you."

But some family members and neighbors grew to like this new vegetable, and tomato vines grown from the seeds that Alexander shared joined the neighborhood gardens.

During the next few years Alexander's medical practice became more profitable, and he bought land until he became one of the major landowners in the Bakshty County. Some was farm land, and some was forest. He read about cultivating an orchard, and on one parcel he planted twenty apple and plum trees. It became a model for other farmers. Count Tyszkiewicz, a nobleman whose spending habits exceeded his income, wanted to sell part of the forest that stood between two nearby villages. Alexander bought several hectares, his biggest land purchase. He was more than Paceviche's doctor. He was hired by the government to run the medical clinic in Bakshty, and he was a landowner. His neighbors elected him to be their representative on the town council. He had been born a peasant, but his children were the offspring of a professional man. They would each have a profession, Alexander thought. Education is the most important gift I can give them. To assure their future Alexander began depositing money in accounts at the bank for each child's schooling.

Danuta, born December 9, 1928, was Katherine and Alexander's first child, and she was followed three years later by Josef in January 1932. The three-room Kowal house was filling up.

That fall Aleksy left for a preparatory school in Molodechno, about sixty kilometers from Paceviche. It was his first step to becoming the family's second doctor.

"Be a doctor. It's an important profession, and in difficult times it can be your salvation. Look at me. Because I'm a doctor, your mother and I survived the war and the revolution," Alexander had told his sons more than once. But Arkady was not as interested in his studies. He loved being outdoors. Hunting rabbits or deer or searching for mushrooms were more fun for him than reading. Alexander agreed that he could become a forester, also a respected profession. But Arkady couldn't go to forestry school until he reached age seventeen, which meant fifteen months between the ending of his schooling in Bakshty and the beginning of his forestry education.

Life was going well, but once again world events were about to intrude on their pastoral life. Reading the newspapers filled Alexander with foreboding. Germany was restless. Defeated by the Western Allies, the Germans had suffered economically after the signing of the Treaty of Versailles. The defeated nation had lost territory and had agreed to pay huge reparations, impoverishing the nation. Most Germans resented paying these large sums of money to the victors. Alexander read about the growing popularity of Adolf Hitler, Germany's new chancellor who played to the German people's anger. He spoke passionately, blaming "international Jewry" for these wrongs against their country. He painted a picture of the Germans as a pure Aryan race. He appealed to the Germans' sense of patriotism and the need to take back what had been lost in the war. Did this mean that Hitler had his eye on Poland?

The United States and Europe suffered financially as the world plunged into economic depression. They were more worried about rising unemployment numbers and stabilizing financial markets than what some fanatical politician was doing in Germany. Alexander read about these ominous events in the weekly paper. Sometimes he talked about them with his friend Tomasz Bogucki, the local police officer and also a member of the intelligentsia class. But the villagers went on with their lives much as they always had. Their livelihoods were not dependent on foreign markets. They grew most of their own food and traded services with neighbors.

Letters from Gregory gave Alexander a window into the financial depression sweeping the world. "My brother who lives in New York lost his job as a welder. People are suffering all over the world, some even more than we are," Alexander told Tomasz. "Gregory's having a hard time finding work, and he's living on his savings."

Alexander's days were filled with caring for patients and managing his land. Katherine took care of their home. Another son, Zbigniew, was born in September 1936 filling Katherine's days with never-ending cooking, child care, cleaning, gardening, and tending the pigs, cows, and chickens. She had little time for Arkady and was relieved when her teenaged stepson wasn't home.

The spring of 1936 had marked the end of Arkady's schooling in Bakshty, leaving him in limbo until he was old enough to start forestry school. He walked in the world of adolescence and without school or a job, he had lots of free time. A popular boy, his social life was filled with friends and parties. Most days he rode his bicycle to visit former schoolmates, spending as little time at home as possible.

His father believed Arkady was happy, enjoying this respite from studying, and looking forward to school. That belief was shattered with Melanie's arrival at the medical clinic in Bakshty early one November afternoon. "I need to see my brother," a pale, shaken, out of breath Melanie said to the receptionist.

The young woman heard the urgency in Melanie's voice, rose, and hurried to the examination room. She knocked and entered. "Your sister's here, Dr. Kowal."

"Melanie?" I'll be finished in a moment."

Melanie took a seat to wait. Her mind was swirling. How am I going to break the news? She stared at the door, and as it opened and the patient left, she rose and rushed to her brother.

"Melanie, what brings you here in the middle of the day?" Alexander paused and looked at his sister whose eyes were filling with tears. "What's wrong?"

"It's Arkady," she choked. "Arkady...."

"Has there been an accident?"

"Yes....No. Katherine...:"

"Is something wrong with Katherine?"

"No. She's fine. It's Arkady." Melanie filled her lungs with air. How could she tell him?

"Alexander, Arkady....Arkady took his own life," she sobbed. "Katherine heard a gun shot and went outside to investigate. She found him by the haystack and ran to my house. We ran back to where he was. He wasn't breathing so she got a sheet and we covered him. Katherine went back to the house to take care of the children, and I came here." The words rushed out between sobs.

Alexander stared at her in disbelief. Arkady? How could this be? "Oh, dear God, no. No! Why would he do this?" Alexander felt his stomach lurch and he clutched the edge of the exam table to keep himself standing. He closed his eyes and turned away from his sister, collecting his thoughts. At last he looked at her. "I'll get my horse and carriage." Outwardly he resumed the demeanor of a doctor always in control in a crisis. Inside he was crumbling.

During the ten-minute ride, Alexander was barely aware of his sister or where he was. The horse headed home from habit. Alexander's thoughts flashed back to Olimpia and the day Arkady was born in Orenburg. Then to Olimpia's last day when she lay in their bed gasping for air. Now their youngest son was gone. He couldn't stop his tears. His first thought was that he had failed Olimpia. He had promised to take care of their sons, and he hadn't. Was Arkady unhappy? Why hadn't he known if he was? Was he angry? Had he not gotten enough attention? Alexander thought about all the times he wasn't home because he was working or managing his property. This was his fault.

Melanie climbed out of the carriage. Knowing her brother would want to be alone, she tied the horse to a fence post and went into the house. In the shadow of the haystack Alexander found Arkady's shrouded body. He knelt next to it and lifted the linen cloth. The boy looked so innocent, so much at peace.

"Why did you do this?" Alexander whispered to his silent son. "Why? Why didn't you come talk to me?" He stroked his son's chestnut hair, trying to absorb what had just happened. Alexander banged his head against the haystack. "Why?" he sobbed. "Why?" He pulled the gun from the boy's hand and pushed it away. "Arkady, I don't understand." He reached under the lifeless body and lifted it into his lap. Tears dripped onto the boy's face as his father kissed his cheeks, wishing he could blow life back into the cold corpse. He held Arkady for a few more minutes before laying him gently back down and covering him with the sheet. Alexander rested his head on his hands trying to comprehend this dreadful happening. The dark clouds that had been threatening snow since morning released gentle snowflakes on the father and his lifeless son. Alexander shivered but didn't want to move. Almost an hour later he slowly trudged to the house.

"I need to see the casket maker and priest to make arrangements,"

Alexander said.

"Shall I go with you?"

"No, Melanie, I must do this by myself."

Alexander's shoulders slumped as he drove a wagon back to Bakshty. He passed the casket maker's first, selected a pine casket, loaded it into the wagon, and covered it with a piece of canvas.

Things didn't go so smoothly at the priest's. An angry and frustrated Alexander drove the wagon with its somber load into the yard through the falling snow. Melanie came out to greet him. Her brother's clouded face told her what had happened before he did.

"The priest won't bury him." Alexander breathed deeply trying unsuccessfully to compose himself. "He made me so angry. I said a lot of things I probably shouldn't have. But this is my son. He deserves respect."

His shoulders shook as he let the horse's reins drop. Melanie picked them up and held out her hand to help her brother down. She put her arm around his shoulders and he leaned against her. "Catholics consider suicide a mortal sin, and he can't go against church law. My poor Arkady."

"I'll go see my Russian Orthodox priest. He might help us. I think maybe he doesn't see suicide in the same way," Melanie said. They took the casket into the house and set it up on the saw horses that Melanie had already brought in from the shed. Then she left to seek out her priest. She returned within an hour.

"He'll perform the service Thursday morning at ten. We can't bury Arkady next to his mother, but we can bury him in the Orthodox cemetery. I talked to Joseph Pakun. He and his sons will dig the grave."

"Thank you, Melanie. I. . ." Alexander choked back tears.

His sister softly touched his shoulder. "We'd better get everything ready. People will be coming tomorrow to pay their respects."

This morning he was seeing patients and thinking about planting more trees next spring. Now in the cloudy afternoon he was planning his son's funeral. "Why?" ran through Alexander's mind as he mechanically walked through the day. Later as they gathered clothes to dress the body, they found Arkady's neatly folded note on top of his small dresser.

> Dear Father and Brother,
> Don't be surprised by what has happened to me. What happened had to happen. Nobody could have prevented it or have helped me. Don't be curious about what made me take this step. There were many reasons.
> My last request is that when I am lying in the casket, please place a picture of Genia Kuzmiczowna over my heart. You will find the picture in my wallet in my dresser drawer. What connected me to this woman you will learn from what other people will tell you. Please fulfill this request. If you choose not to fulfill this request, we will meet somewhere, and I will remind you that you failed to do what I asked. Whatever Genia does, don't stop her.
> Love, Your Son and Brother Arkady

Alexander read the note several times. He had seen this young woman, but didn't know her. "What do you know about this Genia?" he asked his wife and sister.

"She's older than Arkady by four or five years, I think," Katherine told her husband.

"She doesn't have a very good reputation. She's loose. Parties too much." Melanie hesitated, thinking maybe she shouldn't say any more right now. "I think it might be helpful to talk to Konstantin. He's Arkady's closest friend. Do you want me to bring him to see you?"

Alexander was silent for several minutes. "Yes, that would be good. Not tonight. Tomorrow morning." Alexander sank into the rocking chair by the fire. Thoughts of Arkady buffeted in his head. He sat there all night unable to sleep.

Shortly after breakfast Melanie brought a distraught Konstantin to see Alexander.

"Dr. Kowal, I'm so sorry. I can't believe Arkady . . ." the blonde, curly-haired boy choked on the words.

"I know. We can't either. But, please, you must tell me everything you know. What was Arkady's relationship with Genia Kuzmiczowna?"

Konstantin's eyes widened, and then he looked down at the floor. It took him a several seconds to speak. "Arkady.....Arkady liked her, uh, had a crush on her....uh, thought, I guess, that he loved her. They were together at the parties. I think he saw her a lot. She can be very uh. . .." He paused unable to think of the right word or perhaps afraid to say it. But Alexander understood what was unspoken.

"Last week she told him something that really upset him, but he wouldn't tell me what it was." He took a deep breath. "She just plays with men. I don't think she ever…" Konstantin stopped. Maybe he'd said too much, but Arkady's grieving father had asked, and he deserved to know the truth. "I wish I could have done something, Dr. Kowal. I never thought Arkady would do something like this."

"There's nothing you could have done. Don't ever blame yourself. Thank you, Konstantin. Go home." The wind blew a few snowflakes into the house as Katherine bid the boy goodbye at the door. Alexander was suddenly overcome with exhaustion. He took Genia Kuzmiczowna's picture out of Arkady's leather wallet and looked at her dark eyes and smiling face. What's she thinking now, he wondered? Did she have any regrets? Alexander took the small photo to where Arkady's body lay and placed it inside his jacket over the boy's heart. It was the least he could do for his son.

Soon after Konstantin left, neighbors and friends streamed into the house to offer condolences. Some knelt in prayer beside the coffin, some softly sang songs of mourning. Some brought food in an effort to comfort the family. They helped the family keep vigil all night, as was the custom. Genia Kuzmiczowna did not appear. What had Arkady expected her to do? Weep and throw herself on his coffin? Profess her love?

A DOCTOR'S JOURNEY

They buried Arkady on a wind-chilled November day. News of the tragedy had spread rapidly, and the whole village of Paceviche and many people from Bakshty gathered around the grieving family as Arkady was laid to rest. Some people came to support Alexander, and some came out of curiosity.

Rumors inundated Paceviche and Bakshty. Suicide carried a social stigma and was treated differently from other deaths. Alexander was one of the area's most prominent citizens, and his son's suicide was fodder for gossip; but sympathy for Alexander was widespread, too. It was Alexander's nurse who relayed the gist of what was being said. "Some people are saying Genia told him she was pregnant. Others are saying she told him she didn't want to see him anymore."

"I should have known something was wrong," Alexander repeated to Katherine and Melanie again and again. "I was too busy for my own son. How could I have let this happen?"

His wife and sister tried to console him. "None of us really knew what he was going through, Alexander. It's not your fault. It's not anyone's fault. Arkady kept to himself. You know how quiet he was about his life at school and with his friends. And we respected his privacy. He was becoming a young man. Young men don't talk to their parents about their romantic encounters." Melanie paused, waiting for Alexander to say something, but he just stared out the window. "Remember, you were already at medical school for two years when you were his age. How much did we know about what you were thinking?" Melanie stopped, knowing there was probably nothing she could say to make her brother feel any better. He would have to work through it in his own way. She looked out the window towards the haystack, "No one expects to lose a child. Is there anything worse?"

Alexander said nothing, but thought to himself that losing both a wife and a child is worse. The healing scab over his grief at Olimpia's death had shaken loose, and that awful cloud of depression encompassed him again.

"He wrote that you shouldn't blame yourself," Katherine said softly. "You're a good father. He loved you. And he knew you loved him."

The family went through the motions of daily living, but Arkady's absence was a raw space they couldn't fill. It was the first week in December when Alexander took his children's bank deposit books out of his top dresser drawer and another sad truth was revealed.

Alexander opened Arkady's first. He planned to divide the money between the other children's accounts. But he couldn't believe what he saw. The balance was almost zero. He scanned the page. Nearly a dozen withdrawals were recorded. By each one was Arakady's signature. What had his son been doing with his college fund this summer? Alexander stared at the book. What could Arkady possibly have spent all this money on? Perhaps Konstantin knew. He seemed to understand Arkady. Alexander took his sheepskin coat from its hook, pulled on his hat and gloves and walked through the snow.

Konstantin was carrying firewood into the house and invited Alexander in. His mother put a platter of bread and cheese on the table as they sat down. Alexander opened the bank book and showed it to his son's friend.

Konstantin scanned the page. "Arkady was always buying things for Genia. Clothes, scarves, and other stuff. And he took her to parties and bought her liquor. He wanted her to like him as much as he liked her. She really had him under her spell. I tried to tell him that she was just using him, but he was sure she loved him. I'm really sorry. You're right, Dr. Kowal. I don't think he would have listened to anybody."

The winter months were somber as the Kowals went about the business of living. Aleksy came home for Christmas holiday. His presence was a great comfort to his father, but sadness overpowered the holiday. Although Katherine didn't share Alexander's deep grief, she respected his need to be alone and asked for nothing. After Aleksy returned to school, Alexander worked long hours to numb his pain.

Chapter 13

Paceviche, Poland, 1937

At last spring arrived. In May Alexander traveled alone to Molodechno for Aleksy's graduation from prep school. Pride filled Alexander's chest as he watched his son accept his diploma, and he thought of Olimpia. He pictured her smiling at their son. How happy this day would have been for her. At the end of the ceremony one of the teachers approached him.

"Dr. Kowal, it has been a pleasure to teach Aleksy. I'm sure you're pleased that he plans to follow your footsteps in medicine."

Alexander beamed. "Yes, I'm very pleased."

"The faculty is having a reception at the library. Will you join us? Aleksy has done well, and his teachers want to congratulate him. He's one of the shining stars of the class of 1937." It was an unexpected honor and capped a joyful day. Aleksy's graduation was the first glimmer of hope since that painful day last November. Slowly Alexander was finding his way through the cloud. Life had to go on. Too many people relied on him to let grief take over forever. Today was the first time he felt the sunshine of a promising future pushing his ever-present guilt over Arkady's death to the back of his mind.

Father and son went from Molodechno to Vilnius to enroll Aleksy in a month-long preparatory class for the July medical school entrance examination. Alexander was taking no chances that his son might fail.

Aleksy spent most of his summer vacation with his father at the clinic, watching, helping, and learning. In August Aleksy was accepted to Batory University Medical School in Vilnius. "You'll know so much more than I did when I started medical school," Alexander told his son after he had helped stitch a gash in a young forester's leg. Alexander's pride in his son burst from every pore as they worked together, and Aleksy's leaving for Vilnius that fall was bittersweet. Alexander was excited for his son to be going to medical school. At the same time, his absence would leave an empty space in each day. But world events were about to blow a much larger hole in Alexander's life.

Newspapers were filled with stories of Hitler's campaign against the Jews. Alexander's Jewish patients shared stories of harassment and arrest of their families in Germany. Several local Jewish families made room in their homes for relatives who fled Germany to avoid imprisonment.

Without warning on September 1, 1939, waves of German planes bombed western Poland. Warsaw erupted in flames. Poland was under attack, and the Polish army was neither large enough nor modern enough to offer much resistance. Horse cavalries with swords were no match for Nazi iron tanks and airplanes. Thousands of Poles fled to eastern Poland to escape the advancing Nazi troops.

Immediately after the attack, the medical school in Vilnius closed. Aleksy arrived in Paceviche two days later having ridden his bicycle 120 kilometers, stopping only to rest and eat. Alexander feared for Aleksy's safety, and not just from the Germans. If an assertive Polish underground army quickly formed around the small towns and villages, Aleksy would be pressured to join them. If he did, his chances of survival were slim. He'd lost Arkady. He didn't want to lose another son. Three days after Aleksy arrived, Alexander took him to Volozyn where Dr. E. G. Fominski, a friend Alexander had known for many years, was in charge of a hospital. If Aleksy was employed in the hospital as an intern, he would be somewhat protected.

Alexander and Aleksy left early in the morning for Volozyn hoping to encounter few people on the road. "We must be careful, Aleksy. No one can know where you are," Alexander cautioned his son as they rode to Volozyn. "It's just not safe to trust anyone when there's a struggle for power in the country. We learned that during the revolution. Keep your own council." He appreciated his father advice, but it did nothing to allay his fears.

They rode in silence for half-an-hour before Alexander continued. "And it's best that we don't communicate, I think. No letters. If anyone finds out you're my son, the underground will probably find out, too. People in the village know you're in medical school, and they'll ask me where you are. Any underground army will insist that you join them. They'll want your medical knowledge, as limited as it is. I have to be able to tell everyone that I haven't heard from you. As much as I'll want to know that you're well, I won't try to find out."

"How'll I know if you're safe?" Aleksy asked his father.

"You won't. I didn't have contact with your Aunt Melanie for years during the last war, and it may be no different with us. Trust that we're fine. Just be careful. Don't do anything to call attention to yourself. Be a good employee and be courteous to everyone, but don't become too friendly with anyone. It may seem unimportant, but it's not. That's the easiest way to get yourself into trouble. You never really know where anyone's loyalties lie."

Dr. Fominski agreed to take Aleksy into the hospital as an intern. "Certainly Aleksy will be safer here, and I'm glad to have his help. I think we'll be shorthanded as the fighting picks up and people get pulled into the war."

Dr. Fominski looked at the young man who resembled his father at that age. "If an underground army forms, and I believe that's likely if the war doesn't end quickly, they won't venture into the bigger cities to find recruits. They'd be too exposed."

"I remember how it was in the last war. They'll do their fighting where they can squeeze the locals for support and then melt back into the forest." Dr. Fominski sighed. "So much war in our lives, Alexander. We're like bruised and battered balls kicked back and forth in a children's game."

"That we are. In medical school we never dreamed our lives would be shaped by guns, did we," Alexander replied. He looked at his son standing by the window, memorizing his face.

Alexander stood up to leave. "I'm so grateful to you for taking in Aleksy. I hope I can repay you."

"You owe me nothing. He'll earn his keep."

Alexander bid Dr. Fominski and Aleksy goodbye and went home to prepare his family as best he could for the change that he was sure was coming. He would not see Aleksy for six years.

Alexander was right to act quickly. In early 1939 the Soviet Union had negotiated with Britain, France, Poland, and Romania in an attempt to establish an alliance against Nazi Germany. The talks had failed when the Soviet Union insisted that Poland and Romania give Soviet troops transit rights through their territory. This had led to the August, 1939, Molotov-Ribbentrop Pact between the Soviets and Nazi Germany, which had established a secret plan dividing Northern and Eastern Europe into German and Soviet areas of control. One week after the pact was signed, Nazi Germany invaded Poland from the west. Under the pretense of protecting Ukrainian and Belarusians living in Eastern Poland, the Soviets invaded on September 18. The Polish army was vastly outnumbered and provided little resistance. Jews and non-Jews who had fled the Nazis were now in communist Soviet controlled territory. Many Jews fled through ports on the Black Sea, hoping to get to Palestine. Others attempted to flee to other countries that seemed safer, but some had no choice but to stay in eastern Poland.

Paceviche was once again under the Bolsheviks, only now they were called the Soviets, and Paceviche was part of the communist Soviet Union. Alexander was hired by the Soviets to run the Bakshty medical clinic, so his professional life didn't change much. However, he knew he and his family were in danger. He was one of the largest landowners in Bakshty County, and the Soviets considered landowners enemies of the state. Besides that, he was educated, which made him a part of the intelligentsia, also considered a threat to the state. Gone was the freedom of being a Polish citizen, replaced by the tension of living under the Soviet communist dictatorship. The mutable orders of the NKWD, the secret police, and the authoritarian commandants brought daily anxiety into every corner of the district. Using trumped up charges, the Soviets arrested anyone considered a threat. Some Polish landowners were sent to Siberia or mysteriously disappeared. The veil of fear that shrouded Soviet-occupied Poland during the winter of 1939-1940 was as chilling as the frost that killed all of Alexander's fruit trees that year.

The children were in bed, Katherine was hemming a dress for Danuta, and Alexander was reading when a knock at the door broke the silence one night near the end of that bitterly cold winter. "I wonder who's ill," Alexander said as he put down his book.

When Alexander opened the door, a Soviet soldier stepped forcefully into the room. "Dr. Kowal?" Alexander nodded. "Come with me. The commandant wants to see you." Alexander's heart sank. No one was ill. This was it. The commandant was the NKWD officer in charge of governing Bakshty County. My turn to be arrested and sent to Siberia, Alexander thought. It's all over. His mind raced. How much time would they have to gather some belongings? Would he be able to get any medical supplies together? Katherine sat frozen in her chair, needle poised in mid-stitch.

"Bring your bag."

Alexander's mind raced. The Soviets had their own military doctors. Why bring his medical bag? Was he being whisked away to disappear? It didn't make sense.

"I'll be back. Don't worry." He forced himself to sound confident, but Katherine knew he wasn't. He picked up his bag and followed the young soldier outside.

The soldier steered the Soviet truck down the dark rutted road to the east side of Bakshty and turned into the driveway of a house set back from the road and surrounded by spruce trees. "Come with me." The soldier opened his door and stepped onto the snow covered path. Alexander followed.

Another uniformed soldier answered their knock at the door of the main room of the house, which served as the commandant's office. They stepped into a room with two desks, a few chairs and cabinets, and a wood-burning stove in the back corner.

"This is Dr. Kowal, sir," the soldier said to the man seated behind the larger desk. The driver stepped back and awaited further orders. The stout swarthy-skinned commandant with his black curly hair looked like a gypsy to Alexander.

"I'm told that you've been the doctor here for quite some time," the commandant said curtly. Without waiting for a reply, he continued. "You've had success at treating children as well as adults?" He puffed on a cigarette, scowling at Alexander.

"Well, yes, when they've something that's treatable."

"My daughter's ill. I want to know what you can do to make her well." There was no greeting, no courtesy. He was all business. Even through commandant's concern for his daughter, arrogance seeped in. He was used to being feared and obeyed.

"I'll be glad to take a look at her. I can't promise that I can help her. If I can't treat her, we'll have to call someone from a larger town." Alexander was relieved at the turn of events, but he knew this was not a completely safe situation either. The commandant opened the door at the back of the room near the wood stove and beckoned Alexander. It led to the family's living quarters.

A girl who looked to be about eight lay listlessly in a bed at one side of the dim room. She looked at Alexander with feverish eyes. Beside her sat her mother, a plump woman with shinny black hair pulled neatly into a coil at the nape of her neck. Alexander guessed she was in her early thirties, quite a bit younger than her husband. She was placing a water-soaked cloth on the girl's forehead in an attempt to control the fever.

The woman looked up. "She's been like this for two days with a fever and a sore throat. She won't eat and seems to be getting worse."

She beseeched Alexander with her eyes.

The woman stood and Alexander examined the girl. It was evident after a few minutes that she had diphtheria. He gave his diagnosis to her parents who watched from the foot of the bed. "I'll have to inject her with anti-toxin serum. They have some at the pharmacy here in Bakshty. I can't guarantee anything. She's very ill."

"If that is what she needs, do it. The sergeant will drive you." The commandant gave the orders and in less than an hour Alexander was back with the medicine.

The girl cried as he injected the anti-toxin, but her mother soothed her, and she closed her eyes and lay quietly. "If she's going to have a bad reaction, we'll know within a few hours," Alexander told the parents.

"You'll stay here, then, so you can tend to her," the commandant said. It was an order, not a request. Alexander gave the girl an aspirin to help control the fever. The child had no bad reaction, and with nothing else to do at the moment, he went back into the commandant's office, found a chair in the corner of the room, and fell asleep. He knew Katherine must be terribly worried, but there was nothing he could do about it. Shortly before dawn Alexander woke and checked on the child. Her fever seemed less and she was breathing rhythmically. These were good signs, but he knew it wasn't a guarantee that she would get better. Moonlight coming through the uncovered window above the bed cast shadows in the room as he stood watching his small patient. *What will happen to me if she doesn't get well?* He didn't want to think about that, but he couldn't help himself. The commandant could easily have him exiled or shot if the girl died. He could do nothing but wait. He had no control over his fate.

The girl opened her eyes not long after the sun rose. Her mother held her hand to the girl's forehead. The fever was gone. "She's better," her mother said to Alexander. She smiled but offered no words of gratitude for his having saved her daughter's life.

"Your daughter will sleep most of the day," Alexander replied. "Be sure she drinks water when she wakes." The woman nodded.

"Go into my husband's office and get some breakfast," she said dismissing him.

The commandant was sitting at his desk noisily eating sausage and bread. With a greasy finger he motioned to a chair.

"Sit," he said stuffing another piece of bread into his already full mouth. "Have something to eat."

Alexander sat and took some bread and cheese.

"Let's have some vodka." The commandant poured the clear liquid into two glasses. As they ate and drank, the commandant became more relaxed and began to talk about the winter weather.

The vodka and relief also loosened Alexander's tongue. "You know, I was afraid when your driver showed up at my door that you were going to arrest me," he confided to the commandant. Instantly he regretted having revealed his thoughts.

The dark-skinned man said nothing for a moment. He took a deep breath. "Your concerns were justified, Dr. Kowal." He pulled a folder out of the top drawer, and handed it to Alexander. KOWAL, ALEXANDER was printed on the outside. Alexander's stomach muscles tightened. "Open it," the commandant ordered.

The first page was a biography of Alexander—his family, schooling, marriages, and children were all included. He turned to the second page. It listed every piece of land he owned, every county position he had held, including his term as chairman of the County Council. It even included the salary he had been paid for the job. There were some other documents including his army records and medical clinic reports. The last page was a letter.

TO: Bakshty County NKWD Commandant
Deportation orders for Alexander Kowal and family.
Alexander Kowal, a danger to the State, must be relocated to Siberia. You are hereby ordered to arrest Dr. Kowal and his

family, and transport them under guard via train to the Camp 33. All property belonging to Dr. Kowal is to be confiscated and turned over to the State. Dr. Kowal and his family are to be permitted to take with them one bag for each family member and one trunk of personal items for the entire family. This is effective immediately.

Alexander handed the folder back to the commandant. He couldn't keep his hands from shaking, so he put them in his lap and squeezed them together. He was not surprised at the order. The Soviets didn't allow individuals to own property. According to the Communist philosophy, landowners were a wealthy class, *kulaks* they were called, and no one was to have more wealth than anyone else. To make things fair, no individual could own land. Factories, houses, land, and even stores were owned by the State, and all people worked for the State. Alexander's land automatically made him a kulak. Of course the officials all seemed to live in nicer homes than everyone else, but no one ever mentioned that except in private. He waited for the commandant to tell him he was under arrest.

The commandant held the folder for a moment and then walked over to the stove. He picked up the lid handle from where it lay on a shelf near the stove, lifted the lid and threw the folder into the flames. Replacing the lid and putting the handle back on the shelf, he turned to Alexander. "You saved my daughter. For that you'll not go to visit the White Bears."

"Thank you." Alexander felt his heart racing and his knees quivering, but he looked the general in the eye and extended his hand.

The general took his hand. "Perhaps we'll see you again, Dr. Kowal," he said as though this had been a social call. "The sergeant will drive you home."

Chapter 14

Paceviche, Soviet Occupied Poland, 1941

Katherine heard the Soviet truck pull up to the house and peeked out the window. A tired Alexander climbed out, and Katherine's knees went weak with relief. She touched her stomach and felt their fourth child move. The fear of her husband being whisked away, leaving her alone, had robbed her of sleep since the sergeant had appeared at their door. The truck roared off and she opened the door. Alexander stepped into the warm kitchen and collapsed onto a chair.

"We're safe for now," Alexander told her. "There are no orders for our arrest." He told her about the sick child and his ordeal. When he lay down to rest before going back to the clinic, he relived the last day. Once again being a doctor had saved him and his family.

In hindsight Alexander thought perhaps the incident with the commandant's daughter was the beginning of Katherine's emotional decline. A knock at the door, the groaning of a Soviet truck as it passed their house, or an unexpected noise in the night filled Katherine with anxiety and precipitated a panic attack. After Jacob's birth Katherine was sad most of the time. She went about daily routines by rote. Alexander tried to help her, but he had no words or medicine that could dispel her fear or bring light back into her dull eyes.

Then on June 22, 1941, Hitler's army attacked Stalin's army. Their agreement had been a contract among thieves. Each side signed with ulterior motives. Hitler was determined to control all Europe including the areas he had agreed the Soviets could rule. Stalin was surprised. He planned to attack the Germans, but his army wasn't ready. Eastern Europe was once again the battleground for two power-hunger rulers set on European domination.

A DOCTOR'S JOURNEY

Within days of attack, the Soviets fled towards Moscow. The residents of Bakshty County watched from the shadows as trucks loaded with soldiers sped east leaving behind equipment and anything else that they couldn't easily carry. All night Alexander heard the Soviet trucks roaring eastward. By dawn of the second day all that was left of the Red Army was abandoned equipment, some pushed into the marshes to make it unusable by the advancing Nazi forces. Fortune's wheel had turned once more.

Memories of the last war and the devastation when Germans and Russians fought in Paceviche spurred the residents to action. Melanie vividly remembered her struggles to survive and knew what they must do. "Katherine, they'll take whatever they need or want and burn anything in their way. We have to hide what we can—food, equipment, your sewing machine, the bicycles—anything the Germans might think has value," Melanie explained to her sister-in-law who was too young to remember much about the last war.

That afternoon, Alexander, Katherine, Melanie, and Alosha built wood crates. Katherine's sewing machine was taken apart, put in two crates, and buried behind the house after the children went to bed. No need risking the children knowing and accidentally giving up the secret hiding place. Next they took apart the bicycles and buried them in separate crates. In the morning Alexander and Katherine buried sacks of flour underneath the stacked hay in the barn. They dug a hole under another part of the hay and hid most of their rye and barley, leaving just enough to avert suspicion that they were hoarding food.

Alexander saved the most important task until last: hiding his diploma, the instruments he had received when he graduated from medical school, family pictures, Olimpia's and Arkady's last letters, his marriage certificates, and the children's baptismal certificates—his most precious possessions. After giving the instruments a quick polish, he arranged them on the beige linen lining of their soft black leather case, slipped them into their loops that held them in place, and covered them with the linen flap. He rolled his diploma in linen and laid it inside the case with the instruments. Alexander folded the case and snapped the clasp. He wrapped it in more linen and placed it in a metal box with the certificates, letters, and pictures. Fortunately Katherine had saved beeswax for candles which he used to seal the seams of the box. He placed the metal box on a bed of dry straw in a larger wooden box, stuffed it with more dry straw to absorbed moisture, and nailed the box shut. In a dark corner of the barn he dug down about a meter. Sweat dripped off his face as he lifted heavy shovelfuls of dirt. By the time he lowered the box into the hole, his shoulders throbbed. With one last look, he covered the box, tamped down the dirt and brushed it to disguise the hole, and raked hay over the whole area.

Walking back to the house, Alexander thought of Aleksy. He wanted to believe his first-born was safe, but realistically, no place in the country was truly safe from the Nazis. Alexander knew Melanie was worried about her married daughters. Maria lived with her husband's family in a rural village that was probably too small and too isolated to garner attention from invaders. However, Nastia and her husband's home was just a few kilometers south of Bakshty, and Anna and her family lived a few kilometers beyond Nastia. They were most vulnerable. But Melanie and Alexander could do nothing for their adult children now. They had to do what they could to ensure their own survival.

The Kowals' preparations were not a moment too soon. Alexander was putting on his boots the next day when he heard German planes overhead. Explosions shook the ground when the waves of planes dropped their deadly cargo. Rushing outside the Kowals saw clouds of black smoke rising from Bakshty.

"Oh my God! The Germans are doing just what they did to Warsaw before they invaded." Alexander called to Katherine. They stood by the door mesmerized, watching the planes, swastikas emblazoned on their wings, rise in the sky and turn back toward their base. Smoke drifted over Paceviche, its putrid smell filling their lungs.

"I've got to see if I can help. You stay here," Alexander told Katherine. He stuffed bandages, ointment, and a few bottles of medicine into his house call bag and hurried towards Bakshty. The contents of his bag and kitchen cupboard were all he now had to treat patients. The clinic was engulfed in flames.

Most of Bakshty was destroyed. Bodies of all ages scattered the town. Wails of the injured and shouts of those who became rescuers filled the air. Dazed, bleeding people were dragged from what was left of smoldering buildings. Uninjured men and women raced to put out fires with water from those wells that hadn't been hit. Alexander and the other doctor in town set up a triage station in a house that was still standing. All day and all night they did what they could with what little they had to mend unspeakable wounds. It was mid-morning of the next day when Alexander stumbled home, hollow-eyed and exhausted. This was worse than anything he had seen in the war or revolution. This army was vicious.

All that was left of the bridge over the river were a few shattered timbers. Getting to the railway station now required fording the river. Bakshty was isolated. The following day Hitler's army entered the county. When the rumbling and dust of the German tanks grew near, the Kowals and their neighbors fled to the forest, taking as many of their animals with them as they could. They remembered the fighting twenty-five years ago when they were caught in the crossfire. They remembered the haystacks and barns erupting in flames. They remembered the starvation months when they lived in the forest scavenging for whatever was edible. They remembered watching loved ones die of the cold, illness, and despair. The Soviets were gone, so there would be no fighting armies this time. But what would the German army do to the innocent residents left here? If they could drop bombs on these people, what other horrors were they capable of? Disappearing into the forest was the safest course of action.

Katherine, however, refused to leave the house. Jacob was six months old and she insisted that the Germans wouldn't harm a baby and a nursing mother. Alexander pleaded with her to come with the rest of the family. But she was adamant. She would not leave the security of her house. It was familiar, the forest wasn't. Alexander knew she was not thinking clearly, but he couldn't change her mind. The rumbling army was getting closer. He had to be sure the other children were not in harm's way.

"Stay inside, Katherine. Don't try to leave. You'll be safer inside," he told his grim-faced wife.

Danuta and the two older boys in tow, Alexander headed to the forest with Melanie and Alosha. He looked back several times to see if Katherine had reconsidered and was hurrying to join them, but she was nowhere to be seen.

As the Nazi troops rolled through the villages in their Panzers and trucks, they found empty houses. Until they reached the Kowals'. Katherine heard the German tanks rumbling. She, the baby, a few chickens, and the milk cow Alexander had decided to lock in the barn were the only living souls left behind. Katherine pulled Jacob close to her and opened the door in spite of her husband's warnings. Down the dusty lane past the log homes a column of growling tanks and trucks loaded with grey-shirted soldiers thundered. Katherine's heart raced. She held Jacob tighter. As the soldiers and tanks neared the house, the panic that had visited so often in the last year welled up. She scanned the line of armored vehicles and then glanced at the forest that lay on the other side of the field of rye.

Her feet took on a life of their own. Clutching Jacob to her chest, she darted out the door and ran towards the field. A shot rang out and a bullet whistled by her ear. Then another and another. Katherine didn't see the helmeted soldier in the first truck take aim, fire, and fire again. She fell to the ground screaming and sobbing, swallowed up in the tall rye with Jacob held tightly in her arms. Her heart pounded in her ears and she couldn't control her shaking arms. Jacob's whimpers turned to screams as he lay partially under his mother. Katherine rolled off the terrified baby and gathered him to her. Tears streamed down her cheeks as she lay rocking the wailing Jacob. The truck moved on. The soldier rested his warm rifle in his lap thinking he had eliminated one more Pole.

At last the noise of the German column faded. Katherine lay where she had fallen, her mind a gray cloud of emptiness. Hours later a bird chirping in a nearby tree roused her senses. She felt cold even in the warm afternoon. Jacob's screams had subsided and he had fallen asleep. She rose, scooped him up, and scurried on shaky legs back to the house fearing the soldiers might return. She pushed open the door and collapsed with Jacob on the floor unable to make her legs move one more step. He rolled away from her, but she just watched him. He rolled back to her and wrapped his arms around her neck.

When dark descended on Paceviche, the residents, who had been stealthily watching from the safety of the trees, saw the Germans leave. There would be no fighting in Paceviche, at least not now. It appeared to be safe to return, so they slipped back into their homes. Alexander found a traumatized Katherine just inside the door on the floor in a fetal position with a sleeping Jacob cradled in her arms.

Alexander knelt down. His wife's dress was covered with dust and her face smudged with dirt. "Katherine, what happened?" She didn't answer, but stared at him, tears welling up in her eyes.

"Did they hurt you?" Silence.

"Did they come into the house?" Silence. He looked around and saw nothing out of place. He touched his wife's shoulder and she protectively pulled Jacob closer.

Then came a whisper. "They shot at me. At us."

"What? Why?"

"I ran." The words were barely audible. "I was so scared. There were tanks and the soldiers had guns."

That was all she could say. Alexander helped her up, led her to their bed, and covered her and Jacob with a blanket. Danuta and the boys huddled next to the table. Alexander turned to his daughter.

"Danuta, go milk the cow. Give the boys some fresh milk and get them to bed. Boys, wash your faces and hands. Be quiet. Your mother's not feeling well."

With solemn eyes Josef and Zbigniew did as they were told and then sat side by side at the table waiting for Danuta. When at last all his children were asleep and he could hear his wife's rhythmic breathing, Alexander climbed into bed and lay next to her. But fear kept sleep at bay. He had heard accounts of what the Germans had done in Warsaw when they captured it. Alexander knew that the smallest misstep or casual remark could result in death at the hands of the SS. There would be no quietly getting along with the Germans as there had been with the Soviets.

The fighting forces of the Germans moved eastward in pursuit of the Red Army. They left behind the SS, whose task was to subjugate the Polish citizens. The Germans established their *Stutzpunkt*, a command headquarters, in what had been Bakshty's school. Armored trucks and staff cars paraded through the county filled with stern-faced Germans. The troops brandished their weapons and curtly demanded food or supplies from the residents. Tentative peace disappeared, replaced by fear in every thought and action. The few businesses left standing after the bombing closed. Alexander set up his practice in one corner of his kitchen. Danuta became his nurse. People paid for his services with a few eggs or coins if they had them. Alexander again became a farmer. His hands toughened as he, Katherine, their children, Melanie and Alosha tended crops and a garden, cared for the milk cow, chickens, and pigs, and prepared to survive the cold months ahead. The villagers nurtured crops and gardens, remembering the days of starvation in the last war. The Germans waited for the harvest to take what they considered their share. The residents plotted to hide as much as they could.

A DOCTOR'S JOURNEY

Within weeks the Germans' cruelty to certain ethnic groups surfaced. First were the Gypsies. German troops sought out their camps in the countryside, surrounded them, and slaughtered the men, women, and children. The Jews were next. All Jews in Bakshty County were rounded up and sent to live in Borysowka, a small town a few kilometers from Bakshty.

It was on a trip to Bakshty to make a house call on an elderly patient that the plight of the Jews and the cruelty of the SS troops struck Alexander full force. Walking home after treating his patient, Alexander saw SS troops herding a group of Jews down the road, heading to an unknown destination. Not wanting to call attention to himself, he stepped into the shadow of a house and watched them pass. That was when he saw Isaac Romanowski who had owned the pharmacy in Bakshty.

The Isaac Romanowski Alexander had worked with was a tall, broad-shouldered, confident man with laughing brown eyes. He had been a friendly person with an easy smile. But the man Alexander saw shuffling down the road was a broken man. He was crying and his face was etched with terror. His broad shoulders seemed to have shrunk to half their normal width under the cloth bag on his back. Isaac, always careful about his grooming, was wearing mud-splattered pants and a wrinkled shirt. His usually neat hair stuck out in greasy tangles from under a brown cap. None of the other Jews looked any better. Alexander shuddered. What had the Nazis done to this man? And where were they taking him and the others?

"Who's next? What's going to happen to the rest of us?" Alexander whispered to himself. He shuddered. He had never been so afraid. After the Jews and SS men guarding them passed, Alexander stepped quickly onto the road and hurried home.

The people of Bakshty County became the Germans' unpaid workers. Men from all villages were forced to work pulling abandoned Red Army equipment out of the mud in the swamps where it had been left. It was backbreaking work, but under the watchful eyes of armed German SS men, the villagers worked to avoid being beaten or shot. Much of the Soviet equipment was rusted or broken, but any parts that could be salvaged or melted down for new parts were sent to Germany.

In early July a German staff car stopped at the Kowals. Katherine and Danuta were fixing vegetables for the noon stew when a young officer pushed open the door.

In broken Polish the young blond man spoke to Alexander. "Your house is biggest in village. It is now ours to use when we want. Commander will come today. Work here. You will feed us. All of us. We leave when finished. Then you have your house back. Clear?"

"Yes, I understand," Alexander replied. The Kowals' house became the German headquarters on days the SS needed or wanted to be in Paceviche. The officers in their polished black boots moved in and took over the largest of the three rooms. Katherine and Danuta prepared meals for the German staff from their dwindling store of food. It was an effort for Katherine to stay calm and not bolt out the door. The boys were sent to Melanie's house while Katherine and Danuta baked heavy rye bread and cooked stews using as few vegetables as possible.

The SS Troops' presence exacerbated Katherine's anxiety. When they were there, she was a ghost silently cooking and doing the invaders' bidding, her mouth pinched in fear. Sleepless nights were the norm and her panic attacks came more often. The sound of a truck or the barking of a neighbor's dog might freeze her in fear. Danuta took over most of the care of her brothers and more of the cooking for the invaders.

The Kowals never knew when the SS cars would pull up to their door and the SS officers would enter as if they owned the house. Once again the only thing certain was uncertainty.

Katherine's emotional state worsened. She began running into the forest with Jacob when a panic attack struck. When he was home, Alexander would find her, but if he was making a house call, Danuta would leave her brothers alone in the house and search for their mother.

The day after an early October snowfall had blanketed the countryside in white, Katherine heard the honking horn of a German staff car driving by the house and bolted across the rye stubble to the forest with Jacob clutched to her chest. Alexander was in Bakshty. Josef and Zbigniew were playing at Melanie's. Danuta was doing chores in the barn and an hour elapsed before she discovered her mother was gone. Leaving the just-gathered eggs on the table, she ran to the forest.

Blowing snow had covered some of her mother's footprints, and it was well after noon before she found Katherine and Jacob huddled in the snow beside a spruce tree. Neither of them was wearing a coat, and Jacob was shivering violently. Danuta picked him up, tucked him inside her jacket, and led her mother home. Danuta changed her baby brother's soggy diaper, washed his face and hands in warm water, dressed him in clean clothes she warmed by the stove, and gave him warm milk. Jacob's eyes watered, his nose ran, and he began to cough. Katherine sat in a chair by the stove staring with hollow eyes at her daughter.

"Mama, drink this," Danuta said handing her mother a mug of warm milk. Katherine took a few sips but said nothing. "I wish I could make you feel better, Mama."

Katherine looked up at her. "I wish you could, too, but you can't," she whispered.

By the time Alexander arrived home, Jacob had a fever. For the next week he fought for life, but his fever rose and his lungs filled in spite of everything Alexander and Danuta did. Katherine tried to help, but her depression was too deep to do more than hold him and let him try to nurse at her desiccated breasts. Jacob grew listless and died in his father's arms two months before his first birthday.

It was the beginning of the end for Katherine. Danuta took over the household as her mother sat despondently by the stove. The one task Katherine never failed to do was make the family's weekly supply of rye bread every Monday morning. The ritual of mixing and kneading the dough seemed almost comforting for her, but other chores were left for her daughter.

One morning a few days after Christmas while Danuta was in the barn milking the cow and Alexander was at a neighbor's, Katherine left the house and disappeared into the forest. It was now a familiar pattern. Danuta brought in the milk, saw that her mother was gone, and walked to the neighbor's to get her father. They headed into the forest. But this time, their search was fruitless. A light snow had covered Katherine's footprints. They enlisted neighbors to help. By nightfall Katherine was still missing and searching in the dark was futile. At first light Alexander and Danuta left the house. Neighbors joined them. The morning sun had broken through the clouds when Alexander found Katherine curled up under some fallen brush where she had apparently crawled in a vain effort to stay warm.

Katherine was buried in the cemetery near Olimpia and baby Jacob. Alexander now had three children to raise by himself in the midst of the German occupation.

Danuta had to grow up far beyond her years. At thirteen she was a surrogate mother and the family's housekeeper. The first week after her mother's death, the large wooden bowl of rye flour and yeasty starter almost defeated her. Danuta's young arms weren't strong enough to stir the heavy, sticky dough, and her tears dripped into the bowl. Alexander joined her efforts, and together they managed to get the tear-spiced bread mixed, shaped into loaves, and baked. Danuta's courage amazed her father. In spite of life's daily challenges before and after her mother's death, she persevered. Danuta kept the Kowal household running, and cared for her brothers and father. Her courage would be sorely tested in the coming months.

Chapter 15

Paceviche, German-occupied Poland, 1941

Life had to go on in spite of the terrifying German occupation. But it wasn't just the Germans who made life difficult for people. Just as Alexander had predicted, underground armies quickly formed to fight the Germans. Each group had its own political loyalties. Some factions were financed by the Soviets, others fought for Polish independence and wanted all foreigners out of the country, and other groups had a variety of political ties. They contested each other for territory and supplies. Villagers feared them as much as they feared the Germans. At night when the Germans retreated to their camps, underground armies appeared at homes demanding food and supplies.

From Alexander the request was also for medical treatment for the wounded or ill. Refusing or arguing was met with threats or physical violence. Alexander always acquiesced to the partisan's demands giving them food or treating whoever they brought to his door. Their demands for help were always explained as a patriotic duty. They were not the enemy, they were fighting the enemy. The underground army caused the occupying forces as much havoc as they could, but also made life for Polish citizens more tenuous. During daylight they feared the Germans. During the night they feared the partisans.

Alexander had agreed to let one Polish-supported partisan group hide dynamite under the bed in his house and use his barn as a rest stop for men going to or returning home from their missions. Hiding explosives was risky with the SS using the house as their headquarters, but as one of the partisans told him, "Sometimes it's easier to hide things right under the nose of those arrogant Germans." And after seeing the shell of a man the Jewish pharmacist had become under

German mistreatment, Alexander felt hiding explosives was one thing he could do to the people who destroyed his friend.

The knock at the door on a cold November night was not expected, but was also not a surprise. The children were in bed and Alexander was feeling sleepy as he sat by the kerosene lamp reading. He closed the book by Henryk Sienkiewicz, one of his favorite authors, rose, and opened the door. He did not recognize the man standing there.

"I need a place to rest tonight," the ruddy-faced man said in a voice that was almost a whisper. It wasn't a request or a demand, just a statement.

"Of course, come in." Alexander knew without explanation that the muscular man was a partisan on his way home after doing something that would cause the Germans a problem the next day, but he also knew better than to ask what he'd been doing.

The man limped slowly into the room wincing from pain. "What's wrong with your leg?" Alexander asked.

"It's my foot. Infected and getting worse."

"Take off your boot. Let's see what we can do." Alexander pointed at the bench by the table. The man hobbled the short distance and slowly removed his right boot and sock. An abscessed sore oozed pus and blood and filled the room with the stench of infection. Alexander poured the man a glass of vodka, opened his bag and went to work.

It took nearly an hour to drain the sore and dress the wound. The man clenched his teeth as Alexander scraped and cleaned, but remained silent.

"It's fortunate you came tonight. Gangrene was setting in, and you could've lost your foot in another day or two. How far did you walk on it today?"

"Too far. Thank you. It feels better already. I'm Saszka Waniawkin, and I'm in your debt."

Alexander nodded in acknowledgement. "I think you should sleep in the house tonight. I'll check your foot again before you leave. Don't walk any more than you have to tomorrow." Saszka Waniawkin agreed, settled himself on one side of Alexander's bed and was asleep before Alexander blew out the kerosene lamp. Alexander wondered how Saszka had injured his foot, but didn't ask.

Well before dawn the visitor awoke. Alexander woke Danuta to fix some bread and sausage and boil some water for chicory coffee. "You're alone with your children?" the visitor asked his host

Alexander nodded. "My wife died recently."

"I'm sorry. It must be difficult."

"We get by. Lots of people have it worse than we do now. We're still here. The Germans haven't rounded us up and sent us to work camps somewhere or just killed us." Alexander wondered about Saszka's family but didn't ask. He was quite sure Saszka was an alias and the man sitting across from him wouldn't volunteer any personal information. The less Alexander knew the better. But he liked this solidly built man.

The two talked for a few minutes before Saszka stood. "Time to go. My foot is much better. I can make it home before it gets light."

"Put your foot up on the bench," Alexander said. He replaced the bandage with a new one. "Keep it clean. Take this salve and put it on twice a day."

As Alexander watched Saszka disappear into the darkness, he didn't know that this man he had just helped would soon be his savior.

Any day could be unexpectedly shattered in a moment as it did for Alexander a year after the German occupation began. It was early summer and the first small new potatoes were almost ready for digging. Saszka, who had made Kowals a regular rest stop, had appeared at the door once again just as Alexander was climbing into bed. He was here to sleep before heading on to complete his mission. They had developed a friendship during the last few months. Saszka even kept a bundle of blankets in the back room that he pulled out of a chest to use as a bed when he didn't hide in the barn. Tonight the men went quickly to bed without much conversation. Saszka would wake in three hours, be on his way, and be back before dawn to hide and sleep in the barn until dark when he could return home.

The knock at the door just before midnight was not unusual nor was the group of underground soldiers standing there. But their purpose was a complete surprise. They must be here for Saszka, Alexander thought, although nothing had been said of any partisans coming. Alexander groggily opened the door to a group of stern-faced men standing in the shadows. He recognized three of them as men from Ostrowce. In fact, he had known the youngest of the group since he was a baby.

"Dr. Kowal, come with us," the middle-aged man in the ragged clothes demanded.

"I'll get my bag."

"You won't need it. We're arresting you."

"What?" Alexander was instantly wide awake. "Why?"

"You heard me. We know all about what you're doing."

Foreboding gripped Alexander's stomach. Did they know Saszka was in the other room? Did he know about this? Were these his friends or a competing partisan army? Better not mention him in case there was bad blood between the groups.

At that moment Saszka opened the bedroom door and stepped into the room. He scanned the intruders and recognized their rifles as Russian made. "Why are you here?" he asked the apparent leader. They glared, recognizing each other from previous skirmishes between their groups.

"It's none of your business," the man growled.

"It certainly is. Why are you taking this good doctor and where are you taking him?"

"We're following orders." The apparent leader of the group glared at Saszka.

"Show me the orders." Saszka held out his hand. "Show me."

"I don't have to show you anything."

A DOCTOR'S JOURNEY

"If you have orders, show me. Otherwise how do I know you aren't just mavericks causing trouble?" Saszka kept his hand extended.

The leader glowered but took a folded paper out of his jacket pocket and slapped it in Saszka's hand. He read the brief note.

"This is ridiculous. You think he is collaborating with the Germans? He's helping us. Tonight he's letting me hide here. And he let's us keep explosives here. You have the wrong man. If you follow these orders, you'll kill an innocent man. And we need him. He saved my leg and probably my life." Saszka handed the grease-stained paper back. Alexander stood stunned and speechless.

The noise had awakened Danuta. She listened for a few minutes before cracking open the bedroom door and peaking out at her frightened father and the men with rifles.

"We have our orders. Come with us, Dr. Kowal." Alexander looked at Saszka whose eyes were blazing.

The younger man wearing a greasy black cap stepped forward and raised his gun towards Alexander.

"I'll come, but this doesn't make sense." Alexander saw his daughter's eyes at the bedroom door. He took a half-dozen steps to her and pulled the door open a little more. He put his hand on her shoulder. "You're going to have to be strong. Get help from Aunt Melanie. Take care of your brothers. Do you understand?"

He didn't sound as calm and he wanted to, but he sounded more confident than he felt. This heated scene was a lot for a fourteen-year-old to absorb. The frightened girl managed to whisper, "Yes." Alexander kissed her cheek and turned to face the intruders.

"Now you listen to me," Saszka told the leader through clenched teeth. "Don't you dare hurt one hair on this man's head until my commander can talk to your commander. I have to complete my mission tonight, but we'll be at your headquarters in the morning. Is that clear? If anything happens to this good man, there'll be a price to pay that's more than you can afford."

"I'll tell my commander," the leader said. He shrugged. "But I can't promise anything."

"I'll be there as soon as I can," Saszka told Alexander. "They've made a mistake. I don't understand." He turned to the gray-haired partisan. "Surely you can see that he's helping us."

"I'll tell my commander, but we have proof." One of the younger men opened the door and they left.

The four men led Alexander silently in the moonlight on a network of paths at the edge of several villages to Ostrowce. Their pace quickened, and by the time they stopped, Alexander was breathing heavily. He tried to collect his thoughts and find a solution to his situation. That's what he was trained to do. Diagnose a problem and choose the best solution. But his 'arrest' by these partisans defied logic, and he couldn't squelch the panic that filled his gut. They were going to kill him because they had proof he was helping the enemy? That was bizarre.

Silently the group slipped into a log house at the edge of Ostrowce. They took Alexander to the back bedroom of the three-room house.

"We'll shoot him after breakfast so we can all be home on time," one of the men said. Alexander's heart sank. Then the gray-haired man who had arrested Alexander spoke.

"We have a problem. Saszka Waniawkin was at Dr. Kowal's house when we got there. He said the doctor is helping his army, and we shouldn't do anything until his commander can talk to us this morning."

"But we have those statements. You heard what that man told us about Dr. Kowal helping the SS."

"Yes, but Saszka was angry. We should hear what he has to say before we do anything. We don't need those guys seeking revenge if we kill the wrong person. We have different supporters, but the Germans are our common enemy. After the Germans are gone, we can sort out differences. Not now."

The discussion went on for a while, but they made no decision. Then Alexander heard new voices outside the house. Alexander tried to look out the small window but could see nothing in the dark. Someone pounded on the front door.

"We need to talk to you," a familiar voice called. Alexander heard the door open.

"Where's Dr. Kowal?" demanded a voice Alexander recognized as belonging to Jan Lublin, a member of the Ostrowce town council before the Soviets and Germans invaded. "You have no reason to hold him. Release him. Let him come with us." Other voices rose calling for Alexander's release. Alexander was stunned. All these people coming to defend him were unexpected. He wondered how they all knew what was happening. People were shouting at his captors.

"Now listen, you all have to leave." The commander of the Soviet-backed partisans yelled. "We don't want to hurt anyone, but if you get in our way, we'll have no choice. Now leave." Alexander guessed that the guns that had been pointed at him were now directed at the people demanding his release.

There was silence for a moment; then Jan Lubin spoke again, "If you harm Dr. Kowal, don't expect cooperation from any of us. Don't ask us for food or shelter. The Germans are the enemy, not good Poles like Dr. Kowal." He spat the words at the commander. "Do you understand what I'm saying? We'll leave. We won't give you any reason to shoot us today."

Alexander heard the low angry voices fade away as the people left. The door closed. Alexander's captors haggled among themselves about what they should do. They decided to move Alexander to the barn in case the villagers returned. One of the younger men was chosen to escort Alexander across the yard. "You stay with him and guard him," the commander said. "Don't let him out of your sight."

The curly-haired youth led Alexander to a dark corner of the barn and pushed him down into a mound of dusty hay. Alexander felt as though he were in a nightmare and couldn't wake up. He shivered even though the night was warm. So this was to be his last night on earth. What would become of his children? Danuta and the boys had already seen and suffered too much. Would Melanie be able to care for them? And Aleksy? Was he safe? Would he ever get to finish medical school? Despairing, Alexander sobbed. He could do nothing to save himself. Not even being a doctor could help.

Towards morning, Alexander fell into a fitful sleep but woke to the sound of a wagon approaching. It passed the barn and continued, he guessed, to the house. He heard more than one person climbing down from the wagon. Then he heard door open.

"Did you take Dr. Kowal into your custody last night?" It was a gruff voice unfamiliar to Alexander.

"What business is that of yours if we did?" Alexander recognized the voice of the man with the black cap.

"Yes, they did. He was there." It was Saszka's deep voice.

"We've been told that he's aiding the Germans. He's a traitor." Alexander recognized the voice of the highest ranking man who had taken him prisoner.

"I don't know who told you that, but he's been helping us for months. He's let us hide explosives under his bed even though the Germans take over his house some days. He's taken great risks for us."

"Well, that's not what we have been told."

The argument continued and grew more heated. Both sides stubbornly refused to back down. They must have stepped into the house. Alexander heard the door close, and the voices disappeared.

Alexander rubbed his aching hands and tried with no success to find a more comfortable position in the hay. He closed his eyes picturing Danuta, Josef, and Zbigniew. How would they survive this war? Danuta was a strong girl. She had cared for her mother and she took care of the boys. But she was still a girl. How could she survive with monsters like these men roaming the countryside? And Josef and Zbigniew? Orphans, that's what they'd be. "My children, I love you. I love you," he whispered. He wished he'd made better plans with

Melanie. Now it was too late. His chest felt as though an anvil rested on it. Each breath was an effort choked by tears.

Alexander thought most of an hour had passed when he heard Saszka's deep voice talking with two other men. Alexander was afraid to hope that this might be his salvation. The voices disappeared after less than a minute. Outside an owl hooted. The guard opened a door to let in a breeze.

A few minutes later Alexander again heard voices rising in anger deciding his fate. More than an hour passed. Dawn drew near. Alexander knew the argument would have to be won or lost soon. These men shunned daylight when the SS troops in their hobnailed jackboots would leave their Bakshty camp and spread throughout the county. Alexander guessed that Saszka's commander must be losing the argument. How long before they came to shoot him? He closed his eyes and pictured his children and sobbed. The door of the house opened and closed. Footsteps grew louder. Saszka, the commander, and a man Alexander didn't recognize appeared in the doorway of the barn.

"I'm taking you with me." Saszka reached down and pulled Alexander to his feet. "You apparently have a jealous enemy in Bakshty spreading lies about you." Relief flooded Alexander's body.

The commander stepped forward and proffered his hand. "We made a mistake. I'm sorry." Alexander stared at the man's hand but didn't reach for it.

"Some mistake. You were about to kill an innocent man." Saszka grumbled. "Let's go, Dr. Kowal."

Saszka wrapped his arm around Alexander's shoulder to steady him and led him to his wagon. Alexander couldn't stop his body from shaking and Saszka had to lift him into the wagon. As they rode away from the house, Saszka turned back and kept his gun ready in case anyone had a change of heart.

"Thank you," Alexander whispered when they were out of sight of the house. "You saved my life."

"As you did mine," Saszka replied.

It was nearly noon when Alexander and Saszka peered down the road to see if the SS men had taken over the Kowal's house for the day, but no cars were parked in the yard. They pulled up to the house. Danuta and Melanie rushed outside. When Alexander tried to climb down from the wagon, his legs collapsed. The women picked him up and helped him into the house.

Danuta's eyes filled with tears of relief. "It's all right." Alexander put his arm around her. "You did just the right things." He looked at Melanie with sadness. Never again would he see the world in the same way. This night had been the worst of his life.

Melanie took two mugs from a shelf, pulled out a bottle of vodka, and poured some for each man. Alexander met Saszka's gaze. "To you. I owe you my life." He touched his mug to Saszka's. After they had their fill of bread and cheese, Danuta and Melanie helped Alexander to his bed and he fell into a deep exhausted sleep.

Many years later Danuta told her younger half-sister that their father's hair was black when the partisans took him away and gray when they brought him back.

For the next year fear hung over the villagers like a permanent threatening cloud. At any moment the SS might round up villagers, shoot them or march them to the train station, and ship them to Germany to be slave laborers. Every sunrise carried danger.

The grinding gears of German staff cars might mean the Kowal's house was the SS command post for the day. A knock at the door after dark meant one of the partisan armies had arrived to *bombic*, rob whatever they could. The people of Bakshty County knew little of what was actually happening beyond their own village except what the Germans told them, and that wasn't always the truth.

Chapter 16

Paceviche, German Occupied Poland, 1943

It had been more than two years since the Germans had entered Bakshty County leaving their SS Troops to manage the local citizens. The SS men kept the villagers terrorized. The wrong answer to a seemingly innocent question, the slightest suspicion of helping the partisans, a remark inferred as an insult, or a slow response to a request could result in a gunshot to the head. Gypsies and Jews had been the first to be rounded up and eliminated. Then many of the intelligentsia vanished. SS troops emptied entire villages to prepare the land for future German settlements to fulfill their plan to expand German dominance throughout the continent. Some of these villagers were shipped to Germany to be conscripted workers. Anyone could be targeted.

To survive, Poles tried to make themselves unremarkable and invisible to the Germans. But that was almost impossible. It became a cat and mouse game to avoid the SS Troops. Paceviche residents were always on alert watching Germans movements. When it appeared a village was about to be cleaned out, the Paceviche villagers retreated to the forest to hide in case they were the target. They kept stashes of food and blankets in small caves camouflaged with rocks and foliage. Every child knew the routine. Leave the house quickly, quietly and get to the forest as fast as possible.

The Kowals and their neighbors had fled into the forest in June as nearby villages were decimated. They knew their time was coming. Knowing that this time they might have to stay hidden for quite a while, Alexander took the wagon, horse, and milk cow with him. He also had his medical bag and some wooden boxes with bandages and medicines. Danuta carried a small suitcase of clothes with her. At Alexander's urging, Melanie and Alosha decided to slip away to live with Maria and her husband in his rural village

"We've been through this before, haven't we?" Alexander asked his older sister as they prepared to part once again. "We managed to survive the last war. We'll survive this one, too, God willing."

Melanie hugged her brother. "I'll come back as soon as it's safe. I'm more worried about you. I'm just a poor widow. You're in more danger than I am. Please be careful."

"I will." Alexander put a few coins into her hand. "This isn't much. But you may need it to bribe someone." He watched his sister and nephew disappear into the forest. Would they ever see each other again? Alexander couldn't think about that now.

For a month the villagers whose families had lived there for generations wandered the forest seeking the best places to hide. Occasionally at night one or two men sneaked back into the village for supplies they had hidden. In early July the SS troops selected Paceviche for decimation. When they discovered the deserted village, they sent a Polish man who was working for them into the forest with a message. If everyone returned to the village, no one would be punished and everyone would be allowed to stay in their homes. The forest dwellers didn't believe this promise and stayed put. So the Germans swept the forest rounding up the hidden villagers.

The Kowals sat under a tree finishing a late breakfast of dried rye bread and sausage. They were talking about where they would sleep that night when eleven-year-old Josef heard SS Troops. "*Tato*, I think they're coming this way. I hear the dogs." Alexander stopped wiping Zbigniew's face to listen. He heard the dogs barking. Then he saw the dreaded uniforms through the trees west of them.

"Quickly," he said to the children. "We'll go this way." He pointed north as he flung the soiled towel over his shoulder. Then he saw the Germans coming from that way with three of his neighbors in tow.

There was no escape.

"Never mind. We're trapped. We'll have to go with them. Remember to stay with me. And don't talk or cry. Do you understand? We'll be all right." He didn't believe this but knew he had to keep the children as calm as possible. The three terrified children nodded. Danuta quickly stuffed pieces of hard cheese and dried bread into her brother's pockets. She filled her own pockets with what food she could grab and handed some to her father. She looked around their camp, saw her little suitcase, and picked it up. Alexander took each of the boys by the hand. They watched the uniforms draw closer.

Alexander glanced at the rock formation behind the wagon. He had hidden a medical bag and the boxes of medical supplies in a hollow under the rocks. It contained bandages, gauze, ointments, and a fairly large collection of bottles with his name on the labels. He looked away. The Germans would confiscate them if they discovered them.

"I'll leave the medical supplies. They'll just take them," he whispered. Danuta nodded in agreement.

A soldier spotted them. He and the other four soldiers approached pointing guns at the family huddled together. "Don't shoot. We'll come with you," Alexander said looking at each soldier. He raised his hands in surrender, not knowing how much Polish they understood. Three met his gaze, but the other two looked away. Arresting innocent children should make you uncomfortable, Alexander thought. Zbigniew, who had developed a cough a few days before, shook trying to remain quiet, failed, and broke into a spasm of coughs. Please don't shoot him, Alexander thought.

"Give me your papers and walk with them," the tallest of the three soldiers commanded in German-accented Polish pointing at the frightened neighbors who had already been captured. Alexander handed the soldier his identification papers and the family fell in line. The image of the Jewish pharmacist Isaac Romanowski shuffling down the street flashed through Alexander's mind. So this is what it's come to, he thought as he squeezed the boys' hands gently. We're all being led to slaughter.

They were herded to the main road where they joined other terrified villagers. In the distance burning villages glowed against the summer sky. So far Paceviche had been spared. Sporadically a rifle shot rang out. It was at least a five-hour walk to the train station even with the short cuts they were taking on trails through the forests. Very small for his age, seven-year-old Zbigniew soon grew tired. His cough worsened. Alexander made a sling from the towel he had around his shoulders and carried his youngest son some of the time. With each step Alexander thought about escaping. But how?

The sun was sinking behind the trees when the word was passed down that they would soon be stopping for the night at a forest station just outside Juracishki. Alexander saw a rye field about a half-kilometer ahead. Maybe this was his chance.

Pretending to stop and fix his older son's shoe, Alexander whispered, "Josef, when we reach that rye field, we'll walk very close to it. I want you to pretend you have to relieve yourself. Get into the rye and lie flat on your stomach until everyone has passed. Then crawl on your belly to the other side. Go to the little stream you'll hear, and stay there tonight. We'll try to find you before morning. If we don't come, find your Aunt Melanie. You remember your Cousin Maria's village?" Josef nodded but said nothing. He glanced at the field. Alexander didn't really have a plan, but he knew in his gut that somehow at least one member of his family had to escape. Whether they were being gathered to go to Germany to work in the fields or to be shot, staying in this parade was not an option. They walked on holding hands edging towards the side of the road. As they reached the field of rye, they casually veered into it.

Alexander looked ahead and behind. No soldiers were near at the moment. "Now," he whispered to Josef. The tall rye was almost ready for harvest. Alexander let go of Josef's hand and gave him a gentle push. Josef knelt down in the rye. His head disappeared in the waving grain until he was completely hidden. If any of the numbed villagers saw him, they didn't acknowledge it, but just kept walking silently. Alexander turned and kept walking. He put his finger to his lips and looked at Zbigniew. Danuta held her little brother's hand and they trudged on in silence. A lump rose in Alexander's throat. Had he just saved his son or sentenced him to death? Josef's frightened eyes burned in Alexander's mind, but he kept walking. He had no other choice now.

Half an hour after Josef slipped away, the Germans halted the slow procession at the forest station about five kilometers from the Juracishki train depot. A large barn rose on one side of a quadrangle of buildings, sheds on two sides, and the forester's house on the fourth. Families filled the crowded space relieved that their trek for the day was done. Fear and exhaustion sparked short tempers. The law of the jungle invaded the temporary camp. Alexander watched in amazement as people who had known each other since childhood argued over scraps of food.

Someone built a fire in the center of the quadrangle and mysteriously a butchered pig appeared on a handmade spit. Soon the smell of roasting meat filled the air. Children's cries faded as they fell into exhausted sleep. As tired as he was, Alexander knew he had to stay alert if he, Danuta, and Zbigniew were to escape. The frightened people were turning on each other and the SS Troops would not be the only ones he had to trick. Even his fear-filled childhood friends might give him up to the Germans.

Alexander recognized the forester standing on the porch of the house. He had dealt with him several times over the years. Alexander fingered one of his remaining gold coins sewed between the layers of his belt. Time to use it.

Detainees were permitted one at a time to use the latrines. To get to them, people had to walk past the forester.

"Danuta, I'm taking Zbigniew to use the latrine. We'll be right back."

Taking his son's hand, Alexander walked towards the hastily built ditch being used as a latrine. He paused in front of the ranger, slipped a gold coin out of his pocket, and held it in his hand. "This is yours if you'll signal when the night guards are changing. Just stand at the end of this building and light a cigarette." The forester looked at Alexander and the coin. Silently he palmed the coin and slid it into his pocket. The exchange took only a few seconds.

Alexander and Zbigniew took a few steps. "Ten o'clock," the forester whispered. The bribe had worked. At least he hoped it had.

"Danuta, let's move over by that fence before it gets dark. It'll be a little quieter. Since we're going to be here all night, we should at least try to get some sleep." Better that his fellow detainees thought he was just trying to make things easier for his children tonight. They moved through the crowd and settled at the edge next to a field of ripe rye.

Zbigniew grew sleepy as the darkness descended on the forest headquarters. Alexander checked his watch. It was good to let his son get a couple of hours of sleep now. But Zbigniew's cough made sleep difficult. Danuta dozed against a fence post. At nine thirty Alexander touched her hand and she opened her eyes. He leaned over and whispered. "Be ready to leave when I squeeze your hand. I'll take your brother to the forester's to ask for warm milk for his cough. Get into the rye field. Go as fast as you can and make as little noise as possible. I'll be right behind you."

Alexander stared into the darkness towards the headquarters. Inside kerosene lights glowed. Alexander looked at his watch. He searched the darkness to find the guards, but could see only a few of them. Five minutes. The door or the forest station opened and someone stepped outside and walked past one of the glowing windows to the end of the building. The minutes crept by. Alexander took Danuta's hand in his. Then he saw a small glow. The match shined on the ranger's face as he lit his cigarette. Alexander squeezed his daughter's hand. She picked up her little suitcase and walked into the darkness.

Alexander picked up Zbigniew. He looked wide-eyed at his father. Alexander put his finger on the boy's lips, "Shhh. Let's go get you some warm milk." He walked purposefully to the house and opened the front door into a hallway that went all the way through the house to the back door. Alexander looked quickly into the empty rooms on either side of the hallway as he moved to the back door, opened it, and disappeared into the darkness.

Fourteen-year-old Danuta walked silently through the cloudy darkness away from the smell of roasted pork and smoke. People milling around in the area of the fire didn't notice the girl in the shadows. Clutching her suitcase, she walked into the far end of the rye field her brother had slid into hours before. She walked a few minutes, paused and listened. Nothing. She walked on until she heard a faint cough. Zbigniew. She pushed towards the sound.

Her father's outline appeared in the moonlight between the clouds. "Tato," she whispered, but he didn't hear her. She moved closer to his back. Alexander stopped to catch his breath. "I'm here, Tato." He turned. She dropped the battered suitcase and wrapped her arms around him and her little brother. They clung to each other for a moment breathing heavily.

"Where's Josef?" Danuta whispered.

Alexander looked around. The clouds drifted away from the moon for a few minutes helping Alexander get his bearings. "Josef's that way," he whispered, pointing towards a bush-covered hill. "Should be able to hear the stream when we get over that rise. We'll follow it until we find him."

Danuta almost tripped on Josef. He was sound asleep curled up under a bush by the path running next to the stream. In his sleep, one leg had straightened from his hiding place. In the moonlight she saw his shoe and hopped over his foot. Her father froze not seeing why she made such a sudden move. "Josef," she whispered pointing under the bush.

Alexander knelt beside his son and took his hand. "Josef, we're here." The boy startled and opened his eyes. It took a few seconds for sleep to leave his brain. Then he smiled and flung his arms around his father. "You were brave, son. I'm very proud of you." Alexander closed his eyes to keep back tears.

They rested in the intermittent moonlight for a few minutes. Alexander knew they had to keep moving and get into Juracishki as soon as they could. It would be easier to hide in the city. Silently they made their way across country until they came to the road into Juracishki and the Russian Orthodox priest's house.

"Surely the priest will help us," Alexander said as he adjusted a sleeping Zbigniew in his arms. "I've known him for many years. He's an intelligent man. And we've shared more than one vodka toast." His children had walked for hours, and he knew their bodies ached. His did, too. But no one complained. They had to keep moving if they were to survive.

"And if he won't?" Danuta wanted to know.

"We'll have to come up with another plan. Perhaps the Catholic priest. I don't know him as well, although we've met several times. But I think Father Buriatynskij will help."

The Germans shot anyone who hid wanted people, and Alexander was concerned about putting either of these men in danger, but he was desperate. Everyone was in danger for one reason or another.

Alexander found the Russian Orthodox priest's house just before dawn. He and the children collapsed behind the barn and waited until the family awoke. The children slept leaning against each other, but as tired as he was, Alexander was filled with too much anxiety to sleep. He knew that if they were found, the Germans would shoot them. He hoped they hadn't come all this way just to die.

Before the sun rose, the door of the house opened and Mrs.

Buriatysnkij headed to the woodpile. Alexander watched her load her arms with wood and go back into the house. "Stay here. I'm going to talk to Father Buriatysnkij." Danuta started to stand. "Don't get up. I don't think anyone can see us, but we don't want to draw any attention to ourselves." Alexander brushed dirt and straw from his clothes, ran his fingers through his hair, and headed to the house.

The priest answered his knock and opened the door half way. "*Slava Bohu*," Alexander greeted the priest.

The priest did not return his traditional greeting, "Praise God." Instead his eyes moved from the head to the shoes of the disheveled man on his doorstep. "Alexander Kowal? What are you doing here at this early hour?"

Alexander related their situation. "We need a place to hide. Can you help us?"

Father Buriatysnkij's scowled. "Do you know what you're asking? My whole family could be shot if we help you."

"I understand. And my family will be shot if we're discovered. We'll stay in the barn. Not for long. We'll find another place as soon as we can. Please, just for a day or two." Alexander heard the desperate tone in his own voice.

The priest stepped outside and closed the door. "I'm sorry. I can't help you. I don't want to know you now. It's much too dangerous. The Germans. . ." He shook his head and put his hand on the door handle. "The Germans will kill my family and me if they find you here. Please leave before anyone sees you." He stepped back inside. The door squeaked as he pushed it shut.

Alexander stood for a moment staring at the dark wood door. He fought against the spasms of fear that rose in his stomach. He must not let the children see his worry. He stepped off the porch and headed back to the barn.

Danuta peeked around the corner watching her father. She knew the answer before he uttered a word. "Let's go find Father Rodkiewicz before the sun gets any higher. The rectory is only about a ten minute walk." He picked up Zbigniew and motioned towards the dirt road. Josef held his sister's hand. Even though his legs and feet ached, he was silent as he and Danuta followed their father. The boy felt his heart pounding. He wanted to ask what they would do if the Catholic priest also refused to help, but he new better.

Even though no one was up and about yet, Alexander knew the chances of being seen increased with every passing minute. The Kowals slipped into the trees that bordered a small field of rye and large garden behind the barn and sheds of the rectory. In the early morning shadows Alexander looked at his children. They should be safe from prying eyes here. Both boys collapsed next to a tree. A rooster crowed and a goat inside a fence next to the barn bleated a reply. But otherwise the only sound was breeze-blown leaves.

"We'll rest here."

"Will the priest be saying mass this morning?" Danuta whispered. She sat with one arm slung over her small suitcase.

"I suppose so, but I can't see the front of the church or the rectory front door. Maybe it's too early yet."

Both boys slept. Zbigniew coughed, increasing their chances of being detected. Danuta crumpled against a tree. Alexander sat next to the boys. He felt his eyelids growing heavy, but he'd have to sleep later. He heard a door open and stood up staying in the shadows. The priest walked past the cemetery and into the church. The church bell rang. Danuta opened her eyes, but her brothers didn't stir.

"I guess he's saying mass. I hope he's praying for poor souls like us. We'll have to wait until he goes back to the rectory to ask for his help. We can't risk anyone else seeing us. Get a little rest while you can, Danuta." She was asleep almost immediately.

Alexander watched the priest's housekeeper draw water from the well. It made him realize they hadn't had anything to drink since they stopped by the stream last night. No matter what happened, they needed to drink something soon.

Sunlight streaked through the trees when the priest walked back to the rectory. Alexander woke Danuta. "I'm going to the back door now." She watched, afraid to hope the priest would help.

The housekeeper's eyes couldn't conceal her concern as she opened the door to the man with the dirt-streaked face.

"Please, may I speak to Father Rodkiewicz?" Without a word, the housekeeper backed into the house and closed the door.

Alexander stood not knowing whether or not she was fetching the priest. He heard heavy footsteps and the door opened.

"*Niech bedzie pochwalony Jezus Chrystus.*" Alexander greeted the priest in the traditional manner, "let Jesus Christ be praised."

"*Na wieki wiekow. Amen.*" The priest returned the greeting, "For centuries and centuries. Amen."

"Father Rodkiewicz, I'm Alexander Kowal. Perhaps you remember me?" The priest looked closer at the dirty, gray-haired man standing on his doorstep.

"Dr. Kowal, why are you in Juracishki at this hour and why at my back door? Please, come in." Hope reached into Alexander's heart.

The priest led Alexander into the front room of the house. "Mrs. Lubowski, please bring us some chicory coffee," he called. "Now tell me what's going on."

Alexander once again explained what had happened. "Can you help us hide? They took our papers. If we're caught, we'll be killed," Alexander entreated.

Father Rodkiewicz looked at the humbled, frightened Dr. Kowal. "These are terrible times for us Poles. You'd help me if the circumstances were reversed. I can't say no. But you must stay only a few days. The risk is too great. I'll help you find another place. You can trust Mrs. Lubowski." He motioned with his head towards the kitchen. "She lost her son to the German bombs. I'll have her fix some food for you and the children. And we have some blankets you can use. It looks like it's been a while since you've had a chance to clean up. There's an old tub in the barn. Get some water from the well and wash up."

"Thank you. We'll gratefully stay in the barn. No one will know we're here."

"I know. We'll all be cautious. I imagine you and the children are tired and need to rest today."

"Yes, we're exhausted. We walked all night."

It was the beginning of six fear-filled weeks.

The next night as he lay next to Zbigniew in the hay, Alexander was able to think clearly about their survival. He needed his medical bag. Without it he felt naked. He thought about the supplies in the wagon. A plan formed in his mind.

In the morning when Father Rodkiewicz brought bread, cheese, and fresh milk to the barn, Alexander broached the idea of retrieving what they had left in the forest.

"If you'll lend me your horse, and I leave at dusk, I'm sure I can ride to where I left the wagon and get back before dawn. I know short cuts through the woods. I've hunted in that area since I was a boy. It's a lot to ask, I know. We have food there so we won't be such a burden. And I feel that I must have my medical bag. Medicine has been my salvation before, and it can be again."

"I don't know. That's awfully risky. What if you're caught?"

"Living is risky. What if they catch me in your barn? My medical skills are what I can trade for people's help. And the Germans have had their way with Paceviche. They've moved on to some other unfortunate settlement by now. And they never leave their barracks after dark. They're too afraid of the partisans. I'll go tonight if you'll lend me your horse."

The priest pondered the idea for several minutes. "Go if you must. You can use my horse. But be careful." Father Rodkiewicz made the sign of the cross "*Z Bogiem*, go with God, Dr. Kowal."

Still tired from their escape from the Germans, the Kowals napped all afternoon. Alexander cracked open the barn door and looked at the setting sun. "It's time."

Danuta handed her father some dried bread and cheese wrapped in a cloth. "What should I do if you don't come back?"

"I'll be back. But if something happens, go to your cousin Maria's where Aunt Melanie and Alosha are. You remember how to get there, right?"

Danuta nodded. "The back path through the forest, and then the old road." She willed herself not to cry.

In the moonlight and shadows Alexander hurried the horse through the forest. He was counting on the Germans adhering to their habit of always being in their quarters at night except for a few patrols. Only once did he lose his way and have to backtrack to find a familiar trail. His back was drenched in sweat and his heart pounded even though the horse was doing all the work. Several times he was sideswiped by a low tree branch, and by the time he reached the rock formation, scratches covered his hands and face. The wagon stood where they had left it, but the animals had disappeared. He leaned against one of the wagon wheels catching his breath and listening. He heard nothing but the night sounds of the forest. He stood and went to the pile of rocks.

Snap. What was that? A branch breaking? Alexander stopped in mid-step and held his breath. But he heard only silence. Quickly he lifted the rocks and pulled out his bag and box of medicines and transferred them to the wagon. From a hole covered with rocks he lifted two bags of rye flour, some dried cheese, and a bag of dried apples.

Alexander led the horse to a stream nearby and rested while the horse drank. Then he hitched the horse to the wagon and led it. By the time he reached an old forest road that led to Juracishki, his leg and back muscles throbbed. Half-way back to Juracishki his body cried for rest. He stopped and looked at his watch. Almost three o'clock. Less than two hours to get back to the rectory before morning light would make traveling too dangerous. He had to pick up the pace. He urged the horse on and tried to ignore his own crying legs.

The sun tinged the clouds pink when he saw the church. His hands were numb from clutching the reins, the last half kilometer felt like a thousand. He kept constant watch for anyone who might be out this early, but saw no one. Slowly he pulled open the barn door, pulled the horse and wagon inside, closed the door, and collapsed. He'd made it. He was a doctor with the tools of his trade again and he had food for his family.

Every few days the Kowals moved to a new hiding place in someone's barn or shed. They didn't know most of the people who hid them. Some were friends of friends, and at least one turned out to be a false friend. Czeslaw Paszkowski, a relative of a Bakshty acquaintance, agreed to let Alexander and the children sleep in a mostly empty shed on his property. He and his family lived at the edge of town and had no close neighbors. It seemed like an ideal hiding place.

On the second night of their stay a boy with a horse appeared at the door.

"He'll be joining you," Czeslaw Paszkowski told Alexander as he showed the boy where he could sleep. "Jan's afraid the partisans will steal his horse and needs a place to hide," their host explained.

The skinny blond boy eyed the Kowal children with suspicion and said little. He spent most of the next day caring for his horse and napping. When Alexander offered food to the boy, he took it with a curt thank you. This went on for two days. That night Alexander heard the boy slip on his boots, open the noisy shed door, and leave. Alexander decided the boy had to relieve himself, thought nothing of it, and fell back asleep. The next morning the boy and his horse were gone.

Czeslaw Paszkowski shrugged his shoulders at the news. "I guess he didn't think he needed to stay." Alexander was puzzled, but the effort to stay silent and invisible didn't leave time to think about the appearance and disappearance of a young boy who seemed not to have any family. Orphans were numerous in this war-racked country. If anything happens to me, Alexander thought, that could be one of my children seeking shelter.

It was just after midnight on their fifth night in the shed when Alexander was awakened by voices.

"We need supplies tonight. You know we're fighting for our country. You have to do your part, too. Where's your grain?" Alexander's skin crawled. The partisans were here to bombic. Alexander didn't have to look outside to know the family was being held at gunpoint. He looked at his sleeping children. He was helpless to do anything but wait.

"In here? You have more food in here, don't you?" Alexander's heart sank. The door flew open and a bulky, unshaven man holding a torch burst through the door. Alexander sat up.

"So, you have guests. Well, let's see what they have to offer us." He pointed his gun at Alexander. The children woke. Danuta gathered the boys in her arms and sat on the pallet of hay behind her father.

"We have little food," Alexander told the man. He motioned to the bag of flour on the floor.

"Fine, we'll take it. What else do you have?"

"Nothing."

The snarling man held the torch high and moved it from side to side. He spied Alexander's medical bag and supplies. "Look what we have here. We'll take these, too."

"Boys, see what other food is hidden in here. Be quick about it. We have a lot to do tonight."

Alexander watched helplessly as two young men not much older than Danuta grabbed his medical bag and supplies. Two other young men pawed through the things in the corner of the shed and grabbed a bag of barley.

The men disappeared as quickly as they had come. Anger filled Alexander. His medical bag was gone. What did he have to bargain with? He'd lost his means of survival.

"I'm sorry," Czeslaw said. "Lucky for you that you aren't any younger or they may have forced you to go with them and join their gang."

Fear displaced anger after Alexander settled the boys back on their pallets. Life was so precarious.

The next night Czeslaw Paszkowski led them to another house whose owner showed them a place to sleep in his barn.

"How long can we keep living like this?" Danuta asked her father that night as they all lay on the hay between rough blankets.

"I don't know. We can't go home. We have to get papers so we no longer have to hide. Without them the Germans will arrest us. But we've survived so far. We just have to keep hiding." Alexander slept little that night. He searched his mind for some way to get a job that could give him legal status. Until that happened, he would have to rely on the kindness of people willing to risk hiding them.

His medical profession once again saved his family.

The offer came through Father Rodkiewicz a few days after the Kowals had been shuffled back into the priest's barn.

Danuta was in the rectory kitchen fixing her family's food and Alexander was sitting at the table reading one of Father Rodkiewicz's books when the priest came back from his afternoon prayers.

"The Germans are getting desperate, Alexander. They're short of doctors. The railroad station's physician killed himself last week. One of my parishioners who works there told me the Germans need a doctor to care for railroad workers. Their medical people are all with the fighting army. He overheard the stationmaster say they should find a Pole for the job. They need someone immediately, so they aren't asking many questions. It seems pretty chaotic around the station. They might hire you. You should apply, don't you think?"

It was a risk, but Alexander knew he had to take it. What if they asked to see his medical diploma? He had to come up with an explanation. If he didn't get the job, his children would starve in the coming winter. Food was scarce, and no one had extra to share with a displaced family. Alexander shaved and bathed. Danuta brushed his borrowed suit and trimmed his hair. Alexander walked to the railroad station and knocked on the German stationmaster's door.

The flush-faced man sat behind a desk stacked with a disarray of books and papers. A half-full bottle of vodka sat on a pile of papers. "What do you want?" he asked in German-accented Polish.

Alexander removed his hat and approached the cluttered desk that took up most of the small room. "I understand you need a doctor to care for your workers. I've come to apply for the job." Alexander's heart pounded.

The man took off his glasses and looked at Alexander. "You're Polish? Yes?"

"Yes, I'm Polish."

"My doctor died, but my workers don't stop getting hurt or sick. I need someone."

"I've been a doctor for many years. I can take care of them if you have medicine and supplies."

The stationmaster drummed his fingers on the desk and looked Alexander over from head to toe. Alexander clutched his hat, forcing himself to breathe normally and keep his eyes on the man's face.

"*Sehr gut.* The job is yours. You start tomorrow. I'll have your papers ready when you get here. Report to me at eight o'clock. Write your name here." The portly man handed Alexander a fountain pen and pointed to a paper on his desk. He didn't ask to see his diploma. He didn't ask for his papers. The stationmaster seemed to have exhausted his Polish vocabulary.

Alexander signed his name, recognizing that the paper was the official identification document. He handed back the pen. "I'll be here." The stationmaster made no acknowledgement, but put on his glasses and went back to reading. Alexander left quickly, looking around to see if any SS Troops were waiting to arrest him, but no one even noticed his existence.

Alexander rushed back to the rectory with the good news. Six weeks of homelessness and daily hunger were over. They would once again be legal residents. They could move into a house and walk through the town in daylight without fear of being asked for identification papers. At least for the time being, they were as safe as anyone could be under the thumb of the German SS.

Chapter 17

Juracishki, German Occupied Poland, 1943

Rain blowing against the barn woke Alexander before dawn. He lay wrapped in a coarse wool blanket with a softly snoring Zbigniew cuddled in the curve of his legs. Alexander took the boy's bony hand in his. Such a smart boy, Alexander thought. When would this war end so children could once again go to school? Even in the midst of the uncertainty, Alexander and Danuta had taught the child his letters and some simple addition and subtraction. But he should be reading by now, and Josef should be learning algebra and reading literature instead of doing menial chores for friends in return for a few eggs, a loaf of bread, or shelter in a dusty barn. And Danuta should be almost ready for college. Alexander was determined that his daughter was going to be educated. She'd know more than how to sew and bake bread. He tucked the blanket snugly around Zbigniew. At least, he hoped, they'd soon be living in a house and not hiding in fear.

Alexander dozed and woke when Danuta crawled out of her blanket next to Josef. The rain had stopped. Alexander pulled out his pocket watch. Two hours until time to report for work at the depot. He moved away from his son and rose as he heard Mrs. Lubowska at the well. Alexander was grateful for Father Rodkiewicz's help. Somehow he'd found a suit and shirt for Alexander. Last night the priest had told him to come to the rectory to shave and get ready for his new job. This is a man who lives his beliefs, Alexander thought as he walked across the muddy yard and knocked on the door.

Mrs. Lubowska greeted him. "We have extra bread, and milk this morning and even some fresh eggs. Have your children come in the house and eat breakfast." With food so scarce, this was an especially generous offer.

After Alexander washed and shaved and put on the borrowed suit, he went back to the barn. "We've been invited to have breakfast with Father Rodkiewicz. Mrs. Lubowska has both fresh milk and eggs." The children perked up at this good news. Danuta combed the boys' hair and cleaned herself as best she could in the bucket of chilly well water her father had carried in.

"Remember your manners," she instructed her brothers as they crossed the yard to have breakfast sitting down at a table with their hosts. "Tato, are you ready for your first day?"

"Yes. I don't want to be late." He looked at his watch again and then at the boys. "Remember to stay out of sight today. We still don't have papers. And do what your sister tells you," he reminded them.

Alexander arrived at the stationmaster's office fifteen minutes early. No one was there, so he sat on the bench watching workers hurry to their jobs. It was almost a quarter past eight when the stationmaster arrived. His blotchy skin and puffy eyes indicated a night of vodka drinking. Alexander rose and greeted his new employer, "*Guten morgen.*"

"Guten morgen," the stationmaster grumbled. He motioned for Alexander to sit back down, unlocked the door, and went inside. In a moment he returned and handed Alexander a certificate of employment and the signed identification document. The somewhat disheveled stationmaster pointed toward a small building at the far end of the station complex and started walking without further comment. Alexander followed.

The pot-bellied German unlocked the medical clinic door and handed Alexander the key. "This is our clinic," he said in heavily accented Polish. "Your helper should be here soon. He knows what to do. I'm very busy." He turned and trudged back to his office.

Alexander examined the papers in his hand. As of August 18,

1943, he was officially an employee of the German regime. Legal status. No more hiding. He took a deep breath, opened the creaky door, and entered a long-ago painted room. He found a desk and chair in the middle, a bench along one wall, and a canvas cot along the other. A doorway at the back covered by a tattered blanket led to a second room. Alexander pulled the blanket back to reveal an examining room with one blanket-covered exam table, a locked cabinet of medicine, and a few instruments. An empty black medical bag sat on one end of the table. Alexander was surprised at the paltry medications and minimal medical instruments. He expected the Germans to be well equipped. Soon he would realize why they weren't.

His assistant arrived at nine o'clock along with the first patients. Alexander went to work, grateful that the travails of the last six weeks were behind him.

Late that afternoon as he walked back to the rectory, he passed several vacant houses. What looked to be at least a three-room house caught his eye, and he inquired about it at the house next door.

"Jews lived there," the almost toothless woman who answered his knock told him. "They've been gone for a long time. Germans took them. Don't know where they are. Move in if you want. No one cares. Go look around. It probably needs some fixing."

Alexander thanked her and walked to the back of the vacant house. The windows were still intact. He opened the unlocked back door and went inside. A thick layer of dust covered everything. Except for a table, chair and one dilapidated chest, all the furniture had been taken, but the stove was in good condition and cleaning would make the log house habitable. It was certainly better than the barns they had been sleeping in. He hurried to tell Danuta.

"It's a good house, Tato," Danuta said when they went back to look at it. "I think we should sleep in Father Rodkiewicz's barn again tonight, but the boys and I will clean this place tomorrow and move in."

The three rooms weren't as big as those in their Paceviche home, but it was close to the railway clinic. It had a small shed, a root cellar under the house, and the garden in back had good soil and just needed some work. It was too late to plant vegetables for the winter, but perhaps with Alexander's legal papers they could borrow Father Rodkiewicz's horse and go back to Paceviche and retrieve the rye flour, barley, and buckwheat they had hidden under the hay. If there was still cabbage in the garden, Danuta could make sauerkraut. They wouldn't starve or have to rely on the kindness of strangers for shelter. It wasn't home, but it felt safe. At least for now.

They closed the door and stood on the weathered front porch looking at their new neighborhood. "There are more houses on this street than in all of Paceviche, Tato."

"Yes, and less land," Alexander replied. He saw the old woman who lived next door and waved to her.

"Moving in?" Jadwiga Struga asked. She had been checking them out as she gathered eggs and milked her cow.

"Yes, tomorrow. I'll bring our wagon with our belongings after work." Alexander introduced himself and the children. "Do you have extra eggs or milk that you'd sell us?"

The woman's eyes lit up. "Yes. I'm alone since my husband died. My boys are…" She made a sweeping motion with her hands. "Gone. I'm not sure where." Alexander understood she meant they were with a partisan underground army. He nodded.

Mrs. Struga looked at Danuta. "Come tomorrow and I'll give you bread starter." She smiled exposing her shrunken gums and remaining teeth. "It's good to have you next door," she said to her new young neighbor.

Danuta and the boys soon had the house clean and livable. They found wood in the shed at the back of the property. Alexander borrowed a saw and hammer and made a bench so they could all sit at the table. Mrs. Lubowska gave them two ticks and hay for filling to make beds. In the shed they found a battered bucket, a hoe, and a rake.

"My papers don't allow me to live in Paceviche, but I can visit. Father Rodkiewicz said we can borrow his horse and make the trip this weekend," Alexander told his children at supper. The thought of going home, even for a brief visit, lifted the family's spirits.

Josef and Danuta had the wagon ready when Alexander came home from the clinic on Saturday. Also waiting for him was an elderly neighbor who wanted to sell one of his female goats because he didn't have enough hay to feed his whole herd.

"I'll buy her if the hay in our barn in Paceviche is still there," he told the man.

"Now, remember, we don't know what we'll find. The Germans might have destroyed everything," Alexander said as they began the two-hour trip. That tempered the children's excitement. Burned-out villages along the way further lowered their expectations. But when they came over the rise in the evening twilight, they saw their home was still standing, probably because the Germans used it for their headquarters. They approached cautiously, but no German trucks were in the yard. Alexander guided the horse next to the house.

Josef leaped out and ran to the door before the horse stopped. Zbigniew ran after his brother. Alexander swallowed the lump of relief in his throat. He and Danuta followed the boys as soon as the horse was tethered.

"Let's enjoy being home tonight. In the morning we have hours of work to do." In the fading light they explored the barn and sheds. Alexander was surprised that the Germans had taken only a little hay out of the barn and had not disturbed anything in the house except in the main room that they used. It smelled of cigarette smoke and cooking.

Melanie's house was still empty.

At dawn they enjoyed waking in their own beds. Danuta gathered pots, pans, and clothes and put them in the barrels used to make pickles and sauerkraut. She was most happy to take two *pierzynas*, the down-filled thick, tightly woven ticks she and her mother had made years ago. They made beds cozy no matter what the weather. Next to the barn Alexander and the boys tackled the wood pile. Finding wood in the city was nearly impossible, and winter would arrive whether or not they were prepared. Danuta wrapped a few books in skirts and underwear and hid them under the wood. When the wagon was full, they went across the road to the garden Danuta and Melanie had planted last spring. Danuta and Josef dug up some hills of small potatoes and pulled enough garlic, onions, carrots, and beets to have food now. Then they picked cucumbers so Danuta could start making pickles.

The children were reluctant to leave. "We'll come back next month and get the rest of the vegetables. The wagon's full, and we need to leave now if we are to get home in time for me to take the horse back before dark."

Zbigniew fell asleep leaning against the bundle of pierzynas. Danuta, Josef, and Alexander rode silently, each deep in thought.

In mid-September the Kowals returned to Paceviche. They harvested the remaining vegetables in their garden and filled the rest of the wagon with hay for their goat. The potatoes, beets, parsley root, onions, and carrots were ready for harvest. However, the cabbages could have used more time to ripen, Danuta observed as she cut them. They'd still make enough sauerkraut to last the winter. While Alexander was hitching the horse to the wagon, their pig wandered into the yard.

"Looks like we might be able to add our pig to the load," Josef chortled. He grabbed some carrots from the wagon. Holding them in front of the hungry sow, he led her into the barn and captured her. He and Alexander fashioned a pen in the wagon. It took all four of them to lift the squealing animal up into the wagon. When they at last had her secured, they headed back to Juracishki with the new companion for the goat. Alexander slept well that night knowing his family now not only had a house, but some food and fuel for the winter. And he had a job. It didn't pay well, but then, there wasn't much to buy but a few eggs, some cow's milk, and matches to light the stove.

In peaceful times, the children would have started school in September, but the schools were closed. The Nazis had declared it illegal to educate Poles. In Hitler's grand plan for a new world order, healthy Poles would be used as laborers and taught to count to ten and write their names. Only pure-blooded Germans would be educated. In Krakow the university faculty had been called to a meeting to ostensibly discuss curriculum and classes. Instead, the professors were arrested and sent to concentration camps.

Alexander knew he must continue his children's education. Danuta taught her brothers some math and reading using books surreptitiously brought from Father Rodkiewicz's. They were careful to study away from a window, and if they heard voices in the street or if someone knocked on the door, the books disappeared instantly. It was a dangerous exercise of defiance. Had the Nazis caught them studying, they would have paid with their lives.

Danuta longed for the days she and her friends once spent at school in Bakshty. Ever since Danuta had worked with her father at their house in Paceviche after the Germans burned the Bakshty clinic, she had wanted to go to school to study medicine. He had encouraged that dream just as he had for Aleksy, but the money he had saved for his children's education was one more part of their lives the war had taken away. And who knew how long this war would last?

Huddled with her brothers around the stove that winter, Danuta often wondered what her future might be. For now she had to keep the family fed. The sacks of potatoes, onions, and rye flour brought from Paceviche had to last until they could harvest their new garden. With the eggs and cow's milk bought from Mrs. Struga and their store of food, they weren't starving and were grateful for that. They knew that hunger was a guest in many Polish houses. Danuta was already planning her garden for next spring so they would have more food next winter.

Alexander settled into a routine at the clinic. Promises of more medical supplies went unfulfilled, which seemed to confirm the rumors of mounting Nazi defeats. How long before the end? Alexander hoped that when the victors divided German-occupied lands, Poland would be an independent country again.

"To better times." Alexander clinked his mug of vodka with that of Father Rodkiewicz's. They had shared their meager mid-day meal on the first day of 1944. Conversation centered on speculating how long it would be until the Germans were defeated and what might happen then. "The mood among the Nazis is sober," Alexander said.

"Their mood is always sober," the priest replied. Alexander smiled and nodded. "Chess?"

"One game," Alexander replied. For the next hour the men concentrated on their game, which Alexander won. They shook hands.

"It's starting to snow again. Get your coats on, Josef and Zbigniew. We'd better get home and keep the stove filled. It's going to be a cold night." He shook the priest's hand. "I wish I could repay you for all you've done for us."

"I didn't do much," Father Rodkiewicz said, downplaying the danger he'd put himself in to hide the family. "And I'll pray for your oldest son." Alexander thanked him and the family hurried towards home through the wind-swept snow.

Walking home through the snow holding Zbigniew's hand, Alexander remembered holding young Aleksy's hand. Where was his oldest son tonight? Was he warm? Was he hungry? A lump formed in Alexander's throat. He swallowed hard. Months ago he'd heard a rumor that a body in a ditch beside the road near Bakshty looked like Aleksy. Someone had buried the unknown young man and placed a cross there, but the neighbor who shared the rumor had no proof it was Aleksy. Alexander refused to believe it might be true.

Winter ground on. The stationmaster ignored the clinic. He made his way to its door only to hand out monthly pay envelopes or to get aspirin for a headache after a night of hard drinking. Danuta and the boys spent most of their time in the house near the stove trying to stay warm.

The Nazi troops became more querulous as spring arrived. Juracishki citizens took even more pains to stay out of their path. Four years of war were taking their toll on the invaders and the invaded.

As soon as the ground warmed in April, Danuta and the boys turned the garden soil. Neighbors shared seeds, and she had saved some seed potatoes. By mid-May potatoes, radishes, carrots, turnips, cabbage, and onions were peeking through the black soil. Danuta kept the boys busy hauling water from the well to keep the new plants moist. The first fresh radishes and tiny onions were a cause for celebration.

When June weather warmed Juracishki, the German troops' morale deteriorated. Flasks of vodka stuck out of their pants pockets and officers seemed not to notice. Once-crisp uniforms were wrinkled and worn. One day a young drunk soldier offered to sell Alexander his gun. This is a defeated army Alexander thought, watching the young man stagger away.

He didn't know that in January 1943, the tide of the war had turned against the Germans when the Soviets crushed them in the Battle of Stalingrad. Since that time the Soviets, equipped by the United Sates, their new ally in the fight against the Nazis, had been inching their way west taking back territory from the Germans in bloody battle after bloody battle. Cut off from the rest of the world, Alexander and his countrymen also didn't know that in late November, 1943, Stalin had met with Churchill and Roosevelt in Tehran. They agreed to let Stalin set up a puppet communist government in Poland. The three leaders also drew new borders for Poland making the Bug River the Polish eastern border with USSR. The part of Germany east of the Oder and Neisse Rivers became Polish territory. Poles didn't know their fate had been decided by three men sitting in a room thousands of miles away.

Two weeks after he turned down the young German's offer to purchase a gun, Alexander arrived at the clinic to find a dozen trucks lining the dusty road. On the train tracks an engine waited to pull six flatbed cars carrying shrouded loads. Nazi officers shouted orders to grim-faced soldiers who carried boxes and equipment to the waiting trucks. By late afternoon the heavily laden trucks headed west. With a short toot on the whistle, the engineer released the brake and the train chugged away towards the afternoon sun. Alexander looked out the window of the clinic. He had seen this before, but last time it was the Soviets packing up and going east. The clinic had no patients that day; and when the trucks left, Alexander and his assistant went home.

Alexander considered staying home the next morning, but his curiosity got the best of him. The station was deserted. Alexander stood looking at the silent building. The only thing left of the Nazis was what they had discarded as not useful or too heavy or bulky to carry. A tireless truck stood next to the stationmaster's office. "Good riddance," Alexander muttered.

He went to the unlocked clinic, gathered the few medicines, a stethoscope, and a box of bandages that the Germans had been in too much of a hurry to pack. He took one look around the vacant rooms, closed the door, and headed home. I no longer have a job or a salary, he thought as he walked away from the abandoned station.

"Are they really gone?" Mrs. Struga asked, holding a pail of steaming fresh milk.

"Yes, they're all gone." Alexander smiled.

"Thank God!" The woman made the sign of the cross with her empty hand. "We survived those bastards." She held up the pail. "Send one of the boys for milk."

"Thanks," Alexander waved and walked up the path to his house.

"Dr. Kowal," Mrs. Sturga called. Alexander stopped. "What do you think will happen now?"

"I wish I knew." Alexander shrugged his shoulders, waved again, and opened the door of his house.

Residents of Juracishki were jubilant the next day. Vodka flowed freely. Young men scavenged the abandoned Nazi barracks and offices for anything useful. But the celebrations were tinged with hesitation. The Soviets had not been as cruel as the Germans, but their rule was oppressive. Would they return? Unaware of what had already been decided, they speculated about Poland's fate. When the victorious nations sat around a peace table would they make life better here?

The fourth morning after the German departure, Danuta woke at dawn as she always did. She rose from her side of the hay pallet she shared with Zbigniew and let herself out the back door to weed the garden in the cool morning light. She had completed the rows of onions when a low growl interrupted the birds' chirping. She stopped, leaned on the hoe, and listened. It was a sound she had heard before. She went inside.

"Tato, I think the Soviets are coming. I heard them." Alexander stood in front of the broken mirror hanging from the wall, shaving soap in hand. He opened the door.

"Yes, I think you're right." Alexander looked at his boys sleeping peacefully. "Perhaps we can go home soon, Danuta." It was a hope that would be unfulfilled.

Chapter 18

Juracishki, War-torn Belarus, 1944

Mrs. Struga had also heard the familiar approaching roar of an invading army coming west. She, too, didn't have to see them to know that the red flag with its hammer and sickle and yellow star was waving above the tanks and trucks.

Clouds of dust rose in the late June heat heralding the triumphant Soviet army roaring westward through eastern Poland. Except for a few brazen Soviet supporters, Poles discreetly watched the Red Army that three years before had fled east on these same roads. Darkness ended the first day's spectacle, but it began again at dawn when the parade of war-weary Red Army soldiers resumed. Bureaucrats and security forces filled the last two dozen trucks of the miles-long column. While the army that had preceded them chased the remnants of the Fuhrer's fighters, these communists ground to a halt in the center of town. Guns at the ready, they piled out of their dirt-encrusted trucks to scour Juracishki for possible pockets of resistance. They didn't realize the residents were so relieved to be rid of the Nazis that the Red Army was almost welcome. Almost.

Soviet-supported underground militiamen stepped out of the shadows and joined their triumphant comrades. It took them only three days to put Juracishki under communist control and strike terror in Alexander. Walking home beside Josef from a successful fishing trip to a nearby stream with five fish guaranteeing a good supper, Alexander saw what he had feared since the Soviets returned. He recognized two of the half-dozen men in tattered, yellow-star-adorned hats strutting down the road towards them. Their demeanor blazed with intoxication of power.

"Son, let's stop here." Before the men reached them, Alexander took Josef's arm and steered him towards a house set back from the road. Josef glanced up at his father's grim face. "Just keep walking. Keep your eyes on the house." Alexander's grip tightened. Josef said nothing and didn't look back.

The communist contingent took no notice of the fishermen and disappeared down the road. "It's all right. Let's get home." Alexander turned back towards the rutted road.

"Why'd you do that?" Josef hurried to keep up with his father's quickened pace.

"The two men on the left were partisans who accused me of helping the Germans in Paceviche. They'd have killed me if Saszka hadn't intervened. Looks like they're in charge now." Alexander's hardened voice sent chills up Josef's spine. He reached for his father's hand and held it until they entered the door of their house.

"We'll stay here," Alexander told Danuta that night. "It'll be easier for me to be invisible in Juracishki than in Paceviche. Already posters are up around town ordering everyone to register at the Soviet headquarters by next Friday." He tried to reassure her. "They'll give us new identification documents. Maybe I'll be assigned to a job of some kind. We should be safe. But if something happens to me, find your Aunt Melanie. She'll know what to do."

"Are things ever going to be better?" Danuta complained, placing her hands on her hips. "I can't remember when I didn't feel afraid. I just want to go back to being a girl worried about school and what to wear."

It was a rare outburst. Alexander ached to comfort her, but he couldn't lie. "Danuta, I don't know. But I promise that someday you'll go to college. I don't know how or when, but we'll make it happen. War can't last forever. Eventually, one side surrenders and the other declares victory. We just have to survive their fighting." Danuta blinked back tears.

His daughter, although no longer a little girl, needed a mother instead of trying to be a mother to her brothers. Alexander struggled for words. "I understand that your life isn't easy right now. You do a woman's work every day, and I don't know what I'd do if you weren't here. We just have to get through each day as best we can."

"I know, Tato, I know." Danuta went into the bedroom. Alexander stared at the closed door. His heart ached for his daughter, but he was helpless to make things better.

The next morning Alexander took his children to the large house that had been taken over by the Soviet bureaucrats. They joined a long line of grim-faced Poles waiting for their official papers.

"Name?"

"Alexander Kowal."

"Date of birth?"

"March 13, 1892."

"Nationality?"

Alexander paused. "Polish." It was a choice. He was really Belarusian. But he felt Polish. It was a choice that he would soon be very glad he made. He registered the children and waited for the clerk to type up his new documents. The new identification papers were slipped into an official brown cardboard holder by an unsmiling clerk.

Juracishki was awash with rumors and fear in the summer's heat. Within days of taking over, squads of former communist partisans began appearing at people's doors summoning men to the stately house that had once been home to a Polish nobleman. The Soviet victors allowed them to settle disputes and grudges that had been born during the war. Some men were questioned and sent on their way, but others never returned. Those unfortunate souls were imprisoned or shot or perhaps sent to Siberia as punishment for their "crimes." Their families never knew why they now lived with an empty place at the breakfast table. Each night as he lay in bed before falling asleep, Alexander gave a sigh of relief for another day without a summons.

A DOCTOR'S JOURNEY

Alexander's call came on July 8, just two weeks after the German's fled. Danuta and the boys were pulling buckets of water from the well to water the garden. Alexander was in the shed fixing a rake handle. He didn't hear the quartet of communists approaching from the front of the house.

"Is Dr. Kowal here?" the tallest of the quartet demanded.

Alexander stuck his head out of the shed. His heart sank at the sight of the men. "Yes."

"The commandant requests your presence immediately." His Polish indicated he was a former partisan and not a Russian.

Alexander felt the blood drain from his face. Were the partisan's going to get their revenge now? He scanned the faces of the men standing beside the house, but they were all strangers.

"We must go quickly. The commandant doesn't like being kept waiting."

Josef had seen them first and stood frozen holding a bucket of water. "Danuta, Josef, Zbigniew, I have to go with these men." Alexander struggled to keep his voice from cracking. "Danuta, you know what to do."

His daughter nodded wordlessly, her lips pursed. She had expected this day to come. Was this the last time she would see her father? She gathered her strength. "Say goodbye to Tato," she told her brothers. Zbigniew's solemn eyes searched his father's face for reassurance.

"And give me a hug." Alexander spread his arms and attempted to smile. His children gathered around him under the glaring eyes of the soldiers. As he hugged them, he whispered, "Take care of each other. I'll be back soon." They wanted to believe that, but they didn't. War had destroyed their childhood innocence. Alexander put on his hat and squared his shoulders. He wondered if he had just hugged his daughter and sons for the last time. Were the partisans going to finish the task that Saszka had quashed in that barn? His children clung to each other watching the soldiers escort their father away.

The commandant didn't like being kept waiting, but he didn't mind letting others wait for him. His escorts handed Alexander over to a squat soldier with a rifle slung over his shoulder who directed him to a weathered wooden bench in front of the once-elegant house. Under the watchful eyes of this self-important guard, Alexander waited in the partial shade of a tall oak tree for most of an hour. Possible scenarios ran through his mind. The Paceviche partisans had convinced the commandant that Alexander had been guilty of working with the Germans and should be shot as soon as possible. Alexander was a landowner and should be sent to Siberia. His thoughts turned to his children. How would they survive as orphans? Was Aleksy alive? If he were, would he take his half-siblings to live with him or would Melanie take them in? She'd probably returned home by now. Yes, he knew he could count on her if she was alive. The family would be poor, but they could survive if there were no more wars. Once again he felt helpless like he had months before in that barn listening to angry voices arguing his fate.

The front door of the communists' headquarters opened. A Russian-speaking soldier called to Alexander's guard. "Dr. Chufistov is ready for him."

Dr. Chufistov? Doctor? Not the overall commandant but the medical commandant? What did this mean?

Beneath a large portrait of Josef Stalin in the *Rajispolkomen*, the commandants' headquarters, sat the new communist medical administrator for the Juracishki region. The large room was empty except for a wardrobe in one corner, two dilapidated chairs, and a scratched wooden table covered with folders, papers, and an overflowing ashtray. The mustached man peered at Alexander over rimless glasses. "Alexander Kowal?"

"Yes." Alexander's heart raced. He tried with little success to calm himself. Dr. Chufistov opened a folder and scanned its contents. Armed former partisans, some Alexander recognized from Paceviche, wandered into the room and left. Two or three seemed to recognize him but regarded him as though he were a stranger. Waiting to learn his fate, Alexander listened to their echoing footsteps and muffled voices and to the clicking of a distant typewriter. Outside, a small brown bird perched on a branch as though peering in at the goings on in the room.

Dr. Chufistov, in his neatly pressed dull green uniform with frayed cuffs, shuffled through papers. Rows of ribbons blazed on his chest, evidence of his having been a good communist party member. "Our Polish comrades have told me a great deal about you," the balding commandant said in Russian. Had the Paceviche partisans labeled Alexander anti-communist? It they had, this interview was his last.

Doom encased him. He wanted to respond, but no words came from his dry throat. His mind was blank.

"Tell me where you went to medical school." Was this a test to see if he would tell the truth? Later it occurred to Alexander that his inquisitor may not have known as much as he purported to know and was fishing for information. However, at this moment seated in front of the desk with his hat in his hand, fear blocked any critical thinking.

Alexander found his voice and in the language of his childhood explained his medical training. He knew that having attended a school sponsored by the czar might be a strike against him. No doubt Dr. Chufistov was trying to discern Alexander's political views, so Alexander omitted mentioning the czar's sponsorship of the Vilnius medical school where he had graduated more than thirty years ago. It was now a game to say enough to satisfy this man but not say anything that could be interpreted as opposition to Stalin's regime.

"And where have you served as a doctor?"

Alexander recounted the places he had served going back to his first assignment. While he related the chronology of his medical career, Dr. Chufistov glanced at the papers he held, but his passive countenance revealed nothing.

Alexander finished his narrative without mentioning his recent employment by the Germans. Dr. Chufistov wordlessly flipped through the papers.

Only a clicking typewriter broke the silence. At last the doctor looked up at him. "You speak Russian very well, Dr. Kowal. That's good because now you'll work here for us. You'll be in a Juracishki clinic that you'll help organize. You know that in our socialist state everyone is cared for equally." Alexander knew that wasn't true, but remained silent.

"Since you're needed here, you won't be going back to Bakshty or Paceviche, although you may travel there to see family and friends. You can't practice medicine or dispense medications privately. You'll practice only in the government's clinic."

Alexander swallowed. He could go home to his children and sleep in his own bed tonight. "I understand." He was filled with a jumble of relief and apprehension. The memory of the harsh tactics of the Russian revolutionaries a quarter of a century before in Orenburg had not faded. Nor had the face of the commandant who, had Alexander not saved his daughter, would have sent him and his family to die in Siberia. The man he now faced was the progeny of those who had killed anyone in their way.

"I'll walk with you to the clinic and show you around." Dr. Chufistov rose and reached for his hat.

The clinic was in a small two-room house, not far from the Soviet headquarters. Dr. Chufistov held the door open.

A woman in a Russian uniform put down the papers she was reading and rose.

"This is Nadya Kostov. She'll be your nurse."

The gap-toothed, heavy-framed woman with frizzy reddish-blonde hair pulled back in a bun smiled broadly. She reached for Alexander's hand. "Welcome, comrade doctor."

The strange title surprised Alexander. Her fleshy hand was surprisingly strong. He looked directly at her. Although she appeared jocular, her cool hazel eyes were appraising him critically. He repressed a shudder. This woman might be a nurse, but Alexander immediately knew she was assigned to the clinic to keep watch on his movements. That was the Soviet way.

Measure every word carefully, he thought. "Comrade Kostov, I look forward to working with you." Alexander managed an almost smile even while uttering the title constricted his throat.

"Come, let's toast to the success of the Soviet clinic," the nurse chortled. She retrieved three glasses and a bottle of vodka from a drawer in the desk. She handed the men half-full glasses of the clear liquor and picked up one for herself.

"To the glorious Soviet Union." Dr. Chufistov raised his glass, quickly drained it, and put it on the desk. Alexander finished his vodka and perused his new clinic.

The main room was lit by the summer sunshine coming through a dusty window. Behind the square table and three chairs in the middle of the room, newly built shelves lined one wall. They were filled with medical supplies. Alexander looked at them and blinked. Was he really seeing what he thought he was seeing?

"I believe that's your medical bag," Dr. Chufistov said pointing to the black leather bag on the bottom shelf. "You'll be needing it now." He spoke as though this was nothing remarkable.

Fear rose in Alexander's throat. He walked around the table to the shelves. The bandages, gauze, ointments, and bottles of medicine he had stuffed in his bag as he sat by the rocks in the forest were haphazardly arranged on the top shelf. The partisans must have known he was in Paszkowski's shed. But how? Paszkowski? The boy?

His new supervisor stood impassively by the door watching. Alexander picked up a package of gauze and looked at the Soviet officer's cold grey eyes. A storm of thoughts raged in Alexander's head. Had he been set up by Czeslaw Paszkowski? Was he with his feigned kindness somehow connected to the Soviet-backed partisans? Must be. And I trusted him, Alexander thought. No wonder so little of his host's food had been taken from the shed. He turned with his back to Dr. Chufistov and examined the shelves. They're always watching, he thought. He squeezed the gauze tightly, but otherwise showed no emotion. His well-being depended on his ability to appear calm and passive.

Alexander replaced the gauze. Then the bottles of medicine on the shelf below caught his eye. His signature was on most of the bottles. They had been in the boxes in the barn that night. He picked up a bottle and rubbed his finger over the label. You arrogant scum, he thought. Steal my things and then stock your clinic with them and expect me to say nothing and use them as if I didn't know you robbed me? He shuddered. The reappearing medical supplies were a not-so-subtle means of intimidation. Alexander understood the message. We control you and can quash you in a heartbeat.

No longer would he be able to buy medicines from the pharmacy and dispense them to patients as he saw fit. Now the government controlled which medicine would be available and how and when it could be prescribed. An invisible, unyielding cord bridled him.

Alexander picked up his bag. The only outward sign of his anger and uneasiness were his knuckles, white from gripping the handle too tightly. He turned back to look at his new supervisor. "I'll take this home and clean it up." He kept his voice emotionless. Dr. Chufistov's stern face made the uncertainty of Alexander's future clear.

"I don't think there's anything else I need to show you today," Dr. Chufistov said not appearing to notice that Alexander was upset. Or perhaps he noticed and didn't care. "Come to my office tomorrow if you have any questions." He pulled out his pocket watch. "I need to get back now."

"I'll be here tomorrow." Alexander extended his hand for a handshake. He despised this man, but he couldn't show it. His survival depended on the Soviets believing he would be a docile, compliant worker. Of course, he would be a good doctor. He would never consider allowing his feelings about these new dictators to color his medical care. Dr. Chufistov accepted his hand for a brief firm handshake before leaving. Alexander bid the nurse goodbye, picked up his bag, and headed down the road.

He was caught between anger and fear. Anger at being betrayed and fear for not knowing who else might be waiting to betray him.

By the time he reached home, he had swallowed his anger enough to not upset the children. "We'll be staying here," a weary Alexander told them as he closed the door. Danuta's eyes filled with tears. This morning she had been sure they would never see their father again. She recognized the medical bag and raised her eyes to her father's.

He put the bag on the bench. "I'll explain later."

Was he any safer than when the Germans were in control? Probably not, he thought while walking to the clinic the next morning. But he knew he had to make the best of the situation. It was not a time to make those in charge upset. It was a time to be ever vigilant about every word and action.

At least for today he was safe because of his profession. The communists needed doctors to implement their plans, and their own doctors were still busy with the army. The clinic was totally unorganized, so Alexander set about trying to bring some order to the place. He found some comfort in the routine of seeing patients but was always in a state of heightened alertness. When giving directions to his nurse, he was careful to be courteous and circumspect and in every conversation never gave a hint of disapproval of the communists.

Within a few weeks the entire medical system was tested. Typhus, a deadly infectious disease, erupted and spread like a raging fire. To make matters worse, no one wanted to treat the victims for fear of being infected. Alexander was put in charge of quelling the epidemic.

"You'll need to travel to Bakshty and Volozyn, so I've assigned a horse and wagon to you," Dr. Chufistov told Alexander. In the midst of this dreadful plague, this was good news. It meant Alexander could check on Melanie. He still didn't know if she was back home.

Spread by fleas and lice, typhus was an enemy guns couldn't stop. Alexander knew that hygiene and isolating those already ill were two keys to stopping it. At his urging the Soviets converted empty buildings into makeshift hospitals for typhus patients only and assigned Poles to work there caring for the ill. It was dangerous work since typhus was highly contagious. But under this new socialist system, jobs were assigned and refusing an assignment was not allowed.

Alexander's next step was educating groups of women about cleanliness. "Burn all hay ticks and boil all linens and clothes. It's what you can do to protect your children," Alexander told the women assembled in Bakshty, telling them what he had explained in a dozen other villages. "Please tell your neighbors what you've learned today," Alexander encouraged the women. They left grim-faced. He had lived beside these families during so many years of fighting, and now they had to hope their families survived typhus. After the meeting, he drove on to Paceviche, but Melanie and Alosha had not come back. He was relieved. They were probably safer with Maria in the small isolated village.

Typhus victims were immediately sent to the new hospitals. The Americans, now allies of the Soviets in defeating Hitler, sent the powdered insecticide DDT that was dusted on everything from bedding to floors in infected homes. Halting the epidemic was a formidable task. For weeks Alexander left home before dawn and didn't return until dark. Some weeks he had to leave Danuta and the boys home alone for two or three days when he traveled to the Bakshty and Volozyn areas to supervise hygiene education programs and typhus hospitals.

That fall as the epidemic neared its end, a man from Bakshty appeared at the Juracishki clinic and insisted on being treated by Dr. Kowal. He waited nearly an hour before Alexander could see him.

"Cibor Buczek, I haven't seen you in a very long time. Still live in Bakshty? What brings you to the clinic?"

"No, Volozyn. I work for the railroad now and am in town for my job." He followed the nurse with his eyes as she went into the other room. "I have something to tell you," he whispered.

"Are you ill?"

Buczek shook his head. "It's about your son Aleksy," he said softly.

Alexander stared at the man sitting in the exam room. His heartbeat quickened. "Aleksy? You've seen him?" His voice was barely audible. He leaned towards his old acquaintance.

"Yes, he's hiding at the station in Volozyn. He asked me to tell you. The stationmaster is helping him."

Alexander had a hundred questions, but Buczek had no more answers. Even if he did, he wouldn't risk having the nurse overhear the conversation. Alexander's heart pounded from joy. Aleksy was alive. How many times had he been near his son and not realized it? Then fear etched his joy. The Soviets needed fresh soldiers. If they found Aleksy, they'd have him in a uniform before they'd give him papers

"I'm going to Volozyn tomorrow. I'll be back in a couple of days," Alexander told the nurse. Nadya Kostov was glad to have him out of the clinic so she didn't have to work so hard. It was not unusual for him to go to one of the hospitals to supervise patients' care, and she didn't give a second thought to his leaving.

He decided against telling Danuta about Aleksy. Even though his demeanor was calm, he was filled with anticipation and anxiety in the chilly autumn morning air. He gave last minute instructions to his children and left to see his oldest son for the first time since before the Germans invaded. How fortunate, he thought, that he'd been assigned a wagon and this horse.

The man at the Volozyn stable greeted Alexander and assured him he would take good care of the horse. Alexander thanked him and walked in the direction of the hospital, but turned after a couple of blocks and hurried towards the other end of town to the train depot, glancing behind every few steps. He asked for the stationmaster and was directed to a small office at the back of the lobby.

Alexander's knock was answered by a man whose nametag identified him as Stationmaster B. Nowak.

"I'm Alexander Kowal. My son is Aleksy." Nowak's eyebrows rose.

"Come in." Nowak had to be sure this man wasn't from the secret police. Hiding an undocumented person was a crime that merited a prison term.

Alexander understood the unspoken fear and reached into his pocket and pulled out his cardboard identification book. He opened it and handed it to Stationmaster Nowak. "I know you must be cautious."

The tall, thin man looked at the document and handed it back. "Your son is working in one of the back rooms."

Nowak unlocked and opened the door to a large room filled with a conglomeration of equipment and wooden crates. It appeared empty. "Aleksy, you can come out. It's safe."

For a moment nothing happened. Then from behind a stack of lumber the son that Alexander hadn't seen in five years stepped out. He was taller and slimmer than he was when he waved good-bye to his father at the hospital. He looked at the gray-haired man who stood beside his friend Nowak.

"Son, it's me." Alexander felt tears streaming down his cheeks.

"Tato? TATO?" Aleksy rushed to his father and threw his arms around him. "I can't believe it. Buczek did find you." Father and son stood wrapped in an embrace letting tears of joy flow.

"I'll leave you two alone," Nowak said. Neither man heard the door close.

Arm in arm Alexander and Aleksy found a place to sit amidst the machinery and tools.

"How are Katherine and the children?"

Alexander looked at his son. So much had happened. "Katherine is dead and so is Jacob, your youngest brother. We can talk about it later. Danuta, Josef, and Zbigniew are with me in Juracishki."

"Why'd you leave Paceviche?"

"There's much to tell, but for now I'll just say that the Germans were going to either kill or deport us and we managed to escape. How'd you end up here?"

"When the Soviets arrived, Dr. Fominski left to go back to his family home in central Poland, I was out of a job and a hiding place. I was afraid to register with the Soviets. I figured they'd put me in the army or arrest me. Mr. Nowak's nephew was a good friend at the hospital, and he brought me here. I know you said I shouldn't confide in anyone, but I had to. I didn't know what else to do. Mr. Nowak is a very religious person and hates the communists. He's risked his own safety to let me stay here. I'm not sure what I'd have done if he hadn't taken me in. I haven't been out of this room since the night I came. When Mr. Buczek came to pick up supplies, I knew I had to risk asking him for help. Every day I'm here puts Mr. Nowak in jeopardy."

"You were right not to trust the Soviets. Without papers, they'd have had you in a uniform by nightfall. And you did the right thing, asking Cibor for help."

Aleksy nodded in agreement. "That's true about those Soviets. I'm not sure how much longer I can stay here without being discovered. Have you seen the posters encouraging Poles to move west from Belarus to Poland? Maybe Poland will actually be an independent country again."

"I've read them. They say they'll give us documents to get a house equal in value to what we leave behind if we settle in certain places, and there'll be help with resettling. I don't trust the Soviets, and they're in charge here in Belarus." He stopped and rubbed his forehead. "The Polish government in exile wants people to register to go so they can prove there's a big Polish population here and the border should be moved back to where it was before September, 1939. At least that's what I've heard."

"I need to go to Poland, Tato. We've learned enough about the communists to know that they'll takeover everything like they have in the old Russia. And they're vicious. That Stalin will order anyone in his way killed. Besides, I'm Polish. I may speak Russian and Polish, but in my heart, I'm Polish like my mother. I'm not Belarusian."

"You can't go to Molodechno to register." Alexander was already sorting possible solutions. "I don't know exactly how to get documents for you, but I'll figure it out when I get back to Juracishki," he assured his son. Mr. Nowak brought them food, and father and son talked late into the night. Alexander related his experience with the Soviet-backed partisans.

"So, son, once you have legal papers, you'll go to Poland?"

"Definitely. I'll get as far away from the Soviets as I can. I hear the Germans aren't going to last much longer, but that won't stop the Soviets from drafting me. Once they have me in their army, I won't be able to get out. I want to be somewhere west of here. Not close to the fighting, but just farther away from the Soviet border. I've heard that several of my professors were trying to make it back to central Poland. I'm hoping a medical school might open somewhere so I can go back to school. I don't know how safe it is in Poland, but I think it's worth the risk to go. It's just too dangerous to be here. Have you heard any rumors about the Polish underground uprising against the Germans in Warsaw?"

"No, we only get news the Soviets want us to get."

"Well, what I heard was that Poles, mostly students and other young people, were battling the Germans in Warsaw. The Soviets were supposed to help. But the Soviets parked themselves on the other side of the Vistula River and watched the Poles get slaughtered. I don't know if it's all true, but I think it is. It's the story making the rounds according to Mr. Nowak."

Alexander shook his head. "So much useless killing. I hope the border will be moved back. I'd like this to be Poland again." Father and son sat quietly. They didn't know that Roosevelt and Churchill had already promised this land to Stalin.

"Tato, what nationality is on your identification papers?"

"Polish," Alexander said. "I may have been born in Belarus, but I've lived most of my life in Poland, and your mother and Katherine were both Polish and so are all my children. I don't want to live in the Soviet's socialist state. I've already learned what that'll be like. I want no part of it."

"But you don't know if this'll be Poland when the fighting stops. Go west, too, Tato. There's still hope for central Poland. It isn't the Soviets' yet."

"Perhaps you're right, if it's true. But leaving the land of my grandfathers seems like a violation of trust. Our family has lived on that land for generations." Alexander sighed. "For now we must get papers for you."

That night they slept side by side on the hay pallet in one corner of the room where Aleksy had slept since he went into hiding. In the morning Alexander headed back to Juracishki determined to get the documents for Aleksy as quickly as possible.

It proved to be a challenging task. His first inquires about false documents were unsuccessful. People were afraid of the Soviet secret police. They seemed to be everywhere and know everything. But at last a friend said he knew of a schoolteacher in a small village just outside Molodechno. He worked as a clerk in the Soviet's Repatriation Office and had access to official stationary and blank documents. He might be amenable to making the papers. It was a delicate situation. The teacher had to be sure Alexander wasn't trying to trap him, and Alexander had to be sure the man wouldn't report him to the security forces. But at last trust was established and an agreement was reached. Fortunately, Alexander still had gold coins sewn into his belt. The teacher's price for taking the risk and making the papers was one gold coin--fifteen rubles. It was an exorbitant price, but Alexander would have paid anything for his son's safety.

In the chill of approaching winter four weeks after their reunion,

Alexander made the trip on snow-clad roads back to his son. Tucked deep inside his inner coat pocket were Aleksy's "legal" documents, including a permit to move to Poland. He was sending his son into the unknown. When or if he would hear from him again, he didn't know. But for the moment, he hoped he would be safer there than he was in Volozyn, and that was all he could hope for.

Chapter 19

Juracishki, Soviet controlled Belarus, Autumn, 1944

Clutching a small leather suitcase that contained all his possessions, Aleksy climbed the steps of the train and turned to wave to his father standing on the platform bundled in his heavy winter coat against the chilly November air. Alexander saw Aleksy pat his breast pocket to reassure himself that his identification papers and repatriation permit were still there. The forged permit slip looked authentic, but Aleksy was still in danger until he crossed the border.

Alexander wished he could tell Danuta and the boys about finding their oldest brother, but an accidental comment to anyone might end Aleksy's flight to freedom. He couldn't take the risk, and he wouldn't know if or when Aleksy made it to Poland, so the secret had to remain in his heart.

Through the train window Alexander saw his son heft the suitcase onto the baggage shelf and find a seat. Aleksy put his face close to the dirty window and searched for his father. He smiled and waved through the coal smoke blowing over the platform. Alexander raised his hand and made the sign of the cross, just as his mother had done whenever he left home. The whistle blew and the train lurched forward. Aleksy headed toward the unknown. "Please, let Aleksy be safe," Alexander prayed, pushing away the images of soldiers and cannons floating in his mind. His stomach stayed knotted as he hurried towards the station to find Mr. Nowak.

Mr. Nowak's office door was open and he stood when he saw Alexander.

"He's gone?"

"Yes, and I'm heading back to Juracishki. But I wanted to express my gratitude. You saved my son's life."

Mr. Nowak shook his head. "I didn't do much."

"That's not true. You risked your life" Alexander extended his hand, and Mr. Nowak thinking he just wanted to shake hands, extended his. Alexander slipped one of his remaining gold coins into the stationmaster's hand and closed the man's fingers around it. "My son's life is worth more than this, but it's at least a token of my thanks."

Mr. Nowak opened his hand. His eyebrows rose. "No, you don't have to do this." He tried to hand the coin back.

Alexander shook his head. "I want to. I'm sure you can use it somehow. It is not likely we'll meet again, but I'll never forget what you've done for my family." Alexander smiled and backed out of the office, closing the door behind him. The stationmaster stood by his desk looking in amazement at the gold coin.

Holding the reins of the plodding horse, Alexander's thoughts turned to what Aleksy had said about moving west. It was easy for his son who had only himself to worry about. Alexander wondered how he could move Danuta and the boys. Until the war ended, staying in Juracishki might be the wisest choice. However, he decided, it might be a good idea to register for repatriation soon. It might be smart to have the option to leave.

The former partisans now wielding power made him anxious. With no compunction these Bolshevik supporters in charge destroyed lives of innocent people they randomly accused of crimes against the state. They had been ready to kill him once on the word of a man who didn't like him. Images of that dreadful day still came to him in his sleep. Who was to say an upset patient or a report by his nurse wouldn't give the communists an excuse to get rid of him?

The last time the communists were in control, they had planned to send him to Siberia and seize his land. Before the war they had made collective farms of private land in the European part of the Soviet Union. Is that what they had in mind for here? It was hard to understand all the changes and what they meant. Alexander rubbed the smooth leather reins in his hands. I'll just have to be patient and see what happens, he thought. He looked at his pocket watch. Home before dark.

With the typhus epidemic winding down, days at the clinic fell into a routine. But Alexander felt no peace. More former partisans appeared to be taking on a bigger role in the local government. Almost daily stories about them settling old grudges circulated. Alexander found himself looking over his shoulder as he walked to and from work. The puppet government that was run by the Soviet communists ruled through intimidation and fear. Just like the days in Orenburg when he and Olimpia were starting their married life, it was not safe to trust anyone. A neighbor might easily give information, true or false, to the local police in return for a favor. Alexander decided to make the trip to Molodechno, which was the nearest place with a Repatriation Office. It was time to register for a move to Poland. He could always change his mind, but it was better to have permission if he needed it.

The first day of December, he went to Paceviche to retrieve the papers that were buried in the barn in the box with his medical instruments. He'd need proof of being Polish if he was to get permission to move to Poland. All he had were his marriage certificates and the children's baptismal certificates, all signed by a priest. He hoped they'd be enough.

A fresh blanket of snow covered Paceviche. Melanie and Alosha still hadn't returned, and the farm was eerily quiet. Alexander took his shovel out of the wagon and hurried into the barn. He pushed hay away from the hiding place and dug into the cold dirt. His heart pounded from effort and anticipation. Alexander grunted as he reached into the hole and pulled out the box. Holding his breath, he opened the box that held his medical instruments and diploma. He undid the lid and lifted the linen-wrapped leather container.

"It looks like everything is in perfect shape," he said softly to the empty barn. He removed the layers of linen. Unsnapping the clasp, he opened the leather case that he had so carefully wrapped that fearful day. The instruments lay in a neat row inside. His diploma, pictures, church certificates, and letters were safe, too, in their own linen cocoon. He rewrapped his treasures, secured them with ropes behind the wagon seat, climbed in, and turned the horse towards Juracishki.

The next week he took the two-hour trip to the government repatriation office in Molodechno. After waiting almost three hours for his turn, a solemn barrel-chested clerk waved him to a desk.

"I need your identification papers," the man said in Russian. Alexander handed them to him. He had decided to answer first in Polish when asked questions. Speaking fluent Russian might weaken his case.

The clerk copied Alexander's information to another form. "What is your religion?"

"Roman Catholic," Alexander replied in Polish. The clerk appeared to understand.

"Do you have your baptismal certificate?" the man asked in Polish.

"No, mine was lost." The lie slipped smoothly from his mouth. "But I have my children's, and I have my marriage certificates signed by the priest who performed the ceremonies."

After looking at each paper and copying dates and names onto the government form, the clerk handed them back to Alexander. "We'll have to check things. You live in Juracishki?" Alexander nodded. "If you're approved, we'll send the permit to the commandant's office there."

When a Soviet sergeant brought the permit to the clinic a month later, Alexander was surprised. Apparently the communists were anxious for Poles to move to make room for the Belarusians now living in western Poland who had been offered the same incentives to move back to their homeland.

Alexander wondered about Melanie and Alosha. Their house had been vacant each time he had checked on his trips to the area. Perhaps they were still with Maria. If he did decide to leave, he'd make the long trip over rutted roads to that isolated village to tell her his plans.

News of the outside world seeped into Juracishki through rumors and Soviet newspapers that were posted every week on various buildings in the town. Citizens knew the newspapers were propaganda and read them searching for nuggets of real news and truth imbedded in the stories. At the Tehran Conference held a year ago England's Winston Churchill, America's Franklin Roosevelt, and the Soviet's Josef Stalin had given the Soviet Union the eastern part of Poland. The Soviet/Polish border now lay along the Bug River. The western leaders' decision to grant the Soviet's control over the Polish government meant that Poland could never be a corridor for forces attempting to invade the Soviet Union. This was important to Stalin.

In February, 1945, another meeting, between Churchill, Roosevelt, and Stalin, this one at Yalta, cemented Poland's post-war borders, even though the Germans had not yet surrendered. A part of eastern Germany had been carved off and made a part of Poland. The USSR had agreed to permit Poles to move from the eastern part of Poland that was now a part of the Soviet Union to the land that had been part of Germany. The maps on posters Alexander and Aleksy had read made the changes clear.

With the stroke of a pen, the lives of millions of people were affected. When Alexander first read the Soviet accounts of this agreement on the newsprint nailed to the front of the clinic, he wondered if these powerful leaders sitting in warm, comfortable rooms had any idea how their decisions affected all the hungry, freezing people who had no voice but lived the consequences.

When April arrived, warm winds melted the snow and left the streets muddy and passable only to foot traffic. The latest posted Soviet newspaper reiterated the Soviets' willingness to help Poles move back to Poland. Transportation would be provided. Alexander kept his repatriation permit in a drawer at home, but still felt conflicted about leaving. Maybe when the Germans were defeated, America and the European allies would convince Stalin to move the border. Then on May 10th the posted newspaper announced the fall of Berlin on May 8, 1945. The Nazis had been defeated. The war was over at last.

Alexander still had a horse and wagon assigned to him. The typhus hospitals had closed, so officially he didn't need it. Apparently, no one in the bureaucracy had needed it either. I'd better go to Paceviche to see if Melanie has returned before someone decides he wants my transportation back. Had she survived the winter? And Aleksy? Where was he? Alexander shook his head. At least I can check on my sister, he thought.

The next day Alexander told the nurse he needed to go to Bakshty and urged the horse towards Paceviche. Before he reached his old house, he saw smoke rising from Melanie's chimney.

"Melanie, are you home?" Alexander called as he tugged the horse's reins. The door opened and his sister rushed out followed by Alosha and an unfamiliar young woman. A wave of relief and joy swept over him.

Alexander wrapped his arms around his slender sister and remembered her rail-thin frame when he had returned from Orenburg more than twenty years ago. "You're home," she beamed. The fine lines around her eyes crinkled as she smiled and said,. "I've been so worried." She stepped back and clasped his hands."

"And I've worried about you. Each time I came to see if you were back, I was afraid that you might not have made it to Maria's or that her village had been decimated like so many others." He hugged her again. "Thank God you're okay."

"Maria's village was too isolated and too poor to get much attention from the Nazis, thank heaven. And we even came home with a new family member. This is Wusha, Alosha's wife. She was a neighbor of Maria's."

While they shared the midday meal, they filled in the pieces about how each one had survived these past months. At Maria's small isolated village, they'd been spared from the fighting.

"We stayed because we didn't know if there would be enough food to eat here during the winter. Of course," Melanie laughed, "Alosha wasn't anxious to leave after he started courting Wusha. Something good did come from all the bad." Wusha and Alosha blushed and glanced at each other.

"So the Soviets are keeping you in Juracishki? Will they ever let you move back here?" his sister asked.

"No, I don't think so." Alexander looked at his sister. Her hair was mostly gray now, and her dark blue eyes were wreathed in wrinkles. He held her rough hand in his. "Life here now reminds me of life in Orenburg. No one trusts anyone. The Soviet-supported partisans who wanted to kill me are now a part of the secret police. They hand out their own form of justice. It's often just petty revenge. And I know the Soviet nurse at the clinic is really my handler. She reports everything I do to her superiors." He shook his head. "I never know when I'll do something that'll be the end of me. It's tiring."

His sister squeezed his hand. "What are you going to do?"

Alexander shrugged his shoulders. "I don't know. Maybe I should take the children and go to Poland. I have a repatriation permit. But this is home. Remember when I came back after the first big war? As soon as I saw this place, I knew I wanted to bring Olimpia and the boys here. I was so anxious to leave when I went to medical school, and then I was so glad to be back."

Melanie smiled and handed him the bowl of hard-boiled eggs. "Those were good years, weren't they? We didn't realize it."

"I'm afraid it'll never be like that again, but I hate to leave this place. I don't know what to do. You've seen the posters encouraging Poles to move back to Poland?" Melanie nodded. "Well, I put Polish as my nationality when I got my papers from the Russians. I'm pretty sure life isn't going to be easy under Soviet rule. That's why I got the permit. Don't know if I should take the next step with it or not."

"You'll do what's best for your children," Melanie looked at her brother with solemn eyes. "I know you. Family comes first. They're most important now."

Alosha handed his uncle the plate of rye bread "Have you heard from Aleksy?" he asked.

Alexander wanted to tell them about sending his son to Poland. The words were almost to his lips, but he shook his head. "No, I don't know where he is."

Melanie and Alexander's moods were more subdued as they finished their bean soup. He looked at his pocket watch. Time to get back to Juracishki.

"Bring the children to see us as soon as you can," Melanie said.

"I will. They've missed you." Alexander looked out at the black soil in the fields ready for planting. It would always be home, no matter where he lived. Could he really leave this place and move to Poland?

Chapter 20

Juracishki, Soviet-controlled Belarus, Spring, 1945

Alexander walked down the street towards his Juracishki home in the late afternoon sunshine still thinking about his conversation with Melanie. He had left the horse and wagon at the government livery stable but hadn't checked in at the clinic. It had been a long day, and his body ached from the wagon ride. As he approached home, he noticed four figures standing beside the road in front of the house. First he recognized the uniforms of Soviet soldiers. A lump formed in his throat. What could be wrong? Then one of them moved and he realized the fourth figure was Danuta. She was laughing. The four young people didn't see him. He slowed his pace in order to see what was going on.

One of the young men playfully touched his daughter's arm. She grabbed his hand and held it for an instant. Alexander' heart thundered in his chest. Danuta was flirting with these young men. Didn't she realize how dangerous this was? Instinctively he walked faster. Danuta looked up and saw her father. The smile vanished from her face and she stepped back from the men. Alexander thought he heard her say, "Here comes my father."

The young men turned and saw Alexander storming towards them. "Go in the house, Danuta. You should be fixing supper." He glared at the young men and marched through the door behind his chagrined daughter.

"You can't talk to them. They aren't proper young men for you. I don't want to see you talking to any soldiers. That's it. It's not allowed." Alexander's raised voice brought her brothers from the backyard to see what was going on. They stood gaping at their father. Neither boy had seen him this angry.

Danuta's eyes filled with tears. She put the cast iron pot filled with steaming barley and salt pork on the table and the family ate in silence. She felt deprived of being young, but she knew she didn't dare argue with her father.

Neither Alexander nor Danuta slept well that night. Danuta climbed off her hay pallet early the next morning and fixed milk soup for breakfast. When Alexander came to the table, he said nothing. She put the steaming bowls on the table without looking directly at him. Alexander finished his soup and chicory coffee in silence and left for the clinic. The residue of the argument hung over the household like a pall.

Alexander thought about what Aleksy had said. Maybe he should go to central Poland. His children shouldn't have to live like this. "I don't want to leave, but I hate the thought of staying. I don't know what to do," he muttered softly as he walked. The image of the young men talking to Danuta wouldn't leave his mind.

It wasn't a particularly busy week at the clinic. Nadya Kostov's endless chatter filled the stuffy rooms. Some days she was a silent partner as they worked, but this week she seemed to talk constantly. Alexander tried to listen and give appropriate responses, but his mind was filled with thoughts of Danuta and the young soldiers. He wished he had someone to confide in. But he didn't know who he could trust. Father Rodkiewicz was no longer around. The priest had vanished soon after the Bolsheviks returned. Alexander guessed that the Polish underground had helped him slip past the troops, perhaps back to Poland, to avoid execution. Religion was just one more thing the communists crushed for "the good of the people."

Certainly Alexander did not want Nurse Kostov to even suspect he had any worries about his family. If she knew he was worried, she might report it as a weakness to Dr. Chufistov, and who knew how they'd use it against him. The Bolsheviks would use anything to intimidate the people they controlled.

Alexander was filling out one of the endless forms the communist bureaucracy expected when the door opened and a Soviet colonel helped his obviously hurting wife into the room. Nurse Kostov was instantly on her feet helping the woman to the exam table.

"It's my leg, Doctor. I cut it with an ax when I was chopping wood," the colonel's wife explained.

Alexander examined the deep wound, and went to work. Alexander numbed her leg and disinfected it with alcohol before suturing the cut muscle and then the skin. The colonel stood in a corner watching with interest.

Alexander checked the woman's pulse in the back of her leg and foot. "Can you move your toes?" She did. "Your circulation seems fine."

"You're very good at that, Comrade Dr. Kowal."

"I've stitched a few of these, but this is a nasty one." Alexander finished suturing and Nurse Kostov took over cleaning up.

Alexander turned to the colonel. "Keep it clean. Change the bandage every day." He took a small jar from a shelf. "Use this salve. She should keep her leg elevated for a few days. If she runs a fever, give her aspirin. Come back the day after tomorrow so I can check to be sure there's no infection."

The colonel brought his wife back three more times during the next ten days. Each time his wife's leg improved, and he became friendlier. Alexander was cautious, but he liked the man. He wasn't condescending or standoffish like most Soviet officers. Nurse Kostov saw the couple walking towards the clinic coming for the last check up. She scowled. It was time to close for the day.

"No need to stay Comrade Kostov," Alexander said. "It won't take me long to check her wound. I'll lock up." The nurse took her sweater from the hook by the door and was gone before the colonel and his wife reached the front porch.

The colonel's wife came in carrying a basket of stuffed eggs and fresh bread. A bottle of vodka bulged in the colonel's uniform coat pocket. His wife was walking without a limp and the wound was healed enough for Alexander to remove the sutures.

"We're grateful for the good care. Let's have a toast." The colonel removed the top from the bottle while his wife unwrapped the food.

"To your skill, Comrade Doctor" the colonel said raising his glass.

Alexander smiled at the compliment before taking a drink of the good quality vodka. Then he raised his glass and gave the expected response. "To the glorious Soviet Union." They ate and drank and made polite conversation.

The colonel emptied his glass and refilled it. Alexander was careful to not drink quickly.

The colonel raised his glass again. "To the Soviet Union and its ally Poland." He held his glass up and turned to Alexander, "You should go to your Poland as soon as you can." He laughed, drained his glass, and reached for another stuffed egg. Alexander felt the hair on the back of his neck rise. He looked at the colonel wondering if he had actually heard what he thought he had. He adjusted his mask of friendliness being sure he appeared nonchalant. Alexander felt like one of the rabbits he used to hunt. They jumped and hid to avoid being shot. He was always mentally jumping and hiding his true feelings, trying to avoid even a hint of trouble. It was wearing on him. Alexander raised his glass and drank.

Walking home, the colonel's comment ran through Alexander's mind. What did this man know?

That night Alexander couldn't fall asleep. He weighed and reweighed the reasons for moving. He sat up on one elbow and looked at his sleeping children. He wondered where Aleksy was sleeping tonight. Maybe a fresh start would be good. If he stayed here, what future lay ahead for him? He lay back down, his decision made.

Lying on his hay pallet as the sun rose, Alexander felt he'd made the right choice. The time had come to go to Poland. But thinking about leaving his grandfather's land filled him with sadness. In his heart, though, he knew that for the children he had to go. The Bolsheviks were here to stay for a long while. He had experienced their cruelty and mercurial ways before. He wanted as little to do with them as possible and that meant they had to leave. The Soviets had almost taken his land the last time they ruled. If he stayed, they'd do it again somehow, someway.

"I don't see decent schools opening for you to attend anytime soon. I don't want you to grow up here. We're going to Poland," Alexander told his children at breakfast. "It will take a few months to make the arrangements. We'll be better off in Poland than the USSR."

"I think that's a good idea, Tato," Danuta said. She'd heard about other families leaving, but had not wanted to ask her father about it. "If we stay here, our teachers will teach in Russian. Polish is the language we know best. And we can go to church again. I really miss that."

Alexander was grateful for Danuta's ability to see why they should leave the country that had always been home. She would help the boys cope with all the changes. Going to an unknown place might not be easy, but here every day was fraught with struggle.

Danuta finished the last bite of her fried eggs. "Tato, what about Aleksy? How will he find us? It's been so long since we've heard from him." She hesitated, afraid to say what she was thinking, but unable to keep her worry buried any longer. "Do you think he's still . . ." she stopped and swallowed. "Alive?"

Alexander wanted to assure her, but knew he couldn't. "We have to believe he's alive. Maybe he'll go to Poland, too. I promise that we'll search for him as soon as we get settled."

"I think about him so often. Every night I pray that he is safe."

"You can never give up hope, Danuta. I need to tell Aunt Melanie soon that we're leaving. She's wanted me come home to Paceviche, but even if we stay, the Soviets won't let me."

Alexander drove the horse and wagon to Paceviche in June, just a few weeks after the announcement of the fall of Berlin. People, still not totally comprehending all the political changes, were tending their gardens as they had always done.

Melanie saw him coming down the road and rushed to greet him. Alexander climbed down from the wagon. "I'm so glad you're home." Melanie took the horse's reins and tied them to a post.

The siblings stood arm in arm. "Are the Soviets going to let you move home again?" He knew it would be her first question.

"No, Melanie. I've made a decision." He reached for her hand and looked directly at her. "The children and I are moving to western Poland." Melanie breathed deeply. "When I considered the good and the bad, moving to Poland had more good than staying. I wish you could come with us."

Melanie shook her head. "You know we can't. We only speak Russian and our papers list us as Belarusian. The authorities would never let us go." She bit her lip and looked out at the fields. "I've never lived anyplace else like you have. My life is here—my friends, my girls, Alosha and Wusha." Her voice choked. "How many times have I watched you leave? And Gregory? When he left, he was younger than Danuta is now. Is he still alive in America? What was the war like for him? Will I ever know? He'll never come back, and this time I don't think you will either." Her shoulders quivered. Alexander put both arms around her.

"You've always been here for me. I promise that as soon as I can, I'll let you know where we are. It's not safe for me here. I don't see any option but to leave. This is part of the Soviet Union now. Funny how our grandfather's land was in Belarus, a part of czar's Russia, when we were born. Then came a war, and it was declared Poland, and then another war and the Bolsheviks took over, and then the Germans came, and now this same land is in the Soviet Union. But it was always our family's farm."

Alexander's gazed turned to the house where he and Olimpia had sat happily reading by kerosene lamps. He scanned the fields. He remembered the pleasure when some new farming method worked. He looked towards the river remembering Katherine's lush gardens, and then he turned his gaze to the forest. Would there be wild mushrooms in Poland? He looked towards the haystack by the barn where they'd found Arkady. Tears welled up, but he forced them back. "Let's go inside," he said.

While Melanie and Wusha prepared food for the noon meal, Alexander told them about the incident with Danuta and the young soldiers and a little bit about his work. He didn't tell them about the colonel's toast. Melanie worried about him enough; she didn't need any fodder for more worries. Saying goodbye was hard enough already.

"I'll be back in a few weeks to clean out the house and to dig up the things we buried so I can take them with us. We can't take everything. I want you to have what you can use. I hope I can sell a few things. Until I can get a job, we'll need money wherever we resettle."

"I'll do whatever I can to help. I can load my wagon, too, and haul things to Juracishki," Alosha said. Alexander was grateful for his nephew's offer to help. He left feeling more at ease with his decision.

On the way back Alexander stopped in Bakshty to see his old friend and Danuta's godfather, Mieczyslaw Kolenda. They had been close friends since childhood, and he wanted to tell him about his decision. Mrs. Kolenda set out bread and sliced sausages, and Mr. Kolenda poured glasses of vodka for himself and Alexander.

The men related their recent experiences. "Thank God we both survived," Mieczyslaw told his old friend. He hesitated. "Except, of course, Katherine and the baby. Such a tragedy." His wife made the sign of the cross. "And Aleksy? Is he…"

"I haven't heard from him." Alexander paused for a moment. "Things have been difficult for all of us. I don't think I know a single family that hasn't suffered. And you know the Soviets will want to take our land. I've decided to move west to Poland, rather than stay here and watch the communist's grip tighten a little more each day. I've had my repatriation permit for a few months now. It's time to use it."

Mieczyslaw Kolenda looked at his wife who stood by the stove stirring a simmering pot. Her eyebrows rose slightly. She returned her husband's gaze. Then she gave a slight nod.

"I got one, too," Kolenda replied. "I don't know what to do. It breaks my heart to have to give up this land. It's been in our family for as long as your farm has been in yours." He shook his head. "You know I helped the Polish partisans. The Soviet partisans who fill all the offices and the secret police slots didn't always like what I did. They haven't given me any real trouble, yet, but . . . ." He looked at his wife and young son. "My gut tells me we just aren't safe here. You know how they hold grudges for a long time, and they have some against me. I certainly don't trust the communists either. Remember all the awful things they did when they swept in here before? So many good people have disappeared, including the Catholic priest. The Soviets are just like they were before the Germans came. I'm tired of living in fear. It wears on us." He paused for a moment. "When'll you leave?"

"It's going to take some time. But as soon as I can, I think." Alexander looked at Kolenda. "Why don't we go together?"

Mieczyslaw took another sip of vodka. "I don't know. It's difficult to think of leaving my family's land. Stay here tonight. Let's talk about it." Late into the evening the two men discussed the pros and cons of moving, but they didn't make a decision.

The next morning Alexander waited for Mieczyslaw to bring up the subject of moving.. While Mrs. Kolenda prepared breakfast, the men went outside.

"I didn't sleep much last night. I kept weighing both sides. Stay. Go. Stay. Go."

"I think it will be easier to go together, don't you? Whatever village or town we end up in we'll have each other for support. As I understand the government's offer, they will give us documents for another house in return for the one we leave here. So, we'll have someplace to live if nothing else. It would be good to have an old friend in a new place."

Mieczyslaw Kolenda and Alexander stood side by side in silence.

Then Mieczyslaw turned to Alexander. "We'll go with you. I've been thinking about this for a long time, but was afraid to go alone with just my family." He smiled. "You're used to moving to new places, but I'm not, so it will be good to use your experience. Besides, it's always good to have a doctor nearby."

The men shook hands. "We'll be glad to have you with us. I wish I didn't feel like we have to leave," Alexander said looking at the familiar landscape. "Do you suppose they'll move the borders again so we can move back?"

Kolenda shrugged his shoulders. "Will this land become Poland again if the western allies negotiate a new treaty with Stalin? Who knows? The people who make the treaties don't care about us. I keep hoping Americans will take the side of the Poles at a peace conference and move the border back. "

"That's a lot to wish for." Alexander shook his head. "It seems like most of our lives all we've been doing is trying to survive. Maybe life will be better for our children."

By the time Alexander headed home, they had agreed that Alexander would make the initial railway arrangements since he lived in Juracishki where they would load their belongings on the railcars.

"We'll stop by in a few weeks when we go to Paceviche to see Melanie and dig up the things we buried before the Germans came," Alexander promised before he climbed into the wagon for the trip back to Juracishki.

Rye and barley ripened in the hot July sun a few weeks later when the Kowals returned to Paceviche.

"So you're really going?" Melanie asked.

"Yes, we are." He knew she was hoping something would change his mind. "Have you talked to the Kolendas? They're going with us."

"Somehow knowing you'll have a friend with you makes me feel better."

"Me, too. We'd better get started. We have a lot to do today. Let's start with digging up what we hid from the Germans."

Alexander looked over the fields he had tilled as a boy. The image of his father in a sweat-stained straw hat holding a wooden rake in his hand flashed through his mind. Alexander gathered his thoughts and turned to his children who stood in reverent silence. They felt the sadness Alexander was feeling, and the finality of the day overtook Danuta. Her brow wrinkled. She closed her eyes trying to memorize the house of her childhood. But excitement also fluttered in her stomach. Moving was going to be an adventure, a new life. She could see herself in school and having friends her own age.

Alexander broke the reverie. "Let's start with the bicycles. Alosha, do you remember exactly where we buried them?"

Alosha pointed to a small bush behind the house. "We put them over there."

By nightfall the bicycles and sewing machine, all in good shape, had been unearthed. The sewing machine was put back in its boxes for the big move. Alexander and Danuta could use the bicycles as soon as they pumped up the tires.

After breakfast the next morning, Alexander turned to Danuta and the boys. "If you want to say good bye to any friends, now is the time. Danuta, be back by noon. No later." He watched his children hurry down the dusty road, chatting and laughing, hoping to find friends they hadn't seen for months.

The rest of the morning was spent going through the house. Some things Alexander sold to neighbors who saw his wagon in the yard. He gave Melanie what he didn't want to take, and he explained to her that he had to give the government his house in order to get a document for a house in Poland. "But," he said, "your house is yours, not mine. Don't let them take it from you. Some communist party member will probably get mine." He turned to his nephew. "I don't know if your moving into my house might mean that you can keep it, Alosha. Try that if you want. I'd like you to have it."

They had to leave soon, but Alexander had one more thing to do. "I'm going for a walk," he told Melanie. "I won't be long."

Alexander headed towards the Catholic Church, about three kilometers from the house. Birds fluttered in the trees as he entered the cemetery. He stopped first at Katherine's grave. He stood for a moment. "Thank you for three fine children. You'd be proud of them." He stood for a moment and then reached down and touched the small wood cross that marked baby Jacob's grave.

He moved to Olimpia's grave. It had been such a long time. Closing his eyes, he could see her long dark hair and smiling eyes. "Love of my life," he whispered. "I thought someday I'd be buried beside you."

Alexander walked slowly to the Orthodox cemetery. He stopped for a moment at his grandparents' and parents' graves before moving to his second son's resting place. "I don't suppose I'll ever really understand," he said quietly. "I'll always wish I'd seen your pain." He sat on a nearby rock for several minutes before turning back to his boyhood home.

When he returned to Melanie's, Alosha had a gift for him, ten bottles of homemade vodka. "You'll need these to grease the wheels during the trip," he said. Alexander grinned. He hadn't thought of that detail. He would definitely need bribes for officials along the way. It was just a fact of life.

"Thank you. I can't think of a more useful gift."

He hugged his sister. "When we have an address, I'll write to you". This was the last time he would ever see her.

As if he were burning the scene in his brain, Alexander scanned the land his father and grandfathers tended so carefully.

His heart ached as he guided the horse for the last time down the road he had traveled so often. Alosha followed in the second loaded wagon. The children stood in the back among the boxes and bicycles and waved as long as they could see their aunt.

Chapter 21

Juracishki, Soviet controlled Belarus, Summer, 1945

Mieczyslaw Kolenda was standing in the shade of his barn building a wood chest when the Kowals pulled up in the two wagons laden with their worldly possessions. He put his hammer down and waved.

"Are you planning to take all of that with us to Poland?"

"Yes. I think so."

Kolenda surveyed the overflowing wagons. Alexander climbed down and tied the horse's reins to a fence post while the children and Alosha pulled up beside him. Alexander gave them instructions and turned to Kolenda.

"Did you get the notice? The one that gave our departure date as September 14?"

"The magistrate brought it to me last week. That's why I'm trying to get this chest finished. Are you still thinking we should settle in Elk?"

"Well, it's one of the closest places, but I just read a letter from Jan Obuchowicz that the magistrate had given to Melanie. You remember him? He lived over on the north side of Bakshty by the big bend in the river. The Soviets drafted him into the Polish army, but he's out and living in Gryfice near Szczecin, which is almost on the western border. He thinks we should go there."

"I don't know. That seems like an awfully long way."

"True. But we don't have to decide. We can check towns out as we come to them. Maybe Elk will be the best place."

Mrs. Kolenda had seen them pull into the yard and had a pot of chicory coffee, a pitcher of fresh milk, slices of smoked sausage, and thick slices of bread on the table when they walked into the house. "Dzien dobry. That coffee smells good. I hope we'll have enough for the whole trip. We'll need it."

"The travel documents said that we'd each have a railcar. I hope we can get them next to each other," Kolenda said as he sipped the hot coffee. Alexander nodded in agreement.

"I signed the papers giving the State my house and land. Did you?"

"Yes, I went to the magistrate and signed them last week," Kolenda replied.

Alexander took a sip of his coffee. "I wish I felt better about the paper they gave me in return. Will the house I get be as good as the one I'm leaving? Will the land be as good? It's a risk. They are promising a lot of things to us—a house, food, help finding a job. I'm not very confident it will be like they promise. But we'll be safer than we are here, and we'll make the best of it. At least they aren't telling us where we have to settle. And they still haven't had a peace conference. Perhaps those Americans will listen to the Poles and change the borders back."

Kolenda shrugged. "We'll have to make do with whatever we find, I guess. At least I won't always be looking over my shoulder to see who's watching." Mrs. Kolenda nodded in agreement. The men drank their coffee and Mrs. Kolenda refilled their cups.

"I do my final checkout at the clinic August 31," Alexander said. "That'll give me some time to get ready. Why don't you come on the twelfth or thirteenth and stay with us. That way we'll have time to take care of any last minute problems."

Alexander looked at Mrs. Kolenda slicing cabbage. "I know it must be hard to leave the house you came to as a bride. How long has it been now? Ten years?" Alexander asked her.

"Yes, and a little more than seven years since Bolek was born here." She looked at her son giggling outside with Josef and Zbigniew. She smiled. "To them this is a great adventure, isn't it? They don't realize that we're doing this for them. I hope they're all in school in a few months, and I know you do to, Alexander."

"That's true," he replied. He looked at his daughter sitting on a bench watching the boys.. "I promised Danuta that she'd go to college. I intend to keep that promise."

Alexander, Alosha, and the children arrived in Juracishki late in the afternoon, just in time to care for the animals. Jadwiga Struga, sitting outside her house knitting, watched her neighbor and the stranger drive the loaded wagons to the back of their house. Alexander waved to her. "Danuta, let's go tell Mrs. Struga what we're doing. It's best she knows rather than guesses."

Zbigniew scampered across the dry grass ahead of his father and sister. "Mrs. Struga, we're moving to Poland in a few weeks. We have a permit. That's our cousin." Zbigniew pointed to Alosha unharnessing his horse. "He's helping us bring everything from our old house in Paceviche." The words tumbled from the boy's lips. In his nine-year-old eyes, riding on a train and moving was a grand adventure.

Looking at the wizened old woman, Danuta realized she would miss this kind neighbor. The old woman frowned. She liked the Kowals and felt safer with them nearby. The children helped her and made life a little less lonely, and Dr. Kowal had always been sure she had the medicine she needed for the pain in her knees.

"I'll miss you, but maybe life will be better where you're going. God go with you." She made the sign of the cross. "You will be in my prayers." Mrs. Struga had lived in her small log home for almost sixty years. From her front porch she was watching the world change again. These new Soviets might be better than the Germans, but not much. She couldn't leave and knew she would have to find a way to exist with these oppressors.

"We'll miss you, too," Danuta said. She bent down and hugged the frail woman.

Just before noon on the last day of August Dr. Chufistov and Alexander's replacement, a Russian doctor from Moscow, arrived each with a sheaf of papers in a leather binder.

"Comrade Dr. Kowal, this is Comrade Dr. Kuzmenko. He's taking over and will sign for all the medicines and supplies today. We must have a strict accounting of the State's property."

He turned to the nurse, "Comrade Kostov, check things off." He handed her the papers, and the tedious job began. It took until almost three o'clock to complete all the forms. Alexander unhooked the clinic keys from his key ring and handed them to his boss. At last Dr. Chufistov said, "Everything seems to be in order." Inwardly Alexander breathed a sigh of relief.

Dr. Chufistov slipped the clinic keys into his pocket and smiled at Alexander. "Good luck to you in Poland, Comrade doctor."

I won't be your comrade anymore Alexander thought as he shook his supervisor's hand. But he smiled and said, "Thank you." The charade had to continue a little longer.

Alexander turned to the nurse. "We should end with some vodka, just as we began, I think." The nurse quickly pulled out four thick glasses and a bottle she kept in the bottom drawer.

"To the clinic, Comrades." Alexander raised his glass.

"To the glorious Soviet Union." The nurse smiled and raised her glass and drank. "And to your safe journey," she added as an afterthought. The other two doctors lifted their glasses.

Alexander just wanted to leave, but he knew that it was best to end on a good note. As he looked at the nurse's round, alcohol-rosy face, he wondered if she would be staying on to keep watch on Dr. Kuzmenko. Perhaps for a while, but he seemed like a loyal party member. Alexander was quite sure the nurse knew that he knew about her secret job, but no hint of that knowledge ever crossed between them.

"If you have no questions, Comrade Dr. Kuzmenko, we should be going," Dr. Chufistov said putting his glass on the desk. Dr. Kuzmenko followed his new boss out the door. Alexander held it open for a moment watching the two men walk away. That's done, he thought. He took his hat from the hook by the door, said goodbye to Nadya Kostov, and left. He didn't look back.

The Kowals sorted and packed and were ready to leave when the Kolendas arrived on the twelfth. The next day Alosha came with his wagon to help move everything to the railcars and take care of whatever wouldn't fit. When Alexander and Mr. Kolenda went to confirm which cars they would have, they were met with unwelcome news.

"We're short of cars. Families will have to double up. Two families to a car." Alexander and Mr. Kolenda's expressions fell. One car? That would be crowded. "You can wait until the next scheduled trip, but that won't be for at least three weeks," the station agent told them.

Alexander looked at his friend. "We can do it, don't you think?"

Kolenda nodded. "It will be tight, but yes, we'll make do." Who knew what changes in policy might happen in three weeks?

Fifteen *tieplushkas*, boxcars outfitted with three sets of wood bunk beds and a small cast iron stove, waited on a siding track to take them to Poland.

Kolenda pushed open the heavy wood door, pulled himself into car 7, and leaned down to help Alexander up. The odor of dirt and decay overwhelmed them. "Before we do anything, we need to clean this out. My wife will have a fit," Kolenda said surveying the filthy car. "And I'll need to make a ramp from the wagon sides so we can move the animals in and out." One of the things Alexander liked about his friend was that he always looked ahead and solved practical problems.

Near the door the small cast iron stove stood bolted to the floor. Bunk beds were nailed in place at the front end of the dirty railcar. Sunlight filtered through cracks in the sides. This would be home for at least the next two months. The men allocated space, deciding where to put everything before going back to the Kowal's to organize their belongings.

The next morning they swept and scrubbed the railcar, but the smell improved minimally. In the afternoon they piled stacks of firewood and hay and sacks of grain at the back end of the railcar. The cupboard Kolenda had made and another he brought from his house were roped to one wall. Twenty-eight other families were preparing their assigned cars, a few the Kowals and Kolendas knew. It wouldn't be until they were well into their journey that they learned almost all of the emigrants on the train were also leaving because they feared for their lives.

While the men readied the tieplushka, Danuta and Mrs. Kolenda stayed at the house putting fresh hay in the bed ticks and airing the pierzynas. They counted bags of potatoes, carrots, onions, beets, and cabbages that would have to last through the winter. They bathed, too. It would be their last bath until they reached their unknown destination.

Before dawn on the fourteenth, all seven travelers and Alosha were up and loading the wagons for the short trip to the station. The sun was above the horizon when Mrs. Struga came into their yard steadying herself on her cane with one hand and carrying a basket of boiled eggs and dark rye bread. Alexander put the potatoes he was carrying into the wagon and went to the old woman.

"For your trip." She handed him the food.

"That's very kind. Thank you." Alexander took the old woman's hand. "You've been a good neighbor. I hope the next people who live here appreciate you." The old woman smiled, said goodbye and hobbled back to her house without letting Alexander see the tears in her eyes.

By noon the families had moved all their belongings except the animals into the tieplushka. Two tin milk cans had been filled with water; the hay ticks and pierzynas had been spread on the bunk beds. Alexander, Mr. Kolenda, and Danuta each had a bunk of their own. Josef and Zbigniew shared a top bunk, and Mrs. Kolenda and Bolek shared another top bunk. One empty lower bunk became storage for clothes and blankets with a small space for two people to sit and lean against the soft bundles.

There was little room to move around. Most of their journey, they soon realized, would be spent sitting or lying on the bunk beds. Tucked under one bunk among other family belongings was Danuta's small suitcase. She checked it one more time just to be sure everything was safe. She lifted it onto her bunk and opened it. In it she had hidden the rosary given to her by her parents for her first communion. She wouldn't show it to anyone until they crossed the border. But she took the wooden beads from their cloth bag and slipped them into her skirt pocket. She squeezed them and felt comforted.

Carefully she checked the suitcase's other linen-wrapped contents. The framed icon of Our Lady of Ostra Brama that had hung in their house fit snuggly in the bottom of the worn suitcase. It was a hand painted replica of the icon at the gate of the city of Vilnius and had been one of her mother's prized possessions. They had hidden it from the Germans and Russians, but soon they would be free to hang it in their new home. On top of the icon rested the teapot painted with pink and blue flowers that had belonged to Olimpia. Danuta brushed her hand over the linen to assure herself that these precious possessions were safe. She snapped the suitcase closed and slipped it back among the boxes and baskets.

Alexander looked at his watch and then looked west towards the station. An engine was being hooked to the fifteen repatriate cars. "Looks like its time to load the animals, Mieczyslaw. The officer is starting his rounds to check everyone's papers."

One by one the men loaded Alexander's cow and pig and the Kolenda's horse, cow, pig, rooster, and six hens. With parts of the wagon they had made a small pen for the pig, and a fence to separate the cows and horse. Mieczyslaw Kolenda latched the fence and surveyed the car. "That's it. We don't have room for anything else."

A Soviet officer with a Stalin moustache approached car seven. He scowled at Alexander and Mieczyslaw. "Your papers?"

"Right here," Alexander said. They handed the officer their identification papers and repatriation permits. Alexander pulled the bottle of Alosha's vodka out of his pocket and proffered it to the officer. Without even seeming to look, the man took it and stuffed it into his own coat pocket. His two helpers climbed into the car, poked the hay, and moved a few of the burlap food bags searching for anyone who might be hiding.

The officer glared at the women and children huddled silently together just outside the door. Danuta had heard her father's stories of traveling back to Poland from Orenburg. She fingered her rosary in her pocket, put her other hand on Zbigniew's shoulders, and leaned down. "It'll be all right. Just stand quietly," she whispered. The wide-eyed boy stuffed his hands in his pockets and gave an imperceptive nod.

The officer opened his black book and said the name of each family member aloud, looking to see that all were accounted for. "Is anyone else in the car?" he asked his young helpers. They shook their heads no. The officer stamped the documents. "Don't lose these," he snapped.

"No, sir."

"Get in the car so we can lock the door." The women and children scrambled in and the men climbed in behind them. Alexander turned and looked over at Alosha who stood by his wagon stroking his horse's neck. He waved. The officer slammed the door and slid the iron bar across it. The clang of the bar resounded with finality.

The officers headed to the next waiting repatriates leaving the two families in the car lit only by the meager light coming through two opened small rectangular windows and the cracks between the boards in the sides.

"Goodbye Alosha. We'll write as soon as we're settled. Take care of your mother," Alexander called through one of the small windows. Alosha waved, "Go with God," he called back He climbed into his wagon with the odds and ends of the two families' belongings, and urged the horse towards home. It was the last time Alosha would see his uncle.

Mrs. Kolenda started a fire in the blackened stove and put on water for tea. The families sat in the semi-darkness listening to the cacophony punctuated with brief slices of peace. They counted the slamming railcar doors. Each slam brought them closer to leaving. At three o'clock they heard footsteps crunching past the car.

 The whistle blew twice and the train brakes hissed as the brakeman released them. With a jerk that sent the boys sprawling on the floor and the adults clinging to whatever they could grab, the two families left their homeland for a new life. The crowded car was uncomfortable with a smell that would grow more unpleasant with each passing mile. But it was also filled with hope. Hope for a life void of fear of the government, hope for a more prosperous life, hope for the children's future, hope for a fresh start. And for Alexander, hope of finding Aleksy again.

Chapter 22

On the train from Belarus to Poland, Autumn, 1945

The Kowal and Kolenda families quickly discovered that wind whistling through cracks and the creaking and groaning noises of the moving train made yelling necessary for conversations. Except for Alexander, everyone settled into a bunk. He edged himself between stacks of household goods at the side, steadied himself, slid back the wood cover from the narrow rectangular glassless window, and watched the Belarusian countryside slide by. He was remembering his train ride in the fading daylight on his way to medical school in Vilnius. That night he had been filled with naïve excitement and anticipation for a new beginning. This afternoon his looking forward to a fresh start was tempered by life's experiences.

Later, perched in their bunks, they ate Mrs. Struga's bread and hard-boiled eggs for supper. Mieczyslaw Kolenda managed to milk both cows, so they had fresh warm milk to wash down the food. The children fell asleep in their swaying bunks soon after dark. The adults lay awake with their memories, hopes, and concerns.

Just before midnight Alexander fell into a deep sleep but was awakened by the train's screeching brakes. He and Mieczyslaw rose and looked out the small window. They saw a large pile of coal, but no apparent workers.

They heard other repatriates calling out, "Where are we? What's going on?" But no one had any answers.

"I think we'll be here all night. We may as well go back to sleep," Mieczyslaw said. They didn't know that night that stopping and waiting, sometimes for days, would be a part of the fabric of their journey.

In the morning an official unlocked the doors. Local railroad workers loaded coal onto the train. The twenty-eight families soon established guidelines for using available bushes for toilets. The men fed the animals and cleaned the stalls, while the women built fires in the small metal stoves. Mrs. Kolenda made milk and barley soup for breakfast before the train whistle hurried everyone back into the cars.

It took the two families a couple of days to adjust to the jostling and bouncing as the train slowly moved west. When the train stopped during daylight hours, they first cleared out the animal manure and emptied their waste buckets. Then they searched for water to refill their storage containers. At night they slept within inches of each other rocked by the swaying train. It was not a comfortable journey, but every click-click of the wheels took them closer to freedom from Soviet oppression. Mieczyslaw Kolenda unpacked his mandolin and led them in song to pass the time, and they played card games. Sometimes the train halted for a day for no apparent reason. Sometimes they traveled all night. At each stop Mieczyslaw Kolenda slid the wood ramp out the door onto the ground, secured it with large metal hooks, and led the horse and cows down to any nearby patch of still green grass. It took over a week to reach the Polish border.

For two days after the train stopped at the border crossing, nothing happened. The boys romped in the weeds enjoying this respite from travel. Danuta met some girls her own age, and they huddled together under a tree talking and laughing. Mrs. Kolenda gathered with the other women in the sunshine to visit, and the men congregated to wonder why they weren't crossing the border. Tension hovered underneath the conversations. Had the Soviets halted the repatriation program? Would they actually be permitted to leave the country?

Late on the third morning Josef rushed back from a game of hide and seek. "Looks like officers are checking each car, Tato".

The waiting was over. Alexander, his heart beating fast, climbed back into the railcar and slipped a bottle of vodka into his pocket. He checked to be sure he had all their identification papers and permission certificates in the folder tucked in his inside coat pocket. "You have your papers ready, Mieczyslaw?"

He held up his brown leather case. "All set. Looks like this is it. Better get the animals back in the car."

Alexander turned to the families who were gathered around. "It's time. Danuta, Mrs. Kolenda, when the officials reach the car next to ours, spread a cloth on the table and put out sliced sausages and those fresh hard-boiled eggs. Don't look worried or frightened, and don't say anything unless they ask you a question."

Alexander stood in the warm autumn sun remembering leaving the Soviet Union with Olimpia, their sons, and her family almost a quarter of a century before. He had the same queasy feeling in his stomach this time. Just one official taking exception to them could stop their crossing into Poland. Look calm, he thought; don't let them think you're nervous.

With the officials searching each car, it was late afternoon before car number seven was examined. While they were checking car six, Danuta and Mrs. Kolenda arranged plates of food on the small table. Glass tumblers waited for vodka. The officer in charge was all business as he reached them. He frowned at each traveler over the top of his rimless glasses. His two assistants climbed up the ramp. The khaki-clad young Bolsheviks peered into corners and peeked behind the burlap bags of food.

"Do you have your repatriation permits?" No greeting. Just a brusque question from the officious Bolshevik officer.

"Yes," Alexander and Mieczyslaw Kolenda handed him their official permits. Alexander also handed him a bottle of vodka which the man, with nary a comment, slid into his satchel with his papers.

"Two families?" The round-shouldered officer's manner was curt.

"Yes," the two men responded in unison. The officer perused the papers and the two men. He looked into the railcar and climbed aboard.

"Please have something to eat," Mieczyslaw said indicating the food on the table. He turned to the young men, "And you, too, help yourselves. It is a long day for you. You must be hungry." He poured a generous portion of vodka into each tumbler.

The three men helped themselves. The young blond helper looked at Danuta. He almost smiled, but thought better of it and glanced sidelong at his boss to see if he had noticed. Engrossed in stuffing another piece of sausage in his mouth, the officer was oblivious of the young man. He wiped his hands on the cloth Mrs. Kolenda had laid on the table. With a word of thanks, he pulled his black book out of his satchel and continued the inspection.

"Your identification papers?" He examined the proffered papers and handed them back to the men.

"The train will leave tomorrow morning. You may not leave your car. We'll lock it now." His stern countenance made Alexander shudder. Without another word, the taller of the two assistants slammed the door shut. The heavy bar slid sideways and locked. The families were left sitting in semi-darkness.

Alexander's hands shook as he folded the identification papers and repatriation permits and slid them back into the folder. "So far, so good. But until we cross the border and get our approval from the Polish authorities, we're still in limbo," Alexander warned Mieczyslaw.

The next morning after another breakfast of milk and barley soup, the apprehensive families talked quietly. Even the boys played with almost no noise. Border officers' footsteps grew louder then fainter. Alexander and Mieczyslaw took turns peering out the small windows, but they saw little except cows in a distant pasture and hawks circling in the sky. Hours passed, but the train stood still. Periodically doors slammed. Alexander leaned against the side of the car listening to the footsteps crunching on the gravel rail bed. He touched the bottle of vodka in his pocket. The footsteps grew louder. This time when the Soviets reached car seven, they stopped. Eternal silence. Mieczyslaw frowned and with his eyes sought an explanation from Alexander who only shrugged and put his fingers to his lips.

Everyone jumped at the scraping of metal. The young blond man pulled open the door for the Soviet officer who stuck his head inside and scanned the car with blood-shot eyes.

"My head aches," he complained. "All that food and vodka yesterday. It is your fault." He swept his arm indicating all the cars. Alexander's stomach contracted. Were they being uncoupled from the train because of this man's hangover?

He handed the officer a bottle of Alosha's vodka. "I think you'll find the quality of this very good. It is the best thing for a headache the day after."

The flush-faced officer took the vodka. "I'm sure it'll help." He pushed the bottle into his pocket and turned to his young helpers. "Do the final inspection." His minions climbed aboard and looked behind the animals, opened the cabinets, and kicked some of the food bags. The young blond glanced at Danuta, but she never took her eyes off the floor.

He looked at the officer and shrugged. "Nothing." He jumped down from the car.

"You'll be locked in and won't be able to get out of the car until you cross the border," the officer said gruffly.

"Of course." Alexander looked down at the scowling officer. Did he want another bribe? Alexander wished he'd put another bottle of vodka in his pocket. But the border officer grabbed the bar on the outside of the car and slammed it into the locked position. His boots crunched on the gravel. They heard car eight's door open.

"Final Soviet exercise in intimidation." Alexander whispered. "They keep it up to the last instant, don't they?" He sat on a box beside Mieczyslaw and leaned against the side. They looked at each other and shook their heads.

"A parting shot, I suppose," Mieczyslaw sighed. "I wonder if all these guards are grumpy and rude because we're getting out and they're not. Leaving really was the right decision."

Alexander nodded. "Let's just pray the train moves soon and we're still connected. I hope the Polish authorities are not like these thugs." He looked at his children. They had endured so much. It was past time for them to have a real childhood.

It seemed like hours, but was only forty-five minutes later when the engineer blew the whistle and the train groaned and lurched and moved westward. The Kowals and Kolendas looked through cracks in the sides of the car, each trying to be the first to see Poland.

Chapter 23

Poland, Autumn, 1945

The train chugged past the border station and over rolling hills covered with autumn blazed elm and maple trees. Less than twenty kilometers past the Soviet border station, screeching brakes brought the train to a halt.

"Look, Tato, a Polish flag." Joseph jumped up and down. "I saw it first," he said to his brother. "We're in Poland, aren't we?"

Alexander and Mieczyslaw peered out the small rectangular window. The white and red flag hung from the porch of the border station. "Yes, son, this is Poland." Alexander took a deep breath.

A smiling Polish border officer unlocked the railcar door and pulled it open. "Dzien dobry. Welcome to Poland." He smiled at the Kowals and Kolendas. "Your railcar won't be locked anymore" His gaze turned to the children whose eyes following his every move. "It's been a long trip?" he asked them.

Josef looked at his father who nodded permission to speak. "Yes sir."

"Well, it shouldn't be much longer until you find a new home." He smiled at the boys before turning his attention back to the men. "I know you've been traveling many days. I'm sorry we don't have food here for you, but you'll be able to get supplies in Elk."

"Food?" Mieczyslaw asked.

"Yes. The United Nations Relief and Resettlement Agency has basic food supplies for repatriates." Mieczyslaw looked at Alexander. Maybe, they both thought, we'll actually get the help that was promised. They smiled at each other and jumped onto Polish soil. The three boys followed.

It took two days to get all thirty families processed before the train headed to Hajnowka, which had always been a part of Poland and was the first town inside the Polish border. As the repatriates disembarked, Hajnowka residents standing on the station platform stared. Some stepped back. A boy about Zbigniew's age blurted out, "Tato, where are those poor people coming from?" His father hushed him, but the child spoke for everyone. Danuta looked at the clean, ironed shirts and different styled dresses the women were wearing. She looked down at her wrinkled, dirty dress and dusty shoes, then at Mrs. Kolenda in her stained apron and worn dress. Danuta's cotton full-skirted dress and the shabby brown leather shoes with broken laces looked old-fashioned. Color rose in her cheeks. We must look pathetic, she thought.

She turned to her father. "Look at us, Tato, compared to them. We're dirty and we smell awful. We sure don't look prosperous."

Alexander caught the small Polish boy's eye and smiled. "You're right. We've come from behind the Bug River, and it's true, we're poor, but we're glad to be in Poland." He looked at the boy's father. "Could you tell us where we might fill our water cans?"

The man pointed to the back of the station. "You'll find pumps over there." He turned to the boy. "Come on, son, let's finish our errands." The rest of the crowd also dispersed.

After a two-day stop, the repatriates' train made its way from Hajnowaka to Elk stopping for a day or two at several small towns along the way.

Elk, the first larger former German town they reached, was a surprise. Streets were cobblestone instead of packed dirt. The houses were stone and brick and covered with painted stucco, not wooden structures common in Belarus. Many buildings were two, three, or even four stories high. Tall buildings were the norm in larger cities, but not in Bakshty or Juracishki. The children were in awe. "Tato, how do they build them so tall?" Josef asked.

At the repatriation office Alexander and Mieczyslaw were told all the former German houses in town were taken, but houses in the country were still available.

"Mieczyslaw, why don't you take your horse for a ride and see what's available?" Alexander suggested. "I'll look around town."

Mieczyslaw agreed, and they headed back to the train. Alexander noticed a large Red Cross sign on a small white stucco building around the corner from the repatriation office. "Why don't you go on, Mieczyslaw. I want to stop here." He motioned to the Red Cross building.

A sign in the window said: We can help you find missing relatives.

"Tell me about this," Alexander asked the young woman wearing a Red Cross arm band. He pointed to the sign.

"We print newspapers with the names of people searching for relatives and who they're looking for. We send them to all parts of Poland. We also do some radio broadcasts. Do you want to find someone?"

"Yes, my son, but we don't know if we'll stay here."

"Wherever you decide to settle, give the Red Cross office the information, and we'll post your name and his. If he sees the list, he can contact you." Implied in the statement was "if he's alive."

Alexander and the children walked around the town late in the autumn afternoon of their first day gawking at this seemingly prosperous place.

"What do you think, Tato?" Josef asked. "Could we settle here." He was ready to be done with the trip. "It looks like a nice place."

Danuta and Zbigniew agreed.

"Let's see what Mieczyslaw finds," Alexander told them.

At dusk the Kowals headed back to the train. They passed a half-dozen people on horseback and several wagons filled with families making their way to the town square. A curly-haired man riding a sway-backed horse stopped. "Where're you from?" he asked Alexander.

"*Z za Buga*. From behind the Bug River. And you?"

"Me, too, but I live here now."

"Why are all these people coming into town so late in the day?"

Alexander inquired.

"Not safe out there at night." The man waved his hand back where he had come from. "Looters killed three people this month. They clean out what were the German's places, and when they can't get what they want, they attack the new Polish settlers. We camp in the square and go home in the morning. Wish the army would come back. We need their protection. Only safe place is in town after the sun goes down."

Perhaps Elk wasn't the place to settle. They decided to continue west toward Szczecin, the last stop for the train. At each stop they marveled at the stucco and brick houses, the orderly laid-out villages, and the luxuries, such as radios, that some people had. Most buildings in towns had electric lights and indoor plumbing. Even the cows were different—black and white instead of red. Some railcars unhitched as families decided to stay in the lake country east of Gdansk. Some stayed in Olsztyn, but Jan Obuchowicz's letter made Szczecin sound more appealing. They sent him a telegram telling him they were coming.

At each stop in former German territory, the repatriates scavenged deserted German homes and barns for food and supplies. Alexander and Mieczyslaw were uneasy as they foraged through the Germans' barns and fields, but they justified it to themselves because they needed it. "If we don't take this, someone else will, and we're low on food for the animals," Mieczyslaw said as they toted grain and hay back to their railcar. "It'll just rot and go to waste if no one uses it."

Cold November wind and rain that sometimes turned to snow made life in the tiepluska miserable by the time the train reached Gryfice. But the discomfort was a price they were willing to pay for a safe place to live. At each stop they had seen a life free from the Bolsheviks. Gryfice, a town very near the new western Polish border, was smaller than Szczecin and was closer to the Baltic Sea. It was the last stop of the repatriation train for a new beginning.

As the train halted, Mieczyslaw Kolenda swung open the door

letting in the freezing rain. A repatriation worker in a black raincoat splashed up to welcome them. "Hurry into the station to get warm," he called to the shivering families.

The travel-worn, bathless families crowded into the depot waiting room. It was six weeks before Christmas.

"Dr. Kowal, is that you?" Alexander turned his head towards the voice.

"Jan, Jan, yes, it's me." The two men hugged. Jan held his old friend at arm's length noticing Alexander's thinning gray hair and the wrinkles etched in his face. War had aged him considerably.

"I got your telegram. I'm glad you're here. This is a good place to settle. Let me help you with the housing. You remember Franciszek Giermowicz from Juracishki? He's here, too. The other half of his house is vacant now. Let's see if we can get you into it. He was given a small farm for his service, but he's still in the army to help keep the peace."

"Do you remember Mieczyslaw Kolenda? We need a place for him and his family, too."

The men shook hands. "I think there's a house down the street from Franciszek's that's still vacant. Let's get in the line at the repatriation office."

Jan's enthusiasm for this place bubbled over as they walked. "You'll like the fresh fish from the Baltic Sea. It's nice. And it's safe with the Polish army units stationed around here."

Alexander saw the Red Cross office. I'll go there tomorrow, he thought.

With Franciszek and Jan's help, the two families had their possessions and animals moved to their new homes by nightfall the following day. The animals were put in a pen and shed with Franciczek's animals until they could repair the outbuildings at their new homes. For the first time since September, they slept in beds in real bedrooms. Alexander wrote to Melanie telling her they had arrived safely and giving her his new address. He took the letter to the post office and stopped at the Red Cross to register.

As soon as he got back to the house, he told Danuta the whole story of Aleksy contacting him and leaving for Poland. "I hope he's checking those lists," he added as he finished "I'm sorry I couldn't tell you all this before. If anyone asked about him, I wanted you to be able to honestly say that you knew nothing about his whereabouts."

"It's all right. I understand. It must have been tough keeping it secret. I'll pray that he finds us," Danuta said. "And that he's safe."

Food from the UNNRA supplemented the provisions they had left. Canned meat, fruits, and vegetables from America kept them from going hungry. Alexander was anxious to find a job, and went to the regional health care office a few days after their arrival.

The silver-haired doctor held Alexander's diploma and looked at it for several minutes. "I can't accept this. It's thirty-four years old and from the czar's Russia. It doesn't mean anything anymore. I'd offer you a job as a clerk if I had an opening, but I can't certify you as a doctor." He handed the diploma back. "I'm sorry."

Alexander was stunned. "But I've been a physician all my adult life. I've worked in clinics and taken care of private patients. Isn't there some way?" The regional manager wouldn't budge.

Disappointed by this turn of events, Alexander searched for a solution. For now they could survive with the supplies given to them by the UNRRA and what was left of the food they had brought, but that wouldn't last forever. He had to find a job, even if it wasn't in medicine. His next disappointment was the schooling available in Gryfice. The German schools had closed, but Polish schools were not all open yet. Jan didn't have children, so this didn't bother him, but the Kowal children were already behind and Alexander was anxious for them to be in school. Maybe this wasn't the best place to settle. We'll make do for a few months, he thought. But I'm going to have to find a way to practice medicine again.

Christmas was just a few weeks away. Danuta was already making plans for the holiday celebration. Using wrapping from the UNRRA food cans and whatever else they could find, the boys helped her make decorations for the Christmas tree. Diligently they peeled wrappers from the cans and made garlands by folding them accordion style, slipping them on long string with pieces of rye straw. This first post-war Christmas Eve supper meant lots of work for Danuta. She wanted to serve the twelve traditional dishes representing the twelve apostles. She boiled fish and jelled it in its own liquid, put herring in oil and vinegar marinade, and stored them in the lean-to at the back of the house.

Danuta was up before dawn the morning of Christmas Eve making fruit compote, wild cranberry pudding, slicing the last cabbage from Juracishki for the mushroom and cabbage stew, and preparing fish to be fried. Just past noon she stood at the stove stirring the stew. She stared out the window at the falling snow remembering Christmas Eve suppers when her mother did the cooking. A man carrying a brown suitcase hurried up the road.

"Tato. TATO," she screamed. "I think our Aleksy is coming. Yes, it's him. Look, Tato."

Alexander dropped the wood he was fashioning into a stand for the Christmas tree, rushed to the window, then flew to the door and down the steps and to the road. Danuta and the boys followed but stopped at the doorway. Tears of joy rolled down Danuta's cheeks. Her prayers had been answered.

Aleksy ran towards his father. They threw their arms around each other laughing through their tears. Father and son stood in a long embrace amid the gently falling snowflakes.

Chapter 24

Poland, Winter, 1945-1946

Danuta couldn't stop smiling. The fatigue from all the cooking and cleaning vanished. Fish frying, simmering mushroom soup, and the sweet fragrance of bubbling wild cranberries filled the house with Christmas smells. She laid hay on the table to represent the manger where Jesus was born and covered it with the same white linen tablecloth her mother had used on Christmas Eve. Six places at the table, five for the family and one left empty to remember the family members who weren't with them completed the traditional Christmas Eve setting.

Aleksy and Alexander finished the Christmas tree stand, stood the tree in the corner of the small living room, and then helped the boys string the garlands they had so painstakingly made. While they worked, Aleksy talked about his experiences since he waved goodbye to his father in Volozyn.

"I got back into medical school in Lodz, and I'm doing well. I was lucky that some of my professors from Vilnius are on staff in Lodz. They were able to verify the courses I had already taken. I didn't have to repeat anything, so I should graduate in 1949." Aleksy finished his narrative for his family. He took a garland from Zbigniew and put it around the back of the tree. "But, Tato, tell me why you came so far west. This place is peaceful now, but for how long? You know that the western allies and Soviets haven't signed a peace agreement with Germany. How can we be sure the borders won't be changed again? And if they are, you're so close to the western edge, you'll have to leave or stay and be a Pole in Germany. That'd be awful. I really think you should move closer to the middle of Poland. It is much more likely to be stable and safe."

"I suppose. I wanted to be away from those Bolsheviks, but maybe I overdid it." He handed Josef a strand of garland. "Right now I need a job. They won't let me practice medicine here because my diploma is from the czar's medical school. Even so, the whole journey has been worth every challenge. I can't describe what a relief it is to not be looking over my shoulder every day or watching every word I say. And so many people have been willing to help us."

They put on the last of the garland and Alexander stood back admiring the tree. "It's time for the star. Aleksy, you do the honors." He handed his son the tinfoil star Danuta had made from UNRRA food wrappers. Josef and Zbigniew cheered as their big brother tied the silver star to the treetop.

"Boys, I'd better get the *pierogi* made. We can't eat until they're ready." Danuta rolled out dough and spooned mushroom filling. Soon she had rows of little bundles of the traditional mushroom dumplings pinched, sealed and lined up waiting to be cooked.

The house grew dark, and Alexander lit the kerosene lamps. Josef and Zbigniew bundled up and went outside to look for the first star, the traditional signal for the Christmas Eve meal to begin.

"We saw a star," Josef shouted as the boys burst into the house. "Can we eat now?"

Danuta laughed. "Remember when we used to do that, Aleksy? Even though you and Arkady were older, you always came outside with us." Aleksy looked at his father with a sad smile. He feels Arkady's absence today, too, thought Alexander.

"You gave us an excuse to stay as children," Aleksy replied to his sister but continued looking at his father sympathetically. Alexander rubbed his hands together but said nothing. One never forgets a lost child, he thought to himself, even when surrounded by his other children.

"To the table, everyone," Danuta called.

Alexander's reverie was broken and he turned his attention to his children gathered around him. He opened the package of *oplateks*, the embossed, thin, white, rectangular wafers that had been distributed after mass last Sunday. He gave each of his children one. As had been done in Polish families for generations, they walked around the table exchanging small pieces of oplatek and wishing each other good health and best wishes for the new year. Danuta looked at the empty chair at the table. She thought of her mother and baby brother. We've all paid a heavy price in this war, she thought. Thank God it's over.

Once seated, they said grace and the twelve-dish supper began. Danuta scurried between the stove and table. Her father passed the plate of fresh bread wrapped in linen. Cups of warm fruit compote made with dried apples, cherries, and prunes sat at each place. First she served appetizers, herring prepared two ways. Next she brought bowls of clear beet soup and a plate of pierogi, then thick cabbage and mushroom stew, made extra rich with the dried mushrooms she had brought from Juracishki. Platters of fried and boiled fish prepared three different ways followed the stew. Shimmering ruby red wild cranberry pudding and poppy seed dessert ended the meal. They ate until they could eat no more.

A small stack of packages awaited opening before it was time to leave for midnight mass. Alexander had little to give to his children, but had found new mittens for the boys and a soft red wool scarf for Danuta at the UNRRA. Aleksy hadn't arrived empty-handed. He opened his suitcase that was still sitting near the door. He had found a wooden puzzle for Zbigniew, a book for Josef, and a book for his father. He gave Danuta several lengths of cotton cloth and spools of thread he'd purchased at the mills near the medical school. Danuta was thrilled. She could hardly wait to start sewing some stylish clothes.

Alexander went into his room, slipped something out of the inside of his belt, and came back with his closed right hand extended.

"Aleksy, I think you should have this." He opened his hand.

Aleksy's eyebrows rose. "Mama's wedding ring?"

"Yes. I've kept it sewn inside the lining of my belt since the war started. She'd want you to have it. I know you aren't making any money in school, so if you need to sell it to live, go ahead. Your mother was pretty practical. That's what I think she'd tell you."

Aleksy took the small, slim gold band and pictured it on his mother's hand as she read books to him. He squeezed it. "Thank you," he whispered. He closed his eyes. Danuta and the boys sat silently. Finally, Aleksy opened his eyes and turned to his siblings. "How about singing carols? Isn't it time to do that? Let's start with one of Tato's favorites. Remember?"

'*Gloria, Gloria, in excelsis Deo*' they sang. It was an honest thankful hymn this cold, snowy night. Father and children were grateful for God's gift of bringing them together. The blended voices in the room were made richer by Aleksy's beautiful baritone voice. They sang until it was time to leave for midnight mass.

Alexander looked at his children as they sat in the candle-lit church listening to the priest. He didn't have a job, but Aleksy was safe and in school, he and the children were living without fear, they had food to eat, and peace prevailed at the moment. He closed his eyes and whispered his thanks to God. He'd find a job; he always had. People need doctors.

Too soon Aleksy's school break ended. At the train station he put down his suitcase, hugged his father one last time, and made his plea again as he had each day since his arrival. "Think about moving, Tato. If the regional medical director won't hire you, try to get a job closer to the center of the country. You're a good doctor, and there's a clinic somewhere in Poland that needs you. You know, I've always admired the way you bounce back from tough times and look at the good side of things. I hope that when life deals me sadness, I can handle it the way you do."

Alexander walked home mulling over Aleksy's repeated plea. Maybe he was right.

The next afternoon he walked to the Kolenda's to see if Mieczylaw had time for a chess game. While they set up the board, Alexander talked about Aleksy's concerns.

"I think he's right." Mieczyslaw said as he pondered his first move. "An old family friend of ours has moved near Poznan. It's a lot farther from the border than here. We had a letter from him. He likes it there. It'd be safer if the borders change. They still haven't had a conference for a new peace treaty. What's to keep the allies from giving this back to the Germans? I think we should take the train to Poznan to see what it has to offer. Maybe we can get permission to move there. People usually don't get to move once they're settled, but we might get lucky. What've we got to lose?"

Using some of their dwindling money supply for train fare, the two men arrived at the Poznan repatriation office late on a snowy February morning. They sat for almost an hour in the crowded reception room waiting to see a repatriation official when Tomasz Bogucki stepped into the room from one of the offices.

Alexander looked at him and blinked. He wasn't sure he was the Bakshty police officer, but Mieczyslaw was. "Tomasz Bogucki? Is that you?" he asked rising to his feet. Bogucki stopped and turned.

"Dr. Kowal? Mr. Kolenda? What a surprise. Why are you in Poznan?"

It was the stroke of luck the men had hoped for. Officer Bogucki took his old friends into his office. After they related where they'd been and why they wanted to move, he offered to help.

Bogucki pulled a few strings and arranged for the two families' move to Trzcianka, a village near Poznan. He found a house for the Kowals on two hectares and one nearby for the Kolendas. The house had furniture and even some potatoes in the basement the uprooted German family had left. The Kowals and Kolendas moved from Gryfice the last week in April. It seemed like a good omen when the Kowal's sow produced a dozen piglets soon after. They sold them, replenishing their supply of cash. The Poznan repatriation office gave them food. But best of all, Bogucki found Alexander a temporary job as a social worker helping new settlers. As grateful as he was for this good fortune, he was still determined to find a job as a physician.

Politically, Poland was unstable. The supposedly temporary Soviet-controlled communist government, put in place in 1944, still ruled. The Polish government in exile, which had spent the war in England, had sent a representative back. He was campaigning to return the country to democracy, but the Soviet-controlled communist regime was pushing to keep Poland in its grip. A vote on a referendum to test the popularity of the temporary communist government hovered on the horizon.

Undaunted by his current situation, Alexander wrote letters to several regional medical offices closer to the center and the eastern border. A job there would be closer to Paceviche, which still felt like home.

Their garden was growing well as the referendum voting date, June 30th, grew near. "I can't see how we won't be independent," Mieczyslaw said. He and Alexander were sitting outside on a bench enjoying the late afternoon sunshine. "I don't think I've talked to anyone who wants the senate dissolved. That's the first of the three questions on the ballot, isn't it?"

"Yes. No one I've talked to is in favor of just one parliament body like the communists want. And who wants the government running industry? Nationalizing it is a bad idea. The government clogs everything it touches. It'll be run by a bunch of bureaucrats doing nothing but collecting a government paycheck. But I'm in favor of the third question about the western border. It should stay where it is. It'd be a mess to have people move back from where they just settled. I think the communists only set this referendum vote to give themselves time to tighten their hold before we have an election."

It took most of July for the results to be counted. Newspapers announced the results: All three referendum measures passed.

"Do you think they rigged the results?" Alexander asked Mieczyslaw after they played a Saturday afternoon chess match.

"That'd be my guess. They have no scruples. They want what's best for them, not what's best for us." He sighed and shook his head. "Now they've set the election for late January."

"That's crazy, Alexander replied. "It's the middle of winter. People most strongly opposed to the communists are in the villages easily isolated by snowstorms. You can't tell me that's a coincidence."

"All we wanted was to live in peace," Mieczyslaw grumbled. "Now the politicians are fighting for control. And who gets hurt? We do."

"I think we'd better be apolitical until the election. You know those communists. If you voice opposition, they'll find a way to get revenge. Remember when they were in charge in Belarus? They took our land, and we both nearly lost our lives." The men sat silently. Alexander moved his knight, looked across the board at his friend, and smiled. "At least we still have friends from behind the Bug." Mieczyslaw nodded in agreement.

It wasn't until several years later that the truth was revealed. The vote had been overwhelming against disbanding the senate, but the communists controlled the ballot boxes and falsified the results. It was the beginning of the communist's control of Poland, and it would be forty years before their grasp was unclenched.

A few weeks after the referendum results were announced, Alexander received a response to one of his letters. The county physician in charge of the Elk region had two open positions and invited him to visit.

"I have to check it out," he told Mieczyslaw.

"I suppose, but remember how dangerous it was last fall? No job is worth risking your family," Mieczyslaw cautioned. "I'm staying here. The land is pretty good. Maybe I'll exchange my certificate for a house. It doesn't feel like home here, but we're safe and I'm not ready to move again."

Alexander took the train to Elk wondering what he'd find. Happily, Dr. Blusewicz, the county physician, assured him right away that the looters who had terrorized the countryside had been caught or chased away. Walking the few blocks to the county offices, Alexander sensed that Elk residents were not afraid. Businesses were opened and had customers.

"Neither the clinic in Prostki nor Straduny is up and running yet," the neatly dressed Dr. Blusewicz said. He offered Alexander a cigarette from a slim silver case and leaned back in his chair and lit his own. "If you accept either position, you'll have to organize a clinic. The Prostki building needs some repair. A few apartments have occupants and they'll have to leave, but the building's in better shape than the one in Straduny. Let's drive out and look at both of them."

Alexander was not used to riding in a car. Riding in the county's old black sedan with its uniformed driver was a rare treat. It didn't take Alexander long to choose the Prostki clinic. The town was on the train line and larger than Straduny, which was farther away from Elk and accessible only by a dirt road. But even more important, schools in Prostki and Elk were open and the county doctor said the teachers were excellent. Danuta, Josef, and Zbigniew needed to be in school.

"I'd like to be in Prostki. I've organized clinics in Bakshty and Juracishki. I know how to get things done. I've also dealt with a typhus epidemic," Alexander said during supper at the county physician's home.

"You can make the clinic like you want it, within reason. Of course, a doctor with a current medical degree will be brought on board as soon as we can find one. But you'll still have a position as the physician's assistant. You probably have more experience than any doctor we can find, but your medical school work was so long ago. When can you begin?"

"As soon as I move my family." Alexander hadn't felt this eager to start a job in a very long time.

"I have confidence in you, Dr. Kowal. And I think you'll like it here."

Alexander returned to Trzcianka with a hopeful heart. Soon he could again practice medicine and his children could go to school.

Chapter 25

Prostki, Poland, Autumn, 1946

In October, 1946, just a little less than a year after they had arrived in Gryfice from Belarus, the Kowals moved to Prostki with their garden bounty packed in burlap bags, their well-traveled household goods, cow, horse, pig, and chickens. Danuta, Josef, and Zbigniew immediately enrolled in school a month after the fall term had begun. Always in the forefront of Alexander's mind was educating his children. The good schools in this area were the next step.

Feeling invigorated by the new challenge of organizing the Prostki clinic, he set about repairing the building. He found replacement windows and doors for the ones that had been stolen and workers to repair and paint the stucco.

Alexander envisioned a birthing center in the clinic. There was room on the second floor for one and an apartment for a midwife. It was a radical idea for the 1940s in rural Poland. Babies were born at home, not in clinics, but he had read about the lower infection and death rates at these new birthing centers.

The county physician was skeptical. "Even if you put it in, who's going to use it? Women don't want to give birth in some strange room. They want to be where things are familiar. Midwives are accustomed to traveling to people's homes."

Alexander was not to be deterred, and finally his supervisor said, "All right. Put in a birthing room and an apartment for a midwife. We can always use the space for some other purpose when no women come to use it."

A dentist's office and a spacious apartment for the yet-to-be-found doctor occupied the space next to the clinic on the first floor. The

Kowals moved into a two-bedroom apartment on the second floor across the hall from the birthing center, its nursery and kitchen. The midwife and nurse's small apartments took up the rest of that floor. In the attic above were two more small living spaces. With electricity, indoor plumbing, bathrooms, and cold water faucets, the apartment was the most modern place the Kowals had ever lived.

Behind the clinic was a shed with a small fenced yard for animals, a large garden space, and some fruit trees. In the cold, clear November air the week before the clinic was to be officially opened, Alexander stood on the cobblestone street in front of the newly refurbished clinic remembering the beer he took to his first assignment after medical school in Kryviche. He smiled. No party for me this time. He shook his head. "I was so naïve about the world," he mumbled to himself, "then it was the czar who controlled us, now here I am in a part of Poland that was Germany a couple of years ago." He wondered who would be in control after the elections. The democratic government? The communists? Time would tell.

A large crowd gathered outside the clinic on the day of the ribbon cutting. Government officials from Elk and the county physician made speeches. The bright red ribbon was cut and Alexander and the county physician proudly escorted the officials through the clinic. "And this is a birthing center," the county physician announced when they reached the freshly painted white door on the second floor. Alexander opened the door and the officials stepped inside.

The midwife beamed. "Welcome, gentlemen. As you can see, we already have our first baby." She gestured to a young, blond woman lying in bed holding an hours-old baby. "How do you like the center?" the midwife asked the new mother.

"It's wonderful," she said. "I had my first two babies at home, and this is so much better for the baby and me."

The county physician nodded and smiled as though the center had been his idea, and Alexander said nothing. It was enough to know the center would be a success. And it was wiser to let his supervisor take the credit.

Running the clinic took most of Alexander's waking hours. He tried unsuccessfully to hire a decent housekeeper. He couldn't find one who wasn't either lazy or dishonest. In between housekeepers, Danuta cleaned, cooked, and tried to keep up with her studies. Alexander wanted her to be able to devote most of her time to school, so the housekeeper situation was frustrating.

Danuta, Josef, and Zbigniew were working hard to catch up in school. Their home study during the recent tumultuous years had helped them pass some subject placement tests, but they were still behind in others. Ten-year-old Zbigniew and fourteen-year-old Josef were in the elementary school in Prostki, while nineteen-year-old Danuta took a five kilometer train ride to the high school in Grajewo.

Just as he had done in Juracishki, Alexander found himself maneuvering through the Soviet-style labyrinth of rules and regulations. It wasn't the freedom he'd hoped for. Why, he wondered, did the Americans and British agree to let the Soviets supervise Poland until the elections? Fear of the partisans that marked every day in Juracishki was gone, but the communists in charge here were just as capricious. Alexander could never completely quell the uneasiness that harbored within him. Political turmoil simmered beneath the surface of everyday routines. Newspapers were filled with stories about the upcoming election. Rumors spread about opposition leaders disappearing. Alexander concentrated on the clinic and his children and tried not to worry.

One of the first things Alexander did after they were settled was to write to Gregory, hoping he hadn't moved from his last address. Just before Christmas, 1946, the mailman delivered a notice to the clinic. Alexander had a letter at the post office. At noon he rushed through the snow-covered streets the two blocks to the post office, hoping in his heart that after seven years he was about to hear from his brother. He signed for the letter and hurried back to the apartment, but Alexander wasn't the first one to know the contents. The smudged envelope, addressed to him, had been opened as were all letters from "enemy countries." He unfolded the thin paper with anxious hands and read the letter written in his childhood language of Russian.

> My dear brother,
> How relieved I am to hear that you are safe and in Poland, but I'm sad to hear that your wife died during the German occupation. Salomea and I are well. Unhappily, we have had our share of grief. Two years ago our son Walter, while on leave from the army, died in a hotel fire. Our hearts are still shattered. Our son Peter was also in the army. He fought from Normandy to Vienna. They made him an interpreter, so he used the Russian he learned growing up. Thank God he returned safely and now lives at home and works at an electronics firm.
> Peter told us about the destruction he saw in Europe. He says it will take a very long time to rebuild. I think life must be hard for you now. Would you and your children like to come to America? I will be your sponsor. It's time I repaid you for sending me here. If you say yes, we can begin making plans. How good it would be to see you and meet your children.
> Your loving brother, Gregory

Alexander folded the letter and slipped it back into the dirty envelope. Well, Gregory, you didn't mean to, but this puts me in a tough spot, he thought. You wouldn't have written so openly if you knew what it's like here. Having a relative in America was a black mark noted in Alexander's files. A letter asking him to come to America made the black mark darker and bigger.

Go to America? Alexander hadn't even considered the possibility. Was it even feasible? I'll talk to Aleksy when he comes next week for

Christmas holiday, he thought.

Danuta, Aleksy, and their father were sitting at the kitchen table drinking tea while the boys were sledding when Alexander pulled out his brother's letter. "You two need to hear this. It's from your Uncle Gregory."

He began reading. Aleksy and Danuta listened intently. Alexander finished and looked at them. "Well, what do you think?" he asked slipping the fragile letter back into its envelope.

"A chance to go to America? I never thought this could even happen," Danuta said. The ticking of the clock was the only sound for a moment. "Do you want to go, Tato?" Danuta asked. He shrugged his shoulders.

"We're always hearing stories about the golden opportunities in America," Aleksy said. His mind filled with images of life in a country free from government control where you could choose to work where you wanted to work instead of where you were assigned. That must be nice. Then he frowned. Questions washed through him. "How could I practice medicine? I don't know English. Do you think they'd accept my medical degree from here?"

"I don't know. But I do know that if one of us goes, we all go," Alexander said. He paused and looked at them. "We've come through too much to split our family again. We. . ."

Aleksy interrupted. "If we go. . ." He stopped and swallowed. "There's someone I want to take with us." He stopped again and took a deep breath. "I've met a wonderful girl at med school. Her name's Halina. She's going to be a dentist." He smiled. "I was going to tell you at supper that we're planning to get married next June. I want you to meet her soon. I know you'll like her, Tato."

"A sister at last?" Danuta grinned. "This is great news. Congratulations, big brother." She leaned over and hugged him.

This wasn't quite how Alexander had imagined this conversation would go. He offered his congratulations and brought out vodka for a toast. "Of course, Halina should go if we do," Alexander told Aleksy.

"Thanks. I'll have to talk with her. She might not want to leave her family, but she might like the idea of a fresh start in a free society." Aleksy furrowed his brow. "Tato, what kind of job can you get in America when you don't speak English?"

"My career is nearing its end. How many more years can I even practice medicine here? Not many. Your careers are the important ones. If we live with Gregory for a while, I suppose I'll find something. I guess that's a question to ask him. I don't think he'd offer to sponsor us if he didn't plan on us living with them for a while."

"Well, I'd have to learn English. Halina too. It'll take awhile."

"That's true," Alexander agreed. "But then you'd be free to be a doctor wherever you want. Imagine being able to choose to go to any city in America. The government wouldn't be directing your life." This kind of freedom was hard to comprehend.

"And the boys?" Aleksy asked. They'd have to learn English. They're already working hard to catch up. I think another move would be really tough on them." Even though Aleksy was excited by the vision of living in America, his medical training made him look at all the possibilities with rationality.

"They're young," Danuta responded. "Learning English would be easiest for them. It'd be another big change, but they could do it. I'm just beginning my adult life, and if you want to go, I'm ready." Her heart raced at the idea of going to America, but she tried to maintain a calm demeanor and be rational like Aleksy. Freedom. Opportunities. It was almost too much to comprehend.

"I hadn't even considered going until I got Gregory's letter. I just keep thinking about the communists taking over here like they did in Belarus. The election is only four weeks away, and maybe the communists will be voted out, but I'm afraid they won't. I've lived under their repression for so long, and it's…" His voice faded and he looked out the window at the snow-covered trees.

"That's so true, Tato," Aleksy replied. "When I was hiding from the

Soviets, I used to think about Uncle Gregory and how good his life must be without all the fear and restrictions. I never asked why you didn't go to America, too."

"I sent Gregory to keep him out of the army. I saw war coming and knew he'd be killed if he was drafted. But I had a profession and thought I'd be safe." He didn't add that he was courting Olimpia and couldn't imagine leaving her. "When he left for America, Gregory wasn't much older than Josef is now. Today I'm not sure I could send my son off alone like that. Perhaps I'm wiser now. Or maybe a little more cautious."

When the boys came back from sledding, the discussion ended with no decision. Alexander lay in bed that night unable to sleep. He made a mental list of the pros and cons of going to America.

Their talk of emigrating continued for the rest of the week. Leaving, even though it offered golden opportunities, meant giving up the most stable life they'd had in six years. Alexander still hadn't used the certificate for a house to replace the property he'd given up in Belarus. He knew they would have their own house here one day. His children could complete their education in Poland. And that was ultimately most important.

"They can take your land, your house, your money," he told Aleksy and Danuta, "but they can never take what's in your mind. If you have an education and a profession like medicine, you can survive the hard times. Education is what I want for all of you. Danuta, I know you and the boys will go to college here. I don't know enough about America to know if that can happen there. I think we should stay."

Aleksy sipped his tea and nodded. "I agree, Tato. It would be hard for Halina to leave her mother. She's a widow and depends on Halina and her sister. And we'll both have our professions here. If we were to go to America, we'd have to start over. Here as a doctor and a dentist we'll have a decent life. We won't have the freedom it sounds like they have in America, but we will be near family and that's important to us."

"I understand how you feel, Aleksy," Danuta smiled at him. "Going to America sounds exciting, but Halina wouldn't want to leave her mother. I'll have a profession here. If I had to learn English and start over. . . . Well, that would be difficult. Realistically, it's better that we stay here."

Alexander wrote to Gregory thanking him for the offer, but declining to come. He knew the letter would be read by some government clerk. Would his refusal of his brother's offer shrink the black mark by his name? He'd never know. Sometime this bit of family connection might crop up in a way he couldn't even imagine at the moment. Bitter, cold wind blew, numbing Alexander's face as he trudged to the post office through small drifts of new-fallen snow. He held the white envelope in his gloved hand and hesitated before he gave it to the postmaster. I hope I'm doing the right thing, he thought. He put the letter on the counter and paid the postage. Pulling his overcoat collar up around his neck, he went back into the swirling snow. He'd closed the door to leaving Poland.

In February he had cause to reconsider his decision. Newspaper headlines shouted what he had feared. The Soviet puppet government was overwhelmingly favored by the Poles. Anticipating persecution, prominent members of the opposition fled back to England. Increasing tension and control chilled the Poles much more than the freezing winter weather.

"I don't believe these results, Tato," Danuta said. She handed the newspaper back to her father. "Too many people who opposed to the communists couldn't get through the snow to vote. It's been a really bad winter and it was hard for people to get to the polls. But I'll bet the communists falsified the results so only votes in their favor were counted anyway. Who voted probably didn't make any difference. It wasn't a real election." She stopped and sighed. "Is this place going to end up like Belarus?"

Alexander shook his head. "I hope not, but it isn't the free country we thought it would be. Not much we can do about it. We're going to have to learn to deal with the system. It may not be fair, but we have to make the best of it. That's just the way life is. It's probably wise to keep our political opinions to ourselves. You know a lot of people were "convinced" to vote for the communists with threats or bribes."

"That's for sure," Danuta agreed. "A couple families at school suddenly moved to bigger apartments just before the election. But Krystyna's father was arrested. He was very vocal about his support of the opposition. The family doesn't know where he is. Remember the day those soldiers came to the house in Juracishki and took you away? I thought we'd never see you again." Father and daughter slipped into their own memories.

Alexander looked at Danuta and broke the silence. "Threats and bribes. That's how they always operate wherever they seize control. I'd hoped it would be different now, but it's not going to be, I'm afraid. Always be careful who you trust, Danuta." She understood.

"The way you've persevered all these years, Tato, is amazing. You never seem to give up hope that life will be better. I try to be like that, too, but it's not easy."

"It's the only way I know to survive. I choose not to let the day-to-day bruising of living destroy my hope for something better tomorrow. I enjoy my family and my work. I simply choose not to let all that other stuff interfere with those two things." Danuta knew this was true. She hoped she could keep the balance in her life that her father had "And, I've survived. And because I'm a physician, so have you and your brothers," he added.

In spite of the political climate, by 1948 Prostki felt like home. Danuta would graduate from high school in the spring with a teaching certificate and an assignment to teach in a specific school in Elk. But medicine was on her mind. She had become friends with the midwife who lived down the hall. After talking to her, Danuta thought about how much she liked helping her father in Paceviche when patients came to the house.

She confided to her father that she wanted to be a midwife. Alexander was delighted. "I'll do everything I can to see that you can get out of your teaching assignment and go into the medical field." Alexander hated the bribery culture, but a bottle of good liquor to an official brought Danuta a paper giving her permission to go to midwifery school in Bialystok.

"You'll always have a job," Alexander told his daughter, "no matter what the political situation."

The one irritation in his life Alexander could not solve was the constant problem of finding and keeping housekeepers. After he fired the third one for stealing, Danuta said, "Tato, you need to get married. I'll be leaving soon. You need a wife."

"Perhaps you're right," he shook his head, "but where would I find a wife? I don't know any suitable women. I haven't even thought about another wife."

Danuta was resolute. "Ask your friends. There are so many single women."

Alexander looked at his twenty-year-old daughter. She was a young woman now. It would be just the boys with him when she left for school in the fall. He thought of himself at her age, getting ready to go out into the world with such hope. So in love with Olimpia. So excited about his first medical assignment. When he closed his eyes, he could still see Olimpia at that first dance at medical school. How long ago was that, he thought? He did the math in his head. Almost forty years, but her image was still fresh in his heart.

His thoughts turned to his children. I suppose Danuta will fall in love and marry before too many years. The idea startled him. My children are growing up, he acknowledged to himself. Before I know it, the boys will be leaving, too. I'll be alone in a few years.

I guess maybe I do need a wife, he pondered. But where to find one? He considered the women he knew in Prostki and concluded none were suitable.

"I'll think about it," he said to Danuta.

Chapter 26

Prostki, Poland, Spring, 1948

April weather was warm and dry when Alexander decided to take the overnight train to visit his old friends Tomasz and Katherine Bogucki in Poznan. Perhaps they knew a nice woman from home. If he was going to marry again, Alexander thought, a woman from behind the Bug River would be best. Most suitable. Most like him.

Tomasz Bogucki met his old Paceviche friend at the depot just after sunrise. Katherine had a huge breakfast waiting for them. They were nearly finished eating when Alexander brought up the reason for his visit.

"I've decided to marry again if I can find the right woman. My daughter's been encouraging me. I've had a series of housekeepers, and they've all been less than adequate. Zbigniew is almost twelve, still young, and he needs a mother. Danuta's probably right. I should marry again, but I don't know any eligible women. Do you?" He looked first at Tomasz and then Katherine. "I think I'd like to find a woman from home." He took the last bite of the fried eggs.

"I don't. Or at least none I'd recommend," Tomasz laughed. "Katherine, you know more women than I do."

She thought for a moment. "Well, there's my niece Maria. She's a primary school teacher in Karolewo, a small village near Ketrzyn. It's about two hours by train from Prostki. You went through there on your way here." Katherine poured the men more coffee. "Maria moved to Poland with her family in '46. Lucky they got out then. It sounds like the Bolsheviks pretty well shut down the border right after that." Katherine smiled and smoothed her crisply ironed skirt. "Not too smart, those Bolsheviks, to think people would want to live in Belarus when life's better here. Why would anyone want to go back and work on a collective farm when they can have their own land here?" Alexander and Tomasz nodded in agreement. Katherine, dressed fashionably even at this early hour, stood and carried the plates to the sink.

"Maria and her parents, her youngest brother, and sisters got to come because of her oldest brother. He was drafted by the Soviets, and then after the war was given a small farm in Guty not too far from Ketrzyn. He helped the rest of his family get repatriation papers." Katherine waited for Alexander to say something, but he just took another drink of his coffee and waited for her to continue.

"Maria's in her thirties and has never been married. She's smart and has a curious mind. She's an excellent cook and keeps a clean house. And she loves children."

Alexander was quiet for several more minutes. Katherine didn't rush him, but gave him time to think about her suggestion. "All right. I'd like to meet her. How do we go about it?"

Katherine didn't respond for a moment. A debate was going on in her head. Am I doing the right thing? Alexander is almost sixty, an old man. Maria's only thirty-five. An awfully big age difference. But I've already told him about her. I guess she can make up her own mind. Reject him if she doesn't like him. Maria's old enough to know what she wants. Katherine clasped her well-manicured, soft hands together. "I'll write her a letter to introduce you. Since Karolewo is on your way home, you can stop and meet her. Get off in Sterlawki and pay someone to take you to the school house where she lives. It's not far."

Four hours before sunrise Alexander climbed aboard the eastbound night train with a jar of Nescafe in his bag as a gift for Maria. He slept for awhile and as the sun rose ate the bread and hard boiled eggs Katherine had packed. When he arrived in Sterlawki just before noon Sunday morning, he looked for someone with a wagon. He watched a bearded farmer wave goodbye to people on the train and walk to the hitching post where the man's horse and wagon waited. For a few *zlotys* the man was happy to drive Alexander the five kilometers to Karolewo and back to the station later.

"I'll see you at four o'clock," Alexander said to the farmer. The man lifted his hat in agreement and left. Alexander assumed Maria was home. Watching the farmer disappear, it occurred to him that she might not be there. He knocked on the school's front door. A slim, short woman with brown eyes and long chestnut hair pulled back with bobby pins opened the door.

"Maria Kiemlicz?" She nodded. Before she could say anything he continued. "I'm Alexander Kowal. I'm old friends with your Aunt Katherine Bogucki and her husband Tomasz. I knew them in Paceviche." He handed her the letter. "This is an introduction from Katherine. I was just visiting them. She thought we should meet. I'm on my way home to Prostki. He motioned to the farmer headed down the road. "That gentlemen will be back to pick me up in time to take me to the evening train."

Maria opened the letter. The third sentence was the one she paid most attention to. "Welcome our friend Dr. Alexander Kowal just as you would welcome me." Maria smiled. "Please, come in." Her aunt was telling her that this was someone she could trust, a man of good character. Someone who could become a good friend. Maria opened the door on the left side of the hallway that led to her apartment. "You may put your hat and bag over there," she said indicating a hook and bench near the door.

Alexander hung up his coat and from his bag took out the jar of Nescafe instant coffee that Tomasz had procured from UNRRA supplies. "Tomasz and Katherine thought you might enjoy this."

Maria looked at the unfamiliar jar.

"It's Nescafe," Alexander explained. "From America. It's instant coffee, and quite good."

"Let's try some now," Maria replied. "I'll fix ham and bread to go with it. You must be hungry after your trip."

Alexander surveyed the tidy apartment while Maria was busy in the kitchen. Through a partially opened door, he could see into one bedroom with its white iron bed and dark chest. Very clean, he observed. Two other doors, he guessed, led to other bedrooms. "This is a nice apartment," he commented, "and so convenient with the school right across the hall. My children and I have an apartment above the clinic."

"How old are your children?"

"My daughter is twenty and my sons are sixteen and twelve. And I have a thirty-year-old son in medical school.

Maria put the food and two cups of Nescafe on the table. "This will be enough for now while I fix us some dinner," she said placing plates of homemade bread, ham, and butter in front of him." That she had food she could fix for unexpected guests was the sign of a well-run household. Alexander was pleased. And the ham was excellent. They continued to visit as Maria cooked.

"I grew up not far from Paceviche," Maria said. She stopped cutting potatoes for a moment and sipped the hot Nescafe. "Our family farm was about twenty-five kilometers from there. We were deep in the forest. Pretty isolated, but the Germans found us. They gave us a couple of hours to pack whatever we could in the wagon before they burned the house and barn. We had to watch. They wouldn't let us leave until they were sure nothing exploded. They wanted to be sure we weren't hiding partisans' explosives."

Alexander shared his family's war experiences briefly, brushing over the worst parts. "What did you do during the war after your home was burned?"

"I taught elementary school before the war. When the Germans closed the schools, I worked in a sawmill." She noted his look of surprise. "I'm short, but strong. It was hard physical work, but I did it. And compared to what an awful lot of people did to survive, it wasn't bad."

From the pantry Maria brought out onions and yesterday's meatloaf, which she made into meatballs. She grated potatoes and mixed them with leftover mashed potatoes. Then she molded the potato mixture around the meatballs. Alexander's mouth watered. Maria was making *pyzy*, a favorite of his. It was a rich dish, typical of upper class cuisine Olimpia had made long ago. Maria fried bacon and onions while she boiled the potato-wrapped meatballs. Then she put the hot meatballs into the cast iron skillet and covered them with the bacon mixture.

"Pyzy. I haven't had these in years," Alexander said as he cut the first bite. She likes children, her house is neat, and she's a good cook, he thought. For dessert she served slices of spicy honey cake.

They were still sitting at the table talking when the farmer came to take Alexander back to the train station. "I've enjoyed our visit. I'm glad Katherine suggested I stop to meet you. May I come again?"

"I'd like that," she replied. He's well-educated, she thought. And he certainly dresses neatly. And he's interesting to talk to.

"Perhaps three weeks from today?" Alexander asked picking up his bag and hat.

"Three weeks? Yes, that'll be nice." Maria extended her hand. Alexander instinctively took her hand in his and kissed it. Upper-class women expected such social graces, and she was an upper-class Polish woman.

Maria looked out the window at the disappearing wagon and turned to clean up. Only two pyzy remained on the blue flowered plate. Dr. Kowal seemed to like my cooking, she thought as she cleared the table. He was very different from the rich but uneducated farmer whose attentions she had spurned last winter.

Chapter 27

Prostki, Poland, 1947

Alexander wrote a carefully worded letter of thanks to Maria and told Danuta about his visit. She, in turn, told her brothers.

"Tato has a new friend. A woman. She's a teacher in Karolewo. He's going to see her again next month."

"What kind of friend?" Josef asked. "A friend, or more than a friend?"

"They just met." In case this Maria didn't work out, Danuta decided to avoid explaining until later that their father was looking for a new wife.

Maria responded to Alexander's letter telling him she was looking forward to his coming visit and she had arranged for the parent of one of her students to pick him up at the rail station.

When Alexander arrived, Maria had *bigos* stew and boiled potatoes cooking on the stove. "You spoil me with so much delicious food," he told her.

"It's just some Polish cooking," she replied, but she was pleased with the compliment.

Conversation flowed easily. Walking around a nearby lake after dinner, they discovered that they both enjoyed reading and shared a common interest in certain authors.

Alexander next visited the first week in June after the family went to Gostynin for Halina and Aleksy's wedding. At the ceremony, the Kowals sat next to Olimpia's brother Bronis and his son Czeslaw, a Catholic priest. Seeing Bronis brought back memories of Olimpia. Alexander smiled remembering his first visits to the Legutko estate. Bronis' polite disapproval of him that slowly warmed to friendship as his visits continued. Watching Halina walk into the church in her white satin wedding dress, the vision of Olimpia in her gown flashed through his mind. He missed having a companion.

Listening to young couple say their vows, Alexander found himself thinking about Maria. She was a smart woman and they were comfortable with each other. She enjoyed serious conversations and laughed easily. She loved children. And when her opinion differed from his, she readily defended her view, but in a calm manner. He liked her even temperament. He looked forward to his visits. If we married, we could be happy, he thought. His attention returned to the ceremony when Aleksy slipped Olimpia's gold band onto Halina's finger.

Tato, "We've both been assigned to work in Ketrzyn," Aleksy told his father at the reception after the wedding.

"Ketrzyn? It's a nice town. I've been nearby there several times recently," Alexander said. Aleksy looked at his father quizzically with an unspoken 'why' in his eyes. "I've become friends with a woman who teaches in Karolewo," Alexander added.

"A woman friend? Are you courting her?" Aleksy grinned at his father.

"Well, I suppose you could say that."

The news surprised Aleksy. It hadn't occurred to him that his father might like to marry again at his age. "It's not something I anticipated, but I'm happy for you. You've been alone a long time."

"I'd like you to meet her. She's a bit younger than I am, but we are quite compatible." He didn't mention that Aleksy was only four years younger than Maria.

Alexander's regular visits to the brick schoolhouse continued for the rest of the summer. In July, soon after Aleksy and Halina started their jobs in Ketrzyn, he took Maria to meet them.

Alexander saw the surprise in their eyes at Maria's age. While the women were in the kitchen preparing supper, he broached the subject with Aleksy. "I know she's much younger than you expected. But that doesn't bother us. She makes me happy, son. We're good friends. I don't want to grow old alone. Do you understand?"

"If she's a good match for you, then marry her if you want." Aleksy hesitated. He put his hand on his father's shoulder. "I'll get used to the idea that she's close to my age. If she wants to marry someone as old as you, that's her decision."

Now that Maria had met Aleksy, it was time, Alexander decided, for Maria to meet Danuta, Josef, and Zbigniew. The visit was arranged for late August before school started and Danuta went to Bialystok. No mention of marriage had ever been made during his visits or in their letters, but unspoken was the knowledge that if they weren't interested in a lifetime commitment, the relationship would have ended soon after Alexander's first appearance at the schoolhouse.

The Kowals woke before dawn the day of Maria's visit.. Danuta and the boys had spent the last week cleaning and were scurrying to finish the last tasks.

"Now listen," Danuta admonished her brothers. "Be nice to her. And polite. For heaven's sake watch your manners at the table. And, Zbigniew, don't just sit there saying nothing during dinner and then disappear into your room. Talk to her. Answer any questions she asks with more than one word. Maria might be our new mother and we need to make a good impression. Understood?"

Zbigniew didn't remember his own mother. Losing her, running from the Germans, seeing his father taken away by the communists had all been traumatic. The twelve-year old was quiet and somewhat reclusive, seldom sharing his feelings or thoughts with anyone. Danuta hoped that Maria could befriend Zbigniew and give him the kind of love a boy needs from a mother.

Josef and Zbigniew promised to be on their best behavior. "Tato's been seeing her for a long time. I think he likes her," Josef said. "What'll she think of us?"

Alexander met Maria's train on the last Sunday of August. It was a crisp sunny day, and they walked the few blocks back to the clinic. Maria had brought a basket with two jars of wild strawberry jam, and a dozen *paczki*, soft rolls filled with sweet cherry preserves and dusted with powdered sugar, a gift she thought everyone would like.

Danuta had dinner waiting when they arrived. Maria was accustomed to children and with her easy manner, the boys relaxed. For dessert they ate the paczki, which were a hit with everyone. Josef and Zbigniew showed her their school books and some of their homework. Maria and Danuta talked with ease as they cleared the table and did the dishes. Alexander sat back watching. I think they like her, he observed silently. The day is slipping by more quickly and with less tension than I expected. He smiled to himself.

"Your children are delightful, Alexander," Maria said as they stood on the platform waiting for the train. "And they're bright. You're a fortunate man. And to think you raised them practically all by yourself. You've done a good job."

Alexander smiled. "That means a great deal, coming from you. I'm glad you got to meet them, especially Danuta since she leaves for school next week. May I come to visit a week from today?" Maria agreed. She climbed aboard the train. Alexander watched her take a seat. She looked out the dusty window and waved. I miss her when she leaves, Alexander mused.

"Did you like Maria?" Alexander asked Zbigniew.

"She's very nice," Zbigniew said quietly looking up from the book he was reading.

"She's good," Josef said. "And she makes great paczki. You can marry her."

Alexander chuckled. "Danuta?"

"I like her, too. We all do. Marry her if you want, Tato. You have my permission," she teased.

Alexander made his decision. He'd propose marriage next week.

He wasn't as nervous as he had been those many years ago driving up the tree-lined lane to ask Olimpia's father for her hand in marriage, but a few butterflies still seemed to have taken up residence in his stomach. He closed his eyes, and to the rhythm of the train wheels, rehearsed what he'd say to Maria.

Maria's apartment was filled with delicious aromas when he arrived. She had spent the morning making *zrazy*, thin rectangles of beef rolled around a pickle, mushrooms, onion, and bacon. She placed the platter of steaming zrazy, grated beets, and cooked buckwheat on the table. For dessert she'd made an apple pie from apples picked by students. Alexander ate heartily, but his mind was churning. It was a warm cloudless day, so they sat outside after dinner watching the birds and squirrels in the trees that were already beginning to show hints of their brilliant fall colors. "We've come to be good companions these past months, haven't we? I enjoy your company, and I think you like being with me." He paused.

"Yes, I look-forward to your visits and letters." She smiled. "We always seem to find common interests to talk about, don't we? I enjoyed being at your house with you and the children. I like them."

"Well, they like you, too. In fact, they said it was all right if I marry you." He took her hand in his. "Maria, I think we're quite compatible. You're kind and good with children. I've come to love you, and . . . ." He hesitated. "So, I think we should marry."

Maria had felt this question was coming, but now that he had asked, words caught in her throat. She squeezed his hand. It took a long moment for her to respond. "I think we're very compatible, too, and I love you. Yes, I agree. I think we should marry. But I have to finish my contract here." Her voice was soft and her pulse quickened.

Alexander broke into a wide grin. "Yes, of course. How about February? Danuta will be on winter break."

Maria nodded. "February will be fine." They sat quietly for a few minutes listening to the wind rustling the trees. Alexander broke the silence. "We must go to your parents soon and ask for your father's blessing."

The next Sunday Maria met Alexander at the train station in Gizycko. Her father was waiting with his wagon for the hour-long ride to Guty.

"Tato, this is Dr. Alexander Kowal."

"Dr. Kowal from Paceviche?"

"Yes, sir. That's where I grew up and practiced for many years."

"I think we met at Tomasz and Katherine Bogucki's in Paceviche a long time ago. I was visiting and you came to see Tomasz. Katherine's my cousin."

All the way home the two men talked about people they both knew and events they remembered from Paceviche. Maria just listened, pleased that her father and her fiancé were getting along so well.

While Maria and her mother were busy in the kitchen putting the finishing touches on dinner, Alexander brought up the reason for the visit.

"Sir, your daughter and I have been acquainted since last spring. We've become friends, and have many interests in common. We've decided to marry, and I'd be grateful for your blessing. I believe I can offer Maria a good life." He paused. "Of course, we'll be married in the Catholic church in Sterlawki."

Maria's father couldn't hide his surprise, and was speechless for a moment. "To meet someone from behind the Bug," he said regaining his composure. "I never though Maria would marry someone here from home." A smile lit up his face. "Yes, you and Maria have my blessing Dr. Kowal." He reached out to shake Alexander's hand. "Come, we must toast this wonderful news."

The visit was short as Alexander and Maria had to catch the afternoon trains so they could return to work the next day.

Alexander looked out the train window. The visit to Maria's parents had gone well. The children will be happy, he thought. He closed his eyes listening to the rhythmic clacking of the train on the tracks. Should we have a child, Alexander wondered? He thought about it for several miles. Yes, he decided. One child. Maria is young and should have a child of her own, and a child will help cement the marriage. He smiled.

"It's settled, he told Josef and Zbigniew as they ate their supper. You're going to have a new mother in February."

"That's great, Tato. She sure cooks better than any of the housekeepers we've had," Josef said.

"How come you're waiting until February? Why can't she come now?" Zbigniew asked softly. The house was lonely with Danuta at school.

"Well, she has to finish teaching the fall term. The village needs time to find a replacement for her. Would you like to visit her in Karolewo?"

It was, Zbigniew recalled later, a memorable day at Maria's school. She made him her helper and let him ring the bell when it was time to start or end a lesson. "I felt very special," he told his youngest sister years later. "I was glad to have a new mother."

For Alexander, marrying in the Catholic Church was risky. The communists tolerated Catholics, but attending Mass, being married in the church or having a child baptized was seen as a form of defiance. It could be cause for losing a job. As soon as Maria finished the school term, she packed her belongings and moved to Prostki. She and Alexander went to the government office and had a civil ceremony on February 20. In the eyes of the government, they were married, but not in the eyes of the church. Maria was a woman of strong faith, and a church wedding was important to her.

The following week Alexander, Maria, Danuta, and the boys went to Guty. To Alexander's co-workers in Prostki, it was a visit to his new in-laws. But the real purpose was to be married in the Catholic Church. Katherine and Tomasz came from Poznan, Aleksy and Halina from Ketrzyn. Katherine took charge and organized the wedding party. At ten o'clock on a cold winter morning Alexander and Maria and two other couples stood before the priest in the unheated church to say their vows in a wedding mass. After mass the family wrapped themselves in blankets for the hour sleigh ride in the crystal morning air to Maria's parents' home in Guty for the reception. Sleighs and sleds lined up in their yard all the way past the barn as family, friends, and neighbors joined the party. Inside vodka flowed freely and tables almost bent under their loads of food. After having their fill of cold cuts, ham, sausages, pickles, and fresh bread and butter, guests helped themselves to bowls of chicken soup before moving on to the main course, roasted pork loin from the pig that had been butchered for the occasion, potatoes, salads, and sauerkraut. These dishes were cleared, and the layer cakes Katherine had baked and decorated ended the meal. One cousin brought out his accordion and serenaded the newlyweds. It was a noisy, joy-filled day in a house brimming with people celebrating Maria and Alexander's marriage.

The next day the Kowals returned to Prostki to begin a new life. They made no mention of their church wedding to any of their acquaintances.

Chapter 28

Prostki, Poland, 1949

Maria awoke at five o'clock, slipped out of bed in the chilly bedroom, dressed quietly, and went to the kitchen. She lit kindling in the kitchen stove and stoked the fire with coal. An hour later she had milk soup simmering, and water boiling for tea. The rest of the family rose and joined her. She sliced bread and fried eggs for breakfast and made sandwiches for the boys to take to school. Josef left at seven to catch the train to the high school in Elk. Half-an-hour later Zbigniew, bundled up against the freezing February wind, left for the elementary school. Alexander finished his cup of tea and went downstairs to the clinic at eight.

For the first time Maria was left alone in the apartment. She could hear a new baby crying in the nursery across the hall, but when he stopped, it was quiet. Maria finished the breakfast dishes and filled a pot with potatoes and grain to boil for the pig. Before putting anything away, she washed the cabinet shelves until they were spotless. Next she put on her heavy coat and galoshes and went to the shed to take care of the chickens and pig.

Back inside she lit fires in the bedroom stoves and straightened the rest of the apartment, dusting, sweeping, and washing. The last housekeeper had not cleaned to Maria's standards. By the time Alexander came upstairs for his noon meal, the kitchen, living room, and bathroom were sparkling, and Maria had food ready for him. When Zbigniew arrived home from school, the aroma of simmering stuffed cabbages filled the apartment.

Maria added a much-needed woman's touch to the Kowal home. Each Sunday she took the boys to Mass just as Danuta had. Alexander did not go with them. He was afraid he'd lose his job if he was seen at church. Maria's faith imbued the household with a sense of serenity. Winter winds blew outside, but inside life was warm and happy.

Alexander wrote to Gregory, Melanie, and the Kolendas telling them of his marriage. Each wrote a letter of congratulations, but the Kolenda's letter had additional news of their old home. "We heard from my cousins who still live in Bakshty. The Bolsheviks are cutting down the forests. They're taking every tree large or small. They haven't cut yours or ours yet, but they will soon."

Alexander shook his head as he read the letter to Maria. "Don't those Bolsheviks understand what they're doing? Cutting everything is the worst thing they could do. It'll cause floods in the spring, and all the animals will be displaced. And what about the other plants like mushrooms that won't grow? I'm glad I'm not there to watch. It'd break my heart." He bit his lip as he folded the letter. "So many good memories of hunting mushrooms in the forest. And some not so good of hiding there from the Germans."

Maria agreed. "Living here is far from perfect, but it's so much better than what we left."

When spring arrived, Maria planted a garden after the boys helped her turn the soil. Each row of young plants made her feel more connected to Prostki. By July, weeding in the cool early mornings became more difficult. Maria was pregnant with the child Alexander had decided they should have. Her stomach felt queasy for the next month, but she was delighted to be expecting soon after their first wedding anniversary. Alexander was also pleased. It was just as he had planned their life together, and he looked forward to having a baby in the house.

On February 28, 1950, Maria gave birth to John, Alexander's sixth son. *My family is complete*, Alexander thought as he held the healthy boy in his arms in the nursery. *Just one girl, but that's all right.* "You'll always be there for your mother," he whispered, rocking the chubby hours-old baby. "I'll try not to make the same mistakes. I promise."

Alexander said, thinking of Arkady.

When John was two weeks old, Maria took him to church, and he was baptized. There was no party, nothing to call attention to this act of faith, nothing to put Alexander's position in jeopardy. It was part of the game played with the communist rulers. Seventeen-year-old Josef was half-way through his course at the teacher's school in Elk when his youngest brother was born. Twelve-year-old Zbigniew loved having a new baby brother and played with him every day after school.

When John was two, Josef left for college to become a math teacher. Alexander couldn't contain his disappointment. "You're so good at math and science. You'd do well in medicine. I understand your wanting to be a teacher. You know that's what I first hoped to be. But I'm so glad I ended up in medical school. As a doctor you will always survive. Even in the hard times people will pay you in food." Alexander pressed on trying to convince Josef to study medicine. "Things are stable now, but you don't know what it'll be like in ten years. I thought the end of the first war and the revolution meant peace. But it didn't. I lost everything but my ability to be a doctor. Remember fleeing and hiding from the Germans? Sometimes we were hungry and didn't know where we'd sleep the next night, but we all survived because even the Germans needed a doctor." Josef had heard the lecture many times, but his heart wasn't in medicine. He admired his teachers and liked explaining complex ideas to people.

"Doctors need good teachers, too," Josef told his father. Alexander couldn't change his mind, but quiet Zbigniew sitting in the chair behind a book was listening. Alexander didn't know then that the young boy would become the fourth doctor in the family.

The physician's apartment in the clinic remained vacant. Since no doctor was assigned to the Prostki clinic, Alexander remained in charge. However, he knew that when a doctor was found to run the clinic, he might have to move. It was unlikely the government would think the population of Prostki was large enough for two doctors.

Alexander might be assigned to a different job. The future was uncertain, but he didn't let that deter him from making the most of each day at the clinic, always looking for ways to improve the quality of medical service.

The clinic staff was congenial and worked well together. Part of Alexander's job was hygiene and health education. On occasion, dealing with a medically unsophisticated populace proved challenging. At the end of one long day, the nurse told Alexander that a thermometer was missing. The entire staff searched every shelf and drawer to no avail. Several days later a patient arrived at the front desk and handed the clerk the thermometer.

"This thing really works well," she said. "I kept it under my arm the whole time, and now I feel much better."

Working under a repressive system required patience and a certain degree of guile. Fear of the communist officials was always present. Outwardly everyone obeyed the rules and regulations, but each person had his own way of circumventing the system when necessary. Like everyone else, Alexander coped with government hypocrisy, rampant bribery, the necessity of buying things on the black market, and tight control of all facets of life by those in charge. These were all just a part of the fabric of the society, and Alexander did not let them make him bitter as many of his fellow Poles did. In spite of the hardships, the family was happy. All of Alexander's children were getting an education. That was most important. Leaving the farm he had inherited from his father, leaving behind all the land and forests he had purchased between the wars, leaving the place he would always think of as home and moving to Poland were worth it if his children were all educated.

After having been a midwife for two years, Danuta told her father that she was going to go to medical school to become a doctor. Alexander's heart filled with joy.

"I'm tired of having doctors tell me what to do. I want to be the one making the decisions in the delivery room, so I'm going to be an obstetrician," she explained.

A few weeks before Christmas, Maria realized she was pregnant again. Alexander thought she might just be starting menopause. However, he was wrong. The news was unsettling to both of them. "Thirty-nine is old to be pregnant, I know, but I'm healthy," Maria assured him with more confidence that she felt.

"And I'll be sixty-two when this baby is born." Alexander looked at the strands of gray in Maria's hair. "With the pernicious anemia I developed this year, the chances of my being alive when this child reaches adulthood aren't good." Maria watched the cloud of concern wash over her husband's face. "You may have to raise this child without me."

"Every child's a blessing," she replied. "It will be good for John to have a little brother or sister. With the boys gone, he's going to be like an only child. It'll be all right." She didn't want Alexander to be concerned. "Yes, I'll be almost sixty when this baby leaves for college, but we don't know what God's plan is for us." She would just have to take good care of herself, she thought. They ate supper in near silence. While Maria did the dishes, Alexander read a book to John. But when Maria took John into the bedroom to get him ready for bed, Alexander left the apartment and went for a walk in the twilight.

The bare tree branches swayed in the chilly wind. Alexander pulled the collar of his sheepskin coat around his neck and pulled his hat down over his ears. He needed the brisk air to help him make sense of this. A baby. He'd be eighty when the child left for college. If he lived that long. Maria was very accepting of the unplanned pregnancy. He was not. I thought we'd just have one child, not two. Oh, Maria, this certainly changes our life. He walked on in the chilled night air. She has brought so much good to my life, he mused. I'm glad I got off the train that day to meet her. He walked on trying to sort things out. She's a good mother, that's for certain. And she's one of the kindest people I've ever known. And so resourceful. His thoughts were jumbled as he walked. Finally, he decided. Even if I'm not around, she'll be able to take care of this child. And, he realized, he already loved this tiny being. He or she was a sign of hope for the future. He turned toward home in the moonlight.

Aleksy and Halina and their two young sons came for the Christmas holiday. Halina came with a notebook to write down all the recipes for Christmas Eve dinner so she could prepare the dishes Aleksy remembered so fondly. Aleksy's love of traditions and devotion to family pleased his father. Alexander looked around the table at his children and grandchildren and smiled. I'm very blessed, he thought. Very blessed. Maria's right. This child will be another blessing.

Even as her stomach increased in girth, Maria planted the garden. Alexander hired a neighbor woman to help her weed. Zbigniew did his share, too, as did Danuta and Josef when they came home from college. Danuta helped cook and took over doing the laundry, an arduous task that required lifting heavy pots of boiling water from the stove to the washing tubs, scrubbing the clothes on a washboard, then carrying the wet clothes down the stairs and out to the clothesline. Maria was glad to have her stepdaughter's help and to know she would be one of the midwives with her at the birth.

It was a warm July morning when Maria felt the first labor pains. Alexander and Danuta helped her to the birthing center across the hall, and five hours later the newest Kowal came into the world.

"It's a girl," Danuta called out. The nurse washed the baby and wrapped her in a soft, white cloth. She handed the dark-haired girl to her mother, and Alexander came into the room.

"I want to name her Anna," Maria told Alexander looking down at the nursing baby. "It means favored by God."

"It's a nice name," he replied.

He lifted the baby from his wife's arms. The nurse and midwife turned their attention to Maria. Alexander held the tiny bundle close and walked to the other side of the room near a window.

"Anna. If that's what your mother wants, Anna will be your name," he whispered. The baby seemed to snuggle to his chest as he said the name. Alexander rubbed a finger gently against baby Anna's cheek. "I hope you are favored by God, little one. Our family has been through so much, but you, I think, are born into an era of better times. You are my hope for tomorrow, Anna." He watched people in the street hurrying about their business. Someone drove by in a shiny green car. The afternoon train whistled as it left the station. "It's a whole new world out there and it's just waiting for you. Perhaps you'll be the one favored with a life lived in freedom. I hope you'll be the youngest doctor in the family." He held his finger in Anna's hand, and she reflexively grabbed it. Alexander smiled. "My youngest daughter. Yes, you're my hope for a better future."

Epilogue

A new doctor was assigned to the Prostki clinic in 1956, and Alexander was assigned to be a physician in a clinic in Kruklanki, where he finally redeemed his certificate for a house to replace the one he had owned in Paceviche. It was there in 1961 that he celebrated his fiftieth year as a physician. He was correct that he would not live to see Anna grow up. He died in 1971 just before his eightieth birthday. Anna was seventeen. Four of his children and three of his grandchildren became physicians.

Foreign Words Used In the Text

Bigos—(P) [*noun*] a traditional Polish dish consisting of cabbage, sauerkraut, meat, sausage and spices, frequently called Hunter's Stew

Bombic—(local Polish and Russian slang) [*verb*] the act of the partisan groups in World War II in which they demanded food and supplies from local residents

Cheka—(R) [*noun*] Bolshevik secret police force

Dzien dobry—(P) [*adjective and noun*] Good day (greeting for all parts of the day)

Guten morgen (G) [*adjective and noun*] Good morning

Izviestia—(R) [*noun*] One of the Bolsheviks' newspapers

Kulaks—(R) [*noun*] wealthy (for their social class) peasant landowners in the Soviet Union

Mezalians—(P) [*noun*] Marriage outside of one's social class

Na wieki wiekow. Amen—(P) For centuries and centuries. Amen. (used by a religious person as a response to Niech bedzie pochwalony Jezus Chrystus)

Niech bedzie pochwalony Jezus Chrystus—(P) Let Jesus Christ be praised (used as a greeting to a religious person)

Obarzanki—(P) [*noun*] small hard donuts on a string that were a popular treat for children

Oplatek—(P) [*noun*] thin embossed white rectangular wafers families traditionally shared at the beginning of Christmas Eve supper to wish each other a good year

Paczki—(P) [*noun*] Polish donuts filled with fruit preserves and sprinkled with powdered sugar

Pierzyna—(P) [*noun*] feather and down-filled tightly woven ticks used on beds as a thick cover for sleeping.

Pierogi—(P) [*noun*] dumplings that may have a variety of fillings

Pyzy—(P) [*noun*] a traditional Polish dish which consists of meatballs wrapped in grated and mashed potatoes and then boiled and served with fried bacon and onions

Rajispolkomen (R) [*noun*] Soviet local commandants headquarters

Sehr gut (G) [*adverb and adjective*] very good

Slava Bohu—(R) Praise God (used as a greeting to a religious person)

Spirytus—(P) [*noun*] pure alcohol used for making alcoholic beverages and for sterilizing skin and wounds during medical treatment

Stutzpunkt—(G) [*noun*] a local headquarters for German commandants in World War II

Tato—(P) [*noun*] dad or daddy (more familiar and affection than ojciec, which is father)

Tieplushka—(R) [*noun*] boxcar fitted with a small cast iron stove and wooden bunk beds used for long-distance railroad travel

Z za Buga—(P) [*prepositional phrase*] from behind the Bug River

Zloty—(P) [*noun*] Polish currency equivalent to a dollar in the United States

Zrazy—(P) [*noun*] thin slices of beef, wrapped around slices of pickles, mushrooms, onions, and smoked bacon, and then stewed in broth in the oven

P=Polish
R=Russian
G=German